The Tiger and the Hare

THE TIGER AND THE HARE

The Two Years before the Beginning
of the Vietnam War

Jane Miller Chai

iUniverse, Inc.
New York   Bloomington

The Tiger and the Hare
The Two Years before the Beginning of the Vietnam War

iUniverse books may be ordered through booksellers or by contacting:

iUniverse
1663 Liberty Drive
Bloomington, IN 47403
www.iuniverse.com
1-800-Authors (1-800-288-4677)

Because of the dynamic nature of the Internet, any Web addresses or links contained in this book may have changed since publication and may no longer be valid. The views expressed in this work are solely those of the author and do not necessarily reflect the views of the publisher, and the publisher hereby disclaims any responsibility for them.

ISBN: 978-1-4401-2020-6 (sc)
ISBN: 978-1-4401-2021-3 (dj)
ISBN: 978-1-4401-2022-0 (ebook)

Library of Congress Control Number: 2009921074

Printed in the United States of America

iUniverse rev. date: 3/16/2009

CONTENTS

THE TIGER AND THE HARE

To Professor Claude A. Buss, who opened the eyes to Asia

Whatever has happened, the land always lives within us,
The spiritual stream untainted
Poetry still lives; the people are alive
We are the people and we will endure.

Nguyen Duy
"Our Nation from a Distance"

CHAPTER I

Stepping away from the prop plane that had brought her, Linnea flicked aside the moist strands of her hair and zeroed in on a small, furry tree drooping with cotton flocks and red and yellow bulbs below a sign, "Tan Son Nhut." Hit by the absurdity of Christmas in tropical stickiness, she huffed and struggled to breathe. Perspiration stung her eyes. Beneath her feet, the glaring cement apron of the airport tarmac blurred into the whiteness of a sandy beach.

Vietnamese passengers with oversized packages scattered ahead. She followed, trudging toward the Quonset hut terminal. On the way, edging out of her jacket, her silk blouse became glued to her chest. In all the books on Southeast Asia, she grumbled, this boiling heat and suffocating humidity were not so much as mentioned.

In a glance to the side, she saw a tiny tractor dragging her plane by its big black nose—gleaming silver about to be engulfed by waving yellow spears of elephant grass. Carts loaded with crates marked "Made in U.S.A." lumbered past, barely missing her. Swept along, she tripped, her knee clipping the asphalt. Tiny droplets of blood sprouted through a now ripped stocking.

"You had a long trip," a man with a New York accent said as though with an accusation.

Righting herself, presuming he was a similarly exhausted passenger from the same series of flights, she wanted to quip that ducks picked up in Hong Kong made for a foul final leg. But the man scampered away, dismissal in his wake.

Vietnamese military men in the terminal's shadow resembled stage extras in the wings of "The Mikado." Looking closer, Linnea saw faces gleaming as though from demonstrating South Vietnamese worthiness in being America's newest allies in the fight against communism. The men were waiting for her to point out which suitcases were hers. With a wave of her hand over the remaining lot, soldiers clad in the latest jungle green jumped to wrestle them onto a lengthy wooden platform of washboard-like rollers.

It took several seconds to comprehend that an officer's off accented English was instructing her to unlock and open everything. Dripping with gold braid, he pointed to the red leather overnight case in her hand. "Open, pluz." Sweat filled her eyes as she felt in her purse for tiny, tinny keys to fight the locks. "All yours?" he exclaimed as more suitcases piled up, for the first time revealing eyes hidden beneath a thick brown brow.

As though they contained either offal or TNT, a soldier with a lesser amount of gold braid pushed her suitcases past him.

Linnea kept hold of the keys, squared her shoulders, and inhaled as though summoning patience. She had arrived to do something about his country's "police action" in which America was becoming involved, possibly leading her into a better job in journalism if not a position in foreign affairs in Washington. With nose lifted, she stood her ground.

A clean-cut Vietnamese man in a short-sleeved white shirt and dark pants took that moment to approach. With an intelligent look in his eyes, he asked, "Miss Linnea? I am Vinh, your assistant. I will take you to USAID compound." He indicated with an open palm a black car out on the street.

Heading forward, Linnea grinned at officers perplexed by the pile of luggage they couldn't poke into about to be taken away. She anticipated that once out of the heavy mustiness of the echoing terminal the atmosphere would improve. But bright sunlight smacked her hard in the face. Roaring machinery assaulted her ears. Inside clouds of dust she glimpsed huge yellow earthmovers racing back and forth, barely missing each other, laying the groundwork for what might be a mini-Pentagon in the not too distant future.

The black car squatting at the curb was a slung back Citroen sedan. How perfect! A gangster getaway car! Linnea retreated behind windows fogged with reflector film and sank into the cool leather back seat, letting her weary eyes follow Vinh working with her luggage. She began to smile by the way he was first startled by the weight of a particular suitcase and then, after eyeing it, positioned his legs and back for the lift into the trunk. It was too late to tell him about her books. She looked out the other window.

Was she crazy to be here, Linnea asked herself, just before a war, as some said there could be? She'd turned her back on her job with the Associated Press, and she hadn't succumbed to columnist friend Hal's persistent proposals, much as she liked him and admired his WWII foxhole stories of hometown boys, meriting his Pulitzer Prize. She liked the way the AP was family, but amidst the rising swell for women's rights, as Middle Management's "well-heeled, safe bet," she'd been promoted into Newsfeatures writing human-interest stories that didn't interest. She should have been on the foreign desk, using her knowledge of Asia. And so, to prove it, here she was, in South Vietnam.

"Your job with USAID will use your knowledge of the Montagnards," her New York friend Stephen said in a phone call from Saigon. "You already know about the hill people. So, all you have to do is find out what the Hmong want and help them lean in the right direction."

Listening to him back then, looking out the window over Rockefeller Plaza, she'd been grateful for the loud static. She respected Stephen as a thinker and writer, but didn't know how he would be as the USAID supervisor and her boss. "I don't know," she'd answered in a measured tone. "It came over the wire last week that the Viet Cong bombed a place close to Saigon."

"Come on! It's safer here than where you are right now," Stephen had replied with a laugh, referring to the bomb through the mail slot of the Tass office on her floor by a Soviet-hating expatriate of a Central Asian 'Stan country. "This job is a natural for you. Your knowledge of Southeast Asian tribes is probably greater than that of any other American here. It can be a stepping stone for you just as this job may be one for me," he said, referring to what he'd told her, that he might be magazine editor of his international relations outfit after foreign experience, specifically Vietnam.

"Excuse me," Vinh said, opening the driver's door, leaning over the seat, and letting out precious cool air-conditioned air. "I have them all—eight?" After she nodded at his placid, sweating face, Vinh slid into the driver's seat, released the emergency brake, and permitted the Citroen to crawl like a hunched beast into a squirming cauldron of souls.

In every direction people pushed carts and pedaled bicycles, many of them turning inquisitively at the vehicle pushing into their midst. Several came up close when the Citroen slowed and stared blankly at their reflections in windows they couldn't see through.

How could the Vietnamese have energy and motivation in this miserable heat? Just as that thought surfaced, the car air conditioner began to rattle; clearly it was foreign and had to struggle hard, she made mental note, as though it was something to remember.

The Citroen honked and a Vietnamese man's angry face came at her window, making her recoil. Righting herself, she asked, "Americans are welcomed here, aren't we, Vinh?" She remembered wire photos of angry South Vietnamese faces. "Everything's all right here, isn't it?"

"Yes," he said, with a turn of his head. "A recent incident happened in a field, in a rice paddy near here to make people mad. You and I will be in the hills," he said, glancing behind at sweat rolling down her temples, "where it's nice and cool."

Dabbing at her face, Linnea settled back and wondered at the amount of time involved in going into the Hmong hills for USAID when, before that began, there were things she needed to find out, right away, in Saigon. First off, she was to learn the political intentions of the Buddhists in South Vietnam for the father of her close friend Clarissa. And she was to look into the availability of opium in Saigon, in light of the servicemen potentially coming to South Vietnam.

Thirty minutes later, Vinh edged the car into a broad, shaded avenue of tall, thick-trunk trees, evenly placed and heavily leafed. The car slowed in entering an area of old white French-style houses set back amidst expansive green lawns with clusters of oleanders, ferns and rhododendrons. Brilliant scarlet and orange bougainvillea fanned out along perimeters while flowering mimosa splashed against compounds sheltered from the sun-drenching sky by luxuriant lime and ginger trees and the bushy tops of ageless palms.

"Why, this is quite nice!" she said, pulling herself up to the back of the front seat. Unexpected, it brought to mind the mansions and rolling grass slopes of the Pasadena neighborhood of her first ten years, making her feel she might be more comfortable in Saigon than anticipated.

"The Cong Ly district," Vinh said, as he turned the car into gates being opened by a pair of smiling boys in short brown pants. "The best."

"This is the USAID compound? Where I'll be living?"

"Sleep and work. An office is downtown, but Stephen and others do much work here."

The car sank into deep gravel and came to a stop. Linnea opened the door and stepped out under a *porte cochere* that was echoed in the white scalloped-shaped steps underneath. She edged up the steps to push the heavy wrought iron and glass front door that opened into a pleasantly cool interior of marble floors. Polished teak doorframes emitted the familiar aroma of linseed oil.

"Well, so you decided you could make it after all," Stephen said, rushing from a side room with a smile and a nautical blue tie swinging white anchors from his long, lean chest. "I would have met you at Tan Son Nhut, but your arrival time seemed uncertain."

"I cabled the details after I'd arranged all the connecting flights," she snapped.

"Yes. Yes, of course you did. Anyway, Vinh's good at the airport and has been anxiously awaiting your arrival. I trust you're now well acquainted." A dark brown lock fell over the tortoise shell frame of his glasses, making his gently handsome face youthfully professorial. He canted his head close to hers, and in a low voice said, "I'm glad you've come."

The warmth of his greeting surprised her. They had been just friends in New York. Shifting from one foot to the other, she said, "Vinh and I will get along fine."

A heavy-set Vietnamese woman of indeterminate age approached from behind the stairway and, with a disapproving glance at Stephen and not a single word, took Linnea's smallest suitcase to start up the stairs. Linnea watched her ascend, remembering with a sigh her family's warmhearted housekeeper.

Linnea stayed to the side by the wall while Stephen and Vinh relayed her suitcases—Vinh from the car, Stephen from the steps through the door. Finished, Stephen was about to say something when an American woman slightly older than Linnea bounded towards them from the same side room Stephen had come and where it seemed she'd been waiting. She was round faced with wild black hair.

"Well, hallo! Planning on staying long?" Her hands went to her hips with an inspector-like forward bend as though counting a shipment.

"Linnea, this is Susan, USAID's gift to primary education," he said with a skewered voice. "She's been the villa's only woman up until now and is *undoubtedly* glad you're here." Continuing as though following through on something, "As I've told you, Susan, Linnea's work with the Montagnards can make an important difference in America's presence in Vietnam."

Linnea glanced up, wondering what Stephen meant and, even more, if she was in over her head. She would figure that out soon enough. Right now it seemed he and Susan acted like lovers in a bit of a spat.

"That so?" Susan said to the suitcases. "My work taking what's taught in Saigon to the masses in the countryside is both important and already bearing fruit." She threw back her head for crinkly curls to spring out medusa-like. "And my work is definitely ripening! Collaboration, you know." With a lunge toward the door, a strong-arm yank at getting it open, and an overhead backhanded wave, Susan departed.

"Collaboration!" Stephen said in a sarcastic tone.

Linnea felt called upon to say something. "Collaboration is good, isn't it? That's what the U.S. is doing here, working with the South Vietnamese?"

With a change of voice and a smile, "Let's get you upstairs. I'm sure you're tired." He started forward, paused and turned back, "Everything's been straightened up and cleaned."

Linnea recalled the one time in their brief acquaintance she'd been invited to meet him at his place in Gramercy Park before going together to an Asia lecture at the New York Public Library. He'd cleared a path to the couch and adjusted the lighting to hide piles of books. En route she stumbled, releasing clouds of dust, causing her sneezes to overwhelm anything else.

Now, following Stephen up the USAID villa's stairs, Linnea entered upon a gleaming bare wood floor. The room took up the entire side of the top level, pleasantly wide, spare and airy. A beam of afternoon sun bounced up from the shiny yellow, causing her hand to snap to her head, blocking the light. Aware of feeling slightly dizzy, she edged to the back windows opening onto a thick clump of deep green leaves. She leaned out in the hope of finding needed lighter air. Below her, white glazed ceramic elephants tilted at angles to each other, sunk into black mulch along with several huge blue urns overgrown with ferns and cymbidiums.

"I think those are guava and fig trees out there," she said in a barely audible voice that coincided with Stephen's heaving breaths as he struggled in with a load of suitcases. "We had those in the orchard in our back yard," she said, trying to hide embarrassment about her baggage. "And down there, I think, is a pomegranate tree, and a pond with a stone bench." Just then, an oval of water flashed with white and orange. "Koi are in it, too; they're good luck, you know." She turned, but he was already off for another load.

She stayed in place worrying that the number of suitcases might indicate to Stephen she had come for something more than the job with USAID. A couple of government documents given by Clarissa's father might have to be explained, but otherwise the rest were textbooks and monographs, perhaps of use to other Americans here. Shaking her head in a try for clarity, she smelled sweetness in the heavy air. Frangipani, she presumed, the scent bringing forth a memory of lying on her back in the orchard during her high school years, sucking kumquats, dreaming of an adventurous future far away.

With the plop of a suitcase hitting the floor, Stephen indicated he'd finished. Linnea pulled back and turned around. The six flights from New York to Chicago, Seattle, Anchorage, Tokyo and Hong Kong, the twelve take offs and landings over four days, were taking their toll. To steady herself, she placed her hand onto a long board serving as a worktable set on a tall pair of rectangular hi fi floor-speakers. She glimpsed at the far end Stephen's Underwood typewriter resting next to neat piles of paper and some pencils in a Harvard mug. A small, white refrigerator, its brand name in Japanese *katakana,* was perched near the second rear window with his Leica camera and lens.

"Aren't those your things?" she asked, pointing with her hazel eyes. When he didn't answer right away, she waved her hand at the typewriter, "This seems to be your room."

"Yes, it has been. It is large and airy, and will probably suit your needs and style more than mine right now." He mopped his brow with a glance at the suitcases at his feet. "Until I can figure out a space for my desk and files, I thought you wouldn't mind if I leave everything here and use the room, at least for awhile, when you're away, out in the hills."

She shook her head. With everything she wanted to accomplish in a very short amount of time—six months, more or less—she had to have her own space. With no prying eyes.

But she didn't want to begin on the wrong foot. "Well, maybe. But only for a little while."

Stephen made for the large four-poster bed with a canopy spilling white mosquito netting like a tulip-skirted ball gown. Propping up a pillow, "It was quite a challenge getting this Big Bertha in here," he with pride. "With word you were coming, Duong, the woman who brought up your suitcase to get a look at you, had mercy. Seems this bed belonged to a former owner who just hasn't gotten around to coming back for it."

They stared at each other a few moments, Stephen at the bed, Linnea by his desk.

She was tired and didn't really want to start out with questions, but went ahead anyway. "Stephen, in your calls you made it sound like I'll be taking jolly little field trips into the countryside. But what about the Viet Cong I've been reading about? *The New York Times* had a story about recent incidents near Saigon. You said on the phone that the explosions by the VC—calling cards you called them—are just to say they're out there. But…."

"That's right. No worry for you, though. You'll be in the hills with the tribes who are friendly and critically important."

She gave it a moment. "Well, why are the tribes so critically important? You've said our purpose is to help them make progress in their lives," Linnea said, shaking her head, waiting for an answer. "Well?"

"The tribes are important because they're our responsibility. The South Vietnamese government hasn't been getting along with them-and they're significant because of the huge amount of land they're spread over."

"And that's why they're critically important?"

"Yes," he said, moving out from behind the bed. "Some Hmong are helping us by watching what may be coming south from North Vietnam. More Hmong tribes are needed to do that. Our Special Forces medical groups visit and are assisting them in many ways. You'll meet up with them and can help each other to help the Hmong."

"Stephen, we need to discuss a few things," Linnea said, wishing swollen feet wouldn't wobble in the heels they were dying to escape. "You told me USAID wants the Montagnards, the Hmong and all the other hill tribes, to stay in place and start producing crops to sell. I'll try, but it may not be easy to make them change their lifestyles ... like away from the poppies they grow. What am I supposed to do about that?" It wasn't the time or the note on which to turn away from him, but she needed a clear head to tell him what she had been told to worry about.

But, before he could answer, if he was going to, she dashed into the bathroom and shut the door. Freeing hair from the barrette, she bowed her head, letting red-brown tresses encase her classically pretty face. Leaning with hands on either side of the sink, she couldn't tell whether the falling drops were sweat or even tears. After a moment's reflection, she kicked off her shoes, rolled down her ripped stockings and with tepid water sponged her face, neck and arms. With each slow stroke, she sought to assure herself she could handle both her special assignment and the USAID job and do everything fearlessly while staying safe. Finally soothed, even by the orderliness of the black and white tile throughout the huge bathroom—as big as her New York living room—she felt stronger. A lift in spirits even came with the contrast of the shiny new moss green bidet next to the rusted claw feet of a yellowed porcelain bathtub.

"You know what that is, don't you?" Stephen said from his desk holding a large pile of papers, his eyes going past her to the bidet.

"Yes, of course I do," she snapped. "I was just wondering how ... how it's turned on."

"I'll show you," he said, completing the sentence out the door in the hallway with a resolute "later."

CHAPTER II

The distant tinkling of cymbals, accompanied by the soft, steady beats of muted drums slowly brought Linnea awake. The Buddhist monks! She brought herself up with a rub at the eyes. After taking their morning rounds, do they passively pray the rest of the day without any thought or interest in politics? Or are they quietly lying in wait, preparing to act if a situation grows conflicted? They are the key, she remembered Clarissa's father saying. "Find out where the Buddhists stand and you'll be contributing to our efforts to aid South Vietnam."

To sweat and stew beneath clinging sheets, she asked herself, or to rise up and get to work? Her bare feet hit the cool wood floor and carried her to her suitcases. Rummaging through them, she found the Abercrombie & Fitch new "breathable" fiber slacks and long-sleeved shirt. Following a flashlight examination of the already studied Saigon city map, she tiptoed fast down the stairs and out the heavy front door into the compound's courtyard.

Wide-eyed, feeling like a baby bird dropped from a good nest onto unaccustomed fresh ground, she looked about. Straight, tall trees resembled soldiers at attention. A soft, moist breeze sliding through palm fronds made them clap as though with encouragement she could find her way. A harsh clang of cymbals, resembling a crescendo, made her hurry through the villa gates in the direction of the sounds and, possibly, Saigon's main Buddhist temple.

The drumbeats and cymbal melodies seemed strongest from a street ahead, just to the right; she raced for it, but when she got there, the resonance came from another direction. On to another street and one after, but the sounds played tag. She stopped and the beat ceased with her. Was it over? Was she late in finding monks in their pre-dawn rounds? A low-register drumbeat, seeming to be just behind, caused her heart to thump in unison. She swiveled about and walked fast, on and on, until the drum and cymbals became a steady pervasive thudding surrounding her.

Suddenly, the late evening-early morning moon, shining down onto a blanket of fog, diffused light and illuminated two-story wooden houses on her brick and asphalt street. Through the slats in narrow window openings she saw a half dozen pair of eyes following her footsteps. In an area of corrugated metal doors and painted cement walls, she realized she was now in a business area of small storefronts. Over worn wooden doors faded signs proclaimed *parfum* for sale. Pausing under a yellow street lamp to study her map, she became conscious of smells—a heavy, mixture of mold fighting with ammonia.

She sneezed. It was loud and it scared her. She feared she might have lost the cymbal sounds directing her. But the sudden thud of a deep drum felt like it was close, on the next street. She raced to the corner and came into the middle of a junction just as the drumbeat ceased. She stopped, turning slowly around, trying to figure out what had happened. Then, movement caught her eye. Noiselessly, as though they were ghosts carried along in a gray-green mist, a line of saffron swathed monks floated across a cross section of streets. They were thin, slightly stooped, shave-headed and sandal footed. Linnea hurried ahead and rounded a corner at a run, almost piling into a monk bringing up the rear.

The monks had slowed at small dots of fire. A woman in a cardigan sat on a stool beside a brazier at the entrance of a shop with a rolled up aluminum awning. Along with a big spoonful of steaming rice into silver begging bowls, she added a quiet word or two to the bowing novitiates. Another woman a few feet beyond put slices of banana on top of the rice-filled containers that would be the whole of a full day's meal.

Linnea moved parallel to the monks in the hope of reading the profiles of the bare shouldered robed men and the expressions of the devout women serving them. She wondered if these same women got up early every day to give these Hinayana monks their daily sustenance, or, more likely, there were others here and there who shared the task. The monks might have to search each morning for the women wishing to obtain merit on a particular morning, accounting for the monks' hide and seek wanderings.

The monks moved on, their saffron garments melding them together as a single forward thrusting instrument of peace. Linnea hurried to keep up. As she did, the cymbals and drums began to sound different, lighter and more distant, as though about to be put away. Had there been a message in the resonance, calling the monks back? A block or two later, tagging along at the end of their line, she realized she'd arrived into a clearing of rock-strewn dirt at the juncture of several roadways. In the moments that it took for her to look around, the monks vanished. Almost instantly the drum and cymbal sounds ceased with a squeak.

Examining her map, she realized she was where she wanted to be, Saigon's most significant Buddhist temple, the Xa Loi. But it looked downtrodden, neglected, and unimportant. Heading forward she found the earth at the entrance shiny, presumably packed smooth by countless bare feet. Flowing out through the open side of the temple's double-sided wooden doors came the smell of cabbage being cooked. Stepping to the opening and over the ledge into the inner courtyard, Linnea saw through a smoky, foggy atmosphere walls lined with wrinkled old men and hunched old women. Most were snoozing. One or two looked up.

She picked her way past them, edging into a passageway with a worn planked floor and soot-heavy paneling. Her nose wrinkled at acrid smells mixing with burning incense. She paused beside long tables with diminutive bronze statues of bodhisattvas illuminated by flickering votive candles. Bending close to the layout of the statues, she wanted to see if there was a particular instruction in the depictions of the life of Buddha. Then, Stephen's words seeped into mind.

"You've complained your AP story on the great power and goodness of Buddhism in Southeast Asia was editorially destroyed. But Buddhists in Vietnam are weak, only interested in themselves and their nirvana. They're passive and politically uninterested and uninvolved."

"May I help you?" A gentle voice asked from behind her.

Linnea turned. "Oh, I heard the cymbals and drums and followed the monks collecting alms," she said to the short, round figure swabbed in a brown robe. "I thought I'd look inside … to see if I could speak with one of you." She hurried to add, "And the door was open!"

The monk's bushy black eyebrows lifted as he laughed. "Yes, we are open. We always are. And you, young lady, are up a bit early, aren't you?"

"I just flew in—yesterday, I mean—and couldn't sleep." As if reluctantly to leave, she slowly turned.

"It's almost sunrise. Likely your time for tea." His invitation came with a sweep of a cloth-covered arm indicating to follow him down the corridor.

A long, narrow room had several straight-back wooden chairs with cane seats lined up against a wall. A dented four drawer gray metal filing cabinet stood at right angles to a cot. Yellow and orange woven cotton Mandalas depicting Buddha's life hung next to faded photographs of huge Buddha statues carved into the sides of cliffs and sepia pictures of stupas atop cliffs and poking up in tree-covered plains. The room might be a place for the baring of the soul by the faithful. The teapot on the electric burner steamed as though always ready.

"Your English is very good, without much of an accent," Linnea said as she accepted from him a round brown porcelain cup of hot tea. "Did you have education in the United States?" she asked, observing the university crest on a black chair, possibly belonging to the person she intended to contact.

"Yes," he said, the corners of his eyes crinkling as though with a good memory. "Many my age went to France to study. In the last decade, the fifties, though, a few of us started going to America." The long fingers of both hands encircled his huge teacup as though giving it a nice squeeze. He sat back, the shininess of his shaved head obscuring any sign of roots.

"What about now? I've heard that a monk from this Xa Loi pagoda recently returned with a doctorate from Yale."

The monk looked up, a shadow of wariness darkening his face. After several long seconds he said, "One wonders why a simple monk's educational experience is known by or of interest to Americans." He said Americans the French way— *Americains*—and deliberately adjusted wire-framed glasses up his nose, his chocolate colored eyes focusing on her. "You're not just an early arising American out to acquire hot tea and a bit of culture, are you?"

"I appreciate the tea very much," she smiled. "I do want to know more about Buddhism. My education is in Southeast Asia's history and culture," she continued, "*and* the indigenous tribes; I'll be trying to help them, for USAID—United States Aid for International Development. But before I begin my job, I thought I'd like to know more about Buddhism in the government of Saigon." She glanced at the cloth Mandala on the wall illustrating Buddhism as the central core from which authority flows. "I believe Buddhists are the vast majority in South Vietnam and yet you have a Catholic president—Ngo Dinh Diem. I've wondered about that."

She waited measured seconds before continuing. "I mean, as you know, we've just elected a Catholic president, and that's a first for our country. Some Americans have worried there might be an outside power, like the Pope in Rome, to influence and call the shots." She left the teacup at her lips, the way she'd learned to do in interviews to prompt the other person finally to speak.

The monk put his cup down next to the burner. It seemed like he wasn't going to respond as he focused on adjusting his cassock across his knees and legs. Finally he said with ponderous carefulness, "Buddhism is political in this region, as you know, but it does not have to act politically. We Buddhists are cognizant and we observe and we set an example—an example, most importantly, of patience. We Vietnamese Buddhists are very patient."

They talked for a while about where he'd studied and traveled in the United States and his impressions, good and bad. When his brown eyes rested on Linnea with silence, they expressed their conversation had come to its end.

Rising, Linnea said, "I've learned that President Diem was in a seminary in upstate New York for a number of years. Perhaps he's closer to being a monk listening to Rome than is our President Kennedy. I've been interested in President Diem's thinking about how to govern. I've wondered if there's a difference in the way a Catholic Vietnamese heads the country and how a Buddhist would administer it."

"For the present, there is no schism between Buddhists and the Catholics or the way President Diem is conducting things. Rome is not directing Diem," he said and then paused with eyes flaring, "but foreign political interests are trying, as you say, to be in the driver's seat. I fear that President Diem is not listening to his inner conscience."

Linnea tried to keep her breathing shallow and her beating heart quiet as she walked ahead of the monk back down the corridor to the entrance.

Behind her she heard the monk saying, "Your President Kennedy has a very close adviser. His brother Robert is smart and working hard to help his brother, the President. Our President Diem also has a brother who is his closest adviser. You may find that President Diem's brother Nhu also works hard with personal interests with the Montagnards in the hills."

"Excuse me? Would you say that again?"

"Your USAID job with the Montagnards. I hope you will help our hill people. They should not be mere pawns."

A candle had been lit in a side room illuminating a huge brass gong. Beside it in a chair a large mass of saffron cloth swelled and receded in a steady rhythm.

"Our peacefully snoozing monk will be awakened soon by noisy coins dropped into his metal begging bowl by those requesting merit with the striking of the gong. You won't want to be around."

At the double wooden doors, Linnea said, "I hope you won't mind if I consult with you and perhaps others here some time in the future."

"You may, and you don't have to make it at this hour," he said in the same light tone as in the initial meeting. "This is the special time of our day for our meals and prayers." He took her elbow to help her over the entry ledge. "As you say, have a nice day."

Linnea hurried through a stream of nuns in alabaster pink and monks in shades of orange heading toward the temple entrance. She walked with a light step, feeling she'd made a start into her assignment to learn the Buddhists' political attitude toward the Saigon administration. Facing the rising sun as she headed in the direction of the USAID compound, she scarcely noticed a couple of men following with their eyes on her.

Stephen was in her room at his desk. He swiveled around and jumped up to explode, "My God! Where have you been? I searched the villa and was about to go out again calling and looking for you."

His anger highlighted his tan, complimented by the light blue of his button-down short-sleeved shirt. Linnea started forward to share that she'd had an interesting morning seeing Saigon awaken.

As she grew close, Stephen pulled a newspaper over pages beside his typewriter. She came to a halt and stammered, "I heard the Buddhist drums. I couldn't sleep any longer."

"Don't you know it's dangerous?" Correcting himself, "It's not a good thing for an American to go wandering about right now."

"Why not? Americans have been here a while; the advisers and the rest of us are appreciated, aren't we?" Looking squarely at him, "Isn't Saigon safe and charming, the way you've said?"

Stephen didn't answer. He stared at her with an expression that suggested he wondered if he wasn't seeing her for the first time.

Linnea didn't like what she saw, and said in as casual a voice as possible, "Have you been making any progress on where to move your desk?"

"No," he barked. "And there's nowhere in Saigon you should go on your own. I'm responsible for you and I'm going to take care of you."

"Take care of me?" She pulled back with a sour face. "Then I won't need the assistant Vinh?"

"You'll need him all right. In the hills," Stephen said, slapping some papers together.

"I'm set to begin my job," Linnea said. "You've told me I need to make a good effort at accomplishing my USAID assignment in only a very few months. So, I haven't a moment to lose. You need to respect that I'll be working on my own, and that includes here, in this USAID compound. I have my own style, and I need to have my own space. Besides, how does it look that in the very early morning hours you're in here?"

"Dammed it, 'Nea! There's not a soul here to cluck-cluck like your socially warped girl school friends. No one is interested in what anyone is doing here. Vietnam is in no one's consciousness."

Beyond Clarissa and father, only a few AP colleagues knew she was in Vietnam. She looked over at her pile of suitcases containing books and all the clothes not given away. I'm on my own, she said to herself, to do something that may even impress classmates with their primary life goals to secure a husband.

"You've known we'd be working closely together for USAID," Stephen said in an ameliorating tone.

Linnea tried to respond in an agreeable voice, but words belied her. "Stephen, you said I'd have to get the Montagnards to remain in place growing good crops to sell. I can try to do that, but you need to know it may not be easy to make them change from what they've been growing as a way of life for eons."

"I know," he said quietly. "But the effort is important. I'll try to help you." Then, in a wistful tone, "I've looked forward to you and introducing you around after ... after, I suppose, you need to eat."

As they neared the dining room, the aroma of freshly baked bread reminded Linnea that since leaving New York she had only a few airline waxed paper mystery items and a couple of frozen apples hard to bite into and that had made her stomach growl with anger to match her trepidation.

One person remained in the dining room. He was large and spread out over two places.

"Linnea, this is Philco, our communications expert," Stephen said as Linnea quickly slid into a chair opposite, preventing Philco from gentlemanly rising. The platters between them were filled with fruit—yellow, orange, green and purple portions in shapes like kindergartners' blocks. "As you can see, Philco eats light," Stephen continued, pausing long enough for Linnea's head to turn to him, "from very first light, that is, in collusion with cook Duong. This is your second breakfast today, isn't it, Philco?" Stephen answered for him. "Oh, that's right. Communications half-way around the world mean you have to do it in the middle of the night." Stephen leaned into Linnea. "I'm surprised you two didn't run into each other in your early morning quests."

Linnea ignored Stephen and filled her plate. "All this is grown around here?" After several bites, she asked, "Is any of this grown in the hills, by the Montagnards?" When neither one answered, she noisily put her fork down. She glanced at Philco and turned to Stephen.

"It could be," Stephen replied. "And with you, maybe soon the hills will be fruitful."

"The main produce of the hill people is opium," Philco put in, with an eye on Stephen. "More and more of it, I think."

"Not necessarily. Not now. Soon it'll be berries—strawberries and coffee," Stephen sliced the words back at him.

Linnea returned to eating, imagining Philco might be a resource for things she needed to find out.

Several minutes later, Philco asked Linnea, "Stephen said you have a smattering of Chinese. Mandarin or Cantonese?"

"Cantonese," she replied. It pleased her to describe how her patent attorney father became interested in Cantonese because of Chinese inventor-clients. With laughter in her voice, she told how a skinny old waiter in the Chinese restaurant near her father's Los Angeles office and the courthouse was talked into taking the streetcar to Pasadena on Saturday mornings to give lessons. "My father liked to greet Mr. Wong with *Ni Ha* and a big plate of food, to which Mr. Wong always shook his head—the greeting, of course, no longer truly asks if one has eaten. I think my father wanted Mr. Wong to create a new greeting."

After a chuckle, Philco said, "Good it's Cantonese. That's what's used here."

"And Cantonese people are certainly the best cooks, aren't they, Philco?" Stephen said, describing the expansive floating restaurant owned by Philco's girlfriend's family. "Weight means success—prestige, power, and money! So, Philco's magnificence makes a great impression. One of these days the girlfriend's family is going to impress upon him *beaucoup* requests for boatloads of radios, TVs, tuner-amplifiers and air conditioners."

"Is the Chinese population in Saigon very large?" Linnea inserted into what she interpreted as Stephen's transfer of anger at her into ridicule of Philco.

"Their Cholon section just south is practically the largest and most prosperous part of Saigon," Philco replied.

Linnea mused, "I guess when Admiral Zheng He's huge galleons sailed these parts some Chinese got off and stayed."

"You know all about that, don't you, Philco?" Stephen said, launching into reporting that Philco was produced in St. John's College Great Books Program, and that practically all the mail is for him—books on anthropology, archeology, architecture, and right on down the alphabet. "Everything that's utterly useless when we're trying to do something extremely important here in a short amount of time."

Linnea stared at her plate, realizing that a lifeline with Clarissa and her father was what she needed right now. "Is this where letters can be sent and received?" Linnea asked Philco. "A classmate and I want to stay in touch."

"Classmate? Clarissa?   Daughter of JFK's Interior Secretary?" Stephen snarled.

*   *   *

Stephen spread out a large topographical map of Vietnam, Laos and Cambodia onto his desk. He leaned over the map as though with a mountain of thoughts, absently tracing Vietnam's ridges with his forefinger. "You said you're anxious to start your job with the hill people. Well, these are the Central Highlands where some of them live."

Startled by the large map with details never seen before, Linnea yearned to ask why an almost impossible task had to begin and be completed so quickly. Also, to be honest, she wanted to remain in Saigon before journeying up into dark, eerie hills to meet with old stone-age people. A fraud about Indochinese tribes, she suddenly felt she needed to confess. Professor Buss had said Montagnards were potentially pivotal in the Cold War, but she couldn't right now remember why. Researching in the peaceful Stanford libraries, she never expected to have to confront the hill people, and all she could think of right now was that some tribes liked to eat the liver and heart of captives to gain their spirits.

Provinces colored in yellows and browns had penciled notations "hostile" and "unfriendly" that troubled her. She stared at the names Chau Ma, Stieng, Mnong, Raglai, Churu, Rhade and Jarai until they swirled in her eyes like colored pieces in a kaleidoscope. She bent over the map searching for the words Viet Cong or North Vietnamese that in three years might be all over it. Pulling back, blinking, she said,

"Maybe I should compare this map with ones at the back of monographs I've brought," and turned for books in her unopened suitcases.

Stephen caught her arm. "This project has great potential for you," he said, stressing that she would be the USAID agent in the hills and, basically, representing the U.S. government. She'd be safe enough, he said. There would be American military trainers around. "Your in-country work will give you what you want—a fine researching/writing future for yourself."

Linnea swallowed and felt a pinch in her throat. It felt like she was being shoved, at a time not of her own choosing. When Stephen left to get something in another room, she scurried to the front window to stare out into the palm-cluttered courtyard. Ready to fall, a dried palm frond hung down, and the words to "Hang Down Your Head" rolled through her mind. How could she be prepared for this undertaking? Why did Stephen think she could do this job? Why did she? Her knowledge was academic, on culture and history, not the terrain and the troubles in them. She blew air up from a lower lip. Hair strands danced briefly before becoming glued to a forehead gummy with humidity.

Throwing away a good education, she remembered her friends implied at her declared major—Southeast Asia. She'd gone on to get a Master's degree at Professor Buss's urging, remaining on campus after June graduation. Linnea remembered the sun burning off the fog creeping over the coastal range in the mornings, and in afternoons the dashes with friends in open jeeps into the hills. They'd arrive to sounds of strumming guitars drifting out from a gully of swaying yellow wheat, where the gnarled elbows of black oaks seemed like musical clefs. The Kingston Trio belted out songs with the names of local aboriginals, the Ohlones and Coastanoans—names more meaningful at this moment than any Montagnard tribe.

Stephen returned and Linnea made a hurried grab for monographs with attachments. "I'll match these up with your map." She struggled to unfold with moist fingers the tissue paper maps at the backs of foundation-funded pamphlets until Vinh, who had arrived moments earlier, took them from her.

"Thank you," she softly said, seeing him place them over Stephen's chart with the notations about situations in particular provinces.

After several moments of matching the tissue paper maps, and jotting notes, Linnea heard Vinh say to Stephen, "We'll try, Sir. But, it's not easy to find hill people always moving about."

"That's the point. They need to stay in place. Think creatively. Think about agriculture. Find the closest tribe and proceed to the next," Stephen said, moving sideways along his desk, away from the two of them.

Amidst heavy silence, Linnea asked Vinh, "Are we going to visit the leader of each group, so that that person can do the talking with others?"

"We'll begin with the big tribe that is supposed to be off highway 22 to the west," Vinh replied, glancing over at Stephen bent over a pile of folders.

Thinking a Hmong jamboree might help ease her into her job, she asked, "Do tribal members ever come together close to here for what American Indians call a pow-wow?"

Vinh dropped his head to examine his shoes. "A while back at Ban Me Thuot, some Montagnard tribes gathered together. The largest Hmong group arrived in a procession with spears and performing elephants. They brought buffalo to roast. Saigon officials arrived and received earthen crocks with long straws to drink the strong Montagnard rice wine. They got very drunk and then scared."

Linnea nodded. "That's not a reason the Montagnards and the Saigon officials don't get along, is it?" she asked, looking over at Stephen.

"Saigon has other things to worry about," Vinh answered, casting a glance in the same direction.

CHAPTER III

It was barely light when Vinh headed the jeep out of Saigon. Linnea kept her arms folded tight against the chill of dampness while Vinh maneuvered past wagons loaded with baskets of spinach, mushrooms and scallions coming in from the outskirts. In the gray moist air, farmers with lined faces hurried past, carting fidgety, somewhat resigned pigs. A young farmer woman in a loose shirt and baggy black pants, with a yellow conical *non-la* hat tied securely under her chin, sat up straight on an old, stout bicycle. Strapped behind high above her head she carted a cage crammed so tightly with a mass of white feathers that only an occasional orange beak or webbed foot indicated live ducks were headed for market.

Content in watching the extraordinary energy of Vietnamese at the break of day, Linnea remained quiet, not wanting anything to call to mind the reason for her being in the jeep leaving Saigon. But, the longer she didn't speak, the more Vinh's assumption might be that she was apprehensive about what she was about to undertake. It was a correct supposition, if there ever was one, she felt for she hadn't been trained. After they'd progressed through the bulk of traffic hurrying in from the outskirts, she ventured, "Vinh, from what I've learned in books, the word Hmong means free, but I've also read that Hmong means people of the land. Which is it?"

"The Hmong act like all the land is theirs. They wander all over the place, using up the hills. Hmong groups are many. They're not together."

"Do you think it will be possible for the Hmong to make changes?" she asked.

"Mr. Stephen thinks money for produce will make them change."

Rethinking her assignment, "But how can changes happen in only a couple of months' time? That's rather ridiculous, don't you think?" Waiting for a response that never came, Linnea rested her eyes on small, bedraggled brown ponies with drooping mussels and manes trotting the dusty fringes of Saigon. Her brooding mood lightened when she saw a pony with big brown eyes pick up speed to pass for a glorious short-lived moment an older nag overwhelmed by a load of bricks.

Their jeep had to squeeze over a narrow cement bridge at the city's busy edge, letting them come down into the deep gray haze hanging over the countryside. Droplets of dew shimmered in gently waving fields. Dark thatched-roof huts peeked out mysteriously from tight clumps of occluded trees, sometimes mirrored in small ponds alongside the roadway. Like a contradiction, pristine pink blossoms floated on the surface of ponds' murky waters.

"The lotus emerges from filth to bloom in sunlight," Vinh said, slowing the jeep for her to have a closer look. "We think the lotus is symbolic, that we Vietnamese must lift ourselves above troubles toward enlightenment and redemption."

"Enlightenment and redemption? May I ask your background ... your faith?"

"I'm Buddhist," he replied, "and I've had some Western instruction. I admire Christianity, but I adhere to Confucianism—respect."

"Covering the bases?" She'd spoken off the cuff, too early in their relationship for such familiarity. Regretting her effrontery, she glanced over at him.

After a few moments, Vinh proclaimed, "My religion is Vietnam."

25

"Concerning the lotus," she softly said, "with what seems to be coming down from or inspired by the north, do you think the lotus will continue to bloom and thrive in the South?"

Vinh pressed his foot down for the jeep to jump ahead. Almost immediately he had to slam the brakes on at several people scampering onto the roadway pushing wheelbarrows. It was a mile or more before he returned to a steady pace, with Linnea's question lost in the distance.

The green and brown landscape seemed placid and Biblical-like, reminiscent of pictures in childhood religious books. Black water buffalo with scimitar-shaped horns and wide nostrils pulled crude wooden plows, steered by strong-armed farmers just as they had for three thousand years or more. Pure white ibis, crested-headed kingfishers and blue-gray heron dotted the dikes as though standing guard over long rows of women already working in squares of standing water.

Large yellow plaited conical caps concealed women's faces as they bent over, their multi-colored balloon-style pants rolled up their legs. Rhythmically pulling up, separating, and replanting tender green stalks, scarcely a woman looked around as the jeep clanked past. Off to the side a solitary man stood with arms folded as though with a whip, his stance neither protective nor seemingly necessary.

Linnea was about to ask Vinh about the man when her thoughts went to the loud, melodious whistling of a blackbird beating its scarlet and gold wings, sitting on a railing.

"When a bird is under a blue sky, it is difficult for it to repress its song," Vinh said. "A bud just soaked with morning dew, when struck by morning sunshine, can scarcely restrain itself from blossoming."

"Why, Vinh. That's beautiful!" She took a good look at him.

"It's part of something I like to remember."

"Please say it in Vietnamese. *Xin nói bằng tiếng Việt,*" she repeated.

"*Khi một con chim bay trên bầu trời xanh, thì rất khó có thể kìm hãm được tiếng hót của nó. Một nụ hoa vừa ướt sũng sương buổi sáng và khi gặp phải ánh nắng ban mai rất ít khi làm nó không nở ra hoa.*"

26

"I think it might be a good idea if we talk in Vietnamese."

"Tôi nghĩ rằng tốt hơn là chúng ta nói bằng tiếng nước của anh."

After a while, Vinh said: "It is better for us in English."

"Why do you say that?" She proceeded to describe her primary Vietnamese instruction with a very old Vietnamese woman who taught at Berlitz and owned the only Vietnamese restaurant in Manhattan. After the woman passed away, Linnea bemoaned, Vietnamese language had to be learned from a book—*Easy Vietnamese.* "Imagine trying to learn tonal subtleties differentiating meanings without hearing them! I need to practice."

"Okay. But I need to improve my English to help you … and with what is being said by others," Vinh replied.

"What others?"

"Many Americans are here with different ideas about what to do with our country … to make it strong," he added with a glance at her. "Not everybody agrees with Mr. Stephen."

"About my assignment changing Hmong opium to commercial fruits and vegetables?"

Any reply evaporated in Asian timing. The start-stop of their talk nettled, but became assuaged by her fascination with the countryside streaming past. After a while she attempted the poem her teacher made Linnea learn by heart shortly before she died.

"Our lives are like lightning, here and then gone

Spring plants blossom, to be barren in autumn.

Mind not the rise and fall of fortunes

They're dewdrops twinkling in the grass."

"Đời sống của ta thoáng qua như cơn chớp, ở đây và rồi qua đi

Cây cối vào mùa xuân nở hoa và tàn tạ vào mùa thu

Đừng bận tâm về của cải thăng trầm

Giống như giọt sương lấp lánh trong đám cỏ."

"Van Hanh. A great one! He was not just a poet but a statesman," Vinh said with a nod at her jotting the name in her notebook. A few minutes later he said, "You are unusual. You know more about our country than most and want to know more. Do you know our word *Nghia*?" Without waiting for a response, "*Nghia* is, it means, Vietnam's roots, family, the people as a whole."

Grasping the idea, "Do you think Vietnam one day will return to being a whole?" she asked.

Without answering, he slowed to point at a white shrine under a tall shade tree in the center of a village with a gate. The shrine had a lacquered and gilded altar decorated with flowers. "I think you know that the shrine, the *dinh*, connects villages with the Great Spirit beneath the land, protecting it. The *dinh* is why we call our country *dat nuoc*—earth and water. Rivers from mountains flow down into rice fields as fingers, connecting us all together—all Vietnam."

The *dinh's* white shrine with the dwarfed orange tree beside it and a small blue-water pond made a picture worth taking. But Linnea heard something in Vinh's voice that forestalled reaching into her backpack for her camera.

"I want you to know," Vinh said, "that village rules are superior to the laws of an emperor ... or his current imitator."

She glanced over to see Vinh's little finger rise off the steering wheel as though it were President Diem's reputedly very long imperial one. She hesitated and then asked, "Do your family members live in villages like these?"

"They did, but not now." Anger colored his voice.

"Why not?" She saw his cheek muscles rippling.

"Strategic Hamlets," Vinh dropped the strange coupling of words.

"Oh!" Linnea vaguely remembered newspaper articles that connected the two words in something called a *Joint Communique* between the Diem Administration and the United States.

"We all are part of the land," Vinh barked above the motor. "We are at one with it. Our land needs our care and feeding, even if it has to be with blood."

Turning so he wouldn't see her expression, she rested her eyes on squares of standing water becoming mirrors reflecting a light blue sky with just-forming white clouds. The sunrise behind her returned thoughts to Saigon and how Stephen had sent her out without telling her very much, even what he knew about Vinh. Did Stephen know Vinh's temperament or whether he had an agenda that might not include protecting her?

Linnea kept her eyes to the side, trying to immerse herself in the peacefulness of the picturesque gray and brown reed huts dotting the landscape. An hour later, feeling the jeep slowing down, she reluctantly returned to viewing the road and remembering the task ahead.

Vinh changed gears to slow the jeep into a crawl. Fifty yards in front stood men in loose black shirts and pants clustered at the side of the road, leaning over something at their feet. Several eyed their approach before returning to whatever was of primary attention. Vinh geared down and edged the jeep forward. When they were a car length away, black clad bodies turned for dark eyes to slash in the direction of the jeep, as if she was their awaited item for delivery.

Elbows tight to her side, fists clenched, Linnea's feet pushed hard against the forward floorboard. Within a jeep's length of the men, the smell of their bodies and the blood of something screeching in a ditch spilled over onto her. The men closest leaned toward the jeep as though about to snatch, while companions continued poking in the gully at a still living being. Red black blood dripped from the end of poles with threads of pale pink skin dangling.

Eyes sweeping from right to the left, she sought to prepare herself, like jumping to the left and jamming her foot down on the accelerator.

After inching past, Vinh finally shifted gears and gained speed, rocking her exhausted frame forward and back. Linnea swiveled about but couldn't see anything beyond the clump of black. "What is happening back there?"

"Nothing. Just something wild—or foreign."

Gripping the steering wheel, Vinh drove fast down the raised center of the rough, potholed roadway. Several miles later he said, "Your country believes you can control nature, and by controlling land you can control people. President Diem on his birthday proclaimed he would improve the lives of people. What did he do? He said farmers had to leave their ancestral land, their homes and their fields in need of tending, and go into walled compounds called Strategic Hamlets—horrible places. People are unhappy. Kids are sick. Water surrounding the hamlets is a sewer. Are hamlets an idea from your all-powerful America? Is that how it is there?" His knuckles stood out white on the wheel.

With her feet still hard against the floor panel, "No. Of course not! The United States is trying to help Diem demonstrate he cares for his people. The hamlets are to make people safer from the Viet Cong or the North Vietnamese, I'm sure." But she wasn't. And she didn't like the feeling of saying something about an issue she didn't know or have a chance to decide about.

"Safer from what?" Vinh growled. "People fight for what is theirs, not for what they've been forced to move into, and forced to pay for and to build. The hamlets are only to control."

Linnea folded her hands as if to provide herself assurance. "Who can control the hamlets except the people in them?"

"Hamlets are controlled by the man who puts people there," Vinh said, turning as though checking the back seat. "Diem's brother Nhu. Fifteen million farmers in a few months will be in hamlets, controlled by Nhu." Vinh shook his head. "America's big idea!"

Linnea cringed. She remembered her talk with the monk. Were hamlets the foreign instrument doing more harm than good that he implied? She stared toward purple hued mountains where she glimpsed a row of helmeted, camouflage-clad Vietnamese men, loaded with guns sticking out of backpacks walking in a line toward a tall clump of bunched poplar trees. At the front of the column, leading, was a much taller man wearing an Australian-type rancher's hat. Feathers caught the wind, like her father's fly fisherman's cap when he headed for a Sierra stream. That American Special Forces man isn't even carrying a gun that she could see. She wished he'd hurry to train the men and get the work done so that she and Stephen and others might leave with jobs completed.

It was a long while later that Vinh furiously shifted into four-wheel drive as they climbed a steep roadway that resembled a washed-out obstacle course. He manhandled the jeep over and around fallen tree limbs and sinkhole pools of water. Eventually the path became hardened earth, surrounded by thick foliage and many rows of a similarly tall genus of trees—badly neglected and tangled with thick underbrush choking the trunks.

After climbing several hours more, Vinh stopped to compare the odometer with notes on a map. "There was a turnoff around here somewhere," he said, rising in his seat to look around.

"I didn't see anything." She said it to the tall, thick trees hanging down overhead.

"I'll go ahead a half mile and, if necessary, turn back."

"Here!" Vinh said when they reached a barely discernible mushy opening into a jungle of monstrous dark greenness. Forcing a swallow, she suggested that maybe they should keep looking. But Vinh began heading them toward bushes where leaves appeared dry enough for the jeep's wheels not to sink.

"I tried to send a message. No way knowing it was received. We will walk from here," Vinh said, pulling hard the handbrake and, in a swift motion, taking his backpack from the seat behind and hopping onto the ground.

"How far is it?" Linnea could see only a few feet in any direction.

"Don't know. This one may be in close, a good one for our first." Vinh pushed aside a leafy fern, examined the ground, and waited for her to catch up.

It was a well-worn pathway, very narrow, with thick underbrush encroaching on both sides. Three layers of tree canopy permitted only narrow ribbons of light, creating extremes of shadows and as many shades of green as on a painter's pallet. Leaves soft and feathery or brown and leathery suggested science fiction grotesqueries.

Keeping close behind, Linnea made a visual sweep from side to side, following her full multi-colored Mexican cotton skirt. Her outfit's colors and patterns somewhat resembled Hmong costumes seen in a Geographic Magazine photo and she thought might give them ideas for enterprise. At the very least, her bright dress could alert a near-sighted hunter, she hoped, as the question kept hammering as to how she believed she could do this.

Linnea bent to examine a cat's paw prints in the dried mud. She recalled photographs of Montagnard huts on stilts and realized wildcats, rodents and snakes were reasons to be elevated above ground. She scanned the brush and glanced behind, then checked overhead for what might be hanging down or perched on a limb about to leap.

I've got to master this, she said to herself, trying to think of words to convince the headman that his village should stay put and grow potentially profitable produce, like coffee beans. But would she and all she had to say be acceptable? Possibly, she tried to assure herself. The Hmong are a matrilineal society. Women are respected. They inherit property, choose mates, and even can become chiefs.

However, she recalled, women weren't in any of those old sepia photographs—just fierce-looking male Hmong with piercing eyes. And then there is Stephen's dictate that Montagnards hate lowland Vietnamese and think they themselves are invisible.

She plodded along. A large twisting leaf close to the ground caught her attention. Beneath it, motionless, dark splayed toes with cracked white calluses gripped the inky soil.

"Oh, no!"

A man with a short mass of thick, knotted muscles stepped forward, holding an instrument in the shape of a T—a crossbow, certainly that's what it was—pointed right at her.

"My God! Don't shoot!" she screamed with hands raised. "*Troi oi!*" she weakly added.

Large eyes so black they seemed without whites bored through her.

Forcing air back into her lungs, she whisper-shouted, "Who … what is he?"

The skin of the man's bare chest was several shades darker than Vinh's, who was catching his breath, more because of her than from the man's appearance. "A runner. A guard," he said as though she should have known.

The man's only clothing was a piece of hand-woven cloth over private parts, held in place by a narrow reed swath around the hips. She noticed the cloth had a subtle pattern: two threads of red and yellow on a field of black.

Without a word, the guard stepped in front and set out in long, noiseless strides. Linnea followed in line and stumbled. Vinh's head turned but not far enough to see if she was all right, she noted.

After a hurried walk that seemed like a good mile they were in the bright light of a well-trodden clearing, surrounded by a dozen reed huts with thatched roofs built on stilts ten feet above the ground. A few scrawny pigs and chickens worked the dusty earth, every so often startling each other and scooting for shade.

No people were in the clearing, but at hut openings an arm or a leg could be seen withdrawing into dark interiors.

From under the thick ridge of his forehead the guard fixed his eyes on her, indicating with a finger pointed at the ground that she and Vinh were to stay in place. He jogged around the corner of a collection of raised huts, and became lost to sight.

Linnea cast about for a pole that would give this Montagnard village its identity and proclaim its special charms—either to invite in helpful spirits or to broadcast curses onto the unwanted to keep them out. Animistic, the Hmong believe everything's alive, she mused. Good and evil swirling through the jungle cannot be conquered but have to be navigated through, she said to herself. Indeed, that's what's to be done—somehow maneuver through this damned situation to convince people to do something they didn't want or perhaps even need to do.

Vinh led her a few steps to a patch of shade on the corner of a large trampoline-like reed platform under a thickly leafed gingko tree trailing a yellow thread.

"This is center stage for a seer or shaman," Vinh said, "and a resting place for the consumption of betel nut or, more likely, something stronger." He pointed to a small satchel at one corner of the mat, picked it up, and loosened the drawstring. With thumb and forefinger he rubbed a few leaves together and sniffed, and, dismissing, pulled out a small, round brown waxy ball to take a pinch. "This is something you should try," Vinh said.

She shook her head, despite feeling that a stimulant right now might be what she needed. But she focused on the opium bit, and tried to formulate words for the moments ahead.

Linnea rested her backpack on the mat, unbuttoned it and took out her Polaroid camera with the idea that its sounds might attract someone to come out into the open. She clicked a shot of a small, round pink pig panting on its side under one of the huts. But no one poked a head around any dark opening. She fished from the backpack some pencils, fountain pens, crayons and multicolored layered notepads and placed them on the platform.

After what seemed like a very long time, the guard returned and motioned to follow him up an incline. In the far back amidst a group of gingko trees, at a hut like every other except longer, the guard indicated that they were to leave their shoes on the ground and climb the steps hacked into a tree trunk up to an opening.

From the doorway fifteen feet above, a scantily clad old man with a wispy white goatee surveyed them. With an emaciated arm and long, stringy fingers, he motioned to come up, and backed inside.

Vinh slipped off his sandals. His toes were splayed like the guard's, Linnea observed. Looking like he read her mind, Vinh hurried up the steps.

Suddenly alone, Linnea swiveled about to check everything around her. Leaving terra firma, she'd be entering a realm for a task she felt unprepared and unsure about. Taking a luxurious moment and a deep breath, she kicked off her flats to feel the frothy earth rise between her toes like grains on a sandy beach. Reaching back to the good feeling of running on the Balboa shore, she summoned the survival tools derived from those precious times to embark on something beyond the ken of classmates and peers.

When Linnea reached the top, she felt swept into an elongated, dark interior as though sucked by a force. The space was dank with the smell of wet straw. Vinh sat cross-legged to her left. The old man who'd beckoned edged backwards into a dark recess at the center of a semi-circle of slightly younger men. Clearly the most important among them, he appeared to be motioning her to follow.

Linnea started forward but Vinh yanked her skirt for her to sit down exactly where she was, in the light by the opening. He rushed a finger to his lips to prevent her opening mouth from uttering a word.

She wanted to collapse into a cross-legged position like Vinh's. After tries in several positions, she chose to fold a bended knee to one side and one on the other, butterfly style. Somewhat properly settled, she embarked on slow breathing. Soon her nose and throat became irritated by air containing a sweet muskiness combined with the residues of firewood smoke. She glanced at Vinh staring resolutely at the rattan floor mat in front of him and remembered that there would be a preliminary period "for the reading of the soul."

Linnea adjusted herself, intending for her mind to go into neutral, but her eyes had none of it. The atmosphere was dense and it was difficult to see anything clearly except bunches of maize hanging from overhead, appearing likely to drop. With the barest movement of the head, she searched, discerning nothing beyond the loud beating of her own heart. Then she too found the weave of the mat in front of her a place in which her eyes might find comfort.

After what seemed like an eternity of silence, and more than enough time to read her poor battered soul, Linnea involuntarily sighed.

Vinh's head snapped up the same way Stephen's did at the very same thing. She bowed her head and focused hard on the mat ... but her ears heard insects – insects getting louder, circling above and around and sounding like appendages rubbing together preparing to strike. Would her inoculations for the deadly dozen include everything contractible here today?

Scratching sounds drifting up from below at first seemed like that of a chicken but now sounded more like something big, four-legged and feline. She turned to the sunlit opening. Shoes! Were her shoes being taken, preventing a fast getaway?

She glanced at the old man who appeared to be the chief she was to confer with, but he had a blank stare placed onto the space between the semi-circle of men and her. From below came squeals of children, perhaps finding what she'd left on their reed platform. The corners of Linnea's lips curled and just as instantly drooped. What if children thought the fountain pens were candy and sucked them, became ill or were poisoned and died?

A sound came from the corner. With eyes wide, Linnea's head snapped to the left. Gunnysacks, bales of rice ... people?

Linnea stared fiercely at Vinh, demanding that he look and explain. Sweat poured from her scalp and rolled down her back.

Enough was enough. Without caring, she straightened one leg out in front and then the other, rubbing her knees and wiggling her toes, getting ready.

Vinh touched her elbow and she jumped. He motioned for her to proceed up nearer the chief who had now come into the center of the men. She weighed the idea and edged forward.

The chief seemed benign enough with the black and red shawl draped across his shoulders like a loose mantle of power. He looked out from under the gray hairs of his thick superciliary ridge, and it was several moments before she could see luminously black orbits flicking within crescents of white. The taut skin on his bare chest gave him a young, vibrant appearance, despite the gray and white hairs sprinkled on arms and legs. When he began speaking, it was in Vietnamese with more than a few words in French and English.

After a long statement of welcome, the chief reported how many Hmong people lived in the village, their ages, the livestock, and how long they had been in that particular area, about which she made a show of taking notes. It appeared that he already had been interviewed, perhaps by a Special Forces team, suggesting he knew her visit would need that information for a new project. In his concluding words, she was certain she heard in one tongue or another "rights" and "land."

Linnea responded with prepared pleasantries, explaining with smiles and lots of hand motions that she was with the United States Association for International Development and that America intended to help the Hmong. She indicated she might be able to assist them with the Saigon central government, which was going through times of change ... although she was not altogether sure about the changes. She said she wanted the chief to know that the United States was in Vietnam for the purpose of helping "you Vietnamese people."

All of a sudden and too late, she remembered that Montagnards, originally from China's Yunnan Province, didn't think of themselves as Vietnamese. Hastily she said, *"Các Anh Người Mường Ở Trên Núi."* ("You Hmong in your hills.")

The chief's obsidian-like eyes fixed on her like a grandparent forcibly trying to remain patient with an aberrant, unknowing child.

Linnea presumed the chief knew that the Saigon government had already given the United States the responsibility for dealing with the Hmong, glanced at Vinh for confirmation, and proceeded. She talked, listened, and made a few gentle remarks about the beauty of the hills and how with USAID help the land could be highly, beautifully productive.

"You don't know what you're talking about," the chief boomed, with his thin arms flailing the air around him. "These are our hills. The French came, seized our land, made us slaves for rubber, their rubber! They destroyed our earth. The French left and we were promised *our own land back!*" he growled. "Diem now is...." He conferred with Vinh who, taking a glance at her sinking shoulders, uttered for the chief the words Strategic Hamlets. "President Diem is resettling our land as," he looked at Vinh again as though still not understanding, and finally uttered "hamlets ... camps on land, land always ours."

In a dither, confused in trying to comprehend everything, particularly land in the hills as opposed to land in the plains, before Linnea could open her mouth to utter a gentle need for clarification, she heard the chief utter with a bitter rasp:

"Americans, friends of the French, what do you want here?"

Linnea sucked in her breath and tried to straighten. "The United States wants to help you … and the Saigon government." Beginning again, "Our organization USAID wants to help with agriculture, what you grow, so that you will have plenty to eat and even to sell, and can stay where you are and won't have to move around searching for good land. We have seeds and fertilizers, we can help you with wells, and we can assist you with growing what you need and want."

Surprised by her ease in relating unformed certainties, she felt her skin creep and seep from every pore. She felt sticky, dirty, and unclean. She glanced at Vinh who appeared to be examining the mat in front of him as though it might contain an escape route.

The chief's head descended an inch toward the wrinkled backs of his hands knitted tightly together. "We don't need your or Saigon's help with what we grow. Or what we sell. We are our own government." He straightened his forearm and, with fingers together in a flattened hand, swept the space between them. "We are our own nation. We're not part of Vietnam. Saigon is not a friend." He could be seen grinding pink stained teeth.

Summoning USAID pamphlet platitudes, she said, "We the United States want you to retain ... to keep your ... your unique culture. And, if you want ... teachers ... equipment for wells ... seeds for better produce ... threads ... soaps ... radios...." Feeling dizzy searching for the right words, she uttered, "Markets for your handicrafts and ... *and transportation for what you produce and grow.*" (*Bán đồ thủ công và vận chuyển nông sản cho các ông.*)

The chief stared past her.

Linnea swept her forehead with the back of her hand and started again. "Help is always needed for someone sick, a child out of sorts and you ... er, your old people."

For the first time, the chief's face seemed to brighten.

With a slight weave from side to side, Linnea continued, "Things are constantly changing ... progressing. Your children cannot avoid being affected by what's taking place elsewhere. It'll begin with just little things," she said, thinking of Polaroid pictures that would show Hmong what they looked like.

"I brought these for your children," she said, scrambling into the small container with her notebook for a Mickey Mouse decorated pencil. "I've left more on the platform below."

Whispered voices came from the corner! Linnea cast a stern look in that direction and with force said, "Children are curious. And curiosity...." Linnea cleared her voice. "Curiosity can be good. It can lead to education and progress. With our help, Saigon is making progress, and it may be the government your children will have to deal with. In the meantime, you can use me—USAID—with Saigon," and then came one of her unconscious, involuntary audible sighs.

Pale light from the doorway accentuated the chief's sunken cheeks. His jowls twitched.

He jabbed the air with his fingers. "If you and Saigon go away, we can have our land back. We want our land."

"We can help. With our fertilizers and seeds you can grow good things in preparation for your land in the future."

You won't need all the land you think you want, she was thinking.

"Good things! Future!"

"We can help you change from relying on poppies," Linnea said it with a straight back and a clear voice.

The chief was gazing at the corner as though hearing something else. "We have new promises."

Linnea's head swiveled to the same corner. "Be careful," she said in a voice deep and confident. "The French and President Diem may have failed in their promises. But this is a new era. The United States is good and strong and is here to see to it that you in South Vietnam—you Hmong—are free to determine your own futures."

"Fine. The future," the chief nodded. "A quiet future."

"Yes." Linnea stared into the dark corner. Two figures, it was difficult to tell whether male or female, faced her, large, close and forbidding. Could they be Viet Cong? The North Vietnamese?

Linnea turned back to the chief. "We've learned the North and its foreign backers are making promises, promises they cannot fulfill. I've heard you've been promised an enormous amount of land throughout Vietnam. Well, the land isn't theirs to promise."

The chief stared at the doorway as though to indicate the session was over.

Sweat poured from her scalp. Wiggling her toes, she started to rise: "I'm going to be coming back with agricultural experts to show that you can have good things to eat and to sell." She was onto one knee. "Please don't shift your disappointment and dislike of the French onto…"

"Hatred," he growled.

She tipped forward, stopping herself with fingers to the mat. "Okay, hatred," she stammered. "But please don't transfer your hatred of the French onto the Diem government and then onto us. From what I've learned, the Diem government is trying hard. So are we."

The chief squinted. "We'll see." He swallowed and a large bulge bobbed down and up his neck. "America is known for laws. The French made up laws. Saigon uses whatever laws it wants. If law is the path to follow, whose laws?"

"Yes. Well, let's give that some thought," Linnea said almost at full height. "Communists don't have laws. They just make promises—promises they have no intention or ability of keeping."

The chief rocked on his haunches. "We like the government that governs least."

Ah! A familiar line! And so, imagining her late father nodding, Linnea enthusiastically responded, "That's the way we feel, too."

Linnea was first down the steps, feeling like a skirted circus elephant dropping with a tiny parasol. Reaching the mat platform in the clearing, she pulled out the Polaroid camera.

"When next I come," she turned to the chief coming after her, "I'd like to take pictures of the children ... to give to them." After awkwardly releasing the rectangular gray metal into its accordion picture-taking position, she focused on Vinh, who looked distinctly uncomfortable. At the precise moment her sweaty finger pressed the orange hook-shaped switch at the camera's side, Vinh closed his eyes.

The Polaroid sounds resembled a dog gnawing on a bone. The chief sprang forward with arms raised. Linnea folded over, imagining her gray machine and her head about to be smashed. Vinh jumped between them, the chief looking Vinh over as if to see if his soul was intact or had been snatched.

Shaking, Linnea focused on her wristwatch, an action that caused further alarm.

When the prescribed time elapsed, she carefully pulled apart the paper exposing the developing picture. Her fingers flew about but she hadn't enough of them, and so she used her teeth. The chief and guard, at full alert, focused on her, alarmed and ready.

"The picture lets a person see himself; it takes nothing away," she mumbled.

Adhesive on Linnea's fingers stuck to the picture. She waved the square in the air for it to dry. Ungluing herself, she handed the freshly lacquered square to the chief who carefully turned it over as though daring it. He held it sideways and squinted at it. He shook it and, shooting a piercing look at Vinh, dropped the picture face-up on the ground between his feet. With folded arms, he glared at the square and poked it with his toe as though imagining he could step into the photograph.

Flies buzzed and the chief pondered. Linnea folded the Polaroid into her backpack, ready to go. The chief remained transfixed by the photograph. Without looking up, he slipped from his wrist a copper bracelet and held it out to her.

"For me?" Linnea asked, glancing at Vinh. "Thank you. We will see you again soon."

She bowed and, taking the lead ahead of Vinh and the guide, headed for the trail. She yearned for the coolness under the thick canopied foliage, and wasted no time in reaching a large, partially lichen-encrusted rock, starting to round it.

Snarling and hissing like a wildcat, the guide swiped her side.

"Stop!" Vinh shouted, bouncing forward to grab her arm. "That rock has a spirit not to be disturbed. We must go around it exactly the way he wants. He'll lead," Vinh insisted in a voice tinged with disgust.

Linnea glanced back at the chief standing boldly in a shaft of light in the clearing. She considered his pride and began to feel sad. He was an earnest old soul trying to save a sensitive culture in a harsh landscape against a threatening world. Linnea wondered if she'd be able to help him feed, educate and save his people from hostilities that might be brewing.

Vinh was quiet getting the jeep down the hill. Linnea was silent, too, busy replaying in her mind the discourse in the long house. She wanted Vinh's appraisal but suspected she'd have to wait for Asian timing.

When they were almost on flat terrain where the sun blanketed the landscape, Vinh said, "Before I forget, the guard told me that for the next visit you should bring a present. Nothing big or expensive, but it needs to be American."

"Oh. I didn't know to do that. Any suggestions?"

"Well, I've heard a cowboy hat has worked in the past. From Texas."

Linnea examined Vinh's sober face.

When Vinh slowed for a huge flock of noisy white ducks being herded across the road by a young girl waving a long, thin stick, he said, "I suppose you suspected he is the head man of one of the largest Hmong clans. He got that position from wisely dealing with the French."

Linnea wished she had provided the chief with specific information about the hardy seeds and seedlings for strawberries, coffee and limes. "I've heard the North Vietnamese have promised the Montagnards an autonomous region approximately a third of all Vietnam," she said. "So far the Hmong have resisted the communists." She waited for him to comment about the voices in the corner. When he didn't say anything, she asked, "Is it because the Hmong don't want to be obligated? Or do they resist because the Hmong feel Saigon already owes them and that they can get a better deal, maybe with us?"

"Yes, they've resisted," Vinh replied. "Hmong have never gotten along with Vietnamese farmers or the French or Saigon. They don't get along with each other."

A mile or two later, when the pocked roadway had fewer obstacles, like slow, stubborn bullocks or piles of rice stalks spread out onto it to dry, Vinh gained speed. He raced the jeep down the middle of the asphalt cantilevered for monsoon rains to run off into the fields.

Feeling the moment was right, she asked, "Vinh, we need to talk about what USAID wants with the Hmong. Do you think I got the message across, about staying put and growing vegetables? And do you think that if they were told they'd be given back what they say is their land, they'd stop growing opium and start growing better things?"

"You said what you were supposed to say. Mr. Stephen wants particular Hmong, to stay in place, the ones farthest to the west." A few minutes later Vinh added, "The Hmong say they have laws. But they don't have laws, just tribal customs—not the same from one village to another. They're just a worn out, useless people and they're...." He paused. "They're problematic, as your people like to say, and difficult to deal with."

"I don't think they're worn out or useless!"

Vinh countered, "You should know there's not more to learn about or to do with the Hmong. You may see that you should not try."

Linnea folded her arms. Wasn't dealing with them both his job and hers? Wasn't understanding and helping the Hmong to be healthier people, with a better life the objective of the American mission? And didn't cultural comprehension and assistance have a greater chance for success than the confrontation that seemed to be in the minds of so many?

"I'm here to help Montagnards and South Vietnam; and I'm going to assist my country and yours at the same time. If you have a problem, you'd better discuss it with Stephen. And from now on we'll speak in Vietnamese."

CHAPTER IV

After a few more trips into the hills and several Saigon explorations that she didn't want to divulge, Linnea awakened to find Stephen's note under her door for her to meet him at the downtown USAID office towards noon for the talk she said she wanted.

Linnea moved quickly. He's not going to press me this time about where I'm going or why, she said to herself, taking a quick bath, and heading straight downtown to the U.S. Information Service.

The USIS library was centrally located on a tree-lined street in a refurbished French colonial dwelling with white pillars and a flag snapping on a tall flagpole. A Marine at the front door in his blue, white and red uniform was reflected in the full-length glass window behind him like another Marine backing him up.

"I'm with USAID," Linnea said to the plump, gray-haired American matron at the center desk facing the entry. "I want to find out about something called the *Joint Communique* between South Vietnam and our government … and also about the background of the Strategic Hamlet Program. You can help me with those, can't you?"

"The *Joint Communique*, yes, of course. It's a document. I'm not sure how much there is on the other, the hamlet program. I'll see what I can find."

Linnea settled herself into a shiny wooden chair on the left of the first of four long rectangular teak tables stretching down the bookshelf-lined room. Several young glasses-wearing Vietnamese boys with happy chatter picked over volumes on shelves at eye level near the entrance that included Jack London and Mark Twain. Past them, farther down, older Vietnamese men in white with thinning hair and scraggly goatees lifted with bony fingers *Le Monde* from dowels in a stand-up wooden case. A couple of Westerners speaking Spanish poured through the revolving glass entry toward newspapers and magazines along the side in the back. Several teenage girls in *ao dai* ruffled through the colorful covers of *Look* and *Life,* leaving untouched the communist bloc countries' cheap tabloids whose covers splashed harsh reds and greens outside borders and margins.

The *Joint Communiqué's* heavy stiffness indicated its contents were considered important and to be long lasting. The United States would be responsible for helping to protect and secure the villages in the countryside, Linnea read, freeing the South Vietnamese administration to run the government from Saigon. The Strategic Hamlet Program, in contrast, was briefly, vaguely described on newspaper quality sheets.

Linnea made several trips to the reference desk for more information, and then searched newspapers and magazines for clues on the Program's inception and projected length of existence. Waiting in case the matron found something more to fulfill her request, she lifted from dowels the *New York Times,* her daily nourishment in Manhattan. Finishing the first page of the slightly dated issue, her fingers paused on a full page Saks Fifth Avenue winter coat advertisement. A smile crossed her face just as three American men plunked themselves down at the end of her table, presumably to be in the good draft from the air-conditioner.

There are other places in here for them, Linnea wanted them to know, visually pointing to empty tables. But they behaved as though this was their office, and embarked with vigorous voices in discussing policies they were told to follow even though in conflict with village-life in the countryside. Listening, the scene began to remind her of situations with her brother and his friends, when they accepted her female presence as a protestation of innocence if she could just keep her mouth shut.

Faded baseball caps topped three of their leathered faces. The cap on the blond haired man at the end of the table was pulled down tight, sprouting tuffs at the sides like the silk of ears of corn. Appearing like a supervisor, he used his calloused hands to make points. It wasn't long before several friends came in with quick reports about matters that didn't stand out until she heard the word hamlet. With her head down, leaning forward with arms folded over the newspaper, Linnea listened intently.

Three-quarters of an hour later, when she realized she needed to leave to meet Stephen, she rose, and, in a private joke, in a voice the men would definitely hear, she excused herself to them. Startled, the men looked up and stared. "I feel you all must be working hard to achieve something good in rural South Vietnam," she said, folding the *New York Times* with care. "What are your experiences in a Strategic Hamlet?"

The men frowned as though she had broken a trust. Eventually, the man with the corn whiskered ears and penetrating eyes growled in dismissal that he wasn't going to talk about hamlets.

"They are just experimental, aren't they?" she pressed.

The men in unison began discussing supply matters. She lingered long enough for a reconsideration of her question and rushed out. Going along at a fast clip, elevated by the sensation of working a story, she congratulated herself that she'd already survived several trips into the hills and had connected with a number of Buddhists in Saigon with their varied opinions on the abilities of the Saigon government. She was off to a good start to paint a picture for Clarissa's father. Her next move would be to probe journalists.

The USAID office on the second floor of a square concrete building reminded Linnea of the AP "city" pit in New York, with a mishmash of metal desks and wooden chairs, piles of black binders and pads of lined yellow paper. The room indicated American government occupation with its formal framed picture of President Kennedy on the wall. The pungent smell of *nuac mam*, the Vietnamese fish sauce, seeping up from the street below, declared they were doing for their country, as Kennedy wanted, and overseas in a fetid swamp.

Stephen was alone at his desk off in the corner. His hunched back and rolled up shirtsleeves indicated absorption in whatever he was reading. Hearing her enter, he turned, smiled, and took that moment to stretch his back. "From what you've told me, you've been moving into your assignment very well. Maybe you never should have thought of being just a journalist."

"Just a journalist!" She repeated, and headed straight for her desk.

"When I finish this report," he said, "I want to know more about your progress with the Hmong. I know, I know," he cut off anything she might say. "I've had other things on my mind when you started to tell me about Montagnard visits." He remained turned, as though awaiting a response. Above him, the air conditioner sounded like it had a hyperactive hamster running a treadmill.

"The meetings have gone all right," she replied. "The chiefs want the return of land taken by the French and Diem. I indicated we might help, but later. I relayed your offer of transportation for what they grow." She left her eyes on him. Every time she mentioned transportation to the Hmong, it stayed in the back of her mind that she should learn about the mechanics of what she was offering.

Without anything forthcoming from Stephen about commerce in the hills, she cited a few curiousities about the Hmong. When she sensed his thoughts had drifted, she dropped her satchel on the metal desk. Inside, her camera clacked like a colon. Pulling a tissue from the Kleenex box on her desktop for the flow at her temples, "Why is it urgent that Hmong stay in place and change what they're growing—even if it's opium?"

"Even if it's opium?" Stephen sat up. "You couldn't even share a joint at a party."

Linnea shook her head. "Can you tell me the importance behind our helping the Hmong, particularly with transportation, getting their produce down from the hills?"

"You've asked that before. I'll repeat: They're using up a lot of land, always moving around, running up and down the hills with torches burning grasses just to put a few nutrients into the soil that'll last a precious short time. If they start growing coffee and other things they'll make money and stay where they are. And be happy."

"And maybe watch out and track for us?" When Stephen didn't react, she continued, "I'll do my best, but I really wonder if it's not a futile exercise that you've dreamed up."

"I didn't dream up anything." He started turning back to his desk.

Linnea ventured, "I was at the USIA's library this morning looking into the *Joint Communiqué.*"

"Why?" Stephen turned back around and rose, his chair going back with a screech. "That has nothing to do with your assignment!"

"My assignment is to use my knowledge of the Vietnamese people. The *Communiqué* indicates that we, the United States, are to deal with the eighty-five percent of the Vietnamese population who are outside of Saigon—the farmers and villagers in the flatlands and the Hmong in the hills."

"Oh all right," he sighed. "If that's how you have to think of things … but leave it there."

"There's the Strategic Hamlet Program, too."

"The Strategic Hamlet Program is to help protect Vietnamese in vulnerable areas, such as to the north near the demarcation line!"

"But the program isn't just to be up there. It is down here, uprooting villagers all over the place."

"The hamlets are needed and they've been agreed upon."

"By whom? Are troops in the hamlets? Aren't farmers safer at home, in villages they'll want to protect on their own? Whose idea is the hamlet program? Ours? Or was it the idea of President Diem's brother Nhu?"

"Dammit, 'Nea! Don't go there! The Hamlets are outside our bailiwick."

Hamlet construction probably was within USAID's realm, Linnea was pretty sure. "Isn't knowledge of Vietnamese culture my business, my bailiwick, and isn't that why you enticed me here?"

"Enticed you!" Throwing up his hands, "*Enticed you!*" he repeated, smiling. "We definitely need to talk. And we will," he said, turning back to his desk with his final word "Later."

"Later," Linnea said under her breath. *Again, yet, still,* and always *later,* she grumbled to herself. Did he think he could put her off and use her in this damned job? Stephen's string of words was no longer a joke, as it had seemed when they first met.

*   *   *

"May I?" he said, reaching the Asia Society's glass door onto the tree-lined street and walking alongside as though they were already acquainted. At the corner, when he realized she was going straight across Park Avenue, he took her elbow as if it were his direction, too. Heading up the rise to the flower-planted central island, Linnea noticed a slight drag to his right leg.

"Polio," he said to her glance, "and it doesn't slow me down one bit."

Until that moment, she had been going to dismiss him, but self-assurance with an affliction intrigued her. Also, he asked good questions and listened to her responses—a rarity in the males she knew. So she let him walk her past her 64th Street brownstone and across Fifth Avenue and down the slippery cobblestones into the Children's Zoo of Central Park.

"Those splashy seals seem to be the happiest animals here," Stephen exclaimed, pulling her back from a spray of water.

"They aren't seals," she smartly replied. "They're California Sea Lions. You Easterners have simple seals just as you have short, rounded mounds you call mount something or other. We have real mountain ranges," she said, wondering why she was speaking this way.

"Is that so?" He turned to her with a broad smile. "Well, we Easterners are lionized for having intellectually and morally created the greatest peaks in our nation's history."

"Ho, ho, ho," she responded, "but that was then. The west has a future, and it's where people are free to be original, to innovate and be adventurous."

"Oh, my! All that? And are you?"

"Adventurous? Absolutely! I've been skin-diving in Baja California and I've solo sailed out into the Pacific, and I hope to...."

"A sailor! Great! I've found my crew!"

"Your crew? I don't think so!" Then, considering his polio-emaciated leg, she uttered in a soft voice, "Well, maybe. I know how to crew. I helped my late brother skipper and win."

He examined her face. "Then it's settled. I skipper! We'll take my sloop out the East River and sail down the coast to a harbor that's cozy and warm."

When they left the zoo, rounded the Armory, and helped each other up the moss-covered stairs into a cold Fifth Avenue breeze, they continued conversing about Asia, their conversation concluding with Stephen suggesting he might see her yet again, later.

*   *   *

"Pray tell, my irrepressible one, why are you smiling?" Stephen asked, almost up to her desk.

In a voice tinged with nostalgia, she answered, "I was thinking about when we met and how we could talk, and that," she cleared her throat, "I've somehow wound up here."

To Stephen's cocked head, she continued almost wistfully. "Remember how we used to call each other at our jobs to refute or confirm some esoteric fact we'd earlier discussed and then researched? I was just thinking that I miss how we shared things openly and honestly."

Stephen's attention had gone to a young Vietnamese messenger with a cap and glasses standing at the doorway atop the stairs, looking around. After signing, and while reading on the way back to his desk, Stephen then seemed to make an effort to return to what they'd been discussing. "The Hmong headman may have said things to you he would not have with others."

"Why do you say that?" Linnea shot back, wondering if what he had read related to her.

Still perusing, he replied, "Female shock effect. He could have been so startled the U.S. sent a woman that he became more revealing. I'll relay that to the powers that be."Pressing her lips together, Linnea stared at a sheet of white paper. She needed to write Clarissa and she would. Squaring herself in her chair, she wondered what to say about Saigon politics and the Buddhists, Strategic Hamlets, the Hmong opium, and, in particular what questions to ask about where to proceed. She had become close with Clarissa when her mother died of cancer at the same time as Linnea's family suffered tragedies. Afterwards, when Clarissa's father came west to take her to dinner, Linnea was invited along, like she was part of the family.

The relationship developed after graduation, when Linnea joined the AP in New York and Clarissa returned east to live with her widowed father in Georgetown and work in Congress. When Linnea came down to visit, Clarissa's father again took the two girls to dinner. One evening, over dessert at a corner table on a restaurant's quiet second floor, Clarissa's father spoke paternally to Linnea. He suggested that Linnea seemed to have a good opportunity for experience in Asia working for USAID, if she accepted the invitation by Stephen, a brilliant, well-motivated man like himself, he implied. If she would go to South Vietnam, he intoned, "You can be my eyes and ears, providing me with insights on the undercurrent—the stuff that's not in official reports." Linnea had wondered what he really intended from her until Clarissa later told her that her father and, it was implied, the Kennedy administration, needed views in addition to those of the agency and the military.

Dear Clarissa,

My fingers are sloshing the keys as I try to type this to you, and the damned whirling overhead fan is dumping hot, heavy air down upon me and melting the paper. This place is like a sauna! And the weather is supposed to be mild at this time of year!

From what I've seen of Saigon, it's charming and peaceful. My trips into the Hmong hills are going all right. The Montagnards are interesting and challenging, but that's all I'll say about that right now. (Once started, I don't know how I'll stop.)

The political motivations of Buddhists in this Catholic led government appear to be dormant. The monk I eventually talked with (the one your father suggested) has been at Yale and away from South Vietnam, so I'm not sure how well attuned he is. Buddhists refrain from politics, he said, until there is a trigger point. Something in the way he spoke makes me wonder whether a trigger point would be in the actions of the South Vietnam government or in our activities here. The monk agreed for me to talk with him again.

Our USIS library is invaluable for me and, of course, for the Vietnamese. It carries all our newspapers and newsmagazines, and even papers in Russian and Chinese. In the library one day I overheard some International Volunteer Service (IVS) staff members who have been here since World War II, speak the language and are knowledgeable about history and culture. I heard them say our policies in South Vietnam are confusing and contradictory, just as your father suggested they might be. This may relate to the Strategic Hamlet Program, about which your father is probably aware. I can find out whatever he wants to know. The program seems in opposition to Vietnamese culture, from what I can see.

I'm delighted your work for the Congressman is going well. Researching what he needs in his Foreign Relations Committee position makes your job very important. Our Asian studies degrees weren't such bad ideas after all, were they?

> *Hurriedly, with love and a hug,*
> *Linnea*

After locking his desk, Stephen announced they'd be leaving, giving her barely enough time to put her letter into an envelope and seal it before he guided her out the door. With the quickest steps she had experienced with him so far and a continuous stream of remarks, he shepherded her to the broad central square where a hotel loomed into the square like an expansive clapboard monument.

"During the last half year of being here," he said, "I looked forward to showing you around this mesmerizing place, and here is where history begins. This is Saigon's grand old lady, the Hotel Continental, where George Orwell, Aldous Huxley, Somerset Maugham, Victor Hugo, and, of course, Graham Greene sojourned. It's the home of romance, *and intrigue!*" he said with a squeeze to her arm.

Linnea smiled at his old intimation that Helen MacInnes' novels were her *modus vivendi*, and greedily imagined the heady conversations that had taken place on the hotel's wrap-around open-air veranda. With swooping wrought iron and plaster arches and wide porches, the Continental stretched up and out as though to say it was there first and wasn't going to give an inch. Although in need of a fresh coat of paint, Linnea anticipated the colonial relic still had a role to play.

"Greene and pals—like the madams from every continent—loved Saigon and engaged in every sordid activity it offered."

"Like lying back in cozy dark dens smoking the brown bubblies?" Linnea asked, showing off what the hills and research had taught her.

Stephen glanced at her. "Sure, but President Diem stopped all that. With our help, he had a big bonfire of opium and pipes in the streets right here. In the six years since his election, Diem has constructed roads, a north-south railroad, and important waterways—the Dong Tien and Dong Giong Canals—and he's responsible for agriculture being up."

Linnea made a note to herself to check that out at the USIS.

Stephen led her up the steps, first into the shade of the Continental's high parachute-like arches, and then into a musty, wood paneled lobby where once deep red damask on chairs, settees and walls had faded or been worn pink. Crystal chandeliers, heavy with dust, swayed from wobbling, barely revolving wooden fans. Despite open windows and doors, the smell of stale cigar smoke rose from an expansive Persian rug with heavily traveled lanes.

"It's probably just as it was when your writer friends were in residence," Stephen said, "and it's a shame Kipling, Conrad and Greene aren't sitting over there, waiting to greet you."

Recalling Maugham plots and memorable characters, she got into the mood as he magnanimously led her down the Continental's broad wooden steps and onto the square.

While trying to catch her breath in the noonday heat, Stephen pointed to a spot where, he said, the government had had a huge opium burning. "So, President Diem is okay?" she ventured. "Well, that's good. But, didn't Diem also basically dethrone Emperor Bao Dai and repudiate the Geneva Agreement over an election with Ho Chi Minh?"

Stephen may have been about to give a pithy response when noise intervened. As though on cue, motorcycles and cars backfired and high-pitched whistles shrieked. Next, objects of every size, shape and material, going at varying speeds, swirled through the square as though aiming to bump each other as in an amusement park. Rising dust mixing with heavy humidity made it difficult to breathe, and the sun beaming down made it difficult for her to think clearly.

When they reached the square's opposite side, Stephen used his head to point at a woman and young girl rising from a bed of newspapers in front of a door. "Good! The three-hour siesta is over. This is Rue Catinat. Officially it's *Tu Do* – freedom—but everyone still calls it Catinat ... after the first French ship here in the early 1800s," he tacked on with a smile, as though to say he knew she was about to ask.

A block later, Stephen slowed almost to a stop. In a quiet voice, he said, "I'm glad you're independent and have been getting around on your own. Really I am! But please remember that your job is with the Montagnards and that it's unwise to poke into things that are none of your business." He looked around as though checking for someone in the people passing by. "Now, about your project with the Hmong, I'll help you all you want. As you've probably read, opium once was the equivalent of gold here, and Saigon served as its bank. The French had a big production house on Hai Ba Trung Street over there," he pointed, "to supply the dens they promoted, and there were lots of them."

Now we're getting somewhere, Linnea thought. "So, the Hmong opium still comes…."

"The French used opium to pay pensions to civil servants, and they kept it cheap—ten or twelve pipes for less than a dollar. The remaining opium dens are down in Cholon with the Chinese … and no telling what they're up to. Some wonder if Chinese could be a fifth column. Anyway," he placed his hands on her shoulders to turn her, "a remaining den is down this alley here." After she'd had a good look, he said, "And the dragon guards well the holy boughs."

"What? Holy boughs?" she asked.

"From Virgil's *Aneid*. Opium dates from ancient times. That scrawny man down there with the dark half moons under his eyes—he's a regular user and a den watchdog."

The Chinese man with a three strand white goatee and a shiny long black gown put floppy hands on his hips and stared back, his strange eyes seeming to fix on her. Turning away, "I thought you said opium was wiped out in Saigon—by Diem?"

"This den may be a last for old time's sake, to cater to a few, or for show—and for the wasted look on that opium-using watchman to tell the story. Opium here today is just not worth writing home about." With a quick reflection and a check of her face, he squeezed her arm. "You know what I mean."

A hot draft of cloying air made its way into her nostrils, irritating and fascinating at the same time. Feeling something at her back, she snuck a glance behind. The Chinese man had come out onto the street, his opaque eyes following her. "If the Hmong are to grow only enough opium to use or trade, and if they start growing coffee, will opium still be part of the territory?" Will opium remain the worrisome issue Clarissa's father expressed concerning American servicemen coming to Saigon? Linnea wanted an answer and, looking up at Stephen for it, she tripped into a man sitting on a short stool at curbside, his mouth open wide to the sky, his arms and legs fanned out while the filthy fingers of a vigorous man standing inserted a rust-stained chromium instrument into his mouth.

"Dentistry without argument, and probably for only ten cents," Stephen said, pulling her to his side in a voice to express humor. "We'll mark the spot in case my own dentist...." He stopped and looked at his watch. "I have to make a phone call. I'll be right back," he said, slipping into a shop.

Linnea appreciated moments alone to gaze back up the street at billowing silks in glittering sunlight and at the shimmering shades in the faces of a panorama of people. When she focused at the ground, she found in gutters a pair of bare-rump young boys playing in a small pool of dirty water. She looked about. No one seemed to be watching over them, causing the thought to flitter past that those who can have them don't necessarily want them, while those who can't have them....

"Saigon is the Pearl of the Orient, my dear 'Nea," Stephen declared as he rushed out. "As Somerset Maugham said, 'Saigon is a blithe and smiling place.'"

"We're not far from where we're headed, are we?" she asked.

"Just a couple of blocks more."

The Majestic, stated a shiny bronze plaque on a whitewashed wall beneath a high overhead portico. Positioned at the city's principal entryway, across from a main dock of the swiftly flowing Saigon River, The Majestic commanded the junction between the wild and untamed land and the placid sea and a sophisticated world beyond.

Taking a few seconds, Linnea lapsed into a fantasy derived from an old photo: a parade of white suited, long-skirted, parasol carrying passengers disembarking from ships slick with varnished teak decks; refined Frenchmen casually expounded to each other while strolling across an uncluttered earthen street, proceeding up the wide scalloped steps of the magnificent Majestic. Inside, a cool, marbled foyer welcomed with palm trees in life-sized blue and white porcelain pots, finger-like fronds softly fluttering under undulating fans.

Stephen led Linnea upstairs where a most welcomed breeze swirled across a fifth floor open-air lounge overlooking the Saigon River. The waterway surged with a cluster of sampans and lorchas, and brown-hulled junks hoisting maroon sails with patches of faded crimson. An old, mahogany-trimmed oceangoing ship-of-call pointed upstream, its tall, vertical windows flashing pink and blue bubbles in hand blown windowpane, resembling a Tudor estate with leaded windows.

Across the river a luminous tapestry of waving dark blue-green spread as far as Linnea could see. Distant mountains stood prominently within a purplish hue. Close in, banana plants and mangroves decorated riverbanks. The pale blueness of an expansive sky seemed to embrace everything without end.

"A quiche Lorraine and a *petite* salad are on their way." Stephen said, pulling out a chair for her when she returned from the lady's room.

Settling herself, Linnea took a good look at Stephen. As though for the first time she appreciated how his dark brown hairline made him handsome and as distinguished as an ambassador. Looking into the deep lagoon of his eyes, she softly said, I appreciate being here," with you, she came close to saying, "where I hope to do something worthwhile." And, she added to herself, I aim to impress you by achieving beyond your imagination.

"I'm also glad you're here, and I know you will succeed in whatever you want … and I'll be glad if it includes me," he added with a meaningful gaze.

Linnea looked away, as though she hadn't heard.

The waiter arrived with two ice filled glasses and two thicker ones topped by metal devices steeping dripping coffee onto a layer of white at the bottom. "I've ordered Vietnamese coffee— *Cà phê sữa đá* —to introduce you to it. The white stuff on the bottom is milk. We give them the real thing, but the Vietnamese prefer canned Carnation. It's mixed with syrup. When ready, we stir and pour it over the ice."

Wiping sweat dripping from her forehead, Linnea said, "I've been thinking of the movie I saw, based on *"Deliver Us From Evil"* by Navy Doctor Tom Dooley. It was about his clinic for the Catholic North Vietnamese who tromped south in the '54 partition."

"Dooley exaggerated accomplishments, I'm pretty sure, but Catholic Dooley is credited with inspiring Catholic Kennedy to form the Peace Corps. Political Animal Kennedy seems to like unorthodox people like Dooley who's probably also a Damned Democrat."

"Oh, Stephen." She wasn't going to go down that road again, even though they'd laughed about their mutually conservative Republican families. She, however, liked Kennedy and had voted for him.

A while later, dipping a napkin into her water glass so he'd notice and dabbing it on her forehead, "This heat, Stephen. I'm still not used to it, particularly sitting in the open like this. I'd like to go back to the villa," she said

Stephen glanced at the Saigon River and surreptitiously at his watch. "Maybe I should have picked up for you an umbrella or one of those fold-up fans sold all over the place. Hold on! I think I feel a breeze! You'll feel better in a minute," and he signaled the waiter for another round of gin and tonics.

Heat and humidity closed in. Linnea mopped her brow with a fury she intended for him to notice. But, knowing that this was probably the time Stephen had allotted for her to share what was on her mind, she hung on, upset not to be taking advantage of it. Finally, venturing something that might cause Stephen to be angry enough to let her leave, she said, "I respect you and others for thinking that because China recently took a bite out of India it's poised to come down and take over Vietnam and neighboring countries, but...."

"That's right!"

"You may be wrong about that Domino Theory!" she said in a rising voice.

Stephen scowled and titled his head as though to intimate her voice could be heard all the way to the river.

"Aren't you going to say something?" Linnea asked.

"We're here because China wants Vietnam."

"It may want, but the Vietnamese won't let China take over. Way back in 43 A.D.," Linnea said, relating that Chinese General Ma Vien had come down and overwhelmed the defenders, the Trung Sisters, at the Hat Giang River near Hanoi. The Trung Sisters committed suicide because they'd failed to drive out the Chinese. "To drive out the Chinese, Stephen!"

"That was then. Don't count on Vietnamese resistance now."

"Well, think again. When the Chinese built a big pillar in Hanoi they said it would last until the Vietnamese people completely disappeared. Every time the Vietnamese passed by they dropped a rock or stone until now China's pillar has completely disappeared. Doesn't that tell you that the falling dominos theory may be off, that Vietnam is not likely to fall to China?"

Stephen turned to glance at the river behind him. "I have information.... Later, okay?"

Linnea moved to the edge of her seat as though to rise.

Reaching for her hand he said, "You know, there's a Joan of Arc of Vietnam who reminds me of you. She was your age or a little older—24 or 25. And she rode an elephant. Definitely your style."

Linnea slumped as though she was through. "Yes, Trieu Au," she complied. "In the third century she fought for Vietnam's Independence *against China*. Unfortunately she too failed and committed suicide!"

"That Stanford 'junior farm' of yours planted a worthy tidbit or two!"

"There's also a legend about farmer Le Loi who was casting a net in Hanoi's Ho Hoan Kiem Lake when a turtle popped up to put a sword into his hands." With frustration in her voice, "The sword was a sign for Le Loi to raise a peasant army *to repulse the Chinese.*"

"Who were invading," Stephen countered with a shrug and a glance at the river.

"I think you shouldn't be so reluctant to hear what I have learned," she said, vaguely aware that the last drink had clarified her disgust at his avoidance of her belief in the importance of history and culture. "Le Loi defeated the Chinese by *wearing them down, little by little, year after year—* and the sword was snatched back by the turtle and is said to remain at the bottom of the lake until needed again ... *against the Chinese.*"

Linnea fingered her purse on the table, preparing to leave. As a final salvo, "If the United States is in Vietnam for the purpose of making a stand against China over Vietnam, it may be making a mistake. China's not in good shape internally. A French photographer visiting the AP reported serious upheavals in China."

"Think of Tibet!" Stephen said, sitting back as though making a good move.

Linnea noticed several heavy-set Caucasian men with sandy hair using large red hands as though constructing building models. She let her eyes rest on Vietnamese near-by, drinking coffee that continued to look to her like chocolate milkshakes. "Stephen, I'm going back to the villa. Saigon may be magical but its sunlamp is killing me."

Reaching for her hands, "I'll bet you don't know what Saigon means?"

"Stephen, please! I don't want this any more!" She pulled back, mumbling, "This area was part of Cambodia so Saigon could come from *thay gon,* meaning pay back. Saigon also might be the mispronounced Chinese *Tsai con* meaning tribute paid, presumably to China."

Stephen sat up, suggesting he might be ready to go, too, stating that Saigon in Annamese is the name of a tree—boxwoods. Saigon, the village of boxwoods, he said, but he hadn't seen a single boxwood. "See how needed you are!" His glasses had slipped down his nose and he was peering over the rim.

"Maybe this is the beginning of a fine affair," she said, trying for *Casablanca's* final line as her departing words. Rising to full height, her eyes floated to the people on the street below going toward the Saigon River dock. She blinked and the scene became surreal.

Gray steel with large white numbers emerged against a backdrop of gently waving shades of green. A huge, gleaming US Navy ship inched forward, the Stars and Stripes fluttering frantically near the name *Core.* Grasshopper-like helicopter bodies packed its decks with interwoven flopping rotor blades. The bow pushing upstream was about to overwhelm a dock of scrambling bodies jumping into tiny skiffs, sculling hard in surging waters. Hundreds of Vietnamese and a smattering of Westerners poured from side streets, rushing the big ship, cheering blank-eyed sailors standing at attention.

"A warship!" she bellowed at the stunning anachronism. Why a warship with helicopters? Does President Diem want or need them? Or have we decided they're needed?

Dialogue and diplomacy and the work of the Advisors, Special Forces and USAID were supposed to be enough.

"What's on your mind?"

Struggling for an answer, Linnea said, "Oh, just that our being at this moment, in this place, when that thing arrives, it's really rather … intriguing." Linnea held him with her eyes, noticing he seemed somewhat relieved by the appearance of the big gray vessel. "You don't seem at all surprised that we happen to be sitting here overlooking the Saigon River on the eleventh day of December 1961 when it arrives. Why not?"

CHAPTER V

"I thought when you called me in New York you said things here were peaceful and that Viet Cong activity was just a now and then thing to let it be known they're around," Linnea angrily whined from the middle of her room in the villa, aiming at the door, ready to go out.

For some reason she had difficulty facing him—always succumbing to the look in his eyes, she chided herself.

"And do you remember what I said?" Stephen said, getting up from his desk and heading toward her. "I asked if you in Manhattan were receiving hazardous duty pay. Remember the Tass office blown to smithereens, right next to your office? I said it was safer here with me, and that's true. The Ruskies are probably planning to A-bomb New York at this very moment."

Looking at her feet, shaking her head, "Stephen. I have a right to know if things here are not what they seem, not as I've been told."

"I haven't misrepresented anything to you," he replied in a reassuring tone almost up to her.

"You're so quiet, so distant, so...." Mysterious, she wanted to say. "I'm beginning to think, well, that maybe I can't work for you and USAID unless I know what's going on."

"'Nea, there are some things that don't concern you that I can't tell you. So, figure out what's really bothering you and we'll find a time and place for a good give and take. Okay?"

"We used to argue about issues, and we shared a lot." A guilty feeling flittered past that Stephen knew more about her than anyone. With her head down, staring at the floor, "Now you say…"

She wasn't aware he was up to her.

"…you cannot tell me things," she said, abruptly turning, her elbow hitting him in the solar plexus.

"Oh, I'm sorry!" she shrieked as his tall lean frame keeled over with circus performer exaggeration. Flustered, she grabbed the door and banged it shut behind her.

*　　*　　*

"Mr. Stephen told me before you arrived that you like nice things," Vinh said, hurrying Linnea away from the business area of Rue Catinat where they'd agreed to meet.

An hour later, still seething that Stephen probably considered her a powder brain keen on feminine frills, Linnea came to appreciating that Vinh had taken her away from stores with designer frocks on blonde-haired manikins. They were on run-down streets of a hodgepodge of corroded iron grilled storefronts where she had to pick her way over cracked cement and errant children's toys. She reminded Vinh that she wanted a place that might sell a screen to be used to block her books and documents from where Stephen's desk maddingly remained in her room.

Vinh walked quickly, making it challenging to keep up amidst hot braziers spitting pork fat. With eyes on the steps ahead, she asked, "What do you think about the warship that arrived with helicopters?"

Without answering, Vinh raised his head to make an obvious scan for a place or a person.

Checking her shoe for a presumed pebble, Linnea continued, "Does the ship's arrival means anything? Sure, the helicopters are helpful in getting around, but does their arrival indicate something more?"

"What?" Vinh said as though too busy looking around to have heard her.

"Do helicopters suggest the North Vietnamese are at the demarcation line?"

Then, it seemed for the first time that day, Vinh looked directly at her. "Vietnam shouldn't have an artificial line across its middle, like between North and South Korea."

"Maybe so, except if one half is harsh and restrictive, orchestrated by a foreign power with hostile aims, and wants to take over the other half that is open and free."

Vinh's black eyes spun behind brown slits of lids. "The luxury stores Stephen suggested for you. What do they tell you about the open, free Saigon in the southern half? Those things are for the lazy, wealthy people influenced by the rich foreign power feeding it." He turned and marched on.

Linnea trudged after Vinh's brisk pace down streets steaming with fetid smells. "We're entering the Pham Ngu Lao district," she heard him say. It was the first location name he had provided, making her regret that in the rush to depart she had forgotten her city map.

After a few moments, Linnea pursued something else on her mind. "Do you think I should make the Rhade tribe, who don't grow opium, a positive example to other tribes? That tribe's children go to college."

"The Rhade are still hill people," Vinh barked. "Not one tribe contributes or produces anything good."

"Unless it's opium," Linnea groused. Every time she'd suggested to Vinh they learn how much Hmong opium was being grown, he'd lapsed into a record-breaking Asian silence.

Several minutes later, Vinh paused and said, "The Hmong are good at one thing, and that's weaving cloth." He pointed to a collection of women seated cross-legged on a street corner. "You haven't been able to see many Montagnard women, and they don't often come down to the city."

The Hmong women had piles of small multi-colored squares spread across their laps. They were dark in contrast to Saigonese, like the light-skinned slender pair giving them a wide berth as though they were lepers.

Ignoring the Saigonese, the Hmong women bantered to each other in high-pitched screeches like chirping birds, their black tongues flicking between bright red gums and pink teeth. Elongated, curved foreheads, glabrous and gleaming like bullets, made Linnea wonder if it was a particular tribal custom to pluck hairlines back toward the crown. Large silver earrings complimented high-necked, long-sleeved garments of red and yellow on black backgrounds, tightly woven and heavy, indicative of their cooler highland homes.

"*Vieux, vieux,*" a small, bright-eyed woman said when Linnea picked up one intricately stitched square. Primed to hold up whatever Linnea glanced at, the Hmong woman flipped the squares over, back and forth, her cracked brown fingernails scratching at particularly fine appliqué.

"This is very nice. How much is it? *Combien c'est?* Linnea asked, uncertain what language the women might speak, now that she was in the city.

The woman held up three cracked and stained fingers.

"*Đây là đồng bạc Việt nam hay đồng dollars?*" Linnea asked, dong or dollars.

The Hmong woman, with pinpoint black eyes, in a black hat like a nurse's cap, and a black apron over tight, multicolored leggings, poked Linnea's arm and, smiling, lifted both the dong and the dollars from Linnea's hands.

Linnea smiled back and set out following Vinh onto a dirt road with shops that looked like they sold junk. Acting like he had reached his destination, he pointed to a decrepit looking store, saying it might have what she wanted. "Please spend time," he said, stepping back, appearing relieved.

Linnea had to use hands and arms like a swimmer parting water, plowing her way through wicker steamer baskets, dangling wooden spoons, bunches of dried herbs, huge paper fish, long ivory back scratchers, and feathered and scaly creatures, some dead and stuffed—a few surprisingly not. Pausing by iron pots too heavy to push aside, brushing at sweat dripping down her cheeks, about to call it quits, she glimpsed what she wanted.

Spider-webs draped the old four paneled coromandel screen, and yet its rich black lacquer radiated beauty. Struggling up to it, she waved a handkerchief across a surface with mother of pearl and thinly carved agate of incandescent pink, green and amber depictions of the four seasons. The reverse side was etched in white and pale blue like the oldest, finest Chinese screens she'd seen on upper Madison Avenue.

Banging past canisters of tea, jars of candied ginger, and large glass containers with roots, one or two resembling fetuses, she burst back onto the sidewalk with a sneeze and the statement, "I've found what my room needs."

Vinh jumped away from a derelict curbside Renault, and muttered something to a man who slinked off with the shiny blackness of the back of his head a sole identification.

Linnea observed the expression in Vinh's eyes darting from the man to her. Creases made Vinh appear far older than the presumed young man at the airport who drove her to the villa. Right now she experienced a faint mental bell-ringing to figure out how to find out Vinh's politics.

"This looks aged, antique," she said as the screen was brought onto the street. Running her fingers over the exquisitely carved court ladies' gowns, she exclaimed: "The agate's so thin it could be silk. How old do you think it is?"

"I don't know those things," Vinh curtly replied as though dealing with thoughts interrupted. "Anything else?"

"No. But thank you for taking me here. I think I'll also buy that persimmon colored Tibetan rug over there at the front of the store. It came here before the Chinese overran Tibet, don't you think?" she asked.

Instead of responding, Vinh hopped forward to help place rags between the screen's folding panels for protection in transport.

Linnea took note of the area in case it would be good for scrounging for old Chinese scrolls. "This is the kind of thing I like."

"You have much *ly*," Vinh replied, no longer anxious.

"*Ly?*"

"*Ly* is to know the soul of things—the natural harmony deep within."

"Why, thank you, Vinh. Is that Buddhist or Vietnamese?"

"Both."

Linnea hesitated, "Tell me, Vinh, do you belong to a political party or a Buddhist organization?"

After several long seconds, Vinh replied, "I belong to poetry groups."

A while later Linnea said to Vinh, "Thanks for arranging the transportation of the screen, the rug and the rattan chairs. I think I can find my way back from here. I have some thinking to do." Vinh had taken her to places where she could become absorbed while he stepped into a doorway, met a man, or dashed into a shop for a hurried conversation with someone unseen or on the phone, she realized, reviewing the entire outing and wondering about it.

Soon, going from one area to another she imagined making a map of Saigon according to smells—bleach overwhelming mold and mildew in one area; charcoal fire smoke, garlic and ginger on musty streets in another. On Rue Catinat the scents of strong perfume seemed in an all-out heady war with the pervasive aroma of fish sauce.

Slowly cruising, looking into little shops selling the unconnected, like batteries and brassieres, she began to realize that just as Stephen didn't reveal what he was up to, she didn't either.

Stumbling, she scolded herself for again failing to pay attention to Saigon's uneven pavement. This time, though, the impediment came from legs stretching out from an alley.

"Please get up," an anguished voice urged in accented English. A slender woman in *ao dai* was trying to raise the shoulders of a large Western man. "There are people," she pleaded in a whisper.

Linnea examined the woman. She didn't look like a "painted swallow," a loose woman.

"What's wrong?" she asked.

The woman glanced up and then leaned close to the man's head with a whisper that sounded like she was about to cry, "Darling, please. Please get up."

"Is he...?" With that huge Western physique, how could he be ill? Blood wasn't apparent and she couldn't smell alcohol. However, a faintly sweet aroma drifted from his body.

Linnea glanced past the woman down the narrow, shade filled alley to a red paper lantern with black Chinese letters dangling in front of a doorway. The Chinese man with a wispy white goatee stood in afternoon shadows, arms folded over his shiny dark blouse and loose black pants.

"Opium?" Linnea asked, lowering herself onto her own haunches, Vietnamese style. She saw tears drop onto the apron of the woman's *ao dai*. "People usually manage to walk away, don't they?" Linnea asked. The man sprawled on the ground had blond hair in a close crewcut like her late brother's, and he was about the same age, in the late twenties, lying prone the way she had found him. The memory made her snap up as though to be on her way.

On the street, in troubled thought, she ignored a couple of American men sauntering past, saying something to her. "The Orient's temptations," she seemed to hear Clarissa's father saying in Georgetown, "are a danger for our men." Finally she turned back to the sprawled man. Then, sighing, she searched both directions of Rue Catinat for help, realizing at the same time that the street-prowling Americans were her age or even younger, and probably lonesome and homesick. They would appreciate her smile and gratitude for their being in Saigon in behalf of their mutually great land, and would be pleased to be of assistance.

After getting the big American into the back seat of an old Renault taxi, Linnea climbed into the front beside the Vietnamese driver. Speechless, his eyes stayed on her as he released the hand brake for the vehicle to crawl forward.

"Ta hãy hướng về tương lai." "Try looking ahead," Linnea said with a touch of bravado, recalling the time in New York that she demanded a cabbie take her directions of a better route from midtown to La Guardia.

When they were in the newly converted American military hospital, Linnea asked the Vietnamese woman, "While he was having a smoke, what were you doing?"

With her head down, her reply was hard to hear. "… outside. He wasn't long. He had been sad and angry. He said a pipe might take away a horrible memory."

Linnea let several moments pass as she watched the woman's slender hands knead the apron of her *ao dai*. "My name is Linnea, by the way. What is yours?"

"Tam."

"How long have you and your man known each other?"

"Three and a half years, almost four."

"He's been here that long, since 1958?"

Tam nodded. "He's supposed to return to the States soon."

Linnea regretted their communication had started and continued in English. A few minutes later she said, "Was your schooling here in Saigon?"

"No. Hanoi." She looked at Linnea as though measuring her reaction.

Linnea realized the accent in Tam's few Vietnamese words was different.

With slow care Tam said, "My family came south during the separation—the partition. The family for generations has been landowners. *Chữ nôm* —very important to us."

"*Chữ nôm?*" Linnea mused. She knew of the old, the traditional, the classical, but never anticipated hearing a Vietnamese make reference to it.

"Yes," Tam replied with surprise. "You know?"

Linnea nodded. "Your Jim seems older ... or, rather, older than I am," Linnea chuckled, thinking he was more Stephen's age. "You said he has to return to the States. That will be sad for both of you."

"Yes." Tears now fell copiously. "Very sad." She shook her head.

Linnea was thinking the weighty pause that followed was a part of the territory she'd have to get used to, when Tam blurted into her lap, "*Nghĩa.*"

"Oh," Linnea sighed. The *yang* of Vietnamese life: Tradition. Duty. Responsibility. The strongest forces of the Vietnamese being! Straightening, Linnea asked, "Are you still a student, Tam?" Without waiting for the silence that might follow, "A Vietnamese writer has the same name as yours: Nguyen Tuong Tam. I'm sure you know his book, *Breaking the Ties.*" The story about a young woman forced to marry a man she didn't love, forsaken by her family, cruelly treated by her mother-in-law, fighting for unrequited love—*tinh*—stuck with her. The book described a cultural conflict as great as the differences between North and South Vietnam.

"Do you have a job, do you work?"

"Yes. No." She searched Linnea's face to correct any misunderstanding. "I mean I don't have a job for pay. I write reflections, my sentiments in poetry."

"Why, that's wonderful!" Linnea said, turning, genuinely impressed.

"You want to know how we met?" Tam said as though offering a gift, and began describing the afternoon she was reciting one of the great Vietnamese poets, Xuan Dieu. Looking out from the raised platform in the bookstore she saw a tall, blond-haired foreign person at the door, coming in and sitting down. "I thought he wanted to get out of the sun and didn't comprehend, but he knows Vietnamese language and literature very well. He stayed, chatting with the poets, and as I was leaving he came alongside, introduced himself, and escorted me outside toward home. I was surprised ... enthralled."

Linnea kept her mind away from the similarity with her first meeting with Stephen following the Asia Society lecture. "Your poetry, Tam. I'd like to read it. Could you...."

The American doctor who had met their arrival came down the wide, freshly refurbished corridor that in places looked as if white paint had been applied over cockroaches on the move. The black tubes of his stethoscope stretched out a side-pocket of his sweat-soaked, wrinkled whites.

Linnea stepped forward. Tam stayed behind.

"He needs to detox," the doctor said. "And we're not set up for that."

"What do you mean, not set up? This is a medical establishment. Surely you've got men who are drunk ... or had too much grass."

"Yes. But they don't come in here unless they've done something bad and are brought in by M.P.s. Or injured or wounded, of course. And we don't have much of that, so far. Anyway, this guy has been into the high grade brown stuff and we have no facilities."

"No facilities? This is a facility! And this is a medical problem."

"No. No, it's not. It's an indigenous problem. A Vietnamese problem ... a problem with Vietnam."

The doctor seemed to shrivel in Linnea's estimation, his receding hairline going from thin to unattractively balding. "This is an American serviceman who has been bitten by a local bug. It's your responsibility to do something."

The young doctor emitted a long, low sigh. He folded his arms, cast his shoulders forward, and let his head drop so that it looked like he was examining his foot. "We're on the same side, you and I." He looked up sharply. "I can't do anything. I can't admit him because, for one thing, he's probably a ... a higher up ... doing special things."

Linnea's feet moved apart. She folded her arms, dropped her head and looked at the floor, giving the appearance of a similar stance and that she wasn't going to budge.

"There is no other or specialized facility. That's the tall and short of it," he whined. "Not that I don't agree with you. He's probably not the first and definitely will not be the last."

Anger and confrontation won't get you anywhere, an inner voice suggested, and so she sweetly asked, "What do you suggest can be done?"

"I take it he's not with you," he said, nodding toward Tam who seemed very fragile in her seat by the entrance. "If he has a place he can rest, he should go there. He'll need fluids— juice, water, fruits and grains. Powdered milk. Eggs. Quiet.

Darkness. Care. He needs to get word to his ... his whomever that he's sick."

Linnea didn't move a muscle.

"I ... I might help with that. But, he may need to talk with someone." He paused. "Ah! The man in the new field," he said as though psychiatry weren't a part of military medicine. "He has nothing to do. The nuts are weeded out during indoctrination, so he's bored and driving us crazy!"

Linnea smiled.

"Okay." The doctor straightened with a bob to the head. "I can see what needs to happen. The woman will need to have my name and number. She does speak English!" he demanded, and whizzed around on shoes squeaking collapsed arches to speed down the hallway.

The doctor had a definite twang, making Linnea wonder why so many American military seemed to have a Southern accent. She'd seen more Negroes in Saigon than anywhere else, except going through Harlem en route to the airport. Escape Dixie's poverty and prejudice into a military commanded by white Southerners? A cool, dark opium den might be needed.

And she needed to talk with Stephen. The arrival of more and more Americans, as seemed to be happening little by little, meant the Hmong might see less potential in growing peppers than in producing opium for Americans seeking relief.

Linnea and Tam helped Jim into a cab and then into the empty servant's room at the back of Tam's relatives' large compound where she and her family now lived. Even the whitewashed annex seemed luxuriously cool with its thick walls and high ceilings.

"Won't your family know he's here?" Linnea whispered

"My nanny will help me take him early to a place I have in mind."

Linnea scribbled her villa phone number onto a card. "Please contact me. I wish to help," she said, in the back of her mind wanting to talk with Jim about his experience.

"Thank you, I will." Tam said. "I want you to hear our poetry recitations."

Heading toward the USAID villa, buoyant with the sensation of a fortuitous event, Linnea noted American servicemen on the streets searching to address desires in a strange and exotic and tempting land.

She arrived to find Philco at the table at the end of the hall opening packages of books.

"I'm glad to see you, Philco. I've wanted to talk with you. The other day when I was in the USIS library I came across a report about a portable, easy to construct greenhouse for higher altitudes and cooler temperatures. Have you heard or do you know anything about such things?"

"I think they were discussed in a recent *Scientific American.* I'll look for the issue. By the way, some really good fiction just arrived. *To Kill a Mockingbird* is splendid. What say, with your old man's permission, we explore *literature?*" Philco said the word like it was caviar.

"Great!" Linnea replied. "Stephen doesn't read fiction, anyway." Holding him with her eyes, "I'd also like to talk with you about my assignment with the Hmong."

"I've been expecting that, and I'll be glad."

"Incidentally, about books, I seem to remember that the writer Emily Hahn wrote about her experiences in opium dens. Does that ring a bell?"

"*The Big Smoke.* I hope you're not getting ideas."

A sharp crack came with the heavy front door opening and slamming shut. Susan bounded towards them, forehead hair preceding her like the cowcatcher of a train.

"Hello, Susan. How are the schools?" Linnea asked. "And how are you?"

"Functioning, functioning," Susan grumbled, swiping the wrapping paper from Philco's books off the table onto the floor. When she found things addressed to her, she put them under her arm and continued searching.

Pulling her eyes from Susan, Linnea said to Philco, "I'm issuing you a formal invitation for the book reading area I'm creating in my room ... where Stephen somehow still has his damned desk." She glanced at muscles rippling in Susan's jaw, and stifled a smile.

Linnea zipped upstairs to find Stephen pouring over cards on his desk. "With you still here," she said, "you need to know you're going to be cordoned off until you can get out. And behind my screen will be a happy place where I'll be discussing great books and good ideas with Philco." Seeing Stephen cringe, she continued, "And I'm going down to the Cholon Market with Duong to look into Hmong produce potentialities."

Stephen snapped off his desk light, rose and came over to her.

With a slight swagger, she said, "I'm going to see if Hmong *produce* is already being sold in Cholon."

"'Nea, Hmong produce isn't a joke but a key factor in a much larger picture."

"Ah, that larger picture again," she nodded. "Right! Right! I'll keep that in mind."

With resignation in his voice, "I trust Duong's arranged your little outing with the *bep* for a driver and the jeep. Cholon's a way off." He picked up a book and the cards he'd been working on, and headed for the door.

"Yes, Duong made the arrangements," she said, and, as he departed, hurled after him, "So, *later then*," emphasizing his sign off words and enjoying the thought that if she used them often enough he'd eventually realize he was stiff and cold and always avoiding things.

CHAPTER VI

"Cholon means big market, I know," Linnea said as she and Duong headed down the broad Hong Thap Tu Boulevard, "but doesn't Cholon also indicate the entire Chinese district?"

"Chinese need to be together." Pinched mouthed, Duong stated, "Chinese are bad. Cannot be citizens or soldiers or policemen and cannot work for the government. Chinese are free to go."

So often made scapegoats, no wonder the Chinese established themselves close to the nine-talon serpent, the Mekong River, with access to open water, Linnea mused.

The driver maneuvered the jeep around a humanity-choked traffic island before heading onto Minh Mang Street where pale, pocked buildings lined the road on either side. Moldy, fading remnants of once charming two-and three-story French manor houses were packed tightly together. Tangles of black utility wires looped toward ornate iron grillwork on second floors, monogrammed as a flower, an animal or the Roman letters of a family name.

Jammed onto the overhead porches, pots sprouted ferns and what looked like marijuana plants. White shirts and diapers fluttered from laundry lines. Birdcages enclosed feathered creatures as scruffy and hardened as people on streets below.

"Those black birds in cages, what are they?" Linnea asked, pointing and wondering why crows would be caged.

"Parrots," Duong replied.

"Black parrots?"

Rows of small, quaint houses with continental architecture looked as though they'd been built for a substantial number of lesser French bureaucrats living privileged existences.

"Duong, in 1956, when the French left, did they pack up, and depart by plane? Or did they have to leave in a hurry, clambering onto the pier on the Saigon River, trying to squeeze onto a last departing ship?"

"Yes, yes," Duong said with impatience. "They went away."

The roadway split at a triangular central island enclosing a smiling white metal dragon. Worn and weathered living quarters, up three and four stories, were connected by balconies and packed with high-backed rattan chairs, bamboo and rope clotheslines with men and boys' shirts and underwear. Bold Chinese calligraphy declared power and prosperity, while dust and the smells of decay indicated putrid humanity.

Duong began to squirm. She and Linnea were receiving sustained stares. Duong's hand lifted to point at a man in a brown shirt and a brown bowler hat with an enormous diamond patterned skin draped across his shoulders like a shawl.

"My goodness!" Linnea exclaimed. The scaly body the width of a large man's thick leg reminded her that Cholon was called a place of vermin and danger.

At the Dong Khanh Road intersection, the driver stopped the jeep for Linnea and Duong to join people streaming like cattle into dark, narrow stalls beneath a thick, oversized sign in elaborate black and gold—Binh Tay, the 200-year old market. Into an aisle of aged booths leaning into each other as a shaded arch, they flowed with the Chinese shuffling and milling about like worms in a cylinder.

Shiny apples, oranges, lemons and limes, of uniform colors, shapes and sizes stacked in abundance widened Linnea's eyes. In America she had only seen an occasional coconut, mango or papaya, and here there were many. Vietnam is rich!

"Rambutan," Duong said with her hand on a red, oval-shaped fruit she was testing. "Yellow mangosteen, pawpaw, soursop, and that's jackfruit—you've been eating it! And that's grapefruit" she responded to Linnea's fingers on a large oddly shaped fruit with a yellow skin.

"The best. Grown up north. You need to try." She gave *dong* to the man in a 1920s black fedora. "And this is dragon fruit," she said about fruit curiously pink.

Linnea trailed Duong amidst swirls of chattering female shoppers, and then meandered off to discover whether opium, so much a part of the landscape, had its own section for sales. As a vegetable, it had to be close by. However, whenever she asked a question to a salesman in Cantonese, it resulted in a stare verging on fright with no answer. Hurrying on, she entered the fish area. Even as liquid crept into her sandals between her toes from puddles—a putrid mixture of blood, dirt and feces—she kept her head up. A woman sitting up high behind large, slanted flats of ice presenting meticulously arranged fish, rose at the sight of a potential customer, even if a Westerner with a strange expression on her face.

"Were these caught this morning?" (*Ni-di hai-mu-hai gum-jiu-zou zwo-ge?*) Linnea asked. Did a female salesperson mean fish are at the very bottom of the business world and therefore only fit for the lower status woman to sell?

The saleswoman leaned over the wide tray of identical size and shape fish to point to gutted ones with still beating hearts. Linnea took a close look and stepped back, almost knocking over a tin bucket of fish furiously swishing tails, spilling water and reducing time to live.

Nodding she headed on into the poultry area where older Chinese women were engaged in extensive deliberations over a cluster of fowl, with each woman taking into her arms a fidgeting chicken to rhythmically stroke while chatting nonstop. Being cuddled by one hand, the chicken grew calm just as the other hand inserted a slender knife into the chicken's neck. The chicken remained pacified, slowly bleeding to death. Mesmerized, the process reminded her of the way Stephen had talked with her in New York. She stood thinking about that a few minutes and how it is that she is now in a Cholon market in Saigon.

Sighing, she set forth into a spice and condiment area that included orderly white stalls with glass countertops presenting dried stems topped by pale blue bulbs with an areole crown. Sensing she had arrived, she carefully withdrew a poppy stem from a pristine vase and shook it; seeds rattled inside like in a child's toy. The newspaper-reading salesman glanced up.

"You sell *Ya-pien*? (*ni-di hai me-yie*?) she asked, slowly reinserting the dried stem.

The well-dressed Chinese man examined her. His eyes went to string-wrapped brown paper packets resembling packaged meat in a butcher's case.

"How much is a package?" she asked, fingering her purse.

The salesman looked up and returned to his newspaper.

"I'm interested in *good stuff*," she said louder in Cantonese. "I want to know where it comes from, where it's grown, to know if it is the best."

The salesman slowly rose to show himself to men in stalls across the walkway.

Linnea whirled around. Six or eight pairs of dark eyes landed on her in a way that made her shudder. Turning back to the salesman, "Do you sell *ya-pien* in different grades?" she blurted, and, lowering her voice, "Can a batch ever be bad—make a person sick?"

The salesman remained standing, his posture indicating he had no intentions of replying.

Linnea muttered the remembered line of a TV program, "And the mastermind is?" She sauntered off, taking in the location of the stalls and wondering how to learn the volume of opium coming into Saigon/Cholon and the location of its origin. Maybe dens will provide an answer, she thought, her eyes glued upon glass jars on a counter. In the brown liquid red and orange rinds pressed against the sides, like in one of her mother's Old Fashioned glasses. On closer examination, Linnea realized snakes were tightly wound with fruit peels, fermenting, but appearing oddly alive.

"Have a jar," said a smirking youth behind her.

"No thank you," Linnea said in Cantonese (*Mu-shai-le, mu-guai-shai*) and then in Vietnamese, "Không. Cám on."

"Creates loooovvvveeeee!" A jar thrust at her chest made her pull back fearful it might fall and break, releasing snakes suddenly alive.

"Maybe later. I'll let you know," she murmured, heading forth.

Frustrated from not learning what she wanted, she pushed on until she was back into the thick of the marketing crowd where she found Duong selecting bunches of dill, basil, coriander and star anise. When Duong tried to explain to a grocer that the roots of the lotus were wanted along "with seeds and leaves for tea, a sweet dessert, and to wrap sticky rice," Linnea offered in Cantonese the words seeds and stalks (*Ngo xiang mai-di lin-ngao, lin-ji, tung-lin-yip*) and Duong beamed.

Heading for the exit, Duong exclaimed alongside one stall, "Curdled duck's blood custard! A delicacy you will have."

Linnea would try it but only after others. Meanwhile, she'd make a purchase of her own. The tiny action of reaching for her purse alerted a small collection of young boys with upturned faces who had taken up the game of following her. Their sparkling brown eyes stimulated a maternal instinct she usually managed to keep at bay.

"A dozen of those sugar-covered things," Linnea requested.

"*Keo keo,*" Duong provided its name. "The candy contains crushed peanuts."

The boys squealed when Linnea placed the pull sweets into their up-stretched hands.

At the market entrance, ready to cross to the jeep, two old women hobbled arm in arm with swaying, mincing steps in front of them. Duong nudged Linnea with her eyes at the women's tiny embroidered silk slippers.

"Chinese very strange. Feet broken like a lotus! Stupid," Duong said, shaking her head. Then a straight-backed older lady walked regally past in a rich purple silk dress. The lady's pure white hair in a neat chignon highlighted a face proud of being a surviving matriarch.

Chinese women keep their marbles, achieving power by outlasting, while in mother's world immediate financial and social success meant not staying fit or even lasting long, Linnea ruminated, reaffirming a reason she found study of the Orient intriguing and meaningful.

"Good your Christmas is soon. Like Tet, a family feast?" Duong asked when they were unwrapping fruits and vegetables in the villa kitchen.

"Family? Oh, yes," Linnea swallowed. "Christmas is a family feast."

"I will make the *bánh trưng*, the Tet New Year's cakes — steamed sticky rice stuffed with meat and green beans and wrapped in banana leaves. Meantime, I teach you *phở bò*, the knucklebone, roast beef and vegetable soup. Good for a feast! Also, *canh chua* — shrimp, bean sprouts, pineapple and celery! You cannot live without knowing."

Arranging vegetables on the wooden chopping island, Linnea asked with a grin, "What about tender sugar cane wrapped in shrimp? Also easy to make?"

Duong looked up. "For us, of course."

"Of course," Linnea replied with a cock of her head. She exited into the hallway where the long, rectangular altar table for mail was covered with Christmas letters and string-tied, brown paper packages with APO addresses on every side. Linnea's fingers hesitated on top of a pile, as though there might be something for her, and not wanting anyone to know there wouldn't be.

"Cholon was interesting," she said gaily to Stephen, who was once again in her room where a beam of late afternoon sunlight highlighted his cards and snapshots of faces. "Duong and I may go again. She loved the experience." Linnea appraised strain in his shoulders and that he was having a hard time removing himself from his work. So she let him be and slipped to the rattan chair behind her four-paneled screen to pick up a book.

After a while he came over and took the chair opposite. "You look pensive," he said.

Surprised and a bit peeved at that particular moment, she answered, "No, I've been wondering about you, however, always so secretly working on something ... unless you'd like to discuss it here and now."

"I will, once you succeed in the hills."

"Succeed? And in only a few months' time?" She snapped the book closed.

"Your work needs to be successful as soon as possible to benefit a long-range strategy." He peered at her over the rim of his glasses.

"Do you know you resemble a bull clawing the earth when you look that way?" she said.

"It'd be more succinct, Linnea, just to say horny."

Linnea blushed. "Isn't Susan ... don't you and Susan...?"

Without reacting, Stephen rose to scoot over to the part of his desk that had the tuner-amplifier, turntable, and 33-rpm vinyl records vertically stacked in a metal holder.

Linnea watched him fingering the albums of the Kingston Trio, Odetta, Peter, Paul and Mary, and Pete Seeger to a worn slipcover of Mabel Mercer. She'd been with Stephen hearing Mercer in the Village at the Blue Angel singing "Forever and Always." Afterwards they had danced.

After getting the volume where he wanted it, Stephen returned and theatrically bowed. "Shall we?"

Agreeing as though to an invitation by a freshman, she let herself meld into the easy enclosure of his chest and strong arms. Her forehead brushed the scratchy chin of his late-in-the-day beard as she gave his slow leg an extra second to catch up to the rhythm. Dancing with a convenient soul, she had decided, was his way of keeping his right leg muscles active. Later, when she felt fingers descend a bit to the low of her back, she chuckled.

*   *   *

"Vinh, are you sure this is the right way? I don't like this," Linnea said, bobbing to the right and left as the jeep swung from side to side along rutted paths. The occasional sighting of a lone man in black pajamas looking her way made her ill at ease. Being smacked by thick layers of drooping leaves, made her additionally hesitant to continue going on to this particular tribe.

"Their water is running out," Vinh said as he continued the jeep's climb. "All they have until the rains in May or June is in those big earthen jars we've seen. Women are now afraid to drink the water, and they won't let others. They say spirits have been angered by foreigners," he glanced at her, "and that the water is poisoned. The tribe pulls up higher, deeper, still more or less in the same area they're supposed to stay in on your USAID map." He looked at her again as though making a statement. "Maybe they're trying to get closer to a stream. I heard..." He geared down to manhandle the jeep over and around a large rock.

"Cholera?" she asked.

"Your medical teams say it has not happened ... yet."

After few moments Linnea said, "If the tribe has left behind hillsides burned raw so that pretty poppies will grow—they won't be staying put and using fertilizers to grow little old ugly coffee beans." She waited for an easy stretch of road to make a clear statement. "We've had success with small Hmong groups and the Jarai, Raglai, Mnong, and Chau Ma. Chasing after others who scamper about, trying to hide the brown cakes of opium residue they've pounded, is making me feel we've done all we can with some of them." After another swaying stretch without finding signs of the tribe, she suggested, "Maybe we should turn around."

On the path through farms back toward Saigon, Linnea asked about palm fronds arched over entrances of houses by the side of the road.

"Palms with red like that indicate someone in that house has recently been married, *Rước dâu*," Vinh answered. "I'm sure you know the red means good luck."

"*Rước dâu?*" Linnea repeated. "Interesting. *Rước—* welcome, *dâu*—daughter-in-law. Right? Rather nice," she said, and then, thinking further, decided the words were a strange coupling given that mothers-in-law often gave daughters-in-law miserable lives. A vague thought arrived about Stephen's mother. She wondered what she was like.

The jeep sped along, until Vinh, looking ahead, saw something clogging the road and began to slow. Linnea tensed until she heard Vinh say, "Oh, my! You are fortunate! A funeral!"

A dozen men in long, lightly flowing white gowns crowded the roadway holding up by hand bamboo poles with fluttering white banners. They surrounded a scrawny brown, long-mane pony lethargically pulling a clapboard box on wheels, suggestive of a western chuck wagon. Circular cutouts exposed the faces of men in white, peering out with the deceased presumably spread out behind. A soft, continuous clanging of thin tin rings encircled the procession.

"Why is it good luck to see a funeral? Better to see than be?" she asked. Without a response, she pressed, "Well, why are words on the banners in Chinese and not Vietnamese?"

"Respect for the old, the past. A thousand years create strong habits."

"Well, is that a Chinese Confucian funeral or a Vietnamese Buddhist funeral?" she asked.

"Confucian. Most Vietnamese are Buddhist, Taoist and Confucian. A very, very few are Catholic, like *your* President Diem."

Linnea wrinkled her brow. Getting used to that reference, she looked away.

When the jeep was back up to normal speed bringing them into a far-reaching, tranquil landscape, with pristine clouds hanging low under a late day's clear blue sky, Vinh recited:

"They wander lost in the somber darkness of sorrow,
Those fools who follow the footprints of love.
Because life is an endless desert,
And love is an entangling web.
Love is just a little bit of death in the heart."

"That's quite a poem!" she said. "It's not yours, is it?"

"No, no," he said, as though she should know. "The words are by Ngo Xuan Dieu."

With what sounded like a forced chuckle, Vinh said, "Poetry is my political party."

*   *   *

Christmas morning dawned with the gift of a whiff of cool air holding back the soon-to-arrive hot blast of moisture. After knocking, Stephen entered her room in a navy and white striped nautical shirt and captain's cap and with a statement he would sail her away one day.

Laughing and popping out of bed into a robe, Linnea presented Stephen with her gift bought in lower Manhattan's Chinatown—an old, leather bound British volume of *I Ching*, the Book of Changes, with flowery blue ink script in the first page, saying, "From Elisabeth to Harold, December 1913, Hong Kong." Below the inscription she had written her name and Stephen's, December 25, 1961, Saigon." She'd wrapped it in exquisite Vietnamese rice paper hand-painted with birds.

Ripping off the paper, he exclaimed, "*I Ching!* Great! Change is life's only constant. Perhaps as we go along, you'll tell me how things are going and whether you want a change."

"Now, Stephen. You should be getting an idea of how I feel about a lot of things."

"I want you to be happy, and there're bound to be changes."

"As long as there can be honest talk, Stephen."

"I will. We will," he said, pulling out a small package wadded in her pink Kleenex tissue.

"Oh," she gasped, unraveling a delicately carved, dark brown barrette. "Is it tortoise?"

"It looks like it," he said. "But it's from the bone of a very rare animal that Vietnamese hunters sometimes come upon in far off hills, the *Sao La*, which means goat—a rare, solitary, creature never known about or seen until recently. The *Sao La* is unique, like you; one of a kind."

Linnea got dressed in the bathroom and was delighted with the way the dark brown barrette looked holding her red highlighted, light brown hair. Back in her room she heard a loud knock at the door.

"*Pardonnez-moi*, Miss Linnea," came Duong's voice.

"Just a minute, Duong." Linnea ran to the door, but instead of Duong, it was a large object of highly polished amber colored wood slowly edging forward. "Duong?" she laughed.

"From the basement," Duong's muffled voice replied.

The *bep*, the villa's driver and she gradually emerged from behind the French armoire, and backed it against the wall beside her books stacked behind the coromandel screen.

"Oh, Duong. Thank you. I can sure use it."

"Belongs to the owners," Duong said, suddenly serious with a sullen glance at Stephen.

A bit embarrassed about Stephen being there and again wondering the reason for Duong's attitude about him, Linnea strung out thanks and happy holidays wishes as Duong, the *bep* and the driver headed downstairs.

"You suppose Duong knows something we don't? The owners coming back?" Stephen exclaimed with raised eyebrows.

"Francophile Vietnamese like to say we Americans are crude and rude in comparison, and just as stupid. I trust we're not like the French encouraging opium growth and creating a need for it." This wasn't the day she wanted to say it but she did. "In the limited time of my contract, I need answers about opium—how it's able to get from the hills to Saigon—and the relationship between some of our USAID projects and our military."

Stephen had gone to his desk and was fumbling with some papers. All he finally said was, "It's possible that helping the Hmong can be a means to an end."

"What does that mean: means to an end? When? What end? What about their opium? I need information!"

"What information?" He faced her.

Addressing the defensiveness she saw in his eyes, "Information on what we're doing here! What does the U.S. hope to achieve with the Hmong? With your instruction to promise transportation to market, what if vegetables don't grow and opium increases? I'm still a journalist, you know. I need answers, and if I can't get them from you, I'm going to have to talk with … with journalists. I've tried to catch up with a couple of the few who are here. They're never in their offices. I particularly want to talk with those who speak the language."

"Speak the language! And now are you criticizing me?"

"No. Of course not! Language isn't important to you." She took a second. "Foreign language is not part of your job." And she wasn't sure she believed that either.

"Okay, I'll introduce you to a few scribblers. We'll go where correspondents congregate and cook up their stories," Stephen grumbled.

Greeting the aromas of vanilla coffee and buttery *croissants* drifting up from Christmas brunch beginning below, Linnea's shoulders relaxed with a feeling of achievement.

CHAPTER VII

It had taken a month before Stephen fulfilled his promise to take her to a journalist hangout, Linnea reminded him when the USAID driver dropped them off at the dock across from the Majestic Hotel for a walk up Rue Catinat.

A cool breeze curled up from the river and swirled around Linnea's legs and into the sleeves of her short-sleeved blouse. Drawn to the gurgling water, she followed with her eyes the churning currents of the Saigon River, circling narrow brown pirogues, and felt for the scruffy masters sculling hard to bring crafts in to tie up before the sun—so near the equator—began its rapid descent.

"Look over there!" she said, grabbing Stephen's arm to point at several black boats low in the water, with black bodied family members staring sullenly straight ahead toward the sea. The whites of their eyes and the remnants of color in once gaudily painted orbits on the prows stood out from overwhelming blackness. "They're the angriest looking people I've ever seen!"

"They're dredgers, at the very bottom on every scale here, especially survival. They dive down and scoop by hand the bottom of rivers and then take the stuff somewhere to dump or unload out to sea. They live and die on those boats."

Stephen's voice and the way he kept watching the dredgers made her think he might be considering the same thing she was. The gradual increase in American military presence could correspond to Viet Cong infiltration. Dredgers could be so removed from normal life as to see nothing better than to hook up with the Viet Cong. Or, the Viet Cong could pretend to be dredgers and float unnoticed into the heart of the city. Linnea's attention went to the silent men around her, eyeing her as though with something in mind. Catching a rope or securing a skiff, they incongruously had brown bowler hats on their heads. Linnea's hand stayed on Stephen's arm.

The sounds of frenetic sculling became synchronized with the sinking sun. Then, when hues of orange and red streaks receded in the sky, the scene became quiet; the river slipped into an inky blackness with its gurgling growing louder. Heady smells of earth and grasses flowed over from the far side for a brief interplay of the earth's crusty warmth with the river's cool liquidity.

Stephen led Linnea across the broad riverside avenue through a reasonable number of slowly moving people, bicycles and pedicabs.

"Chinese antique scroll shops are snuggled against the back of the Majestic and they're pretty fancy," Linnea gaily said as they passed a dressmaker's shop she'd also visited. "Have you ever noticed that in any American city there's always a Chinese restaurant close by a courthouse or government building, because they're presumably the safest places in town?"

"Only you can make synapses like that," he said, edging her to his side with a conspiratorial low-voice, "If there's ever an onslaught, by all means head for the Majestic. Whoever arrives first orders drinks! When the coast is clear, we'll simply glide across to the dock, commandeer a sampan, and head for the sandy beaches in the Southern Seas."

"Stephen! Who's the romantic?" She smiled up at him. She appreciated that he was guiding her the way she liked, slightly connected but free to be on her own.

Rue Catinat glowed with paper lanterns. A few neon lights installed over a couple of hole-in-the-wall bars had more Western faces heading for them than a few weeks earlier. As they were passing shops with American products, like pastel colored women's hair dryers, Linnea whirled around to look back across the river. A blanket of darkness spread over the countryside, without a single light. It came as a jolt that she should have realized it before. There was no electricity outside of Saigon. She and Stephen and the city were illuminated to no telling what eyes in the darkness!

Loud clucking snapped her head around. Harsh, guttural sounds erupted from male Vietnamese on bicycles, slowly circling in the street alongside a Vietnamese woman walking with a Western man. The woman's red lips mouthed something into the Westerner's ears, an action that caused even louder clucks and grunts.

Stephen interrupted her focus on the developing scene, "Here we are. Brodard's! Where *truth* become fiction."

Before Linnea could respond to an insinuation she deplored, Stephen ushered her through heavily worn teak double doors into what resembled a French style bistro with circling smoke, clinking glassware, clacking overhead fans, and pulsing, animated voices. Faces were a mixture of old and young, most of them Western. Only two or three women dotted the scene, and they were Vietnamese in tight *ao dai*, seated behind American men animatedly talking.

Stephen hurried her past a long, polished brass bar rail of men in light tan jackets and white shirts, with ties swinging as though about to be cast off. Two men sporting large bright red and green insignias on khaki sleeves returned her to thinking about what might be happening in the countryside without soldiers or troops in villages standing guard.

Squeezing through a confusion of chairs, they arrived at a large round corner table.

When they were seated, Stephen pointed his forehead at three tanned and lean young Americans about her same age in business suits, laughing. "You see those men there? Patently smug, aren't they? Their eagerness and self-certainty proclaim they've just arrived as interns in our embassy. And you see those men over there?" Stephen continued. "Now, don't go into your bird dog point and stare," he warned with an old jibe.

Over against the side, a pair of heavy-set, gray-haired, pale Caucasian men thumbed with puffy fingers their tabletop of untouched drinks. Unsmiling and not exchanging a word, their eyes steadily lighthouse-like swept the room, not pausing or reflecting anything.

"What do you notice about them?" Stephen asked from behind his cupped hand.

"Cardboard stiff suits. Totally wrong shirts ... I mean checks and stripes don't go together." Linnea took another look at the slate-colored misshaped double-breasted jackets and realized they could be from the sartorially archaic Eastern Europe. "Russians?"

"Or Czechs or Poles or Bulgarians or Romanians," Stephen acknowledged. "Who knows, they could be Hungarian!" he exclaimed, and, shifting into a low register, intoned, "In order for communism to work, everybody has to be on board, like nations struggling to get on their feet in the wake of colonialism. No doubt those men are in Vietnam to get it under their umbrella."

Before she could respond, Stephen raised a forefinger from his hand resting on the table to point at two Vietnamese men sitting close to a side wall, oddly attired in black leather jackets and incongruous bat-wing reflector dark glasses, taking in everyone and no one at the same time.

"Those two are *Mat Vu* secret police. None too obvious, are they?"

"Saigon has a secret police?" Surprised, she was also peeved he hadn't told her that before.

"Yep. The *Mat Vu* is Diem's brother Nhu's personal police force. I must say: they're doing their job. Brodard's is Radio Catinat. And you see those skinny kids over there?" With his eyes he indicated a table of young men near the stand-up bar. "They're stringers hungry for a story. Bonafide correspondents sometimes throw them a morsel. One night a stringer with his itty bitty tidbit raced so fast for the door he smashed himself and the customer coming in."

Linnea laughed and a moment later contemplated that a stringer might help with an exploration, such as to an opium den.

"Saigon is make or break for journalists," Stephen continued. "They'll either soar or drown, the latter most likely and justifiably!"

"You don't have to keep saying things like that!"

Stephen's attention had gone to a waiter working the tables and appearing to look in their direction. He rose and cupped his hands to his mouth, "Ba Muoi Ba beer," finishing with two raised fingers. While standing, he saw an older man coming through the double doors grinning as though he had a great tale to tell, and waved.

The Westerner nodded he'd seen him. But, known by the customers he was passing, his progress became slow. The man could be over six feet but his slouch and wrinkled attire made him appear broad rather than tall. When he finally arrived at their table, his eyes lit upon Linnea and remained.

"Linnea, meet Hugh," Stephen said, swiftly rattling Hugh's full name and news organization as Hugh bowed to kiss her hand.

"*Enchante*," Hugh declared. Behind layers of lenses, feathery blond lashes fluttered over pale blue eyes. "I'd kiss more than your hand, my dear, but your old man is hovering, probably worrying I'll make off with an arm or a leg."

"Grendel!" Stephen exclaimed. "Finally the right label."

"I'll bide my time," Hugh said, letting his Missouri accent float, as he, more gracefully than his figure gave an indication it could, folded into the chair at her side.

"Hugh is *the* savant of Asia," Stephen explained. "Been here for two decades, probing particular people's peculiar peccadilloes."

Linnea cast a frown at Stephen's alliterative belittling. "In Vietnam all that time?"

Answering for Hugh, Stephen said, "The whole area—Burma, Thailand, Indochina—and, of course, Singapore, Malaya and Indonesia. Right, Hugh? A journalist with one hell of an expense account."

"Now, now! Just because the first round is always on me," Hugh laughed, as sweat flowed from his scalp down craters in his broad red-skinned forehead, and he unfolded a dinner napkin sized handkerchief. Scurrying forward came a waiter with a tumbler filled-to-the-rim with brown liquid and a single melting ice cube in a glass. The tray also had two large beer bottles and mugs.

"Linnea has a masters degree on Southeast Asia and is USAID's point person with the hill people. You've had dealings with them. Any suggestions?" Stephen said, sitting back to survey the room filling with patrons.

Hugh gazed into his drink glass as though at a menu of possibilities and asked Stephen, "Have you told her about the stew?"

"Hugh, you're the man with stories," Stephen responded.

"Well, Miss Linnea," Hugh carefully began, "a couple of years ago a Hmong village invited one of our Special Forces guys to join them for dinner—a mutual appreciation sort of event. Dinner was served from a huge cauldron with lots of vegetables and reams of lean meat.

"It was a very tasty stew with many spices. The aroma, it was said, could be smelled for miles. It was good fare and our Special Forces bloke was having a fine time, happily eating on. When he reached the bottom of his second serving, what did he find?" Hugh paused for a sip. "A hand. Well, the man was an American and consequently diplomatic. He said to himself that the hand had to be a monkey's paw. But, on the other hand, the Hmong were trying to honor him, and since a human is higher on their scale of delectables than a monkey...."

Linnea folded her arms beneath a patient smile. In spite of the pandering of a probable well-worn story, Hugh was just the sort she needed, with years of in country experiences and sources.

"One thing for sure," Hugh added. "Our Special Forces guys are just plain terrific, holding down the stomach while upholding the flag, never losing face or, heaven forbid, a hand."

Stephen and Linnea laughed on cue.

"Lady Linnea, you're definitely a delectable number. It's a good thing you didn't become a savory addition to Hmong culinary adventures."

Linnea gave it a few moments. "The Hmong who were cannibals live up north or to the far northwest and haven't been ... well, not for...."

"You're right," Hugh cut in. "Cannibalism could have faded away a year or two ago, replaced by headhunting," he chortled, "fortunately, not ours. Did you see a crossbow?"

"Yes," she replied, glad that the question might lead somewhere else. "A guard met us with one."

"It takes tremendous strength to use those things," Hugh said, taking his eyes from her to Stephen. "The Montagnards are not as primitive as they look. Crossbows are probably better than our latest toys." Hugh scrutinized several serious-looking military men loudly talking about airflows. "The crossbow kills silently," he continued, explaining that the bow is about two and a half feet long, but a pull of about a hundred pounds is needed to cock its leather string. Arrows are short spikes of bamboo, and they achieve enormous penetration at short range. "The tribesmen paint the tips with something like curare, to kill painfully and, fortunately, quickly." Hugh eyed Linnea and winked.

"There's Mal, your AP bureau chief," Stephen said about the man coming next through the double doors.

"His full handle's Malcolm Browne," Hugh said, leaning into Linnea.

On her other side, Stephen pressed his shoulder to hers. "He's probably scouting for the female just in from headquarters."

Linnea didn't want to lose her AP connection and hoped the management knew she was there and had wired its bureau chief. But Browne was totally different from the bureau chiefs she'd seen coming back from overseas. He looked very young, reflecting that this was a backwater position not of particular importance, and he lacked polish. His red socks would never pass muster in Rockefeller Center, even though they matched his bright red hair. He was skinny and his skin appeared translucent, as though he somehow avoided the tropical sun.

"I see the AP's competition has also arrived." Stephen nodded toward the man just entering. "That youngster is Neil Sheehan, the UPI's man in Saigon."

Sheehan held his slender torso ramrod straight, shoulders back, military attention style. His face gleamed with youthful energy, and his dark brown hair wet-combed into a wavy pompadour shouted dingo cheap. His frayed shirt tucked into crumpled black trousers had the ashen look of having been slept in for days, intimating the UPI was worse off than rumored.

To her suspended examinations, Stephen said, "You and Sheehan share the belief cultural and historical roots determine current events."

"Why, you once must have listened to me after all," she huffed, "and it will be good if you could...."

"Sheehan is a genuine intellectual," Hugh interrupted. "And for someone making history filing fast on the wire, substantiating current events with clues from the past, it's not only remarkable; it's truly laudable. Miss Linnea, you're in good company."

Right at that moment, she wished she could be across the room, learning from Sheehan and the other journalists. "Isn't that what should happen? How can the present be comprehended except by knowing the past?" Sweat crept from her hair onto her forehead.

"That's important, I agree, but there may be a new ball game here now," Stephen replied. "It may not matter that the Vietnamese have been fighting China for centuries."

She reached for her beer to leave her lip in the cool foam on the rim.

Stephen said to Hugh, "Browne and Sheehan may be up to something over there. *Time's* Charley Mohr is joining them. What do you think, Hugh? Collective defense?"

"It may be that the gorgeous Madame Nhu is mad that our correspondents are not writing beautiful things about her," Hugh reported in a measured staccato.

"Maybe she'll expel them, you included," Stephen said.

"Now, now," Hugh snickered. "Have pity! The magnificent Madame is simply a misanthropist who hates husband Nhu and her brother-in-law Diem—all due to her blighted Hanoi childhood. She's just transferring her ire onto every damned one of us—even you, Stephen," he said, adding, "*with whatever you do.*"

Linnea lifted her lips from the mug, looking at Hugh before searching Stephen's face.

Without missing a beat, Stephen said, "Charley Mohr is having trouble with his *Time* establishment, and that's newsworthy, isn't it, Hugh?" Stephen summed up what she already knew, that *Time*'s owner Henry Luce, as the son of missionaries in China, attempted to make the magazine fervently anti-Communist.

"*Time* has *rewritten* Charley's reports, and he's furious," Hugh explained to Linnea. "So, for therapy's sake Charley acts out skits with everybody in them—Diem, Madame Nhu, her husband, Ambassador Nolting, crooks, prostitutes. And maybe one of these days you'll be included, Stephen," Hugh said before devoting himself to a hefty sip.

Into the ensuing silence Linnea said, "I'm surprised so many reporters are here at all."

"Saigon is functioning smoothly, as it always has, but in the countryside things are beginning to heat up," Hugh responded. "Although Diem is granted Confucian imperial respect and is appreciated for constructing temples, he is not...."

"Diem has his hands full," Stephen interrupted with a fist tightening on the table. "He's doing as well as expected. He may not press the flesh like Kennedy. But Diem is learning and he's coming along. We need to give him time."

Hugh shrugged and looked away.

A few moments later, Linnea leaned toward Hugh to softly say, "A while ago you suggested that President Diem and his brother Nhu are different. Well, about things heating up, are you referring to the flatlands and stockade programs? Or are you referring to Nhu and the hill tribes who grow opium and are getting tangled up in being our observers?" She glanced at Stephen.

"Look over there, Linnea!" Stephen indicated a tall, lean older man heading for the table with Sheehan, Browne, and Mohr. "That's Homer Bigart," Stephen's voice rose with disdain, "of the *New York Times!*" Bigart looked substantial in a well-tailored three-piece dark suit, although out of shape and out of place in an attire inappropriate for the tropics.

"'Sink or swim with Ngo Dinh Diem.' That's what Bigart wrote," Hugh said to Linnea, "and it evidently didn't float." With eyes floating over at Stephen, he pressed, "You did read Homer's article on cats! 'American anti-malarial spray kills the cats, that eat the rats, that devour the crops, resulting in agitation in the central lowlands." Finishing with a flourish, "'and hungry, embittered people support the Viet Cong.'"

"Okay, okay!" Stephen snapped. "USAID and I received a lot of flack after that damned piece. We're doing a good job with anti-malarial stuff, and Bigart is totally irresponsible to write about things that shouldn't be advertised."

"You mean Agent Orange?" Hugh asked in a matter of fact voice, squinting at Stephen over the upper edge of his thick glasses.

Appearing to see someone of interest coming in, Stephen shifted in his chair, ready to rise.

Hugh rapidly said, "Want to know why it's called Agent Orange, Stephen? Because the stuff—it's kind of a luminous purple—comes in big orange-colored drums that handlers are told never, never to touch or reuse."

"What's it supposed to do?" Linnea asked.

"Defoliate trees," Hugh spat, "and it must not be very effective, given how much—millions and millions of gallons—has to be repeatedly dumped all over the hills."

A sigh like a groan became drowned out by the backward scrape of Stephen's chair as he rose to leave.

"Which hills?" Linnea asked. "Is it dangerous?"

Hugh gazed down at the last vestiges of bourbon he was twirling in his glass. "If it can take the leaves off of big, strong old trees, I hate to think what it can do to the tender little plants people eat ... or the generations about to be born."

Linnea blinked. A moment later, taking advantage of the chance to talk with Hugh without Stephen being present, she said, "My USAID job is to get the Hmong to settle down and grow things like squash, and in trips with Hmong subgroups so far, I've haven't made much progress. Some of our people here don't seem to care that the Hmong grow opium, even if it's dangerous stuff." Speeding up with what she had to say, "I'm confused. I feel something's going on that I don't know and that I need to find out about right away."

"You may be just what is needed right now." Hugh mopped his brow with his handkerchief and patted her hand. "In short, the South Vietnam administration is shooting itself in the foot and Nhu has the gun. He's a corrupt, disloyal, treasonous little bastard, and a despicable dope fiend."

"Treason? More than with opium from the Hmong hills?"

Nodding, "Opium and every other sordid substance and activity."

"But how can he be Diem's brother and be doing that? Didn't President Diem in '55 or '56 have a huge bonfire of opium and its paraphernalia? Doesn't the president know what his brother is doing?"

Hugh focused on signing for his new drink.

She began, "I'm concerned about arriving American soldiers," and then stopped. Stephen approached with several correspondents clutching glasses, thundering views, and once seated had elbows spread wide over a surface becoming wet with foam. Linnea edged her chair backwards, closer to Hugh's, intending to ask him for a time and place for a talk.

"Linnea here has expertise on indigenous Southeast Asian tribes and is our liaison with them," she heard Stephen say. "If any of you has ever left Saigon's sweet comforts to investigate the heartland, you might know something. Any takers?"

Linnea's face reddened. She barely heard Paul, the young, round-faced correspondent from Chicago when he asked,

"Does she know how Montagnards view our airplanes?" Without waiting for an answer he began:

"A twin engine German Dornier landed on the grass near one of their villages. The Montagnards emerged from the forest for a look. They're in full battle gear, mind you—all of a tiny loincloth and a spear. They walk around the plane and under the wings, look up here and there, and at the rear they stand and point and stare. The Special Forces guys are impressed because they think the mountain people are noticing it's a new, different kind of plane. So, our guys, always helpful, ask what they want to know. Head honcho answers: 'Where are the parts?' Our good guy replies, 'Which parts?' The Montagnard says, 'This is female, isn't it?'"

Linnea laughed along with the rest, and hoped this was the last about Montagnards for whom she now felt increasingly protective and worried. When opinions gained magnitude, Paul leaned over to ask if she was getting used to Saigon's swamp-like heat and humidity.

Thinking about the similarly hot evening with Clarissa and her father in the Georgetown restaurant, she offhandedly replied, "Just like D.C.," and immediately regretted it because of the glances at her and Stephen as if both were spies.

Gradually more journalists with drinks in their hands pulled up chairs and acknowledged colleagues with a succinct statement or a thump on the back. After awhile, senior correspondent Malin asked a friend, "How did McNamara view that *staged* Strategic Hamlet south of Saigon."

Before the correspondent could answer, someone asked, "Are hamlets a certainty? I've heard a third of South Vietnam's entire rural population will be in hamlets by next year."

"More hamlets, more U.S. aid," a correspondent answered for him. That's why they're being furiously built, so that fraudulent funds will wind up fast in Nhu's little kitty. In fact, stand still long enough and barbed wire will be thrown around you and you'll be called a hamlet!"

Imitating the Defense Secretary's voice, a correspondent intoned, "The end is in sight." A few seconds later, "You know, the estimated number of VC in the Delta has doubled in the last six months."

"Cycling down the Ho Chi Minh trail past us, right?" said correspondent Lyman.

"I don't think so," Malin replied. "They're right here, in place, where they've been for the past six or seven years—like teeth in the Greek's Cadmus, sewn into the soil to rise up as men."

Paul in a tone imitating an official, "The VC increasing? Impossible!" In his own voice, "Aren't they decreasing the way they are in Winterbottom's figures?"

"Ah, Colonel Winterbottom's maps!" Correspondent Lyman sighed. "Now you see them, now you don't, like a kid's slate where you lift a plastic sheet and drawings vanish. The VC are less like Greeks than moles," Lyman told Paul. "They spend more energy on tunnels than anything else. It's not just a few of them going down into the cellar of a hut. I think there's a labyrinth spreading all over, maybe all the way into Diem's palace basement."

"Good idea," stringer Paul replied. "Maybe he and Nhu will be carried away with the dirt."

A lull followed, like air let out of a balloon. Linnea edged forward, feeling inundated with questions. "Eisenhower said Diem was the miracle man of Asia. Isn't that true?"

No one said anything until Paul replied, "The miracle of Diem is how much he delegates to Brother Nhu and wife and no one else. But Diem keeps control of one thing—our passports. Write an unfavorable word and...." His hands swished past like a rocket launching.

"If you guys could see your way out of this smoke-filled place you might view things clearly," Stephen's deep voice intoned. "The Viet Cong have killed 1,200 of Diem's provincial leaders; 4,000 good, decent administrators were captured, tortured and assassinated. They're killing teachers in front of children. Do you ever write about that?"

Malin audibly sighed. "We can't write about what we don't see. We're restricted to Saigon; we're phantoms, trying to report on Advisors and Special Forces we're not permitted to see in action. By the way, *sir*," he said to Stephen, "Advisors and Special Forces officers are in the military, aren't they ... or are they also in an agency?"

Linnea, along with everyone else, turned toward Stephen like being drawn by a magnet.

Stephen cleared his throat. "I've been remiss about introducing Linnea who is just joining us. She's a specialist in Southeast Asia and comes with language skills." One or two young newsmen seemed to appreciate the granted look-over.

"I'd like to contact some of you, for background material." Linnea let her eyes rest on Paul.

Paul sprang to life, "Getting back to the mysterious VC never decreasing despite the number killed," he said to Lyman, "maybe the VC increase is due to ARVN desertions. What's your take on that?"

After several seconds, Lyman replied, "There are a lot of ARVN desertions, but more likely they're phantom troops with someone collecting the pay. At least the best South Vietnamese troops are around the city and they're not phantoms."

"No. They're Diem's private army," Malin mused. "And I hope they're good."

"Have you learned something?" Stephen's brow wrinkled.

"Just some captured VC documents," Malin answered, "that indicate the VC intend to demonstrate Diem's weaknesses by isolating Saigon ... on three sides."

Linnea's eyes widened.

Malin continued, "Maybe that's why Diem sent word to President Kennedy that 200,000 American fighting men are needed."

"What?" Linnea came close to shouting. The shaking of heads indicated either disbelief or resignation; she couldn't determine which.

"The first regular ground troops already arrived," Lyman said. "A communications unit, the 39th Signal Battalion."

"I thought that with our Special Forces to instruct and assist, and our USAID work with crops and fertilizers, cattle and radios," Linnea began, "and…."

"You're right. USAID and the Special Forces might save the situation. But if they're phased out, it'll be a catastrophe. Perhaps now's the time for you to rethink why you're here. In fact, I might not wait but get out right away."

"And leave you right here for an exclusive, eh Hugh?" Paul snickered.

"The VC don't have the necessary weaponry for a pincher effort on Saigon," Stephen said, to which Hugh loudly, gruffly replied, "No. Not yet!"

In her muddled state, Linnea heard Hugh tell a fresh stringer that the first American death in Vietnam hadn't been two months earlier, but way back in 1945 when Lt. Col. Peter Dewey of the OSS was killed. The helicopter from the *Core* that was shot down in December and the SC-47 that crashed were not the first incidents in Vietnam involving US equipment, either. "One month *before* the Korean War the United States was supplying the French here with military equipment and economic assistance all over Indochina. Our planes were over Dien Bien Phu. Military Assistance and Advisory Group, MAAG, it was called," Hugh said. "We've really been here a long, long…."

"GOD! What was that?" A loud explosion had her crying out as legs folded her under the table, her arms around Stephen's legs.

Stephen, only briefly startled, began pulling her back up.

"Miss Linnea," Hugh said with amusement in his voice. "It's the Vietnamese custom to use explosives for political expression. On this particular date, however, it's not political but the beginning of TET," he shouted above the din, "and the louder the noise the more lurking evil spirits will be frightened away."

"That's why there's red draped all over the place?" Linnea sputtered.

"To ward off evil spirits!" Hugh nodded.

The racket suddenly ceased. For several minutes a strange quiet settled inside Brodard's and out on Rue Catinat. And then came rapid, loud rat-a-tat-tat popping of multiple strings of firecrackers.

"*Gung Hay Fat Choy*! Happy New Year!" Slipping her his card with a Cheshire cat-like smile, Hugh gave a straight finger palm up regal wave to the waiter who, keeping an eye on him, now instructed the bartender on refills. "Here's to the Year of the Tiger!"

"You're feeling tigerish, I trust," Stephen said, his hand at her back as he headed her for the door.

CHAPTER VIII

It startled Linnea that the streets in downtown Saigon the next morning were eerily quiet. The air reeked of spent fireworks with roads and pathways littered with shreds. Bamboo poles tufted with leaves and paper charms danced solo in spurts of breezes. Fronting doorways, yellow and gold altars sparkled with the lonely flickers of tiny votive candles highlighting shiny white plates presenting segments of fruit, pomegranate seeds and bougainvillea petals.

Stephen kept hold of the arm that Linnea kept trying to pull away. He had had to practically drag her from the villa when her voice grew loud enough to be heard through her room's closed door. Now out on empty streets, with no one to hear, she said nothing.

Holding tight, Stephen joshed, "Can't you be in step with the first day of TET when Vietnamese make peace. Even if one son is a slithering VC and another an angry ARVN, they come together at their *que*, their home."

Linnea heaved angry sighs to match her thoughts: Why are the ARVN angry? Maybe it has to do with their families being in Strategic Hamlets under the control of someone like Nhu.

Stephen, looking ahead, blithely continued that TET would progress into a crescendo of racket after which peace and quiet would follow.

After they'd walked on a ways, "Look around you, Stephen," she said. "The decorations are Buddhist. How does

President Diem connect with the people as the Buddhists do in TET? Instead of connecting, I suspect he and his family just want to control."

"Where did you get this stuff? Lay off Diem, will you, Linnea. He's doing more good than you know. Sure there are problems and things aren't as we'd like. But your news guys are smooth, smart-assed and wrong. We're here to support Diem, who's worthy and needs our support. And we're going to give it to him."

"I'm sorry, Stephen. I'm trying to understand. It's not only journalists. What I've learned at the USIS, and what we heard the other day from your friends where we ate crab, indicates that Diem is a weak figure inside a very strong family. One man called him a loser."

"He is not, 'Nea," Stephen asserted in the determined tone he'd used at the villa when his voice tensed and hers rose decibels. "Diem's dealing with a bad situation. He was strong a while back and can be effective again. He's staunchly anti-Communist and … and the best available."

"The best available? How do you know?"

"Because the communists killed all the rest." In a deep, exasperated voice, "We're here to support Diem and we have to do it."

"Fine. May I ask who really has the interests of the Montagnards and farmers at heart? You said responsibility has been handed to us. Are we to keep them under our control for the special interests of a Diem family member, brother Nhu?"

Examining her with disappointment in his eyes, Stephen said, "Progress takes time."

"Progress? Do you know what I saw being unloaded in front of the Majestic the other day? Radios, televisions, hi fi's, and *water skis*! There were even bags of rice stamped 'Grown in Georgia.' Isn't this place known as a rice bowl?"

Taking a moment, then, with his eyes beginning to sparkle, "Think about it, Linnea. Don't those things tell you that Diem is listening and responding to what people want?"

"What *particular people* want, don't you mean?"

Stephen shrugged and repeated his mantra about focusing on the big picture. Instead of Saigon's dock, he suggested she think about Germany, split apart by a wall with Soviet Russia spreading its communist blanket over all of war-torn Europe. He proceeded to Communist China's claims that maps are wrong and that its better, older ones justify them taking a big chunk out of India and all of Tibet. "Vietnam and all the countries down here are next. We must support those who can hold the line."

"Oh, God. Support a weak head of state to suit our own worldview."

Stephen gripped her arm hard, saying that there could be a wave over vulnerable peoples who would gravitate toward communism because it looks strong and seems good. "South Vietnam is America's ally. We have to show allies as well as enemies that we're reliable and will stand by our commitments."

She walked sullenly on, staring at the ground. "Please, Stephen. I'm growing sick and tired of that line all the time." Snatching a glance at his face, on the verge of telling him how much she disliked his trying out political prose on her, "Do me a favor, will you? Don't belittle my work with the Montagnards by encouraging stories about how primitive they are because they've never seen the sea. And don't suggest that President Kennedy is purely a politico—he's more than that and you know it. And please stop belittling journalists. I still intend to write … it's like you're belittling me too!"

"Oh, dear me," Stephen moaned, slowing to a stop. "I did all that?" He turned her to him, clutching her shoulders. "I'm proud of you for flying across the far Pacific to be under my wing while coming face to face with the stone-age."

"Wing," she huffed, shaking loose to speed ahead down the street. He caught up and grabbed her. Held in place again, she shouted, "Let others find out about me. Let them—and me—ask the questions, and let me state what I believe. You said to the Brodard group that I don't believe North Vietnam and China are aligned. Then you didn't give me a chance to elaborate, to indicate my reasons. What could have been an important issue to discuss was discounted and dismissed. By you!"

"Hmmmm!" His forehead wrinkled but his lips began a slow curl. "Is that so?"

"You've made fun even when I quote something like Edward Lansdale's belief that focusing on 'hearts and minds' makes a difference."

Stephen encased her, his voice soft and serious, "You know, it could be that you sacrificed your great AP job to come to this stinking swamp because you're highly intelligent, very sensitive and want to do some good." For a moment there was a test of strength as he held and she pulled. "And very generously, you postponed your potentially brilliant career to work with a man you might generously consider a soul mate."

A block later, Stephen said, "It just gets my goat that some of the stuff those journalists are cooking up and getting printed is being swallowed whole. It isn't doing any good for South Vietnam or us. And as for accuracy...."

"Accuracy?" in fatigue she shouted. "What about false figures of that guy Winterbottom?"

"Oh, don't pay attention to that. I don't know what the military thinks it's doing fiddling with statistics. Anyway, no one and nothing's perfect."

"Well, unfortunately, little facts like Diem's brother's opium use and, I suspect, his effort to control production and distribution should be included in your big picture."

Stephen's lack of a reply infuriated her so much she wasn't paying much attention when he said, "Everything's closed except perhaps hotels. Shall we revisit the Continental? A little libation to cool the temper before dinner?"

"Dinner! Oh, my God!" Her hand went to her mouth. "I promised Duong that while she's with her family for TET I'd provide the food that she prepared ... with my help. But ... oh, dear!"

"I'll be your second."

"Heat the soup broth, boil the noodles, fry the shrimp and vegetables and ... oh, boy!"

*   *   *

When TET ended a week later, Linnea headed out into Saigon's eastern section with its many streets and curving alleys, all looking alike in a confusing cauldron. Tam had described what she thought were distinguishing landmarks to the apartment she had acquired for Jim.

"You give good directions but I got confused. I'm glad I could find you," Linnea said. Taking a step inside, she felt huge and awkward in the cramped surroundings. "I was able to attend poet Nguyen Dinh Thi's recitation that you suggested," she said, describing how much she enjoyed the poems celebrating Vietnam's majestic rivers and mountains, and remembering how the experience had provided her with a beautiful sense of peace.

"How is he?" Linnea asked, looking down at Jim's large, long body spread out on a floor mattress covered by a thin white sheet.

Tam's hands pressed into the prayer position. "He follows doctor's words but...." Her slender shoulders lifted with uncertainty.

"I'd like to talk with Jim," Linnea said. "I need to ask him some questions." Behind the simple request she wanted to know how he thought opium would help after whatever happened to him.

Tam reached for a straight wooden chair, placing it close to Jim's feet, indicating for Linnea to sit. "He sleeps very much, but not refreshed. He would want to see you."

"Are you feeling better?" Linnea asked after Tam tapped Jim's shoulder and whispered into his ear. Struggling, he raised himself onto an elbow. His face looked yellow against the green blondness of his hair, and the skin covering his upper arms seemed lackluster.

Tam touched his forehead with a cloth.

"I hope you don't mind if I ask a few questions for research I'm doing." Without waiting for a response, "Why did you decide to smoke opium that day? Did you think opium would help with a bad memory?" Glancing to the side, she paused before asking her primary question, "And did it?"

Linnea wondered if the absence of any indication of a reply might be due to Tam on the floor beside him. Continuing, she pressed, "For the others who more and more seem to be coming here. I need to know why Americans might go into an opium den as you did." Then, in a rush, in a resigned tone, "I need to know if opium can take away bad memories."

Jim's shiny, feverish eyes briefly rested on Tam before rolling over to Linnea. In a scratchy whisper, he said, "Two of us had been out for ten days ... in one place, watching, listening ... never moving an inch ... close to being stepped on ... no relief." His eyes flickered at the glare from the window and closed. "When we could pull out...." His heart seemed to heave in the several long minutes before he continued. "Coming back alone my mind needed cauterizing. To forget just for a moment...." Jim let himself fall back down. As though chilled, he wrapped himself in the sheet as if in a cocoon.

Linnea hurried to say, "I'm sorry to be doing this; it's important to know why you became sick and, particularly, if there is an overwhelming urge for another smoke." She waited, but it seemed unlikely Jim would say more today.

Linnea rose and reached into her backpack to remove the heavy volume that had been weighing it down. Anxious to pass it from her humidity-soaked fingers, she said to Tam, "This is the work by one of our greatest poets, Robert Frost."

Tam giggled as she bowed several times accepting it with both hands. She looked thinner than usual in her pale cream-colored *ao dai*. Linnea's first impression of Tam as a typically svelte young Vietnamese woman had deepened with appreciation of her intelligence and devotion. When Tam lifted her head from the book she looked beautiful, even with tears in her eyes.

"It contains the famous poem 'The Mending Wall,' Linnea said, "and also the one Frost wrote for the inauguration of our President Kennedy—perhaps not exactly as he delivered it," she chuckled, recalling how befuddled Frost appeared on that cold Washington day as wind whipped his thin white hair and ruffled the paper from which he was trying to read. "The poem here, though, is as intended," Linnea finished, mentally thanking Philco for helping her obtain the volume.

Linnea's hurried steps down to the alley and street were met by a noisome spurt of wild, humidity-laden wind of a different sort.

Monsoon downpours necessitated that trips into the hills be postponed or cancelled, permitting the pursuit of poetry recitations throughout Saigon at which occasionally she saw colleague Vinh. After one particular session, she approached him to press Vinh into helping her connect with ordinary Saigonese who might be occasional patrons of opium dens. He seemed to hiss after she whispered she intended to learn the volume of opium coming into Saigon/Cholon, protesting that his job didn't include the city. He glanced around as though worried some poetry aficionados might have overheard her request, and quickly vanished.

Without being able yet to enlist Paul or a stringer in her plans, Linnea headed out on her own to Cholon. The frenetic activity of skinny Chinese pushing and pulling overloaded carts with their stringy arms and legs meant they had to seek a dark, quiet place to convene with a substance that removed pain and denied hunger. The part of Cholon that seemed seedy enough to have many smoking dens would be where she would begin.

With her head down, beginning softly and then just loud enough to be heard beyond a few feet, she uttered, "*Ya-pien! Ya-pien!*" ("Opium! Opium!") Grubby men heard her, and didn't break stride, leaving her words hanging in the heavy air. Linnea uttered *ya-pien* again and again, augmenting it finally to "*Yen-yen ya-pien.*" ("I crave opium!")

Raindrops pirouetted on the cobblestones, raising dust devils in tutus of derision. Well-off writers used dens, she said to herself, enumerating the number of authors and outstanding works that suggested an opium benefit without lasting harm. But she wasn't believed, perhaps because she didn't look down at the heel and desperate or the location wasn't right. Making another try before a downpour, she wound her way through more of Cholon's many seedy streets before she would start heading back up to Saigon.

While dodging a vendor offering what looked like seared thigh of dog, Linnea felt an insistent pull at her sleeve. A sallow, wiry old man with two solitary yellowed teeth wordlessly pointed down a narrow, dank alley just behind them, and, curious, she approached. The old man slithered past her for his palm to receive something from the hand of an unseen person behind a hidden doorway. Linnea edged forward, walking to the side of a stream running in a crease down the middle of the stone pathway. At an opening covered by dangling beads, Linnea peered into the putrid smelling darkness. She pulled back, but a hand behind pushed her through.

The musty smell, now recognizable, was paramount. Taking a hesitant step she realized she was on a short wooden level above a staircase leading below. Her hand went to the brick wall at her side, damp and slimy. Cloying bittersweet smoke swirled around her. She edged farther until she reached a ledge overlooking a subterranean cavern resembling an ancient catacomb.

Sloe-eyed men and women sprawled in cubicles atop a wooden platform a foot or two above a dank floor. Spread over hemp mats, on their sides in fetal positions, they moved very little and seemed barely alive. Now and then a soft gurgling came from a vacant soul stretched out in the hazy gray sucking his bamboo pipe like a baby. Hunched hags shuffled wordlessly, fixing the tiny lamp on a short table beside one collapsed customer before going to another.

Linnea's eyes drifted to a cat trying to rise with wobbly legs off of a Chinaman's gaunt chest. Fascinated, she had to remind herself that before anything else she needed a kindly proprietor. If she were willing to be a customer, she might be able to get from him where his opium was grown and how it got to Cholon. She looked around but no one came forward to guide her.

Growing light headed, with a thumping heart, she took a deep breath and felt worse.

Steadying herself she pulled herself up the steps and stumbled out, causing men scattered in the rain-splashed street to crack into grins of ridicule. Wiping her forehead with the back of her hand, she trudged resolutely through puddles developed by a continuous, all pervasive drizzle. Taking refuge in a small smelly market with more than day-old vegetables, she waited for a break in the rain.

The den sampling wasn't dangerous, she decided. Everyone was interested in nothing but his own pleasure, incapable of harming anyone else. But that Cholon den was a dungeon—dirty and smelly—and probably definitely not the kind of place used by a Conrad or a Greene.

Linnea fought the downpour until it let up and she found herself back on Rue Catinat approaching the alley at which she had tripped over Jim. She paused. The den there, so close to the Majestic, was one of the last from the lush age of exoticism. It had to be exemplary! As a surviving showcase, it might have the wide, richly polished large mahogany opium beds to accommodate people like Somerset Maugham and please people like herself.

She fairly marched down the alley guarded day and night by the Chinaman with a wispy goatee and parchment-like tightly stretched cheeks. When she came within a few feet of the hollowed eyed man, his mouth twisted into a hideous sneer, indicating familiarity and as though long expecting her.

"I'm going to go inside," she said in a voice to indicate she would proceed down onto what she knew to be the "velvety couch in a realm of the gods."

"*Dong! Dong!*" he snarled, jabbing skeletal fingers at her purse. "Must pay first."

"Okay, okay!" Humidity swollen fingers caused her to take out dollars instead of *dong.*

The Chinaman's bony hand snatched the dollars while his other hand went to her back, pushing her to the door.

"Yes, yes," she said with a thought flitting past that good research often stems from personal curiosity. Shoved into clammy darkness, Linnea's arms were locked onto by a pair of young girls who whisked her below. "To find someone to talk with," Linnea said to no one in particular, her eyes tearing in the thick, gray haze. The air had a mixture of smells of gently roasted sesame seeds and nicely ripe kumquats, she noted, inhaling until vapors slithering into her nostrils produced a most pleasing, seductive sensation.

The two female escorts had snaked ahead to a lower level past a jumble of cots with indolent, languorous bodies stretched akimbo, and into a small cubicle off to the side. They motioned to her. The only light came from little spirit lamps on trays on low tables, measured distances from each other. Watching her step, she caught up to the girls next to a couch against a brick wall with a cheap tiger scroll hanging over it. Now somewhat weary, Linnea longed to lie down, assured about where she was and what she was doing. *A brief exposure to pipes for my USAID assignment … and for personal pains to evaporate for a clearer view of the future….*

"*Yen poon? Yen poon?*" One of the girl escorts' fingers pressed the question into her.

"*Yen poon? Yen poon?*" Linnea repeated, and the girl slunk away.

Linnea surveyed sprawled flaccid figures, some corpse-like, others with enviously ethereal expressions, and wondered if anyone was familiar. A few appeared to be light-haired Westerners but she couldn't discern the faces in the dim light. On the other hand, no one appeared alert enough to pay her attention or cause her harm.

Her body's heaviness drew her down deep into the woven mat of hemp piled with pillows and a brown shawl that seemed old, familiar and friendly. Barely remembering, she pulled out her notebook and pen and eased into a fetal curl. She closed her eyes.

Hands like claws clamped onto her shoulders. The Chinaman's skeletal fingers drew her up and pushed and punched her back toward the stairs.

"What's wrong?" Linnea groaned, barely conscious.

Shushes swished after them like sweeping brooms. When they reached the top of the stairs and outside, the Chinaman threw the dollars down onto the ground with a spit and a fierce cackle. "Not want your kind."

Linnea's face burned. She stood her ground to stare at the Chinaman with hands on his hips like a short, angry sergeant. Flummoxed, she finally turned to walk down the alley to the Rue Catinat. *Almost!* She muttered as she headed for the Saigon River. If seen as a regular, she might get the information she needed.

* * *

"Duong, are those quail?" Linnea asked, poking her head into the kitchen later in the afternoon.

"Yes," Duong answered, peeling gingerroot without looking up.

"It smells terrific in here. Is there anything I can do to help?"

Duong looked up without smiling. "You can take those scallions, clean and trim them."

"Okay," Linnea replied, putting down her satchel and going over to the sink to wash her hands and the big bunch of green and white. "What is the quail dish called?"

"Lacquered Chinese," she seemed to spit, turning away to place a half dozen medium-sized fish into bamboo strainers over the sink. In a flat voice, "Dinner also will have *cá chien*, fried fish with sesame seeds and spicy *nước mắm chấm*, and also *bánh xèo* crepes with fragrant beef in mint and spinach leaves."

"The usual wonderful mixture of flavors and textures?" Linnea said, wondering about something in Duong's tone. "Spicy, salty, sour, singing and sweet, with everything requiring a huge amount of chopping and slicing." Then she asked, "Where are the girls?"

"I sent them outside when I heard you come in," Duong said, for the first time stopping what she was doing and looking squarely at Linnea. Her expression was hard. "I don't have time for talk. You have been in places you don't belong. In Saigon and in Cholon powerful people do not want businesses looked into or disturbed by trouble-making foreign person. Your actions harm."

Duong's tone was like her mother's. Linnea felt like she'd been slapped.

"Visit central cemetery — where foreigners end." Duong's huge black eyes stabbed.

Linnea couldn't pull her blanched face away from Duong. Long breathless seconds passed before the girls noisily returned. "Thank you," Linnea whispered as she turned for the hallway.

Plodding up the stairs, Linnea asked herself how in the world Duong, always in the kitchen, could know where she had been or what she'd been doing a couple of hours before.

And what had Linnea been doing? Laying the groundwork to prevent future perils of servicemen ... and possibly to relieve personal pains?

CHAPTER IX

"Thank you for meeting with me," Linnea said, dashing up to Hugh under a pair of lacy leafed tamarind trees framing the carved and gilded *CS* over the entrance. "Wow! This is some place."

"*Le Cercle Sportif* has made history," Hugh said, completing a furious wafting of air with a small, carved white ivory fan he proceeded to snap shut and pocket. Taking her arm, "This was the de facto headquarters of most French decision-making, and we know how good that was. Vietnamese were allowed in only as servants." Pushing open the right side of the tall teak double front door, "Come on. Let's see which interesting natives are inside today."

The interior was majestically cool, its entry archway splashed with a cascading pink coral vine that made it seem like the entrance to a wonderland. Shiny teak floors gleamed in aged brown richness. Well-stocked mahogany-paneled reading rooms graced both sides of the main corridor, complete with plush blue and maroon winged chairs. Straight ahead, sunlight illuminated a dozen clay tennis courts, an expanse of green grass with a scattering of white clad lawn bowling men, and a magnificent Olympic-sized pool with Grecian columns.

"In Kipling's day, waiters in starched white jackets swooshed about on their tippy tippy toes tinkling little silver bells delivering messages from the hinterland to their spoiled, sedated colonial superiors." Hugh sighed. "Indeed! Those days were glorious. Come on," he said, steering her toward an informal bar area a few steps ahead on the right. "We need to make sure the Mai Tai's and Pimm's cup are as good as they used to be."

Hugh gave their orders, and Linnea realized they were practically alone. "Who comes here now?"

"Some Vietnamese military leaders like Big Minh spend time on the courts. Also a few American swashbucklers getting themselves into dangerous alliances, like with the Vietnamese military men opposed to Diem. They think their collaboration is good, but I'll bet it's with the wrong people. Now, don't let me get started on that!" Hugh patted sweat on his neck with his handkerchief.

Presently, after taking nourishing sips of his Mai Tai, Hugh leaned back. "Well, dear. What is it you want to talk with me about?"

"I've wanted to follow up on a couple of issues that have arisen at Brodard's," she said, aware with a flash that she was again acting without Stephen's knowledge and that this time it might even involve him. Before getting into opium, she said, "I have doubts about our being here. You stated the problem: we're supporting a president who isn't loved or respected by many Vietnamese or by quite a few Americans."

Hugh carefully wiped his glasses with his handkerchief. "Poor Diem. He thinks of himself as a ruler leading by dint of moral virtue—like a Chinese emperor with the 'Mandate of Heaven.'"

"Why haven't I seen him?" Linnea asked.

"In the fifties, with the CIA's Edward Lansdale's help, Diem visited the countryside, and, from my conversations with him, Diem has known the people in each province and village. But after his friend Lansdale departed, Diem regressed." Hugh shook his head. "He became monk-like, and began to fear criticism and any kind of political activity. And so he's let brother Nhu and Madame Nhu eliminate any challenge to the regime." Hugh took a deep swallow, describing the people of all stripes in re-education camps, jails and horrible prisons. "They're his Brother Nhu's doing—sadly attributed to Diem."

"And then the blame is transferred onto us for supporting the Diem regime?" Linnea asked, to which Hugh nodded.

Linnea described frustrations in trying to get the hill people to take American seeds and advice and to grow vegetables, and said that in the amount of time given to succeed, it couldn't be done. However, she added, "With the promise of transportation for produce, Hmong attitudes seem to warm and the acreage dedicated to opium appears to be increasing. I'm worried about our servicemen, more and more of whom seem to be arriving daily."

"And so, what do you want from me?" Hugh eyed her with a stern face.

Linnea began with a sideline, saying she wanted help for Jim, the American Specific Forces officer sick from opium. She described him as courageous with a friend who is a poetess, not a 'swallow.' "I think the opium poisoned him, a bad batch of 'amber brown bubblies,' the doctor said, and it seems dope's not an acceptable or recognizable ailment for us here."

Hugh groaned. "And that's ridiculous, isn't it? Well, to get him well, I may have a couple of contacts, old Chinese herbalists, who know everything. After all, they've been dealing with the stuff since the British snatched bales of opium in India and sailed them to these parts. Eons of experiences have taught that fried scorpion or snake's intestine will do the trick."

"Thanks." After burying herself in her wide-brimmed Mai Tai a moment, "This place has such an exotic atmosphere, and has attracted many of the world's best writers ... some of whom evidently tried opium and used dens. I've been trying to find out...."

Interrupting as though to avert learning more, "How it gets from there to here and is made into whoopee, right? And maybe who's in charge and the stakes? Perhaps a little checking things out, for career and country?"

Linnea sat back. "The words right out of my mouth," she smiled.

Hugh tapped his fingers. "You like antiques, I've heard. Including old Chinese scrolls?"

"Well, yes, but...."

Hugh leaned back, unashamedly letting white cotton stretch the buttonholes over the bulge of his stomach. He eased into suggesting she should become a regular, interested customer of Fat Wong in the Saigon edge of Cholon, a habitually jolly critter who knows who, when, where, and how, and with her gradual interest, might get her started. "I want you to keep me apprised, though, and I want you to be very careful to stay well clear, you hear me?"

Dull thuds and crisp firecracker rattles in the early morning hours didn't arouse Linnea or anyone else because it was assumed the sounds were associated with a celebration of some sort. Later, at breakfast in the dining room, Philco entered with an announcement.

"A coup was attempted this morning, folks. Vietnamese pilots protesting, quote, Diem's failure to prosecute effectively the fight against the Viet Cong, end quote, bombed the presidential palace."

Blank stares voiced, "Really? Again?"

Philco continued, "They were flying American World War II AD-6 fighter-bombers. Reports are they circled the Palace dropping napalm bombs and strafing with machine guns."

"Damage?" Stephen demanded.

"A mess," Philco replied. "Boulevard Thong Nhat near the palace is evidently in shambles. Smoke is billowing from damaged buildings—the pilots weren't terribly accurate."

Martin, the fish expert, said, "I thought I smelled cordite this morning."

Susan cackled, "Oh, Martin, you did not!"

Screaming sirens and screeching tires could be heard in near-by streets. "Right on schedule," Kevin said with heavy sarcasm.

"Diem, his brother Nhu and Madame Nhu," Philco reported to Stephen, "were, quote, miraculously not harmed, end quote."

At least one person with breakfast in the mouth muttered, "Too bad."

"Well? What's going to happen now?" Linnea asked.

"Nothing! Isn't that right, Steve?" Susan said. "The pilots will be invited in for tea."

The amputation of Stephen's name made Linnea wince, her eyes drifting from Susan to Stephen and back. Philco noticed and became quick to say, "Linnea, last night wasn't a first. Each time there's trouble, even if Independence Palace is greatly damaged, Diem invites the ringleaders over for a chat and chain smokes and talks nonstop until demands are forgotten."

"It would be the same this time," Martin added, "except the pilots and planes have probably already flown to Thailand."

"Yesterday was February 27th," Stephen said as though thinking out loud. "You know who was scheduled to arrive? Army General Paul Harkins." He looked at Philco for confirmation.

"Yeah," Kevin muttered, "And the Army will probably take command of the Special Forces and Green Berets. And that'll be the beginning of the end."

"Or the end of the beginning," Philco added, informing everyone that Harkins in his Caravelle hotel room must have had the best view of the whole show."

Stephen said, "Well, now that he's here, and I don't want to get up false hopes for a positive resolution to problems, a vacation is in order."

Problems? You admit to problems? Linnea stared down at her plate.

"What about the VC's advertised three-pronged pincher movement on Saigon?" Martin asked.

"Their objective, of course," Philco replied, "will be to get to all the goodies and go-go parlors sprouting up along Rue Catinat."

"And that's why Linnea and I will be in the fourth segment," Stephen said, "to the East, Vung Tau and the white sandy beaches of Long Hai."

Linnea's head snapped up with a frown. She had things to do. She was making progress and wanted to keep going. Also, Stephen hadn't asked if she wanted to go to the beach. She glanced at Susan, wondering about her glum face fixed on the tabletop just in front of Stephen's plate.

"Lots of diplomats take highway 50 for Cap St. Jacques, Vung Tau and Long Hai," Stephen responded when they were back up in her room. "A few times very polite VC teams have stopped and just said, 'The National Liberation Front welcomes you and will appreciate your taking these brochures along to read at your convenience. Don't travel at night' — which of course we won't be doing anyway. They understand we're all just hedonists. So, before another onslaught of mean weather, we'll go on vacation. There's nothing to worry about, 'Nea. You can shoot me if I'm wrong."

*　　　*　　　*

The villa driver in the jeep dropped off Stephen and Linnea with their bicycles a good distance east of Saigon. They made their way on an elevated patchwork of roadway, a dike between shiny squares of water reflecting pink and white cotton candy-like clouds.

The scene was tranquil and exquisitely beautiful, Linnea appreciated waving emerald rice stalks reached upwards like little soldiers of steadfast strength. Circling large blackbirds swooped down to pick up debris, tidying the landscape. Men with thick calf muscles glistening in the jack knife bend of their bodies worked their fields silhouetted against the mauve mist of protective distant mountains.

A shiny water buffalo raised his ringed nose, wiggled his ears, and shook his horns; its ribs showed that it was an integral part of a hard-working team. At the nape of his purple-black hide sat a small boy, his legs spread out horizontally, the rest of him swallowed under an oversized yellow reed hat.

The humidity seemed somewhat at bay, and even the high-pitched whine of cicadas sounded melodious. True musical notes, though, tickled the air from a thatched roofed village.

Searching its source, Linnea and Stephen found the sounds coming from boys running after kites with flutes attached to long ribbons serving as tails.

"These people aren't stuck somewhere away from their roots, like in a 'Strategic Hamlet,'" she shouted at Stephen riding ahead of her. "The farmers are doing what their ancestors did, working in harmony with the land. Have you noticed they're not wary of us? They smile and wave, and have answered questions without hesitation."

"Probably because they were asked in their own language. I keep telling you, Linnea: I'm proud of you." After a moment he added, "It could be they're experiencing something new. Linnea, your warm, vibrant style, letting the natives see you're an American *sans* arrogance, inspires the Vietnamese to respond. Maybe with you we can inaugurate something really agitating to the VC—brave, decent, knowledgeable Americans."

She smiled. "Imagine that! Little me, a tool of counterinsurgency!"

After pedaling hard under a strong sun for several hours, they paused under a large clump of trees to eat the lunch that Duong had packed with a bottle of Vietnamese strawberry wine. When they finished the banana leaf wrapped *bánh giò* buns of sticky rice, sausage, and slivers of vegetables, they were more tired than refreshed. They rested their eyes.

A while later, back on their bicycles, drafts of salty sea air suggested they were nearing Vung Tau. Staying as close to the shade of trees as they could, cruising at steady but not great speeds, they challenged each other in nursery rhymes, sung at the top of their lungs.

Stephen chided: "No! No! It's not mairzy dotes 'n' dozey dotes. But," he carefully enunciated, "mares eat oats and does eat oats and little lambs eat ivy."

"Oh, Lord," she replied. "The record...."

"An old glass cylinder?"

Linnea turned to make a face, but her bicycle in the lead hit a rut and propelled her up and over the handlebars and down onto spongy red brown turf.

Stephen dismounted and approached with hands on his hips, appearing to evaluate rather than to be of help. "I don't suppose anything's broken," he said, finally dropping to his knees on the softly fibrous ground. "And where does it seem to hurt, my dear?" His hand started at her leg.

"It's really my esteem," Linnea moaned, rubbing an elbow.

"Yes, you do muster up a bit of steam." Stretching his Brahmin accent into his version of their president's, "Really, my deah. You're supposed to have eyes ahead on the fuutchah."

He inspected a smudge on her forehead and pulled out a neatly folded white handkerchief to wipe it.

Linnea stiffened and pulled back. A figure in a pair of leather, lace-and-hook Jodhpur boots stood a few feet behind Stephen's back.

Slowly turning, Stephen peered over the upper rim of his glasses. He evaluated the tall, gaunt figure standing alone, staring down at them, with arms hanging loose at his side, as apparition-like—conceivably a leftover from the Indochina War, perhaps an aged deserter, and maybe a bit touched.

"*Tôi nghĩ: bạn cần uống một ít gì đi.*"

"Désirez-vous quelque chose a boire?"

"Do you want something to drink?" In probably seldom used English, he said, "My men told me you were here. I think you need something cool." He remained ramrod straight, his aquiline nose an exaggerated prominence. "Perhaps some cleaning up, too," he said to Linnea.

Stephen helped her rise. "We'll be on our way. We're heading for...."

"Thank you. That will be very nice," Linnea interrupted, smiling at the Frenchman, and intimating to Stephen that she'd make the decision this time.

The Frenchman nodded and turned to lead them past row after row of well cared for tall, thick, glossy-leafed trees. Glimpsing the trees when she could, Linnea saw numbers painted in white, with herringbone scars down the trunks to metal cups attached to collect ... latex! That urine-like smell! Of course! Linnea shot Stephen a glance, wondering if he'd somehow heard her retarded deduction. They were in a working rubber plantation, not an abandoned one like those she'd seen approaching the hills to visit Montagnards.

The Frenchman's long strides took him quickly over ridge after ridge, as though he were on an afternoon constitutional. Linnea and Stephen had to scurry to keep their bicycles going up and down the rises of spongy earth. Lizard whistles and high-pitched cicada drones sounded like ridicules of them for being short of breath and sweating profusely.

About to catch up, they abruptly found themselves on a grass clearing with a large two-story white-gray building in its center. They stood and stared. The house was typically old— made of bricks covered by sand, concrete and whitewash, heavily worn—and in stark contrast to clean brown tree trunks, sparkling green leaves and a undergrowth subdued at the lawn's edge. Red tile on the mansard roof sparkled defiantly back at the sun.

Floor-to-ceiling shutters in need of a fresh coat of blue paint appeared to have weathered many monsoons. But a well-tended vegetable and flower garden at the side of the house indicated fresh attentiveness, as did a new appearing, pristine, rectangular swimming pool. Sparkling aquamarine complemented the afternoon sky and invited a running dive.

A Vietnamese woman and a young boy came onto the broad veranda encircling the house. The Frenchman said something and the Vietnamese woman stepped down to meet Linnea, indicating she should follow. An aroma of lavender drifted back from the woman as she led the way inside. The young boy took Stephen's hand to lead to a separate *salle de bain* at the opposite end of a narrow hall at right angles to a wide entryway. Straight ahead, a large dark space suggested an expansive, formal living room. Mildew piqued the air.

Linnea's bathroom was as large as a small bedroom with a square black door lock similar to the one in her childhood home. The yellow and black tile walls were decorated with imaginative vases holding multicolored flowers, still vibrant despite chipped, cracked and missing pieces. Antique copper fixtures in the shapes of fanciful fish spewed water over a green copper drain in a rust stained porcelain sink. Thin white towels with "A de S" monogrammed in yellow dangled from bronzed rods.

Linnea slipped off her shirt to give herself a quick sponge bath. She used a large tortoise shell comb with thick prongs on a linen doily on a triangular corner table, pushing it through her tangled sweat-wet hair.

Pausing only long enough to affirm the grandeur of the interior, Linnea proceeded in the direction of the porch. As she approached, she heard Stephen's rusty French stumble along and listened.

"So your guards saw us. Why didn't they stop us before we went any farther?"

"They said you were singing and that evildoers don't sing songs," the Frenchman replied with a chuckle. "The Viet Cong have songs, but they don't sing in daytime."

"Well, where are your guards?" Stephen said with a squeak of his chair.

"Around. I pay them well, like you do with your mercenaries here and elsewhere."

A second passed. "Our men are all volunteers!" Stephen's voice was deep. "If you're suggesting the South Vietnamese military, we're here as friends and allies of a free south."

Linnea couldn't hear the Frenchman's reply, but thought she heard "Montagnard," propelling her onto the veranda. Stephen made a cursory effort to get up, following the host's full height rise. Slipping toward an old rocking chair facing the Frenchman, she noticed stretched and broken cane in time to put herself down with care. The Vietnamese woman slid a tall iced glass with a crisp sprig of mint into her hands. Overhead a palm frond fanned the air, pulled by a cord in the hands of the boy.

"How long have you been here?" Stephen asked.

"I came to live and carry on when Father died at the end of the Japanese war."

"But this house was built long before 1946," Stephen said, looking around.

"*Mais, oui. Mon grandpere, il arrivait*.... He arrived just before the end of the century. My father was born here but never liked it—not like *grandpere*."

"It must have taken a long time to build this out here." Stephen pointedly examined the veranda's ceiling of blond, brown and black inlaid woods.

"Yes. This place was important then ... and is today. We still export rubber," he said, explaining the importance of natural rubber in gloves for surgery as well as Michelin tires for cars and airplanes. He regarded Linnea's eyes resting upon the sun-splashed lawn against a backdrop of shaded trees. "*Exquisite, n'est pas, Mademoiselle?*"

"*Oui*," she agreed, returning her gaze to an expanse of chartreuse against a backdrop of the deepest, most luxurious blue green.

"There seem to be more Americans here now," the Frenchman said to Stephen. "Many titles—Advisors, Special Forces, Special Operations, Trainers. Surely so many men aren't needed. They must be confusing each other, getting in the way, *n'est pas?*"

"There's a lot of work to be done," Stephen answered with a glance at Linnea who had asked him more than once the meaning behind the titles of arriving groups of Americans.

"What work? The Vietnamese can take care of themselves. Certainly the U.S. doesn't expect to stay."

"We're here to prevent...." Stephen started again, "We're here to help the country and its people to become strong so that they won't succumb to communism."

From under a thick ridge of gray and white eyebrows, the Frenchman looked from one to the other. "What is your job—each of you?"

Stephen explained they worked with the Agency for International Development whose purpose is to help a country become economically, agriculturally and educationally healthy, with a free press, free speech, and free assembly. Then communism won't be of interest and won't succeed, he said.

"*C'est vrai.* Noble and nice." The Frenchman nodded. "But what makes the United States think it knows best for a country far away that it knows very little about?"

Without a pause, Stephen replied, "We know the perils of communism. North Vietnam may not yet know what communism can do to it, including economically. Linnea's expertise is in the indigenous tribes ... and she's providing ideas for commerce for what they produce."

"*Vraiment?*" the Frenchman asked, leaning toward her. "Commercial assistance? Les Montagnards? What they produce?"

With a glance at Stephen, Linnea heard her voice betray false optimism, "We hope to encourage them to grow saleable fruits and vegetables."

"Opium is a vegetable! And you think you are going to goad them into growing something else? Coffee won't have the same *cache.* Or cash." He seemed briefly pleased with the play of words. "*Quel raison?*"

"We're going to help the hill people, the farmers, all the Vietnamese be a beacon of strength and freedom for the entire region," Stephen said, draining his drink.

Linnea looked at her hands. She wished Stephen could see himself as the representative of an upstart nation encountering the envoy of an effete but proud older culture with lessons learned. Beacon indeed! She thought the Frenchman must agree when she thought she heard despair, but it was *j'espere.*

"*J'espère* ... I hope the United States will understand Độc Lập—Vietnamese hatred of foreign control and love of independence. The Vietnamese don't want any foreigners on their land. They've fought the Chinese, the Cambodians, the Japanese and us. Are Americans next?"

"The Vietnamese may have to decide to fight the Chinese again." Stephen swiftly replied.

"And you're here to provide the Eisenhower and Foster Dulles con-tain-ment?"

"Yes, containment," Stephen replied, beads of perspiration bubbling on his forehead.

The Vietnamese woman brought Stephen a fresh drink he immediately began sipping.

As the dialogue between Stephen and the Frenchman continued, Linnea tuned out, resting her eyes on blackbirds pecking at grass on the lawn, and pondered how to probe her host for what he might know about opium routes to Saigon before she and Stephen headed on to the shore.

The boy pulled the cord and the large, wide palm frond soundlessly moved the air. In a period of extended silence came a small squeak. As though on cue, animal shrieks and howls erupted from the trees; chik-chak sounds like human screeches joined in a sequence of rapid clicks and a series of resonating deep grunts.

Immediately the trees seemed a burgeoning dark maze. Anxious to be on the road to Cap St. Jacques, Linnea tipped forward starting to rise. "It's getting dark. We need to be going."

Just then, loud yelps and raucous screeches bellowed from the trees. Shadows swarmed across the lawn. Small puffs of ground fog spiraled upwards at the same time insects swarmed onto the veranda with dive-bomb sounding buzzes overhead.

On her feet, "Come on, Stephen." She pointed at the darkening landscape.

Without moving a muscle Stephen replied, "We've been invited to stay."

Glowering at him, Linnea plopped back down.

The boy went inside and insects started their assault.

"You two are going to be in serious trouble until and unless you understand Ho Chi Minh," the Frenchman said as he led them inside.

CHAPTER X

The Frenchman's dining room sparkled with gleaming contrasts of twinkling white lights and richly polished woods, causing Linnea to sigh at the beauty. Tallow candles pulsed in ornate candelabra, sending fingers of illumination upward to collaborate with soft reflections from alabaster sconces. Small wax candle balls floated in crystal bowls before three place settings at one end of the table, with a fourth by the kitchen door.

Once seated, Linnea caught sight of a pair of geckoes freeze-framed and eyeing her from the pale salmon colored wall. With loud cries, they slithered behind a gold-framed oil portrait of a dignitary with an aquiline nose identical to their host's.

"As a survivor of France's troubles," the Frenchman said to Linnea, "I think my destiny may be to illuminate."

Linnea's eyes met Stephen's: Ho Chi Minh's name means "a bringer of light." Is the Frenchman aligned? Is he a Ho sympathizer, a colleague? Are she and Stephen in trouble?

Their host poured a small portion of red wine into his Baccarat glass, smelled and sampled it, and filled Stephen's and Linnea's goblets with a raise of his glass, "*Bonne sante.*"

The Vietnamese woman and boy brought in soup bowls so eggshell thin that tiny clamshells on the bottom could be seen from a distance. Linnea examined the exquisitely painted Chinese porcelain soupspoon at her place and carefully sipped the aromatic ocher broth. Hungrier than she realized, she finished the soup but noticed Stephen appearing less in need of nourishment than private thought.

"If you go into hills to the Montegnards," the Frenchman said to her, "you need to know about Ho Chi Minh's relationship with the minorities and the peasant farmers in the valleys." He answered a whispered question by the Vietnamese woman and left his eyes on her swaying back as she scurried toward the kitchen. "Ho's passion is nationalism … a whole, neutral Vietnam nation. Your Dulles," he said, shaking his head, "he says people must be for or against, on this side or that, but to be neutral is to be immoral."

Not wanting to get into that right now, she asked, "Did Ho's communism come about because communism had more teeth than socialism? I read that in Paris he switched to a communist cell because it was getting things done." Linnea saw Stephen's soupspoon pause in mid-air.

"This thought you've given attention," the Frenchman nodded. "Ho uses what works. *Il est communiste et un pragmatiste.* To get things done, he practices selflessness."

"Selflessness?" Linnea asked.

"Ho's genius is in taking a native, natural self sacrifice and dusting it with nationalism." The Frenchman carefully uttered Ho's words, "'The Vietnamese soil is the flesh of our flesh, the blood of our blood.'"

"Some Americans say that Ho became our enemy because the U.S. didn't help Vietnam after World War I," Linnea hurriedly said, darting a glance at Stephen.

"The Versailles agreement was *tragique.* The words of your President Woodrow Wilson galvanized people—*self-determination, equal representation, independence for all people.* Great men like China's Sun Yat-sen idolized Wilson and were motivated, believing help would come from the United States. All have been cruelly let down."

The Frenchman continued, describing Ho dressed in a waistcoat and homburg, *exactement comme il faut les delegates,* waiting for Wilson on the steps of Versailles to hand him a parchment written and printed by Ho, of eight points, following Wilson's 14-point program, for creating Vietnam's independence. "Ho was ignored and profoundly affected."

"You know Ho?" Linnea inquired.

"*Oui. Je sais* Nguyen Ai Quoc—that's Ho's real name; it means patriot."

In a flat voice, Stephen said, "Nguyen Ai Quoc is but one of at least a dozen aliases."

The Frenchman resumed without appearing to have heard. "Nguyen Ai Quoc was changed to Ho Chi Minh, the bearer of light, because Ho feels he has to show the way."

Linnea watched her host sampling marinated garlic cloves in a small plate placed between the three of them. Thrilled to discuss the enemy, she asked, "How do you know Ho?"

"On September 2nd, 1945, when Ho declared the independence of Vietnam, I was in Hanoi," he said, looking from her to Stephen and with a smile stressed "by coincidence." Ho is a skinny, reedy soul—like one of those barefoot creatures pulling *pousse pousse,* even though Ho's from a family educated and landowning, he said. "*Il était le jour le plus....* It was the most important day and yet he looked like a poor peasant—shorts, sandals, and a strangely beige painted pith helmet," he chuckled. "Half a million onlookers on Ba Dinh Square—I do not think they knew who Ho was when he climbed up onto the platform to go to that large, round black microphone. By the way, at his side was an American who helped Ho draft words practically the same as your Declaration of Independence."

"Major Archimedes Patti," Stephen provided in a low tone. "And the crowd was far fewer than a half million."

The Frenchman shrugged. "*Bien.* Patti said Ho knew Jefferson's words better than he did himself, and," the Frenchman's cheeks crinkled, "Ho agreed."

"*Oui,*" Stephen said. "And the primary reason Patti worked with Ho was because the US needed help rescuing downed Americans pilots and fighting the Japanese. Ho let himself be useful to secure our weapons and his radio operators training of and, particularly, because of how association with America looked to Vietnamese peasants."

"*D'accord. D'accord. Ho est très agréeable et....*"

"Good at public relations, to legitimatize himself maybe?" Stephen said. "Ho even displayed the photo of Chennault—not presented *to* Ho but snatched *by* him—to suggest America was behind him."

Linnea's head descended toward the flickering candle at her placemat.

"Ho is very patient," the Frenchman continued, refilling Stephen's wine glass and glancing at the kitchen door.

In as light a voice as she could muster, Linnea asked, "Is it true Ho wrote President Truman many times for America to take Vietnam under its wing?"

"*C'est un moment perdu.* Truman called Ho a Fu Man Chu communist."

"Listen!" Stephen said, first looking at Linnea before starting to describe how Truman had his hands full, that the Korean War had started, and communist multitudes were overrunning South Korea. Truman backed France against encroaching Russians with the hope France would become a buttress against communist China here. "We supported you, and France proceeded to lose it." He quickly added, "Besides, Truman didn't fall for nice old Ho who, incidentally, didn't seem to mind France's return in the first place."

Linnea had closed her eyes. She flinched when the Frenchman leaned toward her, "*Pardonez-moi, mademoiselle.* This is what Ho said: 'I prefer to sniff French shit for five years than to eat Chinese dung for the rest of my life.'"

The kitchen door suddenly opened. Steaming aromatic plates of shrimp, scallions and bean sprouts; platters of fried fish fillets covered with sliced oranges and limes; chicken curry afloat with pineapple, green pepper and tomatoes; herb dotted noodles and rice; carved carrots and condiments covered the table in scalloped edged blue and white porcelain.

Linnea observed her host's attention to the woman serving, and appreciated how he and Stephen served themselves and her, putting her in mind to ask an old, unconfrontational question. "Is Ho married? I've heard he has children."

"Ho said to a newsman: 'I am an old man and an old man prefers an air of mystery. No mystery, no interest, and the world will not take notice.'"

Finishing a forkful, Stephen sniped, "Ho certainly has not been celibate. In fact, he's had many women—such as Nong Thi Vang—who mysteriously become dead after being with dear old Ho only a single night."

"Stephen, please!" Linnea said with gritted teeth. His account could be true and she'd check it out, but that didn't give him the right to be rude.

The Frenchman ate slowly and with pleasure. After a while, he sat back to sip his wine. "Ho has seen the world looking like any poor yellow person, and therefore wasn't noticed. I've heard he was in your country at the university Emory, and wrote about Harlem. And he was a monk in Thailand," he said, resuming interest in the condiment plate.

"*Aussi,*" Stephen said, after a deep swallow of wine, proceeding to relate how Ho's tutor in Paris was Karl Marx's son Jean Longuet; how in the Soviet Union Ho's Russian name was Linov; and how in China Ho was a Comintern instigator, responsible for assassinations, pushing poor, war-torn China into being a communist nation. "Ho has made his plans for Vietnam in Pac Bo cave up near the Chinese border, and, guess what? He named the mountain Karl Marx and a near-by stream Lenin. Ho has been a fervent communist before the idea of nationalism ever entered his little head." Stephen shifted his gaze to Linnea who stared at her woven silk placemat like the mat in a Hmong chief's hut. If Stephen could read her soul, as the Montagnards did, he would see her extreme anger and disappointment in him.

Candlelight played around the table and across the Frenchman's broad forehead. "The word communism is like waving a flag red before a toro to you *Americains*. Communism for Ho, *je pense*, is merely a means to an end."

Linnea shifted in her chair. Damn it! There it is again! A means to an end! The Hmong with their opium are only a means to an end with America. She fixed a scowl onto Stephen that he appeared not to notice.

"How do you assess Ho's turning over to your French Surete the names of patriots merely because they might be rivals ... making Vietnamese leaders a scarcity today?" Stephen reported fifteen thousand liquidated—slaughtered—and one hundred thousand imprisoned in North Vietnam just because they owned land of less than two acres.

"Ho has acknowledged mistakes. He corrected landlord classifications," the Frenchman said nonchalantly.

"Great! Reclassification after a person is dead? Let's see: six thousand Vietnamese assassinated in Ho's own native province. *Peut-être*," Stephen said with a thickening tongue, "Ho was living up to his dictate, 'whoever does not follow the line will be broken.' That doesn't sound too selfless to me. Ho's tactics would make Stalin proud—burying people alive and sawing the living in half."

Linnea boiled. What are you doing? Why here and now? Sadness stung her eyes.

"Independence is Ho's goal, " the Frenchman said as though in a coda.

Ignoring the tone of his host, Stephen continued, "What if evil is at the beginning—to be repeated time after time and over time, generation after generation—en route to independence?"

"Can you tell me," the Frenchman said, sounding tired, "how socialism or communism is worse than a dictatorship ruled by a family, for themselves and their friends? Diem is a figure *tragique*. *Mon Dieu!* He should be walking in rice fields, learning how to be loved," the Frenchman said, his hands rising. "Diem and Ho are both nationalists."

The Frenchman pushed his mostly finished plate forward, and folded his hands in his lap.

"Tell me about your President Kennedy," the Frenchman asked Stephen. The Bay of Pigs, *les cochons* ... such a strange name, he said, asking who was in charge. "Was your *Monsieur* Kennedy relying on the C-I-A instead of America's armed forces? Or was it the opposite?"

Stephen rubbed a spot at his temple. "President Kennedy was given conflicting, bad information."

"It is my view President Diem is being supported by a President inexperienced and indecisive 10,000 miles away."

"Kennedy hasn't been president very long!" Linnea pleaded. "Yes, he needs good information about Vietnam," she said first to her host and then to Stephen, whose eyes were on the candlelight, providing her with the old feeling he wasn't hearing her. "Some of us are trying to bring clarity to decision-makers in Washington." Seeing Stephen look up, she quickly added, "Few Americans know about Asia. Your countryman Bernard Fall's book, *Street Without Joy*, may be the only one anyone has read on Vietnam."

"He was the newsman in the interview who asked Ho the personal questions." The Frenchman nodded to the Vietnamese woman who, with the boy, began clearing the table.

Linnea watched candlelight dancing on the mahogany table and wondered if, through her embarrassment, she might be seeing Stephen in his true light.

"I don't suppose you've been in North Vietnam?" their host asked Stephen as remaining plates and platters were being removed.

"No!" Stephen replied with patent astonishment.

"*C'est domage.* We created a fabulous Opera House in Hanoi. We drained the swamps. We built roads and hospitals, and we planted trees and established parks. We made broad avenues and created beautiful cities and capitals. We gave Indochina its heart."

"Opera for poor, illiterate Vietnamese peasants?" Stephen murmured. "*Je pense* a lot done by France, like Michelin tires, was for the benefit of the French."

Linnea's cheeks steamed. Turning from an angry glare at Stephen, she faced her host as if to encourage the Frenchman's launch into pride-fill meanderings. We gave them a future and an appreciation of the past, he said, like Angkor Wat; the French missionary Alexander de Rhodes in 1627 who provided Vietnam its unique written language using Roman letters; the French literature and philosophy contributing to ideas and beliefs: duty to family, land and country — *nghia;* and *tinh,* the yin for life — love, emotion, and intuition.

The Frenchman concluded with a question to Stephen. "Which is better? Duty, or the yearnings of the soul? Neither one is better because each needs the other."

The Vietnamese woman sitting demurely at the far end, with her back straight and not touching the chair, kept attention on the boy clearing the table, occasionally pointing with her eyes for something needing to be done.

"You're wise to be interested in knowing about Ho," her host said to Linnea. "Let me tell you an old tale Ho likes to quote. 'Vietnamese will be like the elephant and the tiger. When the magnificent elephant is strong and rested and near his base, the tiger will slink away and retreat, for the elephant could impale him on his mighty tusks. But the clever tiger though scrawny does not give up. The mighty elephant goes far, far from his base trying to find the tiger. Finally, the elephant grows exhausted from loss of blood and has to leave the territory.'"

Parables often confused her, and this one now worried with foreboding. With blurry eyes the thought arrived as to who would be guests for such an instantly fantastic dinner now that *les colons* were gone. The candlelight and glittering crystal and silver, the delicate and succulent dishes in gleaming porcelain, and the Baccarat wineglasses constantly refilled had created sublime satiation, even submission. She wondered how the dinner could be prepared so expertly and quickly. Once again an idea flirted that Stephen might be behind the invitation, either to impress, to challenge or to establish something.

"May I ask," the Frenchman asked her, "if you are aware of how difficult it will be to try to change the growing habits of the Montagnards?"

Very weary, her reply came with the deepest possible sigh. "We're offering seeds with wells and advice. The Hmong trade opium with each other, as always, but now are beginning to grow more than ever before." She stared at Stephen. "I'm trying to find out how much opium is grown and how it gets to Saigon." She hadn't mentioned her "research" to Stephen because she was beginning to think it could involve him. "Left-over French networks perhaps have been taken over by, by…." She stopped. Suspicions were saved by dessert.

Dishes being brought in contained *che*, the rich tapioca pudding-like concoction made of coconut milk, ripe bananas, and arrowroot vermicelli with crushed, toasted sesame seeds sprinkled across the top. Shiny lichees over slivers of ice were so plump and succulent as to be sexual.

After taking samples the Frenchman said, "Opium was here before we arrived. It was the business of the Portuguese, the Spanish, the British and the Chinese. Our France *used* opium for a purpose, as your government is probably doing the same today."

Linnea believed she saw Stephen flinch.

"Now others are involved … the Chinese and the Corsicans," the Frenchman said, "and they are not all. You should stay clear."

"I'm already involved," Linnea said in a dour voice. "It's my assignment."

With eyes cast down, she nibbled at the delicious dessert. When she'd had her fill she peaked a glance at her host and saw him lift his head to smile at the Vietnamese woman at the end of the table.

"Can you imagine being Monsieur Henri Mouhot trekking through the jungle, struggling with roots and vines and coming upon Angkor Wat's stone figures *avec tetons* peeking out at him!" The Frenchman winked.

"Something like coming upon here," Linnea submitted, instantly abashed.

The Frenchman's cheeks crinkled. "Yes. I guess I and my home are almost ready for the archaeologists." He continued looking down the table before glancing to either side to see that the *che* and lichees were finished. Muscles on either side of his mouth softly twitched.

Linnea saw the woman's palms close next to her cheeks with a tilt of her head.

"Time to retire," the Frenchman said. Rising from the chair with surprising vigor, he grabbed a candelabra and strode into the darkened hallway.

Linnea flashed Stephen a stern "What now?" Stephen pointed with his chin to a slice of total darkness between the curtains. Geckoes reemerged on the walls trumpeted loud agreement.

Stephen made his way around the table to Linnea's side. As she rose, he draped his arm across her shoulders, more as a way of using her as a crutch, than to be gentlemanly which he definitely was not, her face angrily stated. She edged away but Stephen gripped her arm.

"For the flag," he whispered into her ear as together they entered the hallway.

The Vietnamese woman waiting for them at the foot of the stairs pulled something slick from the fold of her tunic. Taking a quick swipe at ancient dust, she pushed the bottle of French cognac into Linnea's hands and with a collaborative smile scooted away.

The Frenchman jauntily headed up the stairs holding high the candelabra of dripping wax. Candlelight accented his profile matching the angular portraits they passed. Threadbare sections of the staircase's Oriental runner had to be watched. Ignoring immediate doors, the Frenchman led them down the long corridor to a room at the far end. He turned a knob and edged the door ajar. He listened, pushed the door farther open and stepped aside.

A vague, high-pitched chirping swooshed out with wings hurtling into Linnea, causing her hand to fly to her face, the bottle with it.

"Bat," the Frenchman said with delight, as though it was a household pet whizzing out to relieve itself. As though dashing in pursuit, the Frenchman passed Stephen the candelabra and, with barely a *bon soir*, left them facing a door partly open to a room emitting a rush of old air.

"We must be brave, my little chickadee," Stephen whispered, lifting high the melting light. "Hark! Who's there?" he gruffly uttered, sounding inebriated and stupidly brave.

Stephen thrust the candelabra at an object that flickered back. "Well, what do you know?" he said to a suit of armor his same six feet. "Surely you didn't see action here." He poked at it as though wielding a sword. "Why in the world are you here?"

The suit of armor lacked an occupant, so Linnea began to feel her way around. She found a wall covered in silk damask, heavy with many years' humidity. The ceiling seemed without end, and, unfortunately, high enough to accommodate a bevy of residents.

"Doesn't this remind you of *Beau Geste?*" Stephen said. "A jewel stolen and hidden in a suit of armor for brothers, covering up for each other, to go off to join the Foreign Legion. Maybe Beau's brother Legionnaires brought this thing here. Maybe a jewel's inside." He jabbed at the metal, making hinges rattle until lifelike it tipped forward.

Anticipating a noisy tumble, Linnea stepped back and tripped on a furry rug, her knees folding as only the limbs of someone high can smoothly do. Stephen heard and saw her. He set the candelabra onto the floor near where she was crawling toward the door.

Anger at his behavior this evening, combined with a growing feeling she'd been set up in her USAID job and used by him, let her kick him as hard as she possibly could.

She wanted another room or at least a second bed. All she had was a large, heavy four-poster bed for defense. With her face and arms tingling in the strange, damp, heavy air, she scrambled beneath it, aiming for the far side. But Stephen, laughing, grabbed the ankle edge of her slacks and yanked. Holding onto a post, as her slacks slipped away, she kicked her hardest, aiming for his head, and scurried to the other side. She was mad. All she could do was burrow under the coverlet and blankets, wrapping up tight in sheets cool and silky and faintly scented with lavender, creating a chrysallis.

Later, when thinking about what had happened, she likened it to diving into the deep blue-green prisms of the Pacific, riding great rhythmic ground swells, down and up with barely an opportunity to reach a surface for a grasp for air. Exploding in unimagined exhilaration, she experienced something she had never known.

After a while she awakened and lifted her head. Stephen was sitting up against a pile of pillows, sipping a glass of cognac. Conflicted, all she could say was, "Do you think the boy is their son?"

"What?" A second or two passed. "Oh," Stephen replied with his care-less voice and a hand to pull her up. "Could be." A moment later, "Linnea, why are you so fascinated with Ho? I worry you have faulty thinking leading you down a wrong path."

Controlling an almost overwhelming impulse to tell him how much he had angered and embarrassed her, she just said, "Well, maybe Ho *is* interesting. Isn't it important to know the enemy … the way old Sun Tse warned?"

Stephen noisily exhaled, "And you don't think I know that?"

"Perhaps, but you're rude and rooted in old beliefs— authoritarianism is better than totalitarianism, dictators can grow into democracts," she said, mimicking what she'd heard him often say. Intending to remind him of Cadmus teeth growing insurgents, she needed fuel. She leaned across to the table for a glass and the bottle. But before she could reach them, he set his glass on the table and pulled her down onto him.

"There aren't going to be battle lines between us," Stephen whispered.

After a while, faint sounds drifted up the stairway, presumably from the living room.

"What's that?" Linnea asked, raising her head to hear *Non, Je Ne Regrette Rien.*

The distinctive, passionate voice of Edith Piaf along with Stephen's hand stroking her shoulder assuaged pent up anger. Confused, she felt thrown into a circumstance that did nothing but cloud her thinking. Still, she curled up at his side and let Piaf's song put her deep asleep.

"I'll send you off in the direction you should have been going," the Frenchman said in the morning. "If you have any trouble or the route gets confusing, don't sing," he smiled. "Shout! Incidentally, my men oiled and tightened your bicycles. No wonder you had an accident!" he winked at Linnea. "Please hold in mind Ho Chi Minh's enormous patience and remember Vietnam's Marshall Vinh Hung Dao's words when the Mongols invaded in 1284: 'The enemy must fight his battles far from his home base. We must draw him into protracted campaigns. Once his initial dash is broken, it will be easy to destroy him, little by little, by attrition.'"

Turning to Stephen, he said, "Don't let the Vietnamese people feel your fight against communism is in opposition to their goal of nationalism. Westerners and Asians fight differently. Ho fights a political war for long-term survival. Like the jungle that cannot be defeated, his forces may only briefly be subdued. Success will be with the natives and their landscape. Be careful and get out soon."

Linnea let Stephen take the lead. Neither spoke as they entered the morning mist rising toward pockets of blue sky in canopies of tall, thick-stemmed trees.

Ahead of them, a 10-foot high fence terminated in an open gate over which spread a boldly carved wooden decoration of tigers and rabbits in a matrix of vines.

A half-kilometer later they came upon a South Vietnamese soldier with a gun pointed at the surface of a rivulet. The soldier had to have heard them approaching, but never looked up from the trickling stream with his fixed bayonet pointing at it. Linnea dismounted, came up beside the soldier and, with hands clasped behind her back, leaned over to peer at water only a foot or more deep.

Patience, such great patience for just a simple fish, she was thinking, knowing that the poverty of ARVN soldiers must be why he was fishing. Then she recalled the Mao Tse-Tung saying that insurgents should swim among people like fish in the sea.

Finished with his bicycle chain, Stephen stretched and looked over at Linnea next to the soldier. Just above their heads, billowing over treetops toward them, dark black smoke spurted into the blue, trailing fiery tongues of red and yellow.

"'Nea!" he yelled. "Get away from there! We have to get out of here!" He swung his bicycle around, yanked hers up and, running up, shoved hers at her. "'Nea, don't dither!"

Several yards later, not going as fast as he, she cried out, "But they see us! They're coming towards us! We've got to stop. They need our help."

Stephen scanned in front, behind and all around. "It must have happened just after dawn."

"*Nói tiếng Việt như thế nào, hả bạn!*" (My friends!) a teenaged girl shrieked, her arms reaching skyward, coming at her. Behind her a young boy sobbed and wailed beside two scorched bodies.

"Can't you call? Isn't that why you brought that radio in your backpack?" Linnea screamed, using her shirtsleeve to try to filter the smell of burning flesh.

"It was to help *us*, if *we* needed it," he said. "Call to do what? What's done is done. Maybe now you can see the reasons for the need for Strategic Hamlets."

"At least let's show we care."

"Come on, 'Nea. The VC did it, and the villagers know it. If we approach, we don't know what we'll be getting ourselves into. And in an instant it'll be our fault."

"If troops had been in their village this might not have happened," she said, mentally castigating Stephen as a hare, running away.

Stephen whirled around, gripped her bicycle seat from behind and pushed, heading them away until they reached fresh, salty air sweeping in from the South China Sea. It was the only time in her life that approaching the ocean wasn't with happy anticipation.

CHAPTER XI

"We need to get a visit with the Hmong in the Central Highlands over with," Linnea fairly snapped when Vinh finally drifted into the USAID office after she had left messages for him all over Saigon. "It's planting season and I need to know about the wells we've helped with and if our seeds are being used. And, this time, I need to know about volumes," of opium, she meant, speaking loud enough for Stephen to hear.

"I'm not sure this is a good time," Vinh replied, his head shaking uncertainly. "Maps are not current. Those tribes ... not important anyway."

"They are, and I've already secured up-to-date maps from the Civilian Irregular Defense Group," Linnea smartly said. "All you need do is let me know of anything we should take to one clan leader or another."

Vinh had been eyeing Stephen. "Remember the recent activity close to Hmong hills. Maps must be fresh the moment we go out," he whined, now turned fully toward him for his words to be clearly heard. "Montagnards are not the only ones moving from place to place. Information must be in hand just when we leave."

"Agreed," she began in a rising voice, aggravated at Stephen's upturned face suggesting he wondered if he'd missed something. "We'll take everything we need for chiefs. And, what about a gun or two for each of us?"

The shriveled Hmong man who greeted them on the trail did so with grimaces. Behind him, the sounds of hurried movements inside the covered area to the side suggested there was a lot the Hmong didn't want seen. It didn't have to be molded brown cakes of opium, ready for shipment, but more than likely it was.

"The seeds take time. Water, water, so much, too much," a hurriedly arriving younger Hmong complained. Tiny orange stitches on his vest indicated clan superiority, and his sawed off black hair swaying like knife blades suggested he could enforce anything, if it suited him.

"Yes," Linnea replied, "seeds take time and water. But we've helped construct your well and once the seeds take root, you can have coffee and melons, along with, maybe, your women's bracelets and embroidery to sell. And that will mean money and a lot of good to come to your people. We'll help you along the way, including transporting your produce and crafts to market."

"We don't know," said an arriving ash-colored older Hmong, his leg muscles rippling with readiness.

With a straightened back and a stern voice, Linnea said, "Opium poppies take a lot of time and much hard work. It is only if you're growing a huge amount that you'll have a chance of profiting. And that will mean trouble for you. You know that. The old days are over. Opium the way the French operated is *fini*." Taking a new tack with a fresh voice, "If you've already grown much opium and pounded many cakes, we can help you." To pick up and dispose of, she was planning. "I don't want things to be bad for you."

The Hmong men were out of earshot when Linnea instructed Vinh that she would stay right where she was, for all to see, and that he was to search out the round brown pancakes, beginning with under the tarpaulin, to calculate the overall volume. Following a low-level dispute with hisses, Vinh headed off to the area behind the huts. In a short while, women's and men's shouts and screams pursued Vinh running with his hair flying.

*   *   *

"The Hmong are okay," Linnea answered the gangly blue-eyed Special Forces medical officer. "Pretty healthy, with the exception of their betel nut pink teeth, and their other habits," she said, handing him a summary of the tribal clans she'd visited.

"My, my!" the medical man chuckled, reading what she'd written. "At least you like one tribe."

"The Rhade are definitely the most advanced," she replied, assessing him the way she increasingly did with everyone, particularly newly arrived Americans. "I'm pretty sure it's because they have no use for stimulants." She hoped he would say something that would indicate whether he had succumbed to the desire for a fast buck.

Intending for him to laugh and then open up, Linnea described Vinh's eyes growing larger and larger as they came to a Rhade village the first time. On top of every longhouse, pairs of plump wooden breasts with snappy nipples pointed up toward the heavens. *Les tetons*, she continued, symbolize that Rhade women lead the clan and can choose a mate, rather than being tricked or forced into a sexual relationship and an eventual unhappy union. "And they don't grow opium. What do you think about that? By the way, what do you think about all the opium growing hereabouts?"

The medical officer's face suggested he didn't know what she was talking about.

*   *   *

Hugh was slouched like a fat Buddha in his customary corner at Brodard's when Linnea and Stephen approached at the end of March. "I understand that following the threat of a pincher attack on Saigon, you two escaped to the beach," he said, looking her over and half rising to greet her. "Well, how was it? Are the world's biggest lobsters still the most succulent?"

"It was wonderful," Linnea gushed, sliding into the chair next to his to be close enough for a quiet talk, if a chance arose. Conscious of her tan glowing in the pale pink cotton halter dress she'd designed for a seamstress to stitch, she blushed, happily remembering Stephen's smooth authority in acquiring "a quiet shore side cabana off from the rest."

Numb from the schoolyard conflagration, she'd acceded to Stephen taking care of everything, including finding out about and ordering local crab specialties and accompanying their dinner with good native drinks. Soft candlelight and gentle evening breezes helped her relax enough to unlock volumes of befuddled feelings, and Stephen's deep brown eyes had encouraged. Stepping out of the cabana the next morning, her spirits soared in seeing free flying gulls having fun over a long white sandy beach washed by gently rolling waves, reminding her of happiest times. With Stephen seated under a thatched sunshade watching, she dove through the crested surf down into the prisms of the sea's clear blue green. Keeping eyes open, like in her youth at Balboa's jetty, classifying all the fish around her, she explored. Breaking the surface like a happy young seal, she felt she was seeing Stephen in a new light.

"There was a night sky so clear the stars seemed close enough to touch—really rather divine," she said to Hugh.

"That describes you." Hugh's blond eyelashes lifted to reveal a bright sparkle in usually limpid eyes. "I know the scenery. The subject was crustacean."

"Yes, yes," Linnea laughed. "The lobsters were heavenly," she said, with a smiling glance at Stephen. "Cap St. Jacques and its towns—especially Vung Tau! What an exquisite, picture-book little village that is, with tremendous potential."

"More visitors and the area will be ruined," Hugh admonished.

Linnea sat back to luxuriate in the way Stephen was taking her in. "We also stayed overnight at a rubber plantation," she said. "The plantation owner was most hospitable and he...."

Stephen interrupted, "He lauded France's great contributions to Indochina without mentioning important little details, like their guillotine in constant use, or the fact that five months *before* Pearl Harbor France gave Japan a

146

base here so that it'd be within easy striking distance of the Philippines, Singapore, Indonesia."

Ignoring him, Linnea leaned into Hugh to describe the Frenchman's plantation, the delicious dinner with beautiful crystal and porcelain, and the perspectives on Ho she said she needed. She stopped when a wave of cigar smoke from a near-by table smelled like traces of burning skin.

Seeing her recoil, Stephen squeezed the hand in her lap. He asked Hugh, "Did we miss anything?"

"Nothing much," Hugh sighed. "Diem issued an edict that no public meetings can take place without prior governmental approval. Madame Nhu whipped up her female paramilitary group, and she's proclaimed that USAID and American advisors treat Vietnamese people 'as lackeys and prostitutes.'"

"Don't exaggerate," Stephen huffed.

"Not one bit. And, adorable husband Nhu has launched Operation Sunrise in Binh Duong province 35 miles north." Hugh put both hands around his cocktail glass to whirl its contents. "That Strategic Hamlet program must be for the benefit of the Viet Cong," he said, taking in Linnea before eyeing Stephen. Linnea also looked at Stephen, wondering about the building supplies for the burgeoning number of hamlets and Stephen's responsibility for them.

Stephen dismissed, "The hamlet program is important and already successful in the north below the demarcation line. Anything else?"

Hugh replied as though with obedience, "Important word about that poor country to the west—Laos."

"Well?" Stephen asked, observing people at the front door. "What's wrong in Laos?"

"It's lost."

"Can't be!" Stephen swiveled back at Hugh. "Our people there are very good!"

Hugh responded, "The battles between embassy folks and the Agency have finally done it: *finit*. Not surprising, considering what we're beginning to witness here between State and the spooks; it's a dirty shame. The Company mavericks worked hard and did an incredibly difficult reconnaissance job using Lao tribes."

"Using tribes?" Linnea uttered with a frown.

Hugh continued, "Despite selective bombing and defoliating trees, indications are the North Vietnamese have been coming down the Ho Chi Minh trail in Laos like it's a four-lane highway."

"Damn," Stephen said.

"The orange stuff that defoliates, does it fall on the Hmong hills next to the trail?" Linnea asked.

"Nothing that falls from planes is always accurate," Hugh said. Returning to Stephen he gave his estimation that the communist forces are growing in strength, supplied by China *and* the Soviet Union. "There's evidence, you'll be glad to know."

Linnea wanted to counter that a photographer had told her in New York that China only had old, used and expendable equipment and that they were only to let Russian trains pass through their country.

"The only way trail travelers can be stopped," Hugh said, "is with armed forces on the trail—American ground troops—which aren't allowed and we can't insert into supposedly neutral Laos anyway."

Stephen's cheek muscles rippled.

Linnea began to wonder if it was the Ho Chi Minh trail that Jim had been instructed to sit by and watch. The trail was partly in Laos. It came to mind that her AP colleague "Pat" Morin, Eisenhower's biographer, told her Ike warned Kennedy that if Laos were lost, all of Southeast Asia would go with it.

With sad disgust in his voice, Stephen said, "Kennedy okayed a tremendous clandestine effort in Laos ... which should have and could have worked."

"Already a fallen domino?" came Linnea's snide remark.

Hugh mused, "For seven years our Advisors have been doing great work, now to be phased out. The military upper brass is chomping at the bit to come on strong. After all, guys from WW2 and Korea need a war for them to retire in style."

"Military men stay in for good reasons and not perks," streamed Stephen in quick reply.

"What about the Lao tribes?" Linnea asked. "How do our Special Forces feel about leaving tribesmen endangered for associating with Americans?"

"They're survivors and will go on surviving," Hugh replied, looking around for the waiter with eyes showing a mind in full gear.

After Hugh completed his order, Linnea asked, "France criticizes us for being here. The Frenchmen were evidently unhappy that France returned here in the fifties and protested. Well, the few Americans who know we're in South Vietnam seem none too happy we're here now, and the French are warning us."

Stephen, with eyes scanning the room, said, "French criticism of the U.S. is meaningless. They've been non-stop angry at us since they laid the groundwork for revolution and ours came first, not bloodied by guillotines."

"Agreed on that one," Hugh said. "The French are best at blowing their own horn."

"And at bringing back heads tied with wire through ears — that's what the French taught the VC and the VC are doing to innocents today," Stephen added.

With her head down, Linnea muttered, "The French brought democracy and individualism to Vietnam with Dumas, Hugo, Rousseau, and Montesquieu, and I…"

Stephen's pat to her hand seemed like a slap. "And French boastfulness established Paris as a Mecca where the best minds in the colonies went to study Marx and Lenin."

"And that's ironic, isn't it?" Hugh responded. "France was the cruelest of all colonizers, and yet French socialist and communist philosophers undermined their own empire."

Gritting her teeth, "Couldn't France's revenge be upon us, in the networks they left behind, that relate to the USAID work I've been assigned?"

Stephen, jotting something in his little black notebook, raised his head to her.

Hugh looked from one to the other with as worried a face as ever displayed. He pulled his white handkerchief out, waving it before blotting at a stream of sweat rolling from his sideburns. As the waiter neared, Hugh said in a loud voice, "Good overhead fans don't cost much. The place already profits! We don't need to be thirstier when we're already imbibing!"

When the waiter moved off, Hugh lowered his voice. "I forgot to tell you, Stephen. Following the palace bombing, Homer Bigart wrote in the *Times*, 'After the *thrilling* bombing of the Presidential Palace, Saigon slipped back into its usual state of apathy.' Diem now wants Bigart out of the country. And Bigart may not be packing his typewriter alone."

The emotion that had entered Hugh's voice piqued Stephen's interest.

"Reporters' jobs haven't been easy, getting copy through translation and to the palace before going out at the cable office. It won't look good to evict journalists," Hugh said.

Stephen snapped his notebook shut as a sign they'd be leaving. His hand was on her chair when Kevin, the most mainstream USAID staffer who escorted high-ranking military and intelligence people into the field, burst through the double doors, rushing toward him.

"You know what that guy Winterbottom did?" the ordinarily ultra-cool Kevin blurted loud enough for many to hear him describe the Colonel of Intelligence as stupid and crazy-assed. Winterbottom reported there were 36 Viet Cong killed in a tree-line, he said, and when Winterbottom was asked how knew there were 36 bodies, he muttered, "'Well, ah, a platoon has 36 guys, see, and the Viet Cong that ran into the trees was a platoon.' The trees were napalmed, so there must have been 36 gooks killed in action.' Another WAG," Kevin concluded.

"A Wild Ass Guess," Hugh supplied Linnea's questioning face.

"Well, wasn't there a platoon?" Stephen retorted, moving Kevin toward the bar.

Linnea checked whether Hugh's glass was at least half full, and softly said, "Hugh, with more troops arriving all the time, I need your help. How, after opium becomes brown pancakes in the hills, is it processed, how does it get here, and how does it work? Does it work?"

Hugh raised his hands in mock surrender. "I'm afraid I'm no use. I don't know how it works. You see I'm a coward. The little bit I sampled," he shook his head, "it wasn't good. I had no control. I was at somebody else's mercy. A terrible feeling! It's different with one of these," he said, fingering the glass, slowly lifting, and taking an appreciative sip. "I know who and where I am and how much I've had."

Why is he saying that when I need him? Linnea wondered. I'm not getting anywhere with Fat Wong and his scrolls, in spite of what Hugh may have done to get him to help me, she mentally whined. Hugh has got to help me! But maybe Hugh said what he did because he sees Stephen returning with a more subdued Kevin.

"Kevin, you've arrived in time," Hugh said. "We were just about to discuss the war."

"Damn you, Hugh! There's no war!" Stephen flat handed the table.

"Stephen, my friend," Hugh said. "Laos was lost in two wars—the power fight between the State Department and the Company, and the war against the muffled feet heading down the trail in this direction. And so, for a meaningful discussion, *conflict* correspondents are needed." He motioned to the next table overflowing with journalists.

"There's no war: just a simple field trip into the countryside," said a wobbly man spilling his beer on his way over. "If there's any fighting to do or the ARVN are asked to move out, they lay down their brand new American weapons for the VC to gather up later, take a three hour siesta, and then go on home. It has no semblance of war with victory or defeat."

A delicate-boned, blond-haired colleague yelled, "Defeat? The ARVN moves so fast away from the action as never to be defeated. More than a thousand government desertions in a single month—that's the going rate. The Psychological Warfare Chief ..."

"On our side or theirs?" stringer Paul inserted.

"... says the situation's a joke."

The AP's serious, deep voiced Malcolm Browne remained standing. "This war has a new face. Insurgency and counterinsurgency—and our leaders don't see it."

Several journalists nodded. "It's a political conflict, and, in fact, a civil war."

"Agreed," Hugh said. "And needed is the intelligence to recognize it."

"I'll bet there are more Intel guys here than Special Forces," Paul commented. "That reminds me about this party I went to. I showered and put on a sincere suit and...."

"Aw!"

Paul described Khmer Kingdom artifacts in an American Intelligence guy's compound. Without anyone saying anything for several minutes, "What really bothers me is that I was set up to see it—the involvement ... the payoff for the stuff, you know what I mean."

Hugh responded to the way Linnea was zeroing in on stringer Paul, and said, "I don't intend to add to your paranoia, Paul, but there must be something you're vulnerable about?"

"God, no. Other than the home office wanting to can me."

Correspondents snickered, groaned, and sought from colleagues the latest directives.

"Linnea, I forgot about someone I need to see," Stephen announced. "He'll be at the Continental right now. I don't know if you want to go with me. It might be a long talk and you'd just be sitting around and waiting. You can go back with Kevin," he said with a pointed look at him.

"No," she said, glancing at Hugh with frustration. "I'll go with you," she replied with the hope of a chance to find out about his mysterious meetings. "If I won't be in the way, of course."

"You are never in the way," Stephen answered. Then a commanding tone entered his voice as he looked at Kevin and added, "I'll feel better this evening if I know Linnea is back at the compound, Kevin."

"I can take care of myself," Linnea bleated with the intention of ditching Kevin and, if possible, seeing where Stephen went and with whom.

CHAPTER XII

Heavy gray fullness rolled off the South China Sea over the Mekong Delta and onto the boiling hot, pinched earth in May. Heat climbed to 100 degrees and humidity became 100 percent. But, when cannon-like thunder claps heralded first droplets, it seemed that Saigon sighed with relief. Streets erupted in frantic mixtures of leaping frogs and fighting crickets with a multitude of little boys chasing after them.

Five thousand American troops were now in South Vietnam. Those in Saigon, the *Stars and Stripes* reported, found respite in front of air conditioners in new "Americans only" concrete apartment blocks, or in the burgeoning military PX, or at the freshly constructed, air-conditioned Alhambra or Capital Kinh-Do theaters.

In Fat Wong's "Old Things" establishment in Cholon, a groaning air conditioner fought to make the viewing somewhat comfortable.

"Is it really Ming?" Linnea asked Fat Wong, rapidly fanning herself. The yellow and brown scroll had a slender Chinese lady sitting sideways to a window with hands folded in serene contemplation. The dozen red seals of former owners indicated it had been treasured. "It's different from the usual four essentials—mountains, water, trees, and a tiny person or hut. And the calligraphy with the upward curving brush strokes also is unusual!"

"You learn well," Fat Wong said. "I selected this one for you. Artist is female. Rare, like you."

Smiling appreciatively, Linnea settled back in the richly lacquered mahogany three-sided chair to indicate serious consideration of the scroll. While focusing on it, she hoped that Hugh, after she'd expressed she wasn't getting anywhere, had given Fat Wong an impetus.

Fat Wong snapped his fingers and a servant girl arrived carrying a tray with teapot and cups. After asking more about the scroll's artist and its age and value, Linnea sighed, "The humidity today must be over 100 percent!" Fanning herself she added, "Is it more humid here because we're so close to water—the Rung Sat Swamp? Have you ever been there?"

Fat Wong frowned. "Rung Sat is Binh Xuyen Pirate hangout." With his high voice rising, "They hold up sampans and come right up here to snatch us poor merchants for ransom. Then sneak back into mangrove dungeons and hide." Shaking his head, inhaling through the separation of his front teeth, "Rung Sat and the Binh Xuyen no good."

"I've heard the Binh Xuyen have business connections around here."

"Not now!" Fat Wong exclaimed, as though a connection might have once included him. "They are like the tide," he said, elaborating on how they came out of the swamp in 1945 and the Japanese then made them police. The Binh Xuyen were bare-breasted, Fat Wong said, with big guns and green berets, carrying enormous banners, 'Binh Xuyen Assassination Committees.' "They strut nine hour," he said, starting to fan with great energy. "Why this?"

"I've heard the Binh Xuyen controlled dens, brothels and gambling casinos until...."

"Yes! Great Profit!" Fat Wong relaxed, saying that Emperor Bao Dai, even with a tiny slice, today has jewels, a yacht and a villa in France. "How is the Emperor? Do you know?"

"He is all right, from what I've heard. And what about the Binh Xuyen today?"

"I not know. Bad, bad people."

Linnea knew that Edward Lansdale and the Vietnamese Army fought the Binh Xuyen in 1955, with many people killed and made homeless. "Is Le Van Vien, or 'Bay' Vien, I guess he is also called, still the leader of the Binh Xuyen?" Linnea heard a faint squeak in Fat Wong's expanding and receding chest.

As though suddenly remembering something, Fat Wong headed for his back room, leaving Linnea facing the Ming scroll. Matching the lady's contemplative stance, she reflected that in order to learn how opium comes to Cholon/Saigon she might have to make a trip into the Rung Sat swamp.

It was after a good while that Linnea's ears picked up the rise in Fat Wong's voice as he talked on the phone. When he returned many minutes later, he handed her a sales slip indicating the price of the scroll with the notation "collector's discount" if she decided to buy it. At the very bottom was an address close by in Cholon.

"Thank you. I'm most interested," she said. Then, examining the slip a second time, she expressed confusion about the notation of the address of a furniture store.

"Store owner long-time opium user knows everything," Fat Wong said, ushering her to the door, his black gown swishing like a broom. "Used to own newspaper; wrote brilliantly after pipe. In English, too." Fat Wong looked up and down the street before backing inside, closing the door and pulling down the shade.

Two large red lacquer pillars on either side of the furniture store's frontage suggested prosperity, but its Chinese owner, waiting at the entrance, looked fairly wasted: skin on neck and arms dried like old leather; chest concave; eyes drained of color. Without a greeting, he turned to lead her, shuffling toward chairs in the back.

Regally seated in his wide, richly polished chair, he began: "Opium is good—and it is essential. It takes us from ugliness of life and carries us up to glorious beauty above the clouds," he said, waving sinewy fingers from the wide thick black silk of his sleeve. With mystical tenderness, he continued, we're transported to a miraculous universe where colors are luminous and the incredible is possible. Fears and hateful memories are banished, and cruelties are erased. "Opium is the most marvelous muse for creativity in the whole world." He finished, scooping his chest toward her as though dipping into her soul. "Is that what you want?"

"Yes, yes," she said, continuing to write in her notebook. "I like the way you express yourself."

When asked what she already knew she replied she'd photographed young opium plants growing as glaucous green leafed plants and, in the next stage, as serrated and fringed petals of gently swaying white and scarlet-colored poppies, until finally the naked bulb had its crown.

The furniture storeowner stopped her and, letting the heavy silk of his blouse fall aside, he used his long yellow fingernail in a vertical swipe as if it was a short curved knife and described the opium oozing out cloudy and white, hitting the air and then flowing like rich black honey. "Like warmed beeswax, your people say. After drying, it is beaten to a tenth of its volume into the brown cakes you've seen." Sounding slightly spent, with a shake of his head, "Fat Wong says you go deep into hills."

"I need to know the steps from brown cakes to the den."

"Why want this?" The skin of his wrinkled brow looked like it might crack.

"Someone I know smoked and got sick. I need to know the process between brown cakes and a couch in a den, and if some opium is … impure."

His gray eyes rolled from side to side as though disappointed. "The cakes have to be heated to a high degree to remove all impurities in producing a base."

"Heated? Where? In the hills?"

He appeared irritated. "Here, in big vats." Then, in a small voice, "Always here until now."

"Where now? In Cholon?" Finally, realizing he wasn't going to answer that question, she asked, "Well, after the base is made, what's smoked?"

"Morphine."

"Morphine? Isn't that dangerous?"

The store owner's head canted back for milky eyes to roll up to the ceiling where they stayed until landing back down on her with a sword-like slice.

Wondering how in the world Fat Wong had inveigled this interview, awaiting a chance to return to what she needed to know, she asked if there was some special reason people smoked in a den rather than at home. He answered that the wealthy with servants smoked at home but that even they enjoyed a den with "the like-minded" and compassionate helpers.

"A dark, quiet place is often needed," the Chinaman said with the gray concentric circles of his eyes revolving, "because eyes and ears change. Here," he impatiently said, pulling over a small table with a tray like a tea service but containing an odd assortment of instruments. "This is a set-up, a *yen-poon.*"

Linnea blushed.

"So you know *yen-poon,*" he said querulously, as though duped. To her vigorous denial he rapidly, laboriously explained that the spirit lamp heats the morphine paste; the scissors keep the wick clipped, and the needle opens the hole in the cup for a clear draw. He picked up a two-foot long brown-stained bamboo pipe sealed at one end, with a jade mouthpiece at the other. The pipe was decorated with colored stones and mother of pearl set in white metal. A hollow porcelain cup three-quarters the way down the pipe, he showed, had a small hole.

His rheumy eyes glanced several times at an empty doorway at the back and appeared relieved by the emergence of a reedy male employee. The furniture storeowner motioned for him to come forward and sat back as the man hurried to his side. "Show her how to smoke." (*"Bei kuei tai ngo-de dim sei nga-pin."*)

The skinny employee's eyebrows went up. Then, obediently, he slid onto a deep bed inlaid with ivory, pulling to him the pipe and tray with its layout. With shaking hands he lit the lamp, replaced its glass cover and curled awkwardly onto his side. He held the cup of the pipe with the paste over the flame and rolled his eyes — more in misery than the touted ecstasy of heavenly enjoyment.

His employer said, "You see, a pea sized amount of the base is taken with the blunt end of the needle, tapped down and held over the flame until it bubbles, swells and turns golden. The smoker pulls on the pipe," he demonstrated. "Care and skill you must have to coax and coddle the paste to perfection." He thought a moment. "It is pure and cannot be smoked quickly. It cannot be rushed! Lying down with a pipe is like caressing ... caressing a lover."

The Chinaman edged to the rim of his chair, indicating the interview was at its end. The employee leaped up to help him.

"More to it than I suspected," Linnea said, rising alongside. "If a dark place with assistants and skills are needed, hard working American servicemen won't have time to use opium."

"Good," the Chinaman grunted.

"Just one more question, please," she said, making a show of putting her notebook away. "President Diem in 1956 burned and outlawed opium in Saigon. His brother Nhu is said to be reintroducing it. More opium is being grown. I need to know how it gets to Saigon/Cholon, and," taking a wild guess, "how you have helped facilitate it. You may wish to pass me onto sources ... as background, of course ... so that America can soon leave and everything can go back to the way you'd like."

For several long moments, the Chinaman remained a motionless figure bent perpendicular.

Linnea extricated herself from the shredded seat covers of the grumbling Renault and struggled through Cholon's tight western streets seething with the odors of sizzling pork and fowl fried crispy in peanut oil. Weaving along with swarms of people, she glimpsed paper and cloth banners, fluttering with black slash announcements, both mutable and eternal. Men in dated dark silk to-the-floor smocks, ballet-like slippers and shiny black pillbox hats rushed past with the same vague awareness of others as New Yorkers passing her by.

When she reached the dim Cholon alley and the innocuous doorway that the furniture storeowner described, it seemed she was expected. An unusually tall and well-attired Chinaman ushered her inside. He handed her off to a succession of bowing elderly women who took her over water-retarding ledges of the anteroom from one high ceiling, incense-heavy space to another, each room more richly furnished than the last. China's long, rich history seemed staged in intricately carved and inlaid lacquered tables and chairs; expansive hanging scrolls of sternly seated court figures in yellows and reds; teeth-exposing ceramic horses in green and brown dripped glaze; and large gray and white porcelain floor vases with ravenously smiling dragons in orange and brown. Linnea slowed to a stop, overwhelmed by the grandeur.

Mesmerized, she was startled when bony fingers grasped her arm to head her into a final richly adorned space. Left alone, she inspected a magnificent carved burnished wood wall cabinet displaying precious objects—deep green jade pendants, intricately carved bronze wine vessels, and translucent porcelain cups.

A slender Chinese woman emerged to stand beside a mirrored half moon. Statue-like in a long pale blue gown with white swallows swooping upwards, neither the heavy gold chains around her neck nor the gold bangles on her wrists gave indication she was there. Her powdered cheeks with soft touches of rouge and narrow black horizontal eyebrows made her ceramic-like. Slits of eyes behind heavy lids followed Linnea's inspections of her treasures.

Linnea smelled her mother's Joy perfume, turned and, with a start, came face to face with her.

The Chinese lady took a step forward, her shiny patent leather high heels bringing her up to her guest. She was several inches shorter. Out from the fold of her rich silk gown she drew a bamboo tube. Taking off a plug at one end, she held it for Linnea to see that the tube held tightly rolled tissue paper sheets.

"Thank you," Linnea said, accepting it without asking anything, as instructed by the furniture storeowner. But now that the materials, presumably about Nhu and his opium dealings, were in hand, Linnea felt she couldn't leave the subject alone. Emboldened by the lady remaining in place without turning away in dismissal, perhaps wishing appreciation for the tiny diamonds sparkling in glossy high piled black hair and the glittering huge stones on her slender fingers, Linnea took a chance.

"May I ask why you're providing this information?" she asked.

The Chinese woman's face stayed an inscrutable powdered mask. The small dark black orbits behind folds moved from side to side.

Linnea stared at the woman staring back, the longest Asian minute yet experienced.

"A horribly tortured family member," came a whisper from between unmoving slices of lips. "My only, my wonderful younger brother. A horrible death! Nhu did it. He killed him." She brought her hands together in a prayer position, turned, and stepped to an almost invisible door in a tapestry-adorned wall. She stopped. Facing the wall, with her regal head high and slightly tilted, "I understand you research personally, alone ... and you want or need more." She may have sighed when she said, "Ask Wu Chou at the front."

Back outside on the street, clutching the bamboo tube, Linnea exclaimed, "Now?"

"Today Binh Xuyen leader Bay Vien in close. Good chance! May be rare time."

Linnea looked around for a Westerner who might be watching her. But, she chided herself, a Westerner wouldn't be down here; it'd be a Vietnamese or a Chinese spying on her. No one right now knows where I am or what I am doing. And it might be nice if someone could know that I've gone this way, Linnea apprehensively concluded.

Wu Chou stood ramrod straight and behaved as though nothing ever happened unexpectedly, including for a young female American to want to go into the dark and dangerous

Rung Sat Swamp, the Forest of Assassins, to meet the leader of the murderous Binh Xuyen.

Linnea's inhale of air resulted in a huge sneeze caused by the massive amounts of ammonia used in fighting moldy Mekong dampness. Her loud discharge made it difficult to tell whether she nodded an okay or if Wu Chou assumed she had.

Wu Chou swiftly headed out through several blocks of outdoor stalls selling varnished ducks, dried lizards, and pickled toads and snakes, noted by Linnea following as fast as she could. At murky watery fringes, huts with slapped-on patches of gray-brown metal sheets haphazardly straddled waters smeared with blue-black streaks of oil.

Wu Chou strode down mossy steps into a dripping tunnel leading toward a tiny opening to a mustard-colored tributary many yards ahead. Trying to keep up, Linnea sneezed again. Her sinuses clogged and her eyes filled. Struggling to breathe, she heard little squeaks. Rats, dozens of them, as large as cats, twirled and scampered over and around each other and off gooey walls on either side. Over her feet they scuttled, causing her to gasp with a congested yelp. Saliva went down her windpipe. She wheezed and coughed and her vision blurred. Stumbling and bumping the slime and growing dizzy, she fought to keep mind, legs and feet moving.

Through swollen, dripping eyes she glimpsed Wu Chou silhouetted at the end of the tunnel. Heaving, she staggered out into gray light and bent over, grasping her knees, coughing, trying to clear her wind passage.

Wu Chou waited without interest or concern. His back was to her as he strode toward the tributary for a craft tied to a partially submerged ramp. The boat appeared slightly more trust-worthy than adjacent ones due to its shiny, new looking outboard motor at the stern.

Linnea approached, step by step, taking in everything in every direction. She waited a weighty second before obeying Wu Chou's hand directions to step in to the craft's middle bench. Clutching the tube like a life-saving buoy, she sat down—too frightened to chastise herself.

The motor spurted into action, and, after a swift, deep slanting turn, its immediate high speed produced a measure of relief from bugs, heat and humidity. The craft's fast forward pace abandoned hesitancies in its wake and perhaps also left behind prying, scolding eyes. Passing makeshift huts flying rags and shreds of children's clothes, they motored on, leaving yellow fields of sugar cane and green and brown patches of coconut trees. The craft swept onwards, out beyond signs of human habitation, until they were deep into a maze of thick mangrove trees.

The farther they went, the more the mangroves seemed animated, possibly alive with snakes and lizards, and the blood-sucking insects she'd heard about. Standing tall, Wu Chou steered the boat around and between islands of snared driftwood and·young mangrove colonies whose roots sank down into shallow waters like the legs of giant spiders. Surrounded by gray-brown water and the many grotesque shapes emerging out of it, their motor sounded reassuring, connected with the world; then it seemed unnecessarily loud, alien and potentially vulnerable.

The sun barreled down and boiled the water until it appeared siphoned up like a reverse tornado into the murk overhead before becoming a great dumping. Humidity wrapped itself around her, crinkling Linnea's hair and melting her scalp. Mosquitoes swarmed and whirled as though from nests rudely disturbed. The smell of rotting fish and decaying roots tightened her throat, her lungs feeling squeezed like a sponge. When something big and gray-brown slithered into the water close by, she didn't flinch. She felt so weak she couldn't even turn to take note of Wu Chou steering.

After what seemed like an interminable distance and a very long time, Linnea was able to pull her head up enough to see a large great blue heron on a near bank, standing tall with a big eye in a side glance following her like a wary sentry. Wu Chou lowered the motor's speed and the skiff wallowed as he edged it into a clutch of mangoes like a tangle of thick yellow brown rope. Linnea turned, saw Wu Chou bend to his knees, and whirled around barely avoiding decapitation. Deep within what could only be described as a briar patch, a black pajama clad man jumped out, cradling a gun. He pointed it at them before lowering it to point at a portion of sandy shore that was just large enough for a skiff to land.

Wu Chou stepped out into mushy sand and pulled up the boat with Linnea wild-eyed and rigid within. Without a word or a backward glance, Wu Chou followed the man, leaving Linnea to bat at insects and work up a sweat that she was absolutely insane to be where she was. What would Stephen think when she was washed up dead on some muddy Mekong shore?

It was a long, agonizing while before Wu Chou reappeared to motion her to get out and follow. In leaving the skiff, Linnea took note of watermarks on the sand and felt there probably wouldn't be enough tidal change to float away the only means of escape.

She followed Wu Chou, stooping under thickly mangled roots on a narrow path. The air heavy, hot and dense intensified fetid smells of rot and decay. With her nose dripping, she kept her eyes on the sand fiber mixture underfoot and the pants leg of Wu Chou a foot ahead. When he abruptly stopped to indicate she was to go past him, Linnea shook her head. The opening he pointed at was low and dark and she would have to be on her knees to enter—probably at an excellent angle for the lopping off of her head. She remained where she was until Wu Chou bent down, almost crawling, going in first.

Darkness was merely in an antechamber that took a sharp turn into a broadcast of light from a huge hole cut through mangoes, exposing a heavy dull gray sky. Linnea shaded her eyes with her hand to look around. A harsh sound at her right came close to flattening her.

"So you think opium is an evil to be eradicated," growled a voice. "You're either a crazy religious half wit or you're an agent. I've dealt with both. So sit down!"

Linnea dropped onto her knees. A thin cushion was slipped under her behind. Abruptly seated, she faced a cross-legged, bare-chested sneering male. Stubby fingers adjusted his slanting dark green beret sporting a badge of a snarling tiger with a thirsty red tongue. Linnea thought out loud, "So you are Le Van Vien, called Bay Vien!"

His hooded eyes fixed on her without answering. His head was round and smooth, and of a light brown shade to indicate Cambodian/Khmer blood. The smoothness of his cheeks made him look more like an altar boy than an extortionist and assassin, perhaps because he once had been a seminarian. A gold earring hanging from an earlobe, a first on a male other than in *Treasure Island*, indicated he acknowledged being a pirate.

"What's your angle?" he asked, his round black eyes flickering. "Are you going to be like Lansdale, bringing me word you're going to squeeze and separate us from our friends on the surface?"

She glanced at Wu Chou off to the side next to the gun-toting, thick-necked assistant with the scarred and welted face. Wu Chou's countenance suggested he, too, had experienced much, feared nothing, and cared less what happened next.

In as strong a voice as she could marshal, "Your friends on the surface? Corsicans? Nhu? The Viet Cong? The North Vietnamese?"

"Ha!" Bay Vien slashed. He nodded at the bamboo clutched in her hands. "I cannot imagine how you did it, but you impressed a lady." A fierce look went to Wu Chou before landing back on her. "What do you want?"

Startled, she said, "I want corroboration that Nhu is responsible for opium production increasing," she said, keeping tight hold onto the tube. "I need proof he controls the journey from the hills and the processing in Saigon—the business that used to be your Binh Xuyen's."

"Ha!" Bay Vien spat at fibers in the sand. "Why? What will you do with information?" Then, as though uninterested in her reply, he switched the stout bundles of glabrous muscles of his legs. "Nhu is a snake. He's ruining his brother—the president *your people* created and keep in power." Shaking his head, "But Nhu's weaknesses will make him temporary."

In the alien silence of the cunning kingpin, Linnea's body seeped washcloths of sweat. "And his weaknesses?"

With eyes streaming at her clutched bamboo like he would snatch it, Bay Vien said, "Weaknesses are ambitions. Maybe you know about that." Still focusing on the bamboo, "The lady who gave you that, her hatreds are Nhu's use of torture and murder. Mine are different." His attention went to his foot, where he picked at the nail of a callused big toe.

Linnea waited. "What are your hatreds?"

His head shot up, "You!" he shouted.

Linnea rocked back as though smacked.

"Your government. Your government gave Diem and Nhu money to fight enemies—the VC and the cadres from the North. American funds were miserly, not enough to do anything about defense. So Nhu connected—was forced to connect—with the Corsicans for cash from the opium business *that was ours*. Our business!" he shouted. "Nhu now reopens *our* dens." Bay Vien leaned forward, his head stretching his neck out like a turtle's from its shell: "Your government makes bad mistakes! It created and is responsible for Nhu!"

"You ... you say President Diem's brother Nhu, working with Corsicans, is running the opium trade to make money to defend the regime?" Linnea asked. "That's what you're saying?"

Bay Vien weaved from side to side. "Opium is the business of making money. Your country knows money making more than any. But your United States is stingy and the Corsican Francisci is not. Rocky Francisci is a businessman; he owns the Continental Hotel, you've probably figured out, and other places in Saigon/Cholon, and he runs investments, including our Binh Xuyen Fund," Bay Vien proudly said with a lift in the corners of his mouth. "So, Nhu is Francisci's silent partner in the opium business to accumulate funds to fight your war."

Uncertain of what she was hearing, she said, "But you, the Binh Xuyen, still have the Hall of Mirrors brothel and the Grand Monde and Cloche d'Or gambling casinos. Aren't you as powerful as Nhu?"

"Not at this moment." Bay Vien said in a less fervent voice.

Linnea tried a new tack. "If you're now not in the opium business, or running the dens, what are you preparing to do about it?"

"Nothing right now. Nhu double crossed us, and he's going to do the same with you!" Bay Vien took from his gun-toting aide a lighted joint. "After your big force with big guns tries to defeat Nhu—take over the opium trade from him—we'll return with a force of our own."

Shaking her head, "You can't be suggesting that the United States right now is fighting Nhu for control of the opium business?" Into her mind crept earlier conjectures. Quietly she said, "Well, any involvement by the U.S. to take over opium is to get rid of something bad."

"Bad? You're crazy! Opium is nature's best creation!" Bay Vien heaved, as though disappointed and suddenly bored. "Opium is good business—the business of peace."

Linnea swallowed. If she survived this, she owed herself a really good rest, at the least on a luxurious opium bed. Searching for oxygen in Bay Vien's suffocating lair, she asked, "The U.S. is trying to suppress Nhu's activities—isn't that what you're saying?"

"Wrong! Talk to your people," he said with a mean glance at Wu Chou. Finally, in a different tone, "Word is that you're unusual. Are you going to look into the CIA effort to take over Nhu's enterprises?" With a penetrating look at her and then his gunman, "You should. But if you don't, it won't matter. You and your folks may not be around much longer."

In a voice beginning to quiver, she asked, "Do you know of a change of opium control from Nhu to Americans?" What information could he have in his smelly, rotten warren?

"We're not without sources on the surface," he said. He waited several seconds. "In answer to your question about Nhu's fatal weakness, he shouldn't have called attention to himself by using opium funds on the *Mat Vu*, and then his political party and military forces, upsetting your people. Little Lady, instead of pursuing who controls opium, you should focus on Nhu's schemes with the North."

Could Bay Vien's effort to get rid of Nhu be so that he could over South Vietnam? "Where can I get more information?" And she meant about his ambitions as well.

Bay Vien turned his head from side to side, recounting schemes and far reaching power plays, and muddying the atmosphere with accusations that seemed to her to include everyone on what he called the surface. He concluded with a sneer, saying, "And you are involved with one of the greatest schemers."

It felt like she'd sunk into the deepest valley of a ground swell, and, frantic to reach the surface for air, she became lost in a vortex that was carrying her down and away.

"Be assured: in spite of differences and antagonisms, South or North, ARVN or Viet Cong, we Vietnamese are the same people. We all hate foreigners in our land!"

Linnea struggled to rise onto one knee and then the other. "If opium is *your* business, aren't you worried the United States will take over and eradicate opium?"

Bay Vien growled. "Our time will come again and it'll be business *without* politics, without the U.S. or your feared Ruskies and Chinese."

In a wobbly, hunched position, ready to exit, Linnea mumbled, "Thank you."

"You're welcome," Bay Vien grinned from beneath his snarling tiger beret. "And remember that if you repeat what I've told you, you'll be finished."

CHAPTER XIII

Wild-eyed, Linnea searched Cholon alleys. It seemed to her it was like making desperate moves in a chess match, considering one roadway and quickly backtracking to contemplate another, searching for a red banner in Chinese, *ya ping*, with a proprietor to provide the prospect of a successful end game. The volume of opium coming from the hills was more than she'd assessed, she was certain now, but she needed to know how it was transported. She firmly believed Bay Vien implicated the U.S. for the purpose of getting rid of Nhu so that he could take over South Vietnam. And his suggestion she was close to someone in charge—well, that had crossed her mind before and would be addressed later.

Pounding the streets, with eyes flickering, a painful bundle of neck muscles indicated she must hurry in figuring things out. Right away she had to get the bamboo tube from her locked USAID desk drawer into the hands of someone Clarissa's father identified. But she needed more details to corroborate that Nhu's network meant the U.S. shouldn't support—was wrong to support—a regime with a brother in activities that could undermine American efforts to help the country. If she could succeed with that, Stephen couldn't discount her conjectures, even if he found out the nature of her correspondence with Washington.

What she needed right now in the northern part of Cholon was a den with a proprietor willing to give her links. Behind men in bowler hats on sidewalk stools, enveloped by halos of smoke, ostensibly playing Chinese checkers, could be a family style den with just such a person. Brushing aside hawkers of fowl who looked, acted and sounded like ravenous birds, she plowed into the back of one potential abode, but instead of a den, she found a little junk/antique shop.

"I've seen you before, at Brodard's and Givrals." The voice was self-assured American.

Linnea's fingers lifted from a celadon urn as if it'd turned red hot. Hovering over her was an American in his late twenties bearing the cocky swagger of an Intelligence officer or an embassy staffer. He had neatly trimmed premature sandy gray hair that matched steely gray eyes. She couldn't place him.

"Your interest in Asian art directs you to interesting places," he said. "I've acquired a few rare items that I treasure. I'm in need of a second opinion about a couple of them. Will you give it a shot? My place isn't far."

It was hot and humid and she was frustrated. Glad to meet someone with an interest in art, particularly an American neatly dressed and reputable appearing, she went along.

Huge old trees, bushy azaleas, thick orange bougainvillea, and purple rhododendron filled the neighborhood of large, stately stone houses, on the same level or even higher than her USAID villa. "This was a French high official's digs," the man said as his *bep* opened the door into an expansive marble hallway with extremely high ceilings. The cold air that greeted her was gratifying and at the same time a bit chilling.

"The art is this way," he said, leading her down the main hallway.

Light coming through vertical slats showed books on shelves in the room on the left reaching up fourteen feet. Looking in, her host bellowed, "We'll be back in a few minutes." Scarcely visible humans, sprawled out on long couches, barely moved. In a different voice, he said, "My trophy room is down this way."

"Twelfth century," he soon commented, pointing at a 4-foot high bronze. "And this is a favorite," he said, directing her to a lovely carved stone Buddha head on a tall teak pedestal.

He permitted her time for appreciation before pointing to the top of a black lacquered Chinese chest bearing large elephant tusks, a couple of curved Lao swords, and two Shan knives with tasseled scabbards, each with a silver mounted hilt ending in a tiger's tooth. Several intricately carved pink and green jades produced the praise he sought, following which he showed an elegant white Chinese ewer with a remarkably luminous gloss.

"Impressive," Linnea remarked, turning to him. "Where did you find all these?"

Instead of answering, her host pushed into her hands a silver-tipped cane. "This is something else I love. It's Malaccan. Without the colonists and the rest of us, good things like this wouldn't be saved." Purposely gazing down at the large, blue and crimson Chinese silk rug beneath their feet, "It's up to some of us to see that things are collected—preserved, really—and taken out of here. Over there the Siamese celadon bowls may be five hundred years old, and look at this pair of extraordinary white Chinese vases! They're Sung!"

"Exquisite," she obediently appraised. "Did you find these in Cholon? I haven't seen a place offering such things. Where did you get these?"

"Let's just say they were gifts—presentations for good work."

"Rewards for good work? Work in Saigon?"

"And work in the field, in the hills."

After saying over and over that she couldn't authenticate the ages or quality of yellowed Chinese scrolls of landscapes, her host headed them back toward the library. He loudly cleared his throat as they approached.

A minimal effort had been made to let in light. American men Stephen's age remained draped and inert on the couches. Long-stemmed pipes lay sprawled over the tables. Nervous movements flowed from the corner where two heavily made-up "painted swallows" sat in tight *ao dais* under the weighty fumes of cheap perfumes.

"Americans are supposed to be here doing good work, helping the Vietnamese people," she said.

"Collecting antiquities is helping the people," her host smartly replied.

"Bullshit!" she growled.

Right back at her, "With your transportation opportunities, more can be achieved and more Vietnamese helped."

"You're not helping people here! You and your friends are probably the same jackasses who go around telling everyone else what to do. You don't even know what's going on!"

He threw back his head to open-mouth laugh at the ceiling. "I know more than you do. You're at the forefront of a fascinating operation. Incidentally, a pipe here may be more to your liking than some dirty old den."

Her face felt itself draining of blood.

"The important thing is that we have similar interests, you and I. We should collaborate ... do mutual good."

"I know some good I can do about you!" Linnea yelled upon reaching the front door. "And don't think I'm not going to do it!" Scampering out as fast as she could, close to tripping down the steps, she found herself getting madder with every stride carrying her away.

Why had she been permitted to see Americans like that? How could he intimate that smoking opium was par for the course? Had he or others really witnessed her searching out dens? Who were they? And how were antiques connected with the production, transportation and delivery of opium? Remembering the frightened Paul at Brodard's describing a similar situation, she slowed, angry for being so abrupt. She should have strung the greedy bastard along to learn everything connected with his activities.

Arriving back at the USAID office in a sweat, grateful, for once, to hear the air conditioner roaring like a musketeer atop a last rampart, she appreciated the sight of Stephen bent over working at his desk. He looked up, smiled, and, either in time with the drumming cooler, or to indicate he'd expected her earlier, tapped his pencil.

She needed to talk with him, but was uncertain where to begin. Besides, anything she might say would probably be considered conjecture and not on a par with what he was doing. At her desk, keeping him in view, she unlocked the lower drawer of her desk and felt with her fingers the bamboo tube tucked at the back. The surreptitious translations she'd achieved with a Vietnamese professor proved that opium activities in Saigon/Cholon, whether or not they were all Nhu's, had a connection with her USAID assignment ... and her feeling she had been set up.

Relocking the drawer, she took out paper and commenced typing a report on Hmong needs, noting that better information on fertilizers and stronger statements on potential markets could make a difference, even though it now seemed futile. Her sweaty fingers smeared ink from one sheet to another, causing her to trash the first draft. Starting again, she stated she had to struggle with twin bureaucracies—the Vietnamese and the American—both standing stubbornly in the way of agreement and action. Before continuing, she realized she often was inclined to by-pass Vietnamese offices because they were inefficient and a waste of time, and now recognized she also avoided the American out of a fear of being disappointed in them.

More needed to be in the written report. She squeezed her elbows back, opening her chest to force air into the heart of the matter—that her USAID Hmong project had little chance of success, whether or not Stephen renewed her contract. But, from the way he now furiously typed, she could see that this would be another time for him again to say *later—we'll talk later.*

In lieu of talking with Stephen, and to get important thoughts where they needed to go, Linnea began a letter to Clarissa. After a polite question or two about her work with the Senator, Linnea described the Rung Sat Swamp experience— making it a humorous river adventure. And then she typed: "I believe the conflict here will not come from a frontal attack—the communist north streaming south, verifying the falling domino theory. More likely there will be an implosion due to dissatisfaction with the Diem administration because of the president's family—his brother Nhu with his abuse of citizens and his opium network. She paused to consider how to mention Bay Vien's claim of Nhu's involvement with North Vietnam.

The situation is perilous not only with what the Diem family is doing to itself, she continued writing, but also because of what some Americans are doing here. Lack of cultural awareness by arriving Americans causes Vietnamese resentment, she was thinking, even though that seemed a trifle in the context of so much else. Tapping a fingernail in rhythm with rain beginning to thud on the corrugated roof of a structure nearby, she remembered the pair of American bureaucrats who wouldn't touch *nuoc mam* in spite of how high in protein she said it was. With a smile she recalled their reaction to her description of how the sauce was made—fish covered by a layer of salt and left uncovered in a large vat for a year under the sun until completely disintegrated. With a grimace, she pictured freshly arrived Americans carrying sack lunches from Saigon so that they wouldn't have to eat the local fare in a village *pho* shop or a family's hut. She returned to typing.

President Diem's brother Nhu is undermining the government of South Vietnam. The evidence I've received on Nhu's murderous activities and involvement in the drug trade, along with reputed actions with North Vietnam, show there's a real danger to our American presence here. As soon as possible, the evidence in the tube—reported in my earlier, rushed note—needs to be in the hands of someone who can recognize how dangerous it is for the United States to be supporting a regime with the seditious power of a President's brother.

Sealing the letter, feeling relieved, she yelled above the air conditioner, "Stephen!"

Stephen swiveled fast around.

"Stephen, I need to talk with you. I really do. The extension of my contract, well, nothing with the Hmong has improved or changed for the better."

Seeing wrinkles develop on Stephen's well-cleaved forehead, she continued, "I'm not making progress with the Hmong to stop them from moving about and growing what they've always grown. And now opium production is increasing. I remember your saying a couple of days ago that Kennedy has ordered McNamara to prepare a plan for withdrawal. If that's so, whatever I'm to accomplish won't make any difference. It won't matter." Including worrying about American servicemen getting hooked on opium and her feeling tormented about Stephen.

"Kennedy is just preparing for his re-election," Stephen said, angling back at his desk. "He may intend for a full withdrawal *eventually*, after re-election, but until then he'll leave things as they are ... for us not to look weak by hide tailing it out of here."

"Oh, Stephen," Linnea whined. "President Kennedy is more honorable than that, and you know it. Haven't your views of communist nefarious intentions changed even just a little bit, so that our presence won't be needed here any more ... or not as much?" She chided herself for the weak tack-on, when she'd meant to say: *So that we can leave!* "I think I've made contributions to American knowledge on the tribes, so...." Let's get out of here, her mind shouted.

"We're to continue as we've been," Stephen said without much steam, jamming a sheet of paper into his typewriter for fingers to explode onto the keys.

Probably producing a good, readable, perceptive report or recommendation without a word needing to be changed except perhaps in a salient perspective at the end, Linnea fumed. She used up so much paper that she had to step on it in the wastebasket to hide the evidence of a mind packed with ideas and the aim to prove her worth.

Dithering, awaiting a time for him to be ready to listen, she flipped through her earlier reports to see if they contained any indication of progress and grist for further work. The copies recorded meetings dates, the Montagnards' locations, their terrain (dry, cracked earth; wet and spongy); the number and kind of livestock (chickens, pigs, cows); the crops and how they were grown (hand-watered from a stream or rivulet). She acknowledged that the observations were in collaboration with IVS and Special Forces personnel.

Vietnamese hill people are relatively few in number compared with people of the densely populated plains, but their territory is larger and the tribes' variety much greater. Many clans are true nomadic hunters and foragers and change locations constantly. A few are sedentary, with written languages and education.

Each Montagnard clan clings to being totally distinguishable from another, demonstrated by village structures, crops, animals, headgear and clothes, embroidery, silver necklaces, bracelets, anklets, ear ornaments, and glass-beaded jewelry. Some women knot their hair over their foreheads; others tie it at the back. Many weave scraps of colorful material through their black hair. The men of some tribes wear their hair long. Others cut it close to the scalp. Some like tattoos....

Deaths are announced by drumbeat, and long, elaborate mournings are marked by ritualistic slaughter of cattle, pigs and chickens—talked with beforehand to request permission to kill them. The most feared death is one that occurs away from the home village with the loss of a body part, particularly the head.

The Halang tribes are often on the move for various reasons; the lowland and upland Hres are big-time betel nut-chewers ... the Jarai in the Pleiku region should be watched out for—they enjoy picking fights, as do the hostile Jehs and the warlike Katu and Bru ... the Koho have slaves from other tribes—fortunately, their sacrifices are livestock bred for that purpose ... the Mnong are forest-dwellers whose fare includes lizards, snakes and rats ... the Raglai are polytheistic with a full complement of sorcerers and shamans; liquor is an important reward, frequently leaving Raglai inebriated from December to April ... the Stieng are spooky and witch fearing ... the Ede or Rhade, tribe doesn't consume substances and is outstanding in many ways.

Smiling to herself, she remembered the good feeling of working like a journalist with the Rhade—asking intimate questions of the women and taking color shots of children and the old in their distinctive tribal costume of striking black and crimson. She'd imagined creating an newspaper or magazine article, pointing out that the Rhade in the savanna of the Darlac Plateau and in the remote M'Drak highlands had students who studied abroad and returned to the tribe—a rarity on both counts. And Linnea would stress that Rhade greater motivation and achievement coincided with their not growing or using substances, or even chewing betel nut.

When she and Vinh returned to a Rhade village, she recalled, it was to bring scholarship information for Quoc, a bright-eyed, strong willed and self-assured youngster. Obtained through Doug at the USIS office in Saigon, the confirmation of the scholarship by a private boys high school in Southern California made the villagers proud, happy and ready to celebrate.

After greeting Linnea and Vinh, the Rhade became unusually formal, announcing that in gratitude for her help, they were going to introduce an important and integral member of their tribe. Linnea got her camera ready, focusing on the brush at which Rhade youngsters were peering. The figure that emerged was an enormous elephant—the largest she'd ever seen.

She hadn't expected what happened next. Several older Rhade youth pulled and pushed her forward and, before she knew it, she was up onto the ample rump of the huge beast. Gripping the ropes of a bamboo platform, she hunched in abject fear.

Vinh and the Rhade, countless old and many young, smiled up at her. She tentatively straightened with a three-finger salute *à la* Hugh. As she did, a sliver of sunlight streaked through the umbrella of trees like sun beaming through a church window. Up high on a beast's hard back in front of a bunch of dark tribesmen, memories of pains in the past skittered completely away.

The elephant raised his head, bellowed, and started out like hearing the call of a ripe and ready mate. Thundering through the forest, mindless of trees with low branches, Linnea bounced from side to side, barely able to hang on. Half laughing and half shrieking, she used every dialect she could mouth to beg the diminutive driver perched between the elephant's flapping ears to make the beast stop. When he finally decided to comprehend, he lightly tapped a little switch to the elephant's thick flank, and many yards later the cross-country rampage rumbled to a stop. It was a long way down and a long way back.

Linnea was smiling when she looked over to measure Stephen's readiness for going out to a place for a talk. He was comparing a page atop a stack on his left with something in hand. Permitting a loud scrape of her chair, she approached.

Stephen rose, appearing glad for the interruption. "I saw you smiling over there a while ago. Tigerish memories?"

"I was reviewing one of my reports on tribes and was reminded of an especially good experience I had with one of them that I may not have had the chance to share with you."

"I want to hear about all your experiences. But right now—well, some damned things have been dumped on me that need finishing. I'm sure you have some poking around you want to do. Let's meet back here around six to test the waters. Okay?"

"All right. I have an appointment for a late lunch anyway," she said, noticing he didn't ask with whom. "We really need to talk, Stephen."

Finding the directions in her notebook to the villa of Tam's relative's, Linnea headed out, taking note of the new neighborhoods passed through, and being careful not to be early or late.

The white two-story compound set back from the street, nestled under a thick collection of tall, leafy flame trees, suggested it was a refuge of tranquility. Welcomed warmly,

Linnea found that chatting with Tam in the hallway was like being with an old college friend.

Tam's mother and aunt and several young relatives scurried from the kitchen to the dining room with a long line of aromatic dishes, taking a curious glance at their rare American female guest.

"Have you ever known a Hmong?" Linnea asked Tam, appreciating how much the pale eggshell yellow of the walls and the high polish of the hardwood floors was in greatest contrast to her own recent rough experiences in the Hmong hills. "The Montagnards are my responsibility, I'm sure you know. What do you think about them?"

Tam sat with hands folded, slightly constrained. "No. They don't interest me."

Linnea noticed an older relative looking her over and remembered Tam telling her that her Hanoi family members were considered second-class by the Saigon relatives.

"I will express my deepest appreciation to your mother, aunt and relatives for this very special invitation," Linnea said as more dishes continued going past. Several moments later, "We have a good cook, but I've never smelled such wonderful aromas as these!" Tiny quail whisked by emitted the aroma of garlic and star anise. The smell of curry in *banh xeo*, the thick crepe stuffed with bean sprouts, chicken chunks, and tiny shrimp, made Linnea's mouth water.

Around the table at each place were plates of *gỏi đu đủ* (green papaya salad), probably presented at the meal's beginning with the thought that Americans were the opposite of French and needed a salad first.

Conversations were about food, and were primarily between family members, with a single question to Linnea about the reason she was in Vietnam. Trying to be entertaining, she briefly described the Rhade tribe and their elephant; it was followed by severe silence.

Later, outside, waiting for a cab, Linnea said to Tam, "This was an experience I'll always treasure. Thank you very much." After a while, when Tam didn't say much of anything, Linnea attempted to explain herself. "There are many hill people, and when they are added with the farmers they are far more numerous than all the people in Saigon, Hanoi and Hue combined. That's why I'm here and the reason for my question whether you've ever visited the Montagnards."

"We're not the same as those people," Tam said, folding her arms as though wrapping herself back into the splendor of the luncheon. "Hmong didn't get along in China. They were pushed out of there and came down here and remained."

"Yes, but that was long, long ago," Linnea replied. "The Hmong are a part of Vietnam now; they make interesting silver jewelry and they have colorful costumes."

"You have tribes," Tam said. "Have you ever visited your Indians on their reservations?"

Linnea laughed. She hadn't, and that concluded the subject. "Will you be reading later today or again soon at another poetry session?"

"My subjects are about nature and feelings and moods. The poetry of others, like in the reading this afternoon, is now political. When our poetry develops that way—although important in making changes throughout our history—it no longer interests me. The discussions that will be following recitations are called Reform and Restoration Meetings. Your people already think our poetry gatherings are communist meetings!" Tam looked sad. "Things are changing quickly."

It was too soon to go back to the office, so Linnea looked for and found the location of the poetry recitation on one of central Saigon's many side streets and, despite feeling clammy, she made herself comfortable on the floor in the front area of a small house. A collection of merchant women and white haired old men took their time looking her over, perhaps reading my frustrated soul, she said to herself.

When the poets commenced, the resonance in their recitations brought a sense of peace she had come to crave. As poems continued, Linnea worked hard to understand the essence of each, but the meaning and significance of many words couldn't be quickly comprehended and the effort finally became exhausting. She became relieved when the recitations neared a close.

About to rise, Linnea heard a poet named Luu Trong Lu started asserting that poetry has a purpose, a responsibility beyond being art.

"My poetry gushes forth into the majestic Bay of Tung;
My feet take one long stride after another.
The offshore wind will keep howling beneath my feet.
While on the other side of the river sits the American-Diem clique,
Their owl-like eyes staring at me provocatively."

After Luu Trong Lu's final words, the room erupted into a potpourri of angry statements.

"How can we achieve anything in the present-day situation?"
"We have to write about and confront what is wrong."
"How can we confront without bringing destruction onto ourselves?"
"We must retain our unique culture and move forward even as the situation gets worse."
"How? We cannot. Our children, the future, are not respecting us."
"Americans are the reason our children don't honor us! Americans have no respect for families."

Linnea departed, agonizing over the tones in the angry words. Heading back toward the office, the usual confusions and congestions seemed to spark with bad ions. The rope around a high stack of crates of chickens on the back of a bicycle suddenly broke just as she was walking past; a cyclo being driven fast by a Vietnamese in dark glasses almost ran her over, with the man never looking back when she fell. At least once a pail of chicken bones, like the scattering of bad talismans, poured down on her from a balcony or were strewn at her feet from out a doorway. She wondered if she was being hypersensitive or being given a message.

Arriving at the USAID office, Linnea expected to find Stephen through with his work and ready to leave for a drink and the talk he promised. Instead, she found a note on her desk that he had to go to the dentist. Heaving her paper and bamboo umbrella into the metal wastepaper basket, she plunked herself down, head in her hands.

"Are you all right?" Vinh asked, coming from the L around the side of the front door.

Startled and disturbed that he'd been in the office without anyone else, Linnea's hand went to her desk drawer. It remained locked. As he came forward, she thought to tell him what she'd heard in the poetry recitation, but then skipped that idea, deciding he wouldn't find comments against Americans all that remarkable.

Pulling up into a straight-back, authoritarian posture, she said, "Our trips have been fairly safe, I guess, because we've been paralleling Special Forces—*American* Special Forces," she emphasized, referring to Kien Tuong province to the southwest and in Binh Long and Phuoc Long to the north. "Now, because we can't venture west any more, I think we should head for Pleiku in the Kontum Plateau." She needed to get out of Saigon.

CHAPTER XIV

On the tarmac of a military base well north of Saigon, an Army CH47 helicopter off to the side began warming up. Compared to other planes lifting off and landing like so many gnats, the CH47 was bigger and noisier and seemed like it might be on its last leg. Its sides were dented, as though rammed by a tractor or the tusks of a herd of elephants.

"Where are they?" Linnea demanded of Vinh about the Special Forces guys supposed to be going with them while she and Vinh contacted a tribe. "They won't want to miss making a delivery to what they consider as poor, dumb tribesmen."

"I'll find out," Vinh replied, running off to a small aluminum hut.

Linnea surveyed machinery taxiing about with men dashing here and there. In light of the increase in military manpower and equipment, her USAID project truly seemed incongruous.

Rotor wind whipped her hair into whacking threads slicing her cheeks, forcing her arms into a wrap around her head.

Vinh ran back with a tall, skinny, hapless soldier doing his blue-eyed best to appear willing and able. Vinh saw the way Linnea looked from the soldier to the CH47, and said, "Don't worry."

If for no other reason than to get out of the whirlwind, the three ran for the CH47 with the pilot at the controls. Almost immediately, the motor went into laborious whining, with twin rotors rapidly turning and exterior red signal beacons blinking, regularly and routinely. Tremendous power went into the tilt-forward lift-off. The sensation reminded Linnea of the Balboa Fun Zone Ferris wheel when greased spokes groaned and propelled chairs into a downward forward slant as they swooped up. Defying gravity, this ungainly machine labored up to 3,000 feet for its blades to flatten out and the ship to attain an even pitch.

Keenly aware of everything at first, Linnea then settled into as comfortable a position as possible in the mesh stretched across the floor, and let noise and vibration lull her into a soporific state. She dozed off into deeper and deeper sleep.

It was hours later, she noted with a glance at her watch. Feeling strong gusts hitting hard from behind, from the southeast, the craft rocked. Shouts by the pilot at the soldier at first seemed for the purpose of overcoming the noise of machinery and wind. The soldier uttered something just as the 'copter began a violent pitching as though being shaken by an angry force.

Canvas webbing agreed to grasping hands as harsh crosswinds buffeted. Linnea felt the wind's violence through her back in the thin skin of the copter's aluminum. Winds alternated from strong and steady to fierce and formidable. She hugged her legs and pressed her forehead to her knees.

 Severe bouncing made her back hurt from banging the sides, and the motor's loud racket ground into her ears and into a headache. She wanted to ask how much longer and farther it'd be, but decided this wasn't the time for an ETA inquiry.

She could see the pilot and soldier checking knobs, buttons and blinking lights. Every few moments the pilot smacked spots on the instrument panel with the heel of his hand.

The wind whistled and roared, harshly pushing the craft and making blades whack their hardest. Covering her ears with her hands, she fixed on the metal strip between her feet.

After an agonizing long span of time, the pilot, half standing and clutching at the partition, shouted back at her and Vinh. "Chip detector light's on. Brace 'selves. 'Goin' down." Slapping the frame, he dropped back into his seat.

Linnea gasped just as the helicopter bounced up and whammed down, a scream flying out her mouth.

Vinh with a wild expression hooked his four limbs deep into the webbing.

A sudden severe drop made insides feel they'd hit the roof of the mouth and exited the nose. Her heart raced. Colored visions flashed. Then a strange quiet overwhelmed.

The pilot disengaged the clutch, throwing the rotors into free wheeling autorotation. The rotors whirled, keeping the helicopter up as though floating on a cushion. The ship began to glide. For long, horrible moments the helicopter eerily cruised in suspension on a vacuum of air.

Blood blasted her eyes. Her ears felt they leaked brain fluid.

The helicopter hit the ground, skidded, bounced, tilted, and shuddered into a stop. The rotors kept whacking as though searching for something to whip. Dust enveloped the machine inside and out. As the rotors slowed, everything became hushed and still.

Linnea gingerly moved her right shoulder; it pained. Her right knee felt hot and tight in the pant leg.

The pilot, sounding oddly calm, spoke into his radio, "Mayday! Mayday!"

Vinh touched the back of his head, and looked over to nod.

The pilot squeezed around the partition. "Okay. Time to get out," he announced, sounding more pleased than worried. "And, oh, yes. Welcome to Laos."

"Laos! How can that be?" she exploded.

"At least an 68 knot Southeast tailwind and a bunged up steering mechanism, that's how," he said, pulling her forward and reaching for Vinh on his hands and knees crawling toward the hatch. The pilot jumped out to put up his arms. Favoring her right side, Linnea fell down to him and into a standing position.

As the pilot and soldier helped Vinh get out, Linnea stumbled away, eyes to the ground, testing her knee. The first couple of steps were rocky and painful. Then, walking some more, the knee worked, sore but okay. She kept going until she realized no one moved along with her. "What?" she asked, turning around to see Vinh, the pilot and soldier standing beside the helicopter staring past her.

Linnea whipped back around. Tall, ashen men, more frightening than any yet confronted in the hills, stood at the edge of the clearing a half football field length away. She blinked through dust at the dark gray skin and black clothing of the large, muscular figures.

To the side, a helicopter perched on the plateau! Smaller than theirs, completely black without markings, it rested smartly like a latest invention.

The sun bounced off a knife blade being edged out and slowly reinserted. More knives were strapped to waists and ankles, with guns at every side in holsters. If they were going to kill, it would already have happened, came her slow deduction.

Without a word, the figures continued lifting burlap bags in a steady rhythm and hurling them into their helicopter. Once or twice the ghost-like bodies shot stern glances at Vinh, the pilot and soldier, cautioning them not to move. Eyes on Linnea pierced and kept her in place.

Unusually tall Montagnards! Sweat sears the skin? Is that a tattoo?

In her central position between three sets of worried eyes and six pairs of disgusted glances, it felt like she was at a tennis match—if not as an umpire, perhaps a mediator. She took a step forward. And as she did, a man a yard or two from the rest gave a hand signal toward a clump of trees. Three typically short and dark tribesmen, their black eyes deep under thick overhanging brows, gave a nod and melted into the forest.

With burlap bags loaded, stares transformed into rapid, well-synchronized movements of men leaping into the small black helicopter. The engine popped, immediately sounding at full power. Throwing dirt in every direction, the 'copter rose, hovered sideways letting something fall out, and headed fast to the northwest.

Linnea, Vinh, the pilot and soldier stared open-jawed after the mechanism as though it were a space ship. Remembering the camera around her neck, Linnea snapped the dot in the sky.

"Who were they?" she asked, presuming they were Caucasians in camouflage and requesting confirmation.

"Did you see that tattoo on the big one?" the soldier said. "A red dragon, I think it was."

Something caught the pilot's attention. He examined the ground where the helicopter lifted off. "They certainly know 'copters. Look! It might just work," he said in an amazed, happy voice, picking up a stretch of hydraulic tubing.

The pilot and the soldier used the radio and worked on the helicopter. When Vinh and Linnea realized they and their inquiries were in the way and that it'd be a while longer, they decided to inspect the eastern ridge. They found an outcropping of rocks with a good view of blue-gray ribbons of mountain ranges. In silence they watched clouds snaking through the valleys below.

Finally, Linnea had to ask, "Do you think that was opium … for Nhu?"

Vinh seemed to shudder. He put his gaze out into the distance. "Possibly."

"How do you think I can find out if it is opium for the President's brother?"

Vinh shrugged. "I don't know." After a few moments, "It's not necessarily his now."

Vinh's little addendum would have to be pursued. Until the right moment, she asked, "Well, Vinh. Did you think we were going to crash?

"No. Not our time, mine or yours."

Linnea withdrew her eyes from the fog-like clouds. "You're sure about that? Were you thinking about anything particular as we were going down?"

Vinh took his time. "My parents, of course. My wish to honor them in death."

"And your family? I mean, what about your wife and children."

"I don't have them," Vinh replied, facing her. "Yet. A wonderful word, your 'yet.'"

"Vinh, I thought the names you occasionally mention are your family."

"They are. My widowed sister and her children."

"Oh! Well, why aren't you married?" Months earlier she wouldn't have dared say that. But, experiences in the hills and fields created a bond. She had grown to like the good burnished teak of his skin and the healthy thickness of brown black hair, and even had realized that because of Vinh she'd seen handsomeness in Vietnamese men on Saigon streets.

"Work to do. I have something to achieve," Vinh said. "I will honor my mother and father and they will help me have a good wife."

"You're certainly a traditionalist. Haven't you already achieved?" She hoped he didn't think she meant success came with working for Americans. "Being educated and intelligent?"

"President Diem and Ho Chi Minh are not married men. I am like them. They have work to do and so do I." Vinh focused far across the ravine.

"Do you think President Diem and Ho Chi Minh will ever work in tandem to bring the South and North together?" Linnea asked. "The North has floods right now, and people are starving. It needs the rice in the South. What do you think? Should the South help the North?"

Vinh left his eyes on distant clouds hugging hilltops and didn't answer.

Linnea put her eyes on the jagged, dark blue gray mountains to the northeast. "Is that North Vietnam?"

"It is—if we're where the pilot said we are." After another weighty pause, Vinh rose. "Come on. Let's explore the other side of this clearing."

"Where those tribesmen were?"

"They're gone and they weren't any more hostile looking than any other." After a couple of seconds, he added, "You haven't seen Laos ... yet," and he chuckled.

Vinh informed the pilot they'd be exploring to the west, and headed toward the spot vacated by the tribesmen. Beneath three layers of tall, thick-leafed trees providing ribbons of light, myriad narrow paths paralleled and intersected. Vinh made quick decisions between fresh tracks created either by man or animal or both, taking descending ones to the Northwest.

"Oh, look," she said when they reached a spot with a clear view of a wide blue-green serpentine river below.

"We soon will need water. Maybe there's a pool or waterfall close. I seem to smell it in this direction," he said, starting out again.

Twenty minutes later she asked, "Are you sure water is what you smelled?" They were aside a live hedge of woven branches at a large furrowed field of pale blue expectant bulbs several feet high; vertical slices down the sides dripped a honey brown resin.

"A large tribal group's," Vinh said. "We'd better...."

Montagnard men had materialized soundlessly to their right and left and, when Linnea turned, she found one on the path behind her. They were very dark and so emaciated that at first she presumed they'd approached because they were hungry.

Vinh tried several dialects to blank stares and finally used his hands to indicate they'd come from the sky. With staccato-like words, Vinh seemed to be trying to say that they were like the people in the 'copter just departed and that they also should be on their way. He took a step but was blocked by a tribesman brandishing a weapon.

Linnea focused on the man. He had a tightly stitched bright red, yellow and black pillbox hat and carried a slender brown firearm as long as he was tall. She presumed he might be the leader. On a scale of one to ten, she appraised, these tribesmen could be a five—neither friendly nor hostile and more dull than dangerous.

The long stock of the leader's gun herded Linnea and Vinh onto a rocky, treacherous trail. It wasn't long before they reached a haphazard collection of huts perched on the sloping edge of an embankment, the roofs a combination of mud and grasses. They were far less orderly or cared for than their *papaver somniferum* poppy field.

The pillbox hat-wearing leader shouted in the clearing, and several extremely skinny men emerged from sheds, blinking and trying to shade their eyes. Staying until their leader passed, they dashed back inside.

The leader poked Linnea and Vinh along uphill to what presumably was his personal hut. They had to stoop to enter the musty enclosure over raw earth. Linnea's eyes fell on the only thing within—a crude pit with scorched rocks. Nothing else reflected human inhabitance until, motioned to sit, she and Vinh noticed and avoided a narrow stream of dampness creasing the dirt.

As soon as the gun-toting leader left, Linnea whispered, "What do we do now?"

"They speak Lao," Vinh finally said, making a circle with his forefinger in the dirt, "with a few words of Yunnan Chinese."

"So? What does that mean? That we're near China?"

Absently, Vinh drew a stick figure in the fluffy soil. "They fight each other, remember. Not us!"

"What do you mean by *us*?" she snarled. "You Vietnamese?" Sweat flowed from her scalp along with a plea from her bladder. After several moments, "Vinh, I need to relieve myself." Thinking further, "With your help, I might get the message across. And then I could slip away to get help from the soldier and pilot."

"Do you smell something?" Vinh asked, when she returned from behind the hut, sullen for not being able to go far. The crackling of wood suggested the tribe was preparing for an early dinner.

"Oh, My God, no!" Linnea groaned, recalling that the leader pulled out his knife from his waistband when he brought them into the hut. Once a knife is drawn, it must always be bloodied before being returned to the sheath, she knew, telling herself it's better to be shot trying to escape than carved up and stewed! "We have to have a plan before he comes back!"

An extremely dark tribesman entered to tower over them, holding coconut shell cups in both hands.

Linnea pulled herself up from her downward curl, "What is it?"

"I don't know, but whatever it is, it's important to accept. I'll try it first," Vinh said of the white gruel with green specks and small chunks of brown. "The green is betel leaf, I think. If I start getting sleepy, maybe you'd better...."

"Yes! What?"

Just then, the leader entered to sit down with crossed legs and watch them.

"Don't worry," Vinh said, scooping out a mouthful of porridge with his fingers. "We have time."

Seething through gritted teeth, she whispered, "Time for what, dammit?"

"Try it. It's not bad," Vinh said, eating quite heartily.

With the leader staring at her, she took a bite of the somewhat sweet and nutty green and brown-specked gruel. A tear dropped. "Fattening us up before....". *And all this simply because I wanted to prove I'm worthwhile!* Her cough down into the dish sounded like she was drowning.

Vinh obviously liked very much what he was munching and accepted even more. When a tankard of water was brought in at his request, Vinh bowed from his waist.

And that did it. "Do you know what's happening to us?" she came close to a soft shriek, causing the Montagnard's muscles to tighten in alarm.

Once the Montagnard relaxed again, she pitifully said, "We're being fattened up for their dinner!"

"Be quiet and enjoy."

"Why, Vinh!"

*   *   *

"What did I tell you," Vinh said, running along a steep uphill path with the superhuman energy of a rickshaw driver.

"Well, what did you tell me?" Linnea asked, almost abreast, close to skipping. More than ever before she loved the smell of trees, the sounds of birds and even the feel of dirt around toes in her shoes.

"You should be grateful to those tribesmen for letting you experience the object of your assignment. Those poor people don't have much. Nothing much grows in their mountains." A few moments later, "I've neglected to tell you how geography is the cause of Vietnam's problems. North Vietnam doesn't have good land. It is mountainous and the mountains cause the people to share what little they have."

"And so they live in clusters, collectively," Linnea said, preparing for "communally," the favorite word in his mantra.

A few yards later, Vinh proclaimed, "The People in the middle, where Vietnam closes in at Hue, are narrow minded, and that's where our leaders have come from."

Through somewhat fuzzy thinking, Linnea recognized that Vinh was referring to Emperor Bao Dai and President Diem, who were both from Hue. "Now, Vinh, you're also from Hue. You're calling yourself narrow minded!"

"No. My head can turn and I can see both ways, in both directions, like a go between, as your people say. The north, *yang*, and the south, *yin,* cannot exist without each other. They must be together."

"Sounds good," she said, feeling benign spirits holding her up and carrying her along. "Are you working on that? Is that what your mysterious contacts and activities are about?"

Vinh glanced behind at the ground to her side without answering.

"Well! Good to see you! We'll have this fixed right quick." The pilot looked them over. "What have you two been up to? Your eyes—you look different!"

"I need to sit down," Vinh said, heading toward a spot on the plateau still bathed in light from the west. Linnea caught up with him. They wobbled, necessitating a mutual assist.

"An experience like that! It makes me think of poetry," Vinh said. "*The Tale of Kieu*, by our great Nguyen Du, is about someone like you—a woman growing and experiencing *nhan* and *nghia*, trying to understand."

Linnea folded her hands in her lap, ready to listen.

After a few moments of thought, Vinh sat up to begin, but then slumped, seeming on the verge of crying, "Oh, no! I cannot remember all three thousand lines!"

"Oh, my dear Vinh," Linnea laughed. "Do whatever you can!"

He repeated favorite lines that included:
"Our lives are like lightning, here and then gone
Spring plants blossom, to be barren in autumn
Mind not the rise and fall of fortunes
They're dewdrops twinkling in the grass."

Once airborne, the helicopter rose to a height where the sun in the west appeared below, ready to rapidly descend for darkness to spread over the landscape.

With Vinh snoring in the back, she reviewed the aftermath of eating opium bits, appreciating how well she'd felt afterwards and that untoward thoughts had not come to the fore. Whenever she had had too much to drink, bad memories made her shout in her sleep and sometimes even awake. And so, the focus of her worries—opium—maybe wasn't that abysmal after all, she began to think.

She crawled to the space between the pilot and co-pilot soldier to look ahead through the windshield. "What's that over there?" She pointed at a line of charred, jagged incinerated tree trunks silhouetted against the deep orange western sky.

"It's caused by one of those defoliants."

She remembered a strong defoliant had the name of a color and wasn't effective because a lot had to be used. She had worried about its effects in the Hmong hills and now made an urgent mental note to mention defoliants in her next letter to Clarissa and her Dad.

As their helicopter whacked its way closer to Saigon, it joined a procession of other helicopters, reminding Linnea of childhood days in her sailboat towed in a long line of other boats back up the bay after a race down by Newport's jetty. While pulled along, she bailed, coiled the ropes, and prepared the craft ready a freshwater spraying in front of her bay front summerhouse. Then, after a good day in winds and waves reaching the finish line ahead of boys older than she, she would ready herself for family evening challenges she never won.

How extraordinary to return to sophisticated Saigon in time for a good bath, a tasty meal, and a comfortable bed, she thought. It's probably like returning in a cab from the front lines in World War I for an evening in Paris. And how ironic it is that the increase in American presence in Vietnam produces a surge of nostalgia for things French.

Saigon, positioned between the Saigon River and the Delta's myriad waterways, could be seen from a distance. In the increasingly dark sky, bright floodlights beamed upwards, panning back and forth as though proclaiming that city people were superior—using heads rather than hands like farmers who, after working all day, had no electric light against the night.

Saigon glared so brightly against the sea of black that it looked like an island surrounded by a reef without openings into the surrounding ocean; only one or two faintly lighted roadways suggested access to the countryside. The closer the helicopter came, the more the municipality resembled a boiling cauldron, with headlights of roaming vehicles coalescing like a tiger turning into melted butter.

The next night Linnea talked Stephen into taking her to the Eiffel Restaurant. They stepped from their cab onto the mica-glittering sidewalk of the Eiffel's elegant entry, and as Stephen parted for Linnea the heavy blue damask curtains at the entrance, she felt she might be entering a new chapter in her life.

"The Eiffel takes itself so seriously!" Linnea playfully whispered just inside. An unsmiling proprietor's assistant, focusing on her reservation book, delayed looking up as though about to say that the almost empty Eiffel was full up. The assistant's two-piece suit in heavy, ivory-colored silk bore two vertical lines of black buttons, connecting loops of shiny black cord across the bust like the uniform of a martinet. At her desk, fully opened roses in a cut glass vase appropriately suggested a French Impressionist still life.

The maitre d' led them toward their requested table in the back. On the way, giddily, Linnea pointed out the extent to which the Eiffel theme was carried out in hand-colored old photographs, antique lithographs, and etchings of the 1889 Eiffel Tower on all the walls. Bar stools in the shape of the tower, lamp bases tower-shaped, and tiles behind the bar all were in black, gray and white. Leading upstairs, a wrought iron and wood banister bore Tower emblems; the empire-style curtains cascading from black wainscoting completed the Eiffel theme.

"It's strange," she said. "Nowhere in this place does it indicate that Gustave Eiffel designed the bridges in and around Hanoi. Is that because of politics?" Without anticipating a response, "Did you notice that the maitre d's goatee is black, gray and white? His red carnation, though, stabs the tuxedo when it should be white."

Stephen's smile seemed to stroke her face like with the palm of a hand. His handsome tanned and freckled forehead glowed a lyrical Irish heritage, and his cheeks and jaw proclaimed a strong Puritan angularity that she'd grown to love. Refractions in his brown eyes reminded her of lightning far out at sea, mysterious and yet rich with the music of a sensitive percussionist.

Linnea's filmy silk organza gown of her own design, in soft shades of peach and beige, made her feel elegant. She seldom dressed this way any more. Tonight, though, she wanted to be as sexy as a Marguerite Duras in colonial Saigon, and even to imagine that she could be a match to a Vietnamese in clinging *ao dai* captivating a jaded Graham Greene.

"I'm glad I didn't buy it," Linnea said, using an expression recently acquired.

Stephen pulled his eyes away from the menu with one of his gentle 'what's that, Kid?' looks. "You are rather ravishing tonight, Lady Linnea."

"Thank you. Stephen," she began, but something caught in her throat. "I'm glad I'm here with you. I...."

"Yes," he said, leaning forward to take her hand. "It means everything to me that you are safely here with me."

A moment later he raised an empty wineglass to alert the waiter he was ready with a selection.

Several refills of wine later over the first course of very thin fish filets sautéed with crushed fennel produced a pleasantly glib and jovial Linnea.

Then, finishing the main course, Stephen asked, "What are we going to do about your report? I don't see how you got all the way up to Laos. Yes, yes," he continued, cutting her off with a raised hand. "I know: strong winds, mechanical troubles. But some might think it a deliberate act of snooping."

"Snooping, eh. Well, isn't that what I'm really doing? Going out there supposedly to get the Hmong to grow strawberries while actually seeing to it that they aren't taken in by the North Vietnamese or Vietcong." She coughed as though Lao dust still clogged her throat. "I've reported the best information possible under the circumstances." Focusing on the linen tablecloth, she mumbled under her breath, "Everything gets turned around all the time. Communications are lousy. We...." She looked up. "Our forces don't know what we're doing."

"I shouldn't have said snooping. I'm sorry." Stephen leaned into the table. "But I interrupted. I want to hear everything again."

Linnea took in his tender smile and the soft creases around his eyes, and realized she didn't want at this time to be her old confronting self. It was still early for the Eiffel's clientele, even though after 9 p.m., and quiet, and might be a chance to share a few things. But if she began, she feared she'd describe a trail leading back to him.

"What I want to know is what you did with your photographs," Stephen said. "You do still have your film, don't you?"

"Yes. Well, no," Linnea replied. "I mean, I turned it in for developing."

"To Jerry? You gave the film to Jerry?"

"No, Stephen! He wasn't in so I gave it to Jerry's assistant."

"Tell me again exactly what you saw," he said, pushing back the cuticle on a thumb.

"A half dozen men dressed completely in black. Blackened faces, everything painted black—even their guns and knife handles."

"Go on."

"Well, the man off to the side who seemed in charge lifted rubber-like binoculars to look at a clump of trees, and then glared at us to not move. When the haul was finished, he got on board and their chopper departed like Buck Rogers. That's it! That's all!"

"What were they like?"

"Tall—your height, six feet or more."

"Some Montagnards are six feet—you've reported that yourself," he said. "Milk drinking Vietnamese are tall. The men *could* have been Vietnamese or Lao Hmong."

"I don't think so. They were obviously Americans, in an American helicopter. They would have shot us if they'd been North Vietnamese, Chinese or Russian. Or Laotian. Wouldn't they?"

"Maybe you scared them as much as they scared you. You'd made a hard landing, were shaken up. Hardly a threat! Besides, American military aren't permitted in Laos. But the North Vietnamese are there, and we've had reports about Chinese and Russians and North Koreans."

Shaking her head with slumping shoulders, "Our pilot radioed distress signals so it was known who we were. The smoke-covered ones had to be Ameri...."

Cutting her off, "And they painted themselves black?" Stephen lifted a fork to make stabs into an embossed Eiffel Tower butter square in a dish of slivered ice.

"The physiques were American."

"You may think you're an expert about mine," he snickered, "but I doubt others. The Viet Cong wear black, so do the men of Laos."

"True," Linnea said, "but they don't fly helicopters."

"Well, the North Vietnamese do, and so do the Chinese."

"They had Western features, damn it, Stephen."

"They could have been Russian."

"I'm positive they were ours."

"And I suppose you still think they were loading opium."

"Absolutely." Linnea replied, settling back. "I've seen it growing, being collected, and the residue drying and getting molded." With a stern face, "But not carted away, until Laos." She toyed with asking him about USAID helicopters— what they were like—or revealing she'd consumed opium as morphine bits when she seriously feared becoming a Montagnard dinner. Instead, miffed and frustrated, and with eyes blinking, she merely said she had been thinking of him when the helicopter was going down.

Noise erupted with a large entourage at the Eiffel entrance. Stephen twisted to the side and turned back around, leaning forward, his mouth hidden behind cupped hands. "As the saying goes, don't look now—and for heaven's sake, 'Nea, don't go into your bird-dog point and stare. It's Diem's brother Nhu, Madame Nhu and their cronies."

Her eyes swarmed over them: a Vietnamese man slight in build with a good head of black hair and pasty white skin spoke with thin, icy lips to the maitre d'. Nhu had a narrow, chiseled face with eyebrows bushy, dark and upturning at the outer edges, giving him a distinctively sinister appearance. His skin stretched unnaturally tightly across prominent cheekbones, accenting heaviness in lines about the mouth and eyes, the look of an addict.

The women in the party had hair piled high in lacquered, voluptuous arrangements inserted with pearl and diamond combs. Madame Nhu was short, barely five feet tall, wearing extremely high, shiny emerald green heels. Petite and beautiful, she gave the impression of being in charge by the way she behaved with the maitre d'.

Linnea appraised Madame Nhu, just as a journalist had described her, as the anti-goddess in a movie, Hollywood make-up studio perfect, and deadly. Her dazzling primrose yellow *ao dai* splashed with brilliant green weeping willows plunged at the bodice—a unique design to highlight full or assisted breasts. Large sparkling jewelry beamed from her shoulder, wrists and fingers, confirming husband Nhu's reputation for graft.

"Diem's primary problem is those people, who he thinks are his only friends," Stephen morosely said close to a whisper. "Because Diem didn't get hurt in that palace strafing coup attempt, he thinks he has divine protection." Stephen lifted the bottle of wine and poured, causing the waiter standing at the side to make an aborted effort to do his duty.

"Brother Nhu over there is Machiavelli incarnate," Stephen said, "totally cunning and malicious. I think he's smiling because he's up to something, like ruining us."

"Yes," she said, sitting up. "I've been trying to tell you that. I think Nhu's involvement in the opium business is undermining the Diem's regime ... and our work here." She waited a couple of moments. "Stephen, there's something else I need to talk with you about."

"Later, when we're alone." Almost immediately, Stephen signaled the waiter for the check. Barely examining the bill, he left a pile of *dong* to lead Linnea swiftly out the door.

Susan was in the hall going through her typically huge pile of mail when they arrived back at the villa. Rushing past her, Stephen took the stairs by twos, leaving Linnea behind. Watching Susan, she could visualize Susan's rough-and-tumble younger brothers printing the misshapen APO addresses on envelopes that Susan ripped open to accumulate on the floor.

"You look pretty snazzy," Susan said, her eyes peeking out the sides without a lift of her head. She wore a typically mismatching outfit, suitable neither for field nor town. Her curly hair, already with strands of kinky gray, needed a good cut, but that might upset her well-established, unique appearance.

"Thanks," Linnea answered. She had grown to appreciate Susan's lack of inhibitions and even to envy her self-confidence, derived, no doubt, from her close Northeastern family—similar, probably, to the cohesiveness of Vietnamese families she'd grown to admire.

Susan read one letter while opening another, standing with legs apart as though in need of balance, faced with so much news. Her family's duty appeared to be keeping Susan current with *Time, Newsweek, Look* and *Life,* a thick pile of movie magazines, plus Peanuts cartoons carefully cut out with penned notations of relevance.

"I suppose you're waiting around for this," Susan said, handing over a magazine with a cover of Jackie Kennedy holding John-John tugging at a string of pearls. Linnea examined it without moving off. How extraordinary to have a president's family the subject of both hard news and movie magazines simultaneously!

"I wasn't expecting it, but thanks."

"For now, okay?" Susan said with eyes glued to a wide-lined sheet of paper with large printed words.

As Linnea headed upstairs, it occurred that the Kennedy dual media attention jibed with Stephen's appraisal of the president as part show and part substance. She would grant him that tiny bit and keep the magazine out of sight.

When she entered her room, she found Stephen eyeballing the placement of objects on his desk and measuring something on the two-drawer cabinet containing his profile cards. He bent forward for a second look.

"Someone's been in here. I'm sure of it."

"Is something gone?"

"I don't know. But there's going to have to be a good lock on the door from now on." He spoke without looking at her, running his fingers through the phonograph record jackets, opening one and shaking it and then peering into the back of the refrigerator.

"What would anybody be after?"

He stopped, rose to full height and turned to her. "Perhaps the cards for my book ... or, it could be something relating to you, something you're doing."

A sudden cool draft of night air careened past the blush rising on her face without providing relief or a direction to her thoughts. She faced her feet. She wanted his reasonableness and, most of all, she wanted his honesty and whatever respect he had for her.

When she looked up, she was a little whiter. "May I have a drink and maybe some music?" she asked, edging behind the Chinese four-paneled screen to a chair. "Could you come here to talk for a little while? I believe I have some things to tell you."

CHAPTER XV

The next morning, showered and preparing to go out, Stephen came into her room to place hands on the pillow on either side of her head, leaning down to say they were on the same side, that she shouldn't worry because everything was going to be all right with regard to the Hmong. They would talk later about what she called an opium network and culprits, he said.

"My dental appointment won't take long. I'll be back in a short while," he asserted.

Linnea smiled at him, but when the door closed, she was up, mentally replaying their talk the night before. She had revealed some of the incriminating data on Nhu as a torturer in the tube and how she had obtained it, and she had summarized Bay Vien's assertions about Nhu's opium network and dalliances with the North, without describing the swamp or Bay Vien or where he'd pointed the finger.

She didn't have to suggest that the Nhu material might be the reason for the room having been entered and searched; Stephen accepted that as a possibility. Linnea wanted Stephen to recognize that the Nhu material meant America might rethink its involvement in South Vietnam. But Stephen didn't ask what she'd done with the Nhu material. Instead, as she nervously went on with one thing after another, he seemed to be more interested in her than in what she was telling him.

By late morning Linnea realized she might have stretched it to suggest that the trespassers in her room might be

American Intelligence agents, such as an antique collector and his opium-smoking colleagues, mavericks up to no good. She had even implied that the Intelligence outfit in the villa next to their USAID villa, always watching even with binoculars their every move, could have been the trespasser.

By half past noon, without Stephen's return, Linnea realized Stephen hadn't revealed much of anything about his work, what he was in charge of, such as helicopters.

At 1:30 p.m., when Stephen finally returned, Linnea snarled, "How was your appointment with the dentist?

"What?" Stephen replied, obviously distracted as he placed his heavy valise on the floor.

"Your teeth," she shouted from where she'd been reading, her magazine smacking the floor.

"Yes, yes. Teeth! Thank you. Yes, my teeth are just fine. In fact, I was told to do a lot more lashing with the tongue," he said taking exaggeratedly long strides over to her. "Maybe the dentist said to have more tongue in the lashing."

"Nice try, but you're not going to succeed by never asking me the right questions about important issues, never answering my questions, and then trying to escape into fun and games!"

"Whew! Do you think tangling with you is a cake walk?"

It sounded funny and she wanted to laugh, but it hurt. The thought re-emerged that he'd had liaisons, possibly recently with Susan or currently with someone else in Saigon.... "Stephen, I think you're seeing someone."

"Yes, I am. The dentist."

"That's a lie," she seethed. "You have no complaints, before or after."

Stephen calmly said, "I do go to a dentist's office."

"Well, why? Who's ... what's...?" she sputtered, shaking her head. "Stephen..."

Stephen pulled up the chair opposite hers, knee to knee, taking her hands for his thumbs to massage the back of them. "Linnea, don't let your mind go screaming down the wrong path. I visit the dentist, and the dentist is a he. Certain discussions need to take place away from an American facility and the scrutiny of others, that's all. A dentist's office is where talks can take place painlessly."

"You could have told me that! And, what's so important that it needs to be done in secret?" With a frown she waited. "Oh, I see," she finally snapped. "I'll bet you're going to say you don't have to answer, that it's none of my business, and that that's for my own good."

"There's nothing for you to be concerned about. But you need to know that I have a lot of worries, especially about you." He looked almost sad. "I've had reports of sightings, as though you're some exotic bird that needs to be tracked and recorded. Personally, I think you need to be steadily coaxed, coddled, and, when necessary, overwhelmed."

"Whose reports? The thugs who follow me? When you talked me into coming here maybe you didn't know me well enough. I can sense and see things that maybe you and others cannot. With sights focused far ahead," she looked at the ceiling, "at the big job of fighting communism, you think you can *contain* a situation in South Vietnam by molding the country into a little America. You hate the French, and all they wanted were the rubber and rice. Well, maybe America's reason for not wanting the communists to have Vietnam is its gold, its tin or its oil, if it has any, while we meanwhile extract Vietnam's soul."

"Whew! Linnea, what on earth is bothering you? You've done extremely well—far better than you possibly know, and I'm proud; so should you be. But you seem to be all over the place—like the visit to someone's villa and those poetry gatherings with questionable people. You're my responsibility and I'm worried about you."

"Your responsibility?" She pulled herself up to a standing position and fought a gnawing urge to say she was certain he was responsible for helicopters transporting opium from the hills. "Have you had me followed? Have I been leading you and your damned dentist office colleagues to the fine Saigon intelligentsia, so that Nhu's secret police can pick them up, imprison and torture them? You know what? I think you, your friends and others may sell out the very people we're here to help ... and trip up us all at the same time!"

Stephen was slow to respond. "Maybe I've been remiss and have led you on." In a slow, measured voice, "You and I have a lot more to talk over." He rose to go over to his desk, finally specifying the address of the dental office where she should meet him in the afternoon.

*   *   *

"Led you on!" He actually said that! Over and over Linnea threw the words at rain lunging at her in horizontal swipes. Searching for a signpost in the wet morass, she stepped into a large puddle to complete the sensation of all over wet-cat fury.

She found the grill-and screen-covered door for the poetry recitation and plunged in. Close, hot dampness steamed with vengeance enough to make her gag. Dropping her poncho, she edged to the back with an eye out for Tam and maybe even the recovering Jim. But she wasn't disappointed not to see either one of them. She wanted to learn more and needed to be alone with the soothing cadence of poetry. Recalling how the opium-addicted furniture dealer described a reason for dens, she said to herself that she needed to be with like-minded people.

Linnea tuned her ears to appreciate words and phrases in a language deep in beauty and meaning. The long, gentle beginnings of poetic recitations became soporific until, at the end, the atmosphere changed in the electric exchange of two esteemed poets.

"The situation is getting worse. It's not the fault of President Diem. The trouble is the United States."

"Don't be dumb. Before it was the French, and now you say it's the Americans. Children see things differently. They want change. That's the way it always is."

"Change? That's all America thinks about. They tear down to build up. Our ways have carried us well for countless generations.

If there's no honor or respect for us and our ancestors, everything will be lost."

"Nothing will be lost."

"The Americans have done this. They've ruined us. America has assumed that the raison d'etre of our government is to promote American interests."

"No they haven't. We've needed them. Diem needs them."

"They're destroying us. We'll lose our past and our future at the same time."

The words jarred. She had to get out of there. After waiting for someone else to exit so she wouldn't be the first to leave, she stood, ready to slip out, and then heard:

"USAID means United States Assistance in Interrogation Detention. Torture happens in USAID built structures: arms broken like matchsticks; fingernails pulled out by pliers; men and women hung by their thumbs; eyes scooped out with ladles. Now is as bad as with the French."

Linnea burst onto the street. The rain had let up, but the poets' words drummed. She had to figure out how to get their sentiments across to Stephen, and, without seeming alarmist, also to Clarissa and her Dad. Leaving the curving street going onto a primary road, she maintained a steady pace on rain-slick paths when she heard steps running up behind and a car door opening. She swiveled in time to see a pair of men in dark glasses and leather jackets near a Citroen with red paint slashes on its tires just as a second pair similarly attired leaped out, blatantly focused on her and ready to follow. She walked faster. Unfamiliar with the neighborhood, she started running, frantically looking down one alley and then another. None seemed to offer an escape or even the refuge of a dark den. Dripping with sweat, she rushed down a narrow lane too slender for a car but just right for being a well used play yard, and headed for the shop at the far end. Hearing screaming behind her, she ran with all her might, slipping through the shop and out the other side.

With vision blurred by sweat stinging her eyes, she finally found the street that Stephen said the dental office was on or near and where he said she should meet him.

"Are you okay?" he asked when he caught up with her moping along with her head down.

"Sure."

"I was longer than anticipated." A minute or two later, sounds of a man splashing fast through puddles behind them caused her to grab Stephen's arm.

"Linnea, this is a colleague," he said without giving a name to the confident-appearing American with amber eyes and a bullet shaped head covered with quarter inch gray bristles.

The American insisted they avoid the incipient downpour by coming to his office a short distance away. He led them to an older but still luxurious former colonial mansion set back deep in a large courtyard behind tall, heavy-leafed, thick-trunked trees. Expecting a richly furnished book-lined teakwood library office, Linnea was surprised and disappointed to be headed to a door opening onto a dark passageway going below.

Rushing to turn on lights, their host explained with false laughter the circumstances for his basement study. "Time is all important," he said as he poured water into a small metal drip *espresso* pot. "My little abode reminds guests to be quick with what they have to offer."

Linnea looked around and didn't at first comprehend the meaning of the man's words, *explained consequences in advance*. Her eyes gravitated to rusty links of chain attached to large round metal rings imbedded in concrete walls. Deep red rectangular oriental rugs dotted the floor and between them dark brown stains filled cracks in worn, shiny stones.

"Of course you and your USAID are being very helpful constructing facilities in hamlets where ARVN can interdict. The supervision of Viet Cong interrogations is going pretty well, don't you think, Stephen?" His jaw appeared to click in time with his fingers snapping ivory mahjong pieces together on his desk. "Stated consequences make a difference, don't they, when within sight of consequences?" He nodded at the place Linnea's eyes were glued.

Linnea glowered at Stephen whose face was turning red. He reached for her arm to indicate they were leaving. Touching her, she flinched.

She didn't relax until they were up the stairs and out and a good distance away.

"'Nea, I'm sorry. I had no idea that man is sick enough to live in the site of French atrocities. I've," he audibly swallowed "always maintained French colonialism is a lesson in how not to behave."

If Stephen could now realize that the U.S. is following in France's footsteps in more ways than one, maybe he'll listen, she decided. "Stephen," she hoarsely whispered. "I've heard that the information collection places are called...."

"USAID is only responsible for construction, not what happens inside."

"Like Speer?" It rolled out before she could hold it back.

Stephen stopped. "Oh, my God, no," he said, shaking his head with his face darkening. "No. No. No. Mavericks and craziness exist everywhere, at any time. No one can oversee or control everything. But only a very, very few Americans, I pray, are ever as bad as the French. I only see that things get done."

Now! Linnea's mind pleaded. Now is the time to confront him about helicopters and U.S. opium involvement, somehow under his aegis. But Stephen is down. His tight hold on her arm seems to beg for support. Also, the large puddles left by the slackening rain need to be attended to—to maneuver around. And Stephen's right leg is dragging.

"There's more here than I bargained for—for you or for me." He slowed. "It hurts to the core to know what people do to each other. Like links in an endless chain, somebody does a horrible thing to someone and then that person does it worse to someone else. You've got to remember and believe that you and I have the same values and that we basically view things the same way."

"You wanted me to keep my eyes and ears open," she said, working on how to begin.

"Do you know what we're passing right now?" Stephen asked a while later.

"Of course. The Botanical Gardens. You brought me here once. I'll never forget where we've gone together."

To her somber face, he said, "Believe me, I didn't know it before, and I don't want to know it now. But a jail is under the Gardens over there. From what I've heard, it's where Nhu's torture machinery has reached a high, horrible artistry."

Linnea's mind screamed: Nhu! Nhu! You've got to listen to me, Stephen, to see him more than as the simple troublemaker of a brother. She couldn't tell whether the screams were in her imagination or from the Gardens.

Low-hanging pewter-colored murk closed in upon them. Stephen slipped off his jacket and cupped it over her head.

Rushing along, peeking up at him, she said, "I've been out on Hai Ba Trung Street to the French Foreign Legion Cemetery. One of the grave markers is well tended, and not overgrown like the rest. It has little white stones and fresh flowers. In spite of how some Frenchmen behaved, whatever they did, someone here still loves and remembers." She didn't know why she said that. She felt vulnerable and put her arm around his waist, pressing her cheek to his side.

CHAPTER XVI

Monsoon rains swirled through the streets in the first days of October until abruptly stopping, with attention refocused onto President Diem—what he was doing or not doing in his Saigon administration.

Then, overnight, the focus whirled back across the Pacific to the Southeastern corner of the United States.

Linnea, Stephen and most of the USAID staffers read news bulletins to each other in voices of disbelief:

"Russian nuclear missiles are in Cuba, aimed at Washington, New York, and defense locations up and down the eastern seaboard."

"A showdown! Soviet Chairman Nikita Khrushchev and the Russians are challenging the United States by audaciously sending nuclear missiles to Cuba, 70 miles off the American shore."

With incredulity, they shared snippets of reports:

"Bomb shelters proliferate in backyards."

"Water and food stockpiled; shortages expected."

"Families make compacts with neighbors—pool water in exchange for dried provisions." "Disclosed: Air raid shelters in every major city are inadequate or unprepared."

"Multiple market baskets by single customers with odd selections—14 large boxes of detergent—expose national malaise."

"Tensions are at a crisis level!"

"Fights break out across the land. Paranoia and secretiveness abound."

"Two doctors in the basement storage area of a Seattle hospital staff complex got into a fist fight over bottles of distilled water that one or both had pilfered."

"Bizarre police statistics: A Florida judge stopped for speeding, heading inland, remembered his wife and kids had been left behind."

Whenever they could, colleagues gathered in the USAID villa dining room to discuss whatever news anyone had gleaned. One day Susan entered, listened a brief while, and ran out, saying she had to phone home. Philco didn't say much before lumbering upstairs to his radios. Martin's monosyllabic mutterings provided nothing except an opportunity for ridicule.

Linnea's thoughts gravitated to what she'd be doing if she were in Manhattan. She had barely known her neighbors in the brownstone, had little room for more than a few days' supply of food, no bottled water, and only a spider and rodent infested basement as a potential shelter.

Looking around at her companions, she wondered if everyone else had also accumulated fears of nuclear annihilation from grade school years. Her school across from Caltech was a known Russian target, and duck and cover—curling under a desk with arms overhead—were regular morning exercises. After school, after seeing Albert Einstein with his head down walking toward Lake Avenue, nuclear fear became a part of her life.

Upstairs in her room, Linnea exclaimed to Stephen, "My God! It could be like *On the Beach*," she said, referring to the movie about the aftermath of a nuclear war with men in a submarine surfacing after hearing tapping on a Teletype machine and hoping to find a survivor of the contaminated wind curling the globe. The tapping by a Coca Cola bottle caught in the cord of a blown-out window shade, bobbing up in a breeze, spelled the end of the world.

When she didn't hear anything from Stephen at his desk, she read aloud that Senator Fulbright stated the President's naval blockade of Cuba is the worst action, and that it's better to invade Cuba than provoke the Russians and light a tinderbox. House Armed Services Committee Chairman Carl Vinson, she reported from her sitting area, declares the U.S. should strike Cuba and the Russians with all we've got and get it over with. She looked up, wanting Stephen's reaction. Without being able to tell anything, she resumed: "Here it states that the largest American invasion force since World War II is assembling in Florida. Right this minute!" She fingered sheets backward until she found something else. "Air Force General Curtis LeMay says the blockade and Kennedy's political actions with the UN and the OAS are leading right into war."

Stephen rose and came over to her. "Demonstrations and appeals for peace are taking place in every American city, including right in front of the White House, and that may be for the good," was all he said.

"Why? What good?" Linnea looked up.

"Kennedy's ear is always to the pulse of the people."

"And that's going to stop Khrushchev? The Mutual Massive Retaliation Agreement between the U.S. and the U.S.S.R. that you wrote about can mean the end of civilization!"

"It can also mean a standoff," he said. "Anyway, we're safe here." With a throat in need of clearing, he said, "But, if anything happens, if there's fallout, it'll take a while for a cloud to reach Vietnam, and it could be dissipated by then."

That evening, Linnea succeeded in getting Stephen to sit down with her in the little reading area in her room. Drinking more than she should, Linnea began by sharing memories of happy days sailing, skin diving at the jetty and body surfing down at Corona. She described the movie stars whose yachts were moored in front of her beach house and whose voices carried over the water in early morning hours, introducing her to four letter words. Continuing with California experiences, some of which Stephen already knew, she found herself thinking of her brother and equating his alcohol with Jim's opium and the harm done to both.

They finished the evening dancing to the slow tempo of a Nelson Riddle arrangement.

In the days that followed, Linnea moved about with morose awareness of how different she was with no one back home to worry about or to worry about her. That realization brought Stephen into clearer focus—that he might have been more important to her than she realized. She had saved every note he had sent her in New York, written on any scrap of paper, and had brought them with her.

One day, when Stephen wasn't around to observe her, she placed his missives into a tight tin box for burial in the mushy soil by the old overgrown fountain and clay elephants in the back garden. She included his much-heralded 1961 article that caused the Council to urge upon Stephen experience in Vietnam, before taking up editorship of the Council's journal.

"Fidel Castro, the opportunist, is turning tropical Cuba coldly communistic, inviting in the Russians with their military. The Russian Yuri 'I am an Eagle' Gagarin, is circling the globe overhead, right over Manhattan, proclaiming Soviet technologic superiority. And Russian and Chinese communism, spreading over the recovering weak in Europe and the freshly colonial free in Asia threatens the U.S., which practically alone is trying to stop them. A war could erupt at any moment! It would probably be nuclear, and it could be the end."

As the crisis days of October ground on, Linnea became aware that Stephen changed his tune about Kennedy. "Khrushchev may consider JFK young, naive, and only surface deep," she heard him say, "but the bully will be making a stupid, tragic mistake. Kennedy will have to show he has the strength and cleverness to back the Khrushchev tick out of the skin, without Khrushchev feeling humiliated or getting angry and escalating the situation."

A week later, in the afternoon in the USAID office downtown, Stephen asked her, "Are you sure you're okay? Where are you going now?"

"Just down to the AP office," Linnea replied, almost out the door.

"Why?" He caught up to grab her arm. "And be the first on your block to know the searing flashpoint with a radioactive mushroom cloud is on its way?"

Linnea gulped. "Maybe."

Stephen grasped her shoulders. "Khrushchev is no fool."

Shaking her head, "Shouldn't we have a plan?"

"I guess so. First, we'll have to scratch the Majestic rendezvous idea. Instead, we need to commandeer a vehicle to head for the hills. 'Nea, I told you you're invaluable. Since you're in tight with tribes with elephants who can carry us to a secluded cave, we'll have a head start. As the world becomes stone-age again, we'll already be in with the stone-age...."

"Damn you, Stephen. This isn't funny. Air and water will be contaminated; there'll be nothing to eat or drink...."

"Then we'd better go to the Majestic after all."

Linnea trekked to the cluttered and banged-up Associated Press office and then to the storefront shared by the UPI and *The New York Times*. Amidst constant clacking of wires and the ringing bells of bulletins, she observed work continuing apace and grew envious of journalism's focused demands. Exiting back into busy streets with Saigonese oblivious of possible oblivion, she felt both glad and guilty to be so far away from New York.

But she thought of New York and special memories. She recalled being on Central Park's most photographed granite boulder where she and Stephen had spread out with chins on knuckles and discussed things, including nuclear build-ups and fears of a missile gap—that America was technologically far behind the U.S.S.R. Later, it was on a park bench that Stephen told her he had to go to Vietnam. Stunned, she had felt dismissed, abandoned, and very sad.

Then, after talking with Clarissa and her father, she accepted Stephen's USAID invitation and, it now seemed, from the moment of her arrival, she had been goading him— about Diem and Nhu and opium and for him to recognize

Vietnam's unique culture. Now, in October, nothing seemed to matter very much any more, so she let up. Stephen was also in a delicate zone. Every afternoon at 5, coming into her room, he poured them both a drink and, to her surprise, sat down to take her hands and hear what she had to say.

Finally, after almost two weeks of horribly tense days, Stephen quipped, "Well, that was a damned stupid little probe!" He reported that the Russians were backing off, their ships turning around from heading towards Cuba, and said a nuclear holocaust now was less likely.

Linnea hugged him like he had achieved it all by himself.

In the aftermath of the October crisis, Stephen grew more outspoken, saying that the missile crisis proved that the west must hold back Russian machinery and global ambitions. We've got to block their red tide from advancing, he said, for if we don't check them here and now they will unleash their aggression and take over. Then, as often as not, Stephen would say to her, to USAID villa-mates, and even to unknowns at Brodard's, the Caravelle, Givrals, and elsewhere: "We must stand firm; our mandate is clear."

Linnea lapsed back into what she'd been doing before: collecting data, as much as humanly possible, on how much opium was being grown in the hills. In Saigon, she used all her wiles to learn the means and volume of opium coming to Saigon, going so far as to browbeat medical officers and helicopter pilots.

One day, when Stephen was at his desk in her room and she was reading in her chair, Stephen suddenly turned and said that she had changed and was different somehow. Linnea felt her blush might be visible through the coromandel screen.

Coming over to her, "You must have heard the thump-thump, whack-whack helicopter noise rolling in waves over the villa indicating something big is happening, and you didn't react or ask if it was a coup," he said about the big exercise in Tayninh Province to the north, near the Cambodian border called Operation Morning Star.

"Morning Star?" she said in a sudden relieved voice, feeling frisky. "That's the name of a huge schooner in Balboa!"

"That was a crazy response, 'Nea. What's wrong?"

"I have a lot on my mind," she said. "It seems like things are building up … have built up, making my USAID agrarian efforts totally inconsequential."

Sitting down opposite her, Stephen said without much steam, "Progress takes time. South Vietnam needs whatever we can do to help the people and thwart opposing forces."

"Yes. But using the tribes as look-outs and transporting their opium?" she asked.

*   *   *

Eight days later, in the dining room, Linnea and Stephen were present when USAID colleagues discussed 'Morning Star.' Five thousand South Vietnamese troops with American advisors were ferried in U.S. helicopters to a place known as a guerrilla collection point near the Vietnam-Cambodian border, it was reported.

"'Morning Star' was a complete wipeout, a total failure. Our side," Kevin said.

"Fifty-six aircraft went to where the Viet Cong were supposed to be, and 17 water buffalo were killed. And now water buffalo are an enemy statistic!" He made it sound funny. "The lack of ARVN motivation in fighting for their country is a sure sign for us to depart."

"Stop that!" Stephen said, getting up to go upstairs.

Stephen was at his desk, working on his "Cast of Characters" cards when Linnea arrived. Although dying to know who was in the cards, and knowing better than to ask, she suggested, "The *Mat Vu* should be in your cards. They're bumbling and potentially brutal."

Stephen turned.

"The *Mat Vu* followed me yesterday," she continued. "I was in a hurry to get to a store before the owner closed for the long lunch. Behind me, I heard screams and yells and the ringing of bicycle bells. The *Mat Vu* tailing me ran smack into a man whose cart was loaded with oranges and grapefruit. They tried to kick the man as the cart turned over and flattened the *Mat Vu*," she said with a weak chuckle.

Stephen smiled and shook his head.

Swiftly she asked, "Are the *Mat Vu* really Nhu's? Or could they be ours?" Or Stephen's? Or an Intelligence outfit dealing in opium? She had questions enough to feel about to burst.

"'Nea, your adventurous spirit may have led you astray. It's not just that the *Mat Vu* are suspicious of Americans with Vietnamese friends, but American outfits are also wary of American-Vietnamese relationships. I've told you that!"

Linnea felt her face redden. "Well, dammit, that's why we're here, isn't it? We should have empathy and humility and behave as a friend to Vietnamese, appreciating them and their culture. I'm setting a good example—and I'm learning a lot." But she didn't feel she was getting anywhere.

At the end of October, following what were now coined as the Cuban Missile Crisis and Operation Morning Star, Linnea and Stephen agreed to go to Brodard's, each for a separate reason. Putting her next to Hugh, Stephen took off to talk with someone at the bar. Hugh continued giving a tip to a stringer standing at his side, making Linnea feel forsaken. Frustrated, she let her eyes rest on a man whose long legs, large frame, and many plates of food seemed too much for his tiny table.

Finishing his chat, Hugh observed where she was gazing. "His name is David Halberstam. He's bright and a good talker, and just in from the Congo. Before that he was in Dixie writing about police chiefs with German shepherds, fire hoses and pitchforks. Harvard, you know," Hugh said, stretching the "A's," and reporting that Sheehan and Halberstam were on the Charles River together, working on the school paper. "I'll introduce you, but first, obviously, the poor man must eat."

"No food in the Congo?" Linnea asked. Halberstam simultaneously talked to a colleague and swallowed in a steady rhythm. His close-cropped, thick dark hair made him ruggedly handsome. His glasses, however, were a round plastic drugstore variety, taking on the light blue of his plaid shirt. His long-arm gestures coincided with sharp-eyed sweeps of the room.

"Six foot three, 185 or 190 pounds. His mama probably told him to feed Feed FEED those brain cells," Hugh chortled.

"It's interesting," Linnea responded. "Two Harvard journalists here in the boondocks at the same time. I had the impression in New York that correspondents worked their way up from paper boy or, only recently, from a journalism school in Iowa."

"Two Harvard—or three, if you count Stephen—and only one Stanford. You're outnumbered, my dear. Think you can handle it?" Lowering his voice, "And does your research indicate you are?"

Although almost desperate to pass on to him the latest opium acreage figures, Linnea said, "It's good the Establishment is well represented," and with a change in tone, "in such a damned confusing, dangerous, and difficult...."

"My dear! Whatever could be confusing about this utter mess? Is it that we're all constantly harassed by the *Mat Vu* and by our own people so that we can't do decent work? Or is it that the South Vietnamese military, fully armed and who should be motivated, won't fight or even hang onto the weapons we keep giving them? Or could it be that with our enormous American might, we don't know how to fight, or whether to stay in the game or go home?"

"That's part of it."

"Lord! Part of which part?" he sighed. "Oh, don't tell me," he said. He signaled to the bartender and let his body sink back into the rattan as though with the completion of a strenuous task. "It's best to drink and not think."

Linnea observed Stephen talking elbow-to-elbow at the bar, forgetting about her and never even glancing back to see if she had a drink. Turning to Hugh who had ordered her one, "Since you've brought it up, why, when you have such perspective and know so much, do you seek to drink and drown it?" She caught herself. "We need you."

Hugh's blue eyes blinked fast as though momentarily stunned. "Saigon is a great place to lose the past. For some in this room, Vietnam will make their futures and become their pasts at the same time. Others will lose out altogether."

"Yes, but what about you? Don't you want more than to be considered a curmudgeon? You provide so much valuable background. I've seen you point green correspondents in the right directions, saving them countless hours and frustrations. Saigon couldn't your past?"

Hugh didn't answer.

Worried of having offended, Linnea slid her hand over Hugh's.

"I drink because I'm a big bright boy and bored."

"With us? This place?"

"Not by Saigon, or even this little exercise, this damned stupid conflict. Just life."

"But you're loved! You have a daughter somewhere, from what I've gathered. You're respected and don't have to scramble like the rest."

"Lots of things sound or look good on paper. Therefore, young lady, what I do is my prerogative. Chalk it up," he said, lifting his fresh glass, "to challenging the edge." After a good swallow he leaned over to her, "Now, what can you tell me?"

Linnea made certain Stephen was still occupied and began with a matter of courtesy. "My Vietnamese friend Tam, for whose friend Jim you kindly provided the stuff for his bad opium session, is from a well-educated, formerly high ranking mandarin family from the north. They're nice people and...."

"I'll bet they're none too happy with your friend Tam being friendly with a foreign devil," Hugh said in the way he used to speed up someone to get to the point.

Linnea nodded. "From lunch with Tam and her family and poetry readings I've learned how Vietnamese feel about President Diem. Tam's family is Catholic. They and other Catholics try to express themselves to the Diem administration and they're shunted aside and harassed, and called communists or communist sympathizers. Which they're not."

"How do you know?" Hugh snapped.

"I don't. But they're Catholic, and Diem promotes and puts into high places those who are Catholic, but because my friend Tam's family came from the north they can't get jobs. Some of them were nationalists of the old school, probably sympathetic to anti-French groups, like the Vietminh. They're frozen out, but, if someone worked for the French, even in a low capacity, he can get a good position from Diem." Taking a deep breath, "If they worked for the enemy they're employable, whereas...."

"Whose enemy—always a good question. Yes. You've summed up what we've known."

"I've taken too long with this; I'm sorry. I have some statistics written out I'd like to have you see—somewhere else. I have more information on Diem's sibling's dealings with the North. Sometimes I think I'd like to meet President Diem."

"Not a bad idea. I'm not now a fan of Diem but sometimes I think he's getting a bad rap ... due to that sibling. He feels we're belittling his country and he's aware we have intelligence outfits talking with and listening to his foes. Anyway, I'll work on a meeting. Meanwhile, you're dying to tell me something else, aren't you?"

Linnea smiled. "The incriminating evidence I have should be enough to incarcerate Nhu. I've also collected information on people associated with him. It is going to the right place. There's something else. The Binh Xuyen leader told me to focus on transportation and I've discovered we...." She glanced up, repeating "that we...."

Stephen, fast in their direction, caused her to pull away from Hugh and, in a voice loud enough for him to hear, said, "It came over the wires that Senate Majority Leader Mike Mansfield says two billion dollars have been pumped into South Vietnam in the last seven years and it's a total waste with nothing accomplished."

"And just what was that supposed to mean?" Stephen said as he dropped into a chair. "I think you two have been up to something," he said, sounding pleased with himself and leaning into Linnea with Scotch on his breath.

"It's about a coup, Stephen my man," Hugh casually replied, leaning back, eyeing him.

"Is that so? Well, whose and when? Important little details, you know, Hugh, old man."

"Maybe soon, and the *coup du jour* may not come from the ARVN military, as perhaps expected," Hugh said.

"Anyway, it's not Diem who should be deposed," Stephen said.

"Well!" Linnea remarked. "You're moving right along! Nhu's activities certainly justify him for disqualification from the Diem government, don't you think?"

"To talk with Diem about Nhu wouldn't do any good," Hugh cautioned. "He doesn't trust us as he did when Lansdale was here, and Diem probably regrets what he's let happen— American gung-ho, let's-do-it involvement, overwhelming his country."

"Could Lansdale come back and help with Diem about his brother?" Linnea asked. "Incidentally, is Lansdale military or CIA?"

"Both," Stephen murmured as though to dispatch the subject.

"And that's not so very unusual, now is it, Stephen?" Hugh said.

"History shows that disaster follows a leader overthrown," came Stephen's swift reply, as though following up on a conversation at the bar.

"Well, then," Linnea said. "I guess I again want to know who is making the decisions? Who is the top authority—Diem and the South Vietnam government, or our military, or our ambassador, or our CIA? Who's in charge? I need to know!"

Stephen stared at her as though shouting: Not here, not now, and why in the world?

After hooking eyes for several moments, with Linnea thinking about the Strategic Hamlets that needed army protection from within at night, she submitted, "The Vietnamese feel that instead of being defended they're being assaulted. By us," she looked at Stephen, "and also by Madame Nhu whose edict—the Family Doctrine—regulates sexual relations ... contradicting Buddhist beliefs!"

"Mine, too," Stephen agreed with a squeeze to Linnea's thigh.

A newly arrived journalist came to their table with a pair of stringers, and, sounding like throwing out bait, said, "We shouldn't be in Vietnam."

Halberstam, coming up at the same time, surveyed the journalist and stringers with small, dark, quick-moving eyes, and nodded at her. After cursory chatter, in a deep, distinctive voice he said, "It's right we're here in Vietnam. If South Vietnam falls, the pressure on the other shaky nations will be intolerable." With the lens of his glasses blinking, he quipped, "But if you want to debate methods and foolishnesses, self-delusions and a host of other things, please be my guest."

It impressed Linnea that Halberstam developed such a perspective in the short time since his arrival.

"Have you heard General Harkins' pronouncement?" said a small man named Paine with a foghorn voice and a bureaucratic demeanor. "'Orientals respect power, and bombing makes the peasants afraid.' How's that for stupidity? Our bombs will frighten farmers so they'll burrow underground and join up with the VC."

"A general told me," Halberstam said, "Vietnam is a great war game."

"A well-positioned anonymous source," said correspondent Paul coming up, "told me that an atomic bomb would do the trick and clear a 900-mile swath of vegetation at the 17th Parallel to contaminate the area into a hot zone the VC couldn't pass through."

"Yeah, and the VC will just go around the contamination and get onto Ho's trail in Laos and Cambodia and come right on down, speeding into Saigon," a stringer said.

"That bomb-the-hell-out-of-'em is nuts," uttered a young crewcut anxious American, pulling up a chair. "It's the constipated thinking of conventional warfare freaks. This isn't that kind of a war."

"It's not just Vietnamese who are dying," Paul yelled through the subsequent din. "One hundred nine Americans have already been killed here."

"This place is a putrid mixture of ambitious young officers who are frustrated like John Paul Vann, and dueling military services and government agencies and paranoid intelligence outfits," the handsome Neil Sheehan summarized.

"See here, there are 20,000 guerrillas," Paul said with a sarcastic Southern twang. 'Okay, 20,000 are killed. Next day, 20,000 more guerrillas! I tell you, it's puff the magic dragon land."

"No wonder opium thrives," Hugh agreed, turning as though with a crick in his neck, "and not just as a holiday treat."

CHAPTER XVII

The USAID villa's juvenile palm tree in a pot by the front steps looked like it wept from being so heavily draped in red and white Christmas bulbs and a mass of tinsel sent by Susan's family. It struck more than one that the tree reflected the anachronism of the American presence in Southeast Asia—more and more massive material swamping a fragile landscape with a taproot weak and incomprehensible.

Christmas morning began with Stephen anointing Linnea his "giggling lover" (she accepted the giggling part but didn't know if she had skill to fit the latter). They exchanged agreed upon gifts of prose. Hers were Manhattan memories and Saigon vignettes on a hand-painted rice paper Vietnamese country scene card. Reciting his, he was cryptic and funny whereas Linnea's verses were serious but sincere.

Melodic refrains from below made them hurry to head downstairs, passing Philco coming from his room in a huge red Mickey Mouse t-shirt. His natural adipose encouraged a gentle punch he graciously received. The twinkle in Philco's eyes suggested he would play Santa some day to offspring similarly jovial and rotund.

Philco's "Ho Ho Ho" was followed by a refrain with collegial augmentations "Ho Ho Ho, Go Go Go, Go Ho, Go Ho, Go Chi Minh, Yeah!" The servants, who had seen Philco perform Santa Claus before, remained in doorways smiling. Heaving his sack from behind, Philco dropped it onto the dining room table with a clunk. As though there could be something alive in the pillowcase, he peered inside and jiggled before yanking out a seductively curved silver metal item not immediately identifiable, bearing a large red tag attached by red electrical wire.

"Ah, ha. This is for Martin. Santa writes, 'Wind direction is important to check when standing at a sloop's stern to relieve oneself.' This handy little pee pot will solve the problem."

To complaints of "Yes, Martin," Martin jumped up to grab the urinal.

"What's this?" Philco said, edging a tiny parcel out from his bag. "Ah, yes. What any energetic young thing shouldn't be without! Trojans! For you, Susan dear, and your rushing, thrusting, forgetful friends."

With anger spiking her unruly hair, Susan snatched the packet, her face a shade darker.

Linnea hoped for a quick take on whatever Philco might have for her. She nibbled on fruit, very much enjoying villa mates who seemed like family with personal foibles accepted.

"Billy, this cigarette pack is for you," Philco continued, holding it up for all to see it didn't contain cigarettes. "The joints are rolled in Old Glory." He pulled a couple out and passed them to the left and right around the table.

"Isn't there a ruling about desecrating the American flag?" Kevin asked.

"Doesn't count here," Martin answered. "We're already wrapped in...." He spelled out his favorite four-letter word. "Anyone know the law?"

Eyes went to Stephen who shrugged he didn't know or care.

"This is for you, California," Philco said to Linnea. "It's good to have you on board."

Linnea dashed around the table to accept the rice paper wrapped book-sized package. She carefully unwrapped it to find a hand-made cookbook with a dedication by Duong and pencil drawings of yellow and orange vegetables, green and gray herbs and the instructions and ingredients of dishes.

Linnea kissed Philco on the cheek, and ran into the kitchen to thank Duong already working on their Christmas dinner.

Philco's Santa Claus presentation had ended when she returned and he was heartily eating. Servants brought more pitchers of fresh orange juice with chilled magnums of *Moet et Chandon,* and poured them into fast-melting frosted glasses.

"What did he give you?" Linnea asked.

"Here," he showed her. "One is by Herb Albert and the other Odetta, for both of us. Very thoughtful."

"He is. We should do something for him," Linnea said, thinking it was again time for a multi-course Chinese dinner in Cholon.

Chatter subsided to be replaced by the sounds of eating and drinking, as though thoughts had drifted far away across the Pacific.

Without a family to miss and few good Christmases to recall, Linnea was hesitant to break in. "You know, we're lucky. We can have three celebrations: today, New Year's and then TET."

"TET? Susan wrinkled her nose. "Why should we celebrate TET?"

"Because TET honors birthdays—everyone's, all together—not individually. Since we don't know each other's birthday, maybe we should celebrate all of ours together."

"I can just see telling my family, no birthday cards from me, folks! I celebrated yours at TET," Susan said to quick laughter.

Kevin, as though missing something, said, "For TET, let's drape the front fence and gate with strings of fireworks and set them to go off when all the rest do all over the city. Pow!"

"How about my getting a bazooka?"

"We can make, or rather get Duong to help us make, *bank chung,* the sticky rice cakes filled with bean paste and pork," Kevin said, "and then make a presentation of it at one of the temples, right along with the Vietnamese. And be blessed."

"Aw!"

"Cozying up Kevin!" someone commented.

"Perhaps we could offer the *bank chung* here," Linnea suggested, "at the hearth for the Ong Tao spirit to report on high that we've been good little soldiers." She glanced around.

"That's a good idea. Let's go Vietnamese—no work for at least four days," Susan said. "We'll stock up at the PX because there's not supposed to be any shopping during TET, right?"

She looked at Linnea.

"But drinking's all right," Martin declared.

"What's the exact date for TET this year?" Jamie asked.

"The new moon will be around January 23rd. I'll check," Martin said, pulling a card from his wallet.

"I remember the racket last year. Fireworks all over the place and rockets filling the sky! And suddenly afterwards the streets were empty and eerie."

"Maybe a few VC will change their mind," Stephen said, "when they hop back into the home nest."

"Don't count on it!" someone said.

"TET will be on the 23rd," Martin announced. "The new year nineteen sixty-three will be the year of the hare, the hero in local folklore. The year just ending, of course, was the year of the cat or tiger. Hmmm. So the hare is after or follows the tiger. That's a switch or is it?" He glanced at Stephen whose eyes were on Linnea.

"Last year there was cockfighting on the first day of TET and chess matches with people as live chess pieces on court squares," Linnea said in a lilting voice. "We could dress up as knights, bishops, pawns!"

"Yeah. The streets will be empty anyway."

Soon Jamie and politically astute Kevin set up the house chessboard. Others stuck around, sharing stories and avoiding the usual negative chatter about the military build-up.

"This is much better than fighting over which ball game to watch or how something should be prepared in the kitchen after an endless mass," Susan said.

*   *   *

In the afternoon, by prior agreement, Linnea and Susan went to Christmas services at the Cathedral de Notre Dame, the huge orange brown Moorish-looking structure facing the Presidential Palace.

Linnea, an Episcopalian, dabbed the water, crossed herself like everyone else, and genuflected entering the pew. After wiggling onto a pillow on the cool stone floor for a long session of kneeling, she looked around. Overhead, large bronze chandeliers twinkled with many lighted candles. Stained glass windows of red, blue, yellow and green permitted prisms of gentle light. The figures had Caucasian features unlike the thoughtful faces of the Vietnamese who were repeating Latin prayers they didn't necessarily understand. When the service droned on into the litany of communion, Linnea excused herself, indicating she'd see Susan back at the villa.

Outside in the bright sunshine, as the only one coming down the steps, the eyes of black-suited chauffeurs and bodyguards and men with the dark glasses of the *Mat Vu* followed her. She hailed a taxi that edged forward, its driver looking from side to side at the many men watching him. In the time it took her to describe the address of Tam and Jim, her formerly crisp linen shirtdress was a wrinkled mess.

The raw dirt streets in the eastern outskirts were lined with sidewalks of uneven wooden boards. Two-story, clapboard structures cut up into apartments provided space for small shops to sell bottles of soda pop and one or two essentials. Laundry fluttered from balconies.

Formerly graceful entrances on the main street had been blocked off, and from prior trips she knew that to reach the upper floor she needed the stairs around the side in the rear alley. Turning the corner, she felt the throb of Taoist drums beating in a cloistered pagoda near by. She stepped carefully around collections of young boys playing *soc dia* with coins under inverted bowls over plates, or casting marbles and small stones at a tin. On the far side by a wall several small crowds of men and boys squatted on haunches in the dirt, squabbling over dice, with bottle tops and pebbles thrown down in lieu of *dong*.

Linnea found herself facing indistinguishable doors, not one with a mark she could remember.

From overhead came the faint voice of a young woman, leaning over a rail and pointing toward the door underneath to the side.

"I didn't recognize you," Linnea greeted Tam at the top of the stairs. "When did you start wearing glasses?"

"Yes," she said in the usual way Vietnamese begin to answer a question. "I thought Jim would not like me in glasses." Tam smiled. "He says he prefers it this way."

"You appear like the successful poetess I feel certain you some day will be. I like your latest poetry very much. You have sensitivity and depth, including in describing the complex feelings of the Vietnamese people today."

Tam covered her mouth with her hand.

The sound of water heating on a two-burner electric cooker on a wooden corner table indicated it was ready for tealeaves from glass jars on a shelf above. Movement began in a pile of dark gray material in the corner. A tiny, old woman with a tightly pinched face emerged bowing as she glided to attend at the table.

Linnea fished in her oversized purse. "I brought these," she said, lifting out bottles of vitamins.

"You knew she likes them," Tam gleamed, nodding to the woman who now rushed forward, bowing up and down.

Linnea said to her, *"Xin cám ơn nhiều vì đã giúp người bất hạnh này, người Mỹ này. Chúng tôi rất đội ơn."* "Thank you very much for helping the unfortunate person, the American man."

Her black eyes shining like buttons, "Most pleased," the diminutive woman said as she backed with her gift to the table to resume fixing the tea.

Shifting on heels she seldom wore, Linnea freed from her purse the heavy box with a ream of high-grade paper. "I'm pleased to give this to you," she said with a laugh, gratified with Tam's immediate delight. A few moments later, she asked, "Please tell me how Jim is? Did he have a relapse? Is it serious?"

"Yes," Tam replied. "Chinese man you sent brought herbs we've boiled as directed and Jim sleeps well afterwards. He talked by phone many times with the man the military doctor recommended." Tam's slender arms waved as though clearing the air to impart something else. "He talks about his partner." Her voice dropped to a whisper. "Sometimes he screams his name—Brent. He cries he caused him to be caught and killed … and 'I want to die.'"

"I'm so sorry." And Linnea genuinely was. She waited several seconds. "I've been curious, Tam. You said you've known Jim over two years. You told me he hadn't used pipes before the day I found you both. Did Jim have a bad time with opium because of not knowing how to smoke, or because he was already ill, or because of bad memories?"

"I don't know," Tam's anguished face looked down. "Jim and his partner were in the hills a long time. Jim was asleep in a trench. When he opened his eyes his friend's head was on a pole, this far from his face," her thumb and forefinger stretched two inches." In a questioning voice, "He said a distant superior didn't know the assignment."

"What was he assigned to do?" Linnea asked.

Tam didn't answer. Finally, she said, "Jim proposes marriage with me."

Her mind elsewhere, Linnea was slow to say, "Why, that's wonderful … isn't it?"

"My family threatens I will disgrace all our ancestors and all future generations." Tam pulled a handkerchief from her sleeve. "We were substantial in the North." She twisted the handkerchief. "My family now talks of suicide." A tear ran down the side of Tam's cheek.

"Oh, no!" Linnea exclaimed. "Look, Tam. Your family— their respect, don't lose it." She felt odd giving advice to a person older than she. "I'm afraid we've brought a lot of new ideas that must be overwhelming and confusing." She hesitated with the flash of a personal memory. "But family is all we'll ever have … and just once. Please be patient and understand."

Tam got up and went into the other room. Returning, she said, "He's willing for you to talk with questions, but not today. He'd like to greet you, though, so please come."

Jim edged up from a cot. "Thank you for the Chinese herbs the man brought. You won't believe it by the look of me, but I'm making progress." His blue eyes glowed.

"I'm glad. Relieved, in fact." And she was. "When I come again, if you feel like it, I'd like to ask about your experience smoking … for research I'm doing."

"I'll do what I can," Jim replied, elbowing his way back down.

Linnea's gaze stayed on him. He reminded her of her brother, also wounded by a drug. Accused of the gas tank explosion of their Dad's yacht, killing him and his new wife, Fred's congenitally bad heart failed. Told of his death, their mother had a fatal stroke. At the AP she'd feared some enterprising reporter would figure out that the Linnea of the family tragedy was the journalist Linnea who wanted to be on the foreign desk focusing on Asia.

Scurrying back into the front room, "When I am able to talk with Jim I want to know if opium took away bad memories," she blurted, beginning to sweat profusely. With more faith in the cab driver downstairs than she felt, "I have someone waiting on the street." Searching her purse, she pulled out a slender red ribbon-wrapped box with a delicate gold necklace selected from a display case in the new PX. "This is for you — for all you've been going through."

Tam pressed the box to her chest.

Stepping to the door, Linnea said, "Thank you for giving me the locations of the poetry readings and discussions. I'm learning a great deal from them."

"Wait!" Tam dashed over to books the corner. "I want to thank you for Mr. Robert Frost. I've read and reread everything. One question, please. Here." She opened to the poem written for the Kennedy inauguration and, pointing to a place, began reading:

"They are our wards to some extent
For the time being and with their consent

To teach them how democracy is meant
A democratic form of right divine."

"What does Mr. Frost mean by 'wards' and 'right divine'? Do Mr. Frost and Mr. Kennedy think of us as wards of the U.S.?"

Linnea didn't remember those lines delivered in the inauguration. How strange, she thought. Surely the president and Frost didn't adhere to Kipling's "White Man's Burden." She lifted the book to reread the lines, feeling like a student hearing bad English in a revered teacher. "I don't know what 'right divine' means," she said querulously. Did her country consider itself a patron of Vietnam?

Tam nodded to the little woman in gray who trundled forward with a slender bound volume of rice paper sheets that Tam handed to Linnea. "I saw your face glow when Ho Xuan Huong's poetry was read at the poet's gathering a month ago. Ho Xuan Huong was very brave when she wrote in the Le dynasty."

Linnea saw Vietnamese written on the left sided pages with English on the right, facing page. She smiled her delight and appreciation, clutching the volume to her chest.

"Ho Xuan Huong's *Confessions I, II and III.* I hope they please you." Tam smiled. A moment later, "You asked if I'm going to church today. Yes, I am. I went to confession yesterday. I have much to be thankful for, especially you."

"Thank you, Tam. Because of you, I've learned some of the most important things I know. Merry Christmas," she said, and hurried downstairs.

* * *

"How was church?" Stephen asked when she arrived back at the villa.

"Oh, fine. Catholics are very long-winded, you know."

"Susan's been back for hours. Dammit! You lie to me. Where were you?"

CHAPTER XVIII

"Okay! Okay!" Linnea stopped Vinh from continuing with a raise of her hands. "So we can't go north and we cannot go west! Well, what about south, into the Mekong Delta? It's peaceful there, isn't it?" Anger had entered her voice as she succumbed to the need to get out of Saigon, even though not yet Vietnam. Abandoning ire at him for not helping her more with her "research," she appended, "I've heard the soil there isn't good for the stuff growing in the hills that's causing me so much trouble."

"A lot grows in the Delta," Vinh said as though preparing to express a particular message. "You shall see the abundance."

The journey out of Saigon south on highway 4 into the Mekong Delta was Linnea's gift to herself—a reward of sorts. Resting her head back to face up at serous clouds floating lazily across a clear blue sky, she let wind blow her hair into tangles that seemed like the mess inside her skull.

The road was well traveled and smooth, letting her feel that the peaceful beauty of South Vietnam's countryside would be a salve and an imperishable memory. The farther they went from Saigon, passing through arches covered with fuchsia and pink bougainvillea that looked like wedding boughs, the more the confrontations with Stephen seemed to dissipate. Going along at a good clip, one crumbling yellow clay French fort became followed by another and then another, each one at a precise kilometer from the next. The forts linked across the broad alluvial plain with the regularity of a knotted cord.

"They seem much more ancient than having been left here just eight years ago," Linnea said, sitting up to take a closer look.

"They weren't meant to last long, I think," Vinh replied. "The French went into their forts and stayed there—and that's where the Viet Minh found them."

Deeper into the Delta's broad expanse, like a newly engaged tourist, Linnea delighted in the variety of the fruits and vegetables being grown—rice, bananas, mangoes, pineapples, papayas, pears, sugar cane and coconuts. "This area is very rich!"

"Yes, things grow quickly here. Delta farmers don't have to work hard and can take it easy," Vinh said.

Linnea seemed to hear "lazy" and "spoiled" in his voice and awaited his refrain that the people in the North worked hard in poor terrain and soil.

Driving on, Linnea began taking notes. Khoai-sap plants swayed wildly along the sides of canals and roadways, their leaves dully slapping like elephant ears. Stands of dua lop breadfruit trees had branches crowned with spiraled clusters of ribbon-like leaves. Nipa palms and other wild vegetation thriving on brackish water decorated the edges of rivulets. Some palm trunks angled horizontally as though reclining hammock-like, while nuoc palms with feathery leaves rose straight up twenty to thirty feet like an arm rising high in a good stretch.

Barely clothed children waved from floating boards, or gave a shout as they jumped from the open sides of dwellings built on a slice of land in one of the nine fingers of the Mekong Dragon. While young children splashed, older siblings helped fathers pull in and stitch aged fishing nets. Peace seemed to be flowing through the open sampans and riverbank hovels that resembled derelict houseboats with fluttering laundry in shades of gray.

"You know," Vinh said, "fish are so plentiful down here they can be caught with bare hands. But," with a change of tone, "life in the Delta is not easy; the people are poor." After going a distance further, he slowed the jeep. "You should see how the people here live."

They parked and walked along the narrow raised dike between rice paddies up to a square of land where a thatched roofed small brown clay and bamboo hut perched under an old, gnarled pepper tree. The hut was picture perfect amidst fields of pale yellow and bucolic green.

"Won't we disturb someone?"

"No. They're out working."

The interior of the shack was dark, and in the middle of its dirt floor stood a single item—an old, scarred wooden table.

"They cook, eat, repair and even sleep on this table. It's all they have," Vinh said.

"You're saying people in the Delta's rich rice bowl are not as rich as their landscape."

"Delta people eat hand to mouth. By living alone, scattered about, they have no one to help them and they live cruelly."

Anticipating that Vinh's next words would express that people in the north lived better because they lived in communes, communally, with neighbors helping neighbors, Linnea prepared to listen with one ear. But gunfire was what she heard in both.

A loud exchange sounded from behind a thick clump of sugar cane to the right of the embankment they were standing on. From overhead came the whack-whack of helicopters flying low, startling Linnea and Vinh who started walking back, presuming the activity was an exercise, for it was in daylight on a bright, sunny day. But the irregularity of the bursts of weaponry and the erratic swoops of the helicopters indicated it could be something else, so, with Linnea in the lead, they hurried.

To the right, coming at them through the middle of his carefully planted field was a farmer, perhaps the one whose hut they'd just visited. His arms were out in front as if beseeching, his legs sawing up and down, his eyes white with fear. A single shot rang out and the man's heaving chest exploded in a red splash out his front, slowing him as though he was dazed. He stared ahead, confused and sad, and collapsed onto his face.

"My God!" Linnea screamed.

"We'd better get out of here," Vinh said, squeezing around her to run toward the jeep. Getting the motor going when she reached it, "Something strange is happening."

"No. No," Linnea said, turning back at the man spread out in the watery field and an old woman shrieking and running toward him. "We need to help."

"I don't know," Vinh said, looking anxiously in every direction.

"Just do it. We're in the middle anyway."

Hunched over the wheel, Vinh had the jeep inching back around when Linnea shouted, "Look! Over there! Neil Sheehan and the Reuters guy Turner!" The reporters ran in one direction and then whirled around to go in another, caught in gunfire from two directions!

Helicopters swooped low over Sheehan and Turner, then banked and flew sideways toward a hedgerow, heading upwards without thrust. Shots came from behind a thick clump of trees; first one and then another helicopter circled erratically, going round and round and then dropping, folding into a heap, in the farmer's field near his body.

"Stop. We've got to help."

Leading the way through the field toward the downed 'copters, Linnea heard more than felt the shot that clipped her hat above her right ear, making her fall flat and remain that way until Vinh, minutes later, pulled her up out of the mud.

Over many hours, Sheehan, Turner and a few Americans, whose clothes indicated they were cooks brought in from somewhere, lifted up and lay out beside each other five dead American pilots and three dead advisors who'd been in the helicopters. They carried the sixty-six bodies of ARVN soldiers who appeared to have been shot at close range from behind and brought them over with the rest. It had been difficult work in a hot and muggy day.

Sheehan and Turner and a couple of newly arrived Advisors sat on the ground a respectful distance from the bodies, quietly waiting for the arrival of trucks. Linnea and Vinh, who'd helped as well as they could, put themselves down between the newsmen and the dead soldiers. Linnea tried to staunch her sweating body and stinging eyes. Finally she rose and went over to stand by the dead. The Americans were her age and she might have seen them on Rue Catinat the day before. Their healthy, muscular bodies looked like they could get up and walk away. But they wouldn't, and with that realization her teeth ground and her eyes smarted. Shoved into an unwanted realm, she bowed her head, clasped her hands together and gave a prayer for them and for herself.

A while later, still waiting, she overheard the Advisors saying:

"Colonel Huynh van Cao was in charge of this region and presumably is in the area."

"Don't count on it. The mandarin legacy of sharp distinction between officers and enlisted men gives a colonel the right not to have to go into the field."

"This was another example of the same mistakes being made over and over again the same damned way."

"General Harkins says the Viet Cong can be whipped if they'd only stay and fight. From what I could see, the VC did stand and fight."

"Diem pumped up the ego of that damned Colonel Cao, telling him he's the Tiger of South Vietnam. Well, Cao's 7th Division troops were less than a mile away and they didn't engage. I could see John Paul Vann up there in that little white spotter plane, going back and forth like a Mad Hatter, and I can imagine what he was yelling at Cao over the radio. It must have finally gotten through, for Cao then pounded the area, wounding and killing his own men."

"And our helicopter pilots—five out of fifteen—and three advisors with them."

*   *   *

Excited to such a degree that her tongue got in the way, Linnea shouted at Stephen, "While Diem's brother Nhu undermines the regime with opium and ambitions, Diem's government forces can't even fight."

"I need to drag you along this evening to find out about Ap Bac," Stephen said in a tone suggesting possible concurrence.

"Yes, Ap Bac," she replied. "Forty miles southwest of Saigon, the place of disgrace."

"Your sarcasm, Dear Linnea, sometimes overwhelms the message. I know Ap Bac is the subject of a dispute as to whether it was a success or a failure. Diem forces and our military, primarily Harkins, call it a victory; but some of our mid-echelon officers and your news pals describe it otherwise."

"Neil Sheehan was at Ap Bac. Maybe you should pay more attention to journalists who, despite obstacles our military throw in their way, do get out and see things."

"Okay! Okay! And that's why I want you with me when Ap Bac is discussed, probably at the Officer's Club at the Rex. We'll start there and maybe go on to Givral's."

"Why not also to La Cigalle?" she said, indicating she knew it was the Intelligence community's watering hole. "Isn't that where your kind hangs out?"

With a faint sigh, he gripped her arm. "Not a bad idea. I think La Cigalle has a piano with ivories anxious to be tickled."

"It will be a treat to hear you play again," she smartly replied, remembering the time at the Village Gate when Stephen had shown a side of him thought to last. She was game for anything that might assuage her anger for not being able to confront Stephen about opium and helicopters!

The Rex Hotel top floor Officer's Club was cavernous, providing an institutionally expansive bar capable of accommodating the long row of muscular backs at its trough. Red and brown bandoleers draped across shoulders complementing bright green berets perched like crowns on men whose physiques suggested epaulets and chest boards of ribbons.

"This place has a dance floor!" Linnea exclaimed in a whisper. A revolving silver and glass ball suspended from the ceiling bounced colored lights over the room's three levels— the dance floor; the table area; and the much livelier bar that they were passing. "And a live band!" she added as eight plump Filipinos with bored expressions came from behind a curtain onto the bandstand. Abruptly they began trumpeting a discordant imitation of the Tijuana Brass.

Stephen led her down one level to an unoccupied small table close to the dance floor and took a quick look back at the men along the bar. Taking a moment to study two couples dancing, he rose and, to her astonishment, pulled her out onto the floor.

Drawing her to his chest, he held out her arm as though steering a wide-handled bicycle, making her think he might be trying to make her laugh or to take attention away from the drag of his atrophied leg

"You're smooth, you know, Stephen, as good as anyone," she said, frustration dissipating a bit in his strong arms as the band segued into an imitation of a Nelson Riddle arrangement of a Sinatra hit.

"Don't bend over backward being truthful, Kiddo. Anyway, it's a rather fresh experience, isn't it, that the next step doesn't lead to something else."

Linnea's forehead went to his shoulder.

A Glenn Miller piece began and became followed by a late '50s fast one. Linnea expected they'd quit, but several men arriving caused Stephen to turn her around, keeping his eyes on them. When the music stopped, he swept her past their table to snatch her purse and up to where he lifted her onto a tall stool at the far right end of the bar.

A clean-cut, blond-haired officer in his early thirties was speaking. "The ARVN soldier cannot tell his officer what's happening because that just isn't done here. Also, of course, the officer cannot be found because he's out of reach in the *Cercle Sportif.*"

"The ARVN officers don't know what they're doing and the poor ARVN grunt knows it and doesn't want to go into the field anyway," the officer next to him said. "Morale, to put it mildly, is one heck of an ARVN malaise."

"What about ours? Going into action with ARVN soldiers whose first thought is to avoid the enemy! What a cockamamie situation this is!" grunted a sunburned young man.

The blond-haired officer suggested as a matter of fact, "Frontal assault may not be the ideal tactic. This war calls for discrimination ... discrimination in killing. The knife is best. Barring a knife, maybe a rifle ... because you need to see the face of the person you're killing."

Linnea leaned forward to see the man who described killing so casually.

Stephen's hand on her shoulder squeezed the message to stay back out of sight.

Statements came rapidly, piling on top of each other.

"By giving ARVN jet fighter planes and helicopters, motorized riverboats, armed personnel carriers and the most modern radio equipment, we've let them pick up very bad habits. They need to be in the swamps learning how to be men."

"Agreed. Non-selective terror by artillery and air strikes is no good. I'd be happy if we took every plane and every cannon out of the country."

"The major Viet Cong problem is weapons," said a shaved headed officer sounding rather weary. "The ARVN have got to stop arming the VC by abandoning equipment all over the place."

"Weapons? The Viet Cong are probably most successful when they aren't carrying any and are going into the villages as Father Shrink, letting the peasant complain and making him feel like a man. Misery, my friends, is the VC's ally. VC agents make farmers' troubles their own, the opposite of what Diem's troops are doing."

"Colonel Cao at Ap Bac epitomized the problem," the blond-haired officer said, sounding like he was barely controlling his anger. "Do you know he said gunfire gets on his nerves? Colonel Cao should be serving in an opera company, not with soldiers with live ammunition in a real battle. Cao said there were seven Russian advisers with the Viet Cong. Was he close enough to see them? Cao whined, 'I don't take orders from Americans.'"

"Three companies of Viet Cong at Ap Bac simply walked away," spat the bandoleered officer.

"Diem's newspaper the *Vietnam Times* wrote that we gave Cao's forces contradictory orders, and that therefore ARVN showed 'considerable bravery' staying where they were. And that lying rag declared Diem forces humane to let the Viet Cong escape."

"There might be hope here if ARVN officers could strategize."

"Wouldn't matter. Diem is the one who decides who fights where, how and when."

"Isn't that what Hitler did?"

Heard the entire length of the bar, the blond haired officer bellowed, "Ap Bac shows there's little chance of *victory*."

"Victory! Yes, Ap Bac was a great victory," responded a senior officer entering with a potbelly constrained by a thick belt.

"Victory?" snapped the junior officer closest to him. "Twenty-five hundred troops with automatic weapons, armored amphibious personnel carriers, supported by helicopters, to defeat a measly 300 guerrillas ... who escaped with no losses?"

The buddy next to him took over, "Our 'copter guys died trying to save each other and the Vietnamese. The ARVN wouldn't even pick up their own dead."

A tall officer closest to the older man stood up to tower over him. "A victory? Goddamn it, tell us: how and whose?"

"We achieved our objective," said the older officer amiably. "The Viet Cong left their positions and that's a victory!"

"I don't believe this!" The blond-haired officer muttered in a low, sad growl, "We're in a guerrilla war, damn it, not a cockamamie textbook fight with tanks and battle lines."

"On top of old Ap Bac, all covered with blood...." junior officers up and down the rail started humming the tune to "On Top of Old Smokey."

As soon as they were outside and on the street, a petulant Linnea said, "Well, I hope you learned something from that."

"Yes and no. I want you to know that I, too, talk with Vietnamese," Stephen said with confidence, looking straight ahead. "For instance, I was told that Colonel John Paul Vann, advisor to Cao's 7th Division, in an observation plane overhead, phoned the captain commanding the armored division and screamed that if he didn't get his vehicles across the canal he'd have him jailed. As you keep telling me, the Vietnamese are sensitive. Well, from what I've learned, the ARVN tank group went up and down the canal but couldn't cross because it was swampy and they'd get stuck. And so, my courageous, inquisitive friend, in any battle there are at least two sides and lots of views."

Maneuvering around stalls selling flowers and books, they passed children playing with stones alongside fathers dealing cards. A merchant shouting his offering stepped sideways with a pole across his shoulders and a basket at each end with cups of jelly drinks and cooked tapioca. Gray smoke and an enticing smell of garlic floated up from an old woman on a stool in front of a sizzling brazier stirring pork fat, meat, scallions, sugar, and fish sauce in a dented iron pot.

When they were in the clear again, Stephen said, "I agree with you, Linnea, that arrogance and belligerence don't accomplish much. The reason I want to know more about this John Paul Vann is that something isn't quite right. I'm sure Vann is a fine soldier, ambitious and probably frustrated. But he's giving interviews to newsmen that...."

"Newsmen clarify things," she interrupted, coming to a halt. "Ap Bac was a battle between Vietnamese. This could be developing, you know, into something like a civil war—something we shouldn't be involved in."

He gripped her arm and started her forward. "It's far, far bigger than that. Anyway," he intoned with his eyes panning the streets, "let's remember that the mission tonight is piano."

Linnea gave Stephen's stated plan a few seconds. "It could be that our standard old way of doing things may not work in the situation here, and is turning people off."

"You could be right," he sighed. He was concentrating on helping her pass through women loudly hawking pork and rice steamed in banana leaves, and children in high pitched voices selling *banh cuon*, the rice crepes with sausage. "It may fit in with your incipient anti-authoritarianism, Linnea, that...."

"Didn't what we just heard suggest that our higher-ups aren't always right, that they don't know what's happening?" she cut him off. "Ambassador Nolting says correspondents are writing frivolous, thoughtless criticisms, and General Harkins maintains correspondents are prevaricators."

"Linnea, listen to me."

"Listen to you? If you listened, you'd know that Sheehan was at the airport and met up with your Head of Fleet, Admiral Felt. Sheehan asked Felt if Ap Bac was a victory and Felt said that the stuff he was reading was a bunch of lies, in particular the stories by a Neil Sheehan. Sheehan then identified himself and Felt shouted that Sheehan should talk to people who had the facts. And.... And...." She hated it when she stuttered. "And Sheehan answered Felt, 'You're right, Admiral, and that's why I went down to Ap Bac.'"

"All right," Stephen responded. "It seems our military higher ups didn't venture out of Saigon for that one. However, middle echelon military like Colonel John Paul Vann have been feeding information to journalists that's not completely accurate and that's been printed."

"Dammit, Stephen. The situation here is ... is ... is murderous! Diem's *Vietnam Times* had a picture of Sheehan in a military uniform under the banner caption: 'American Adviser Sheehan; What Does He Really Want?' as ... as though he's responsible for the Diem regime's failures. That's malicious."

"Yeah. Okay. Agreed."

"Sheehan and other journalists have had their rooms ransacked and their phones tapped, I think you should know." Linnea suddenly thought of Sheehan's beautiful Vietnamese girlfriend; an attack on Sheehan would be an attack on her. "Doesn't that tell you that even people like me, doing a little research and listening to a few poets, are in danger?"

Stephen examined her face with a thought he didn't convey. Finally he said, "It's possible the Diem household— Nhu—may have gotten the impression from Nolting, Harkins and Felt that it's all right to go down hard on journalists."

"And researchers! I, too, am scared, you know!" And she really was.

Americans in their gathering spots, Givrals and La Cigalle, were either too angry or too tight to answer Stephen's questions about Ap Bac. Stephen took a Minox headshot once or twice without the subject knowing.

On the way to Rue Catinat for a likely spot to catch a cab, a piano's tinny strings drifted out to them, trying out go-go and twist rhythms.

"Ah! The seamier side! Perchance I've been remiss, my Dauntless 'Nea."

Before she could respond, Stephen pulled her through a narrow opening covered by tinkling beads and a filthy cloth that smacked her like a fly swatter. Inside, the atmosphere was close with a distasteful mixture of strong cigarette smoke and cheap perfume. One harsh white light beamed down on a small, empty, semicircular stage. She heard a piano sadly plucked, somewhat accompanied by a thickly strummed bass, a sour trumpet, and a zither, also poorly played.

A flashlight covered with red cellophane and a rubber band led them through body-cluttered darkness to a tiny table by a wood planked wall. Just as they were seated, an unusually tall young Vietnamese female in an abbreviated Western-style vest and shorts came onto the stage. Shimmering straight black hair reached down her back to the uppermost of her thighs. Glossy strands undulated as her petite buttocks waved. Prancing in red satin sling-back slippers covered with sequins and elevated by several inches of thick platform, the dancer teased, her gold ankle chain glittering its tiny red stones.

To male hoots coming from the dark, the winsome face began a grind that reached a frenetic twisting with the room wildly screaming. At a final lurching screech from band's brass, the performance ended, with the dancer slithering between curtains held apart for her escape.

The instant the stage light went out, pale orange house lights snapped on to expose the tawdriness of the place. As Linnea's eyes adjusted, she began noticing the debris on the floor around them into which came the calfskin shoes of a Westerner who seemed to know Stephen.

"I was following you," the American said in a hard to hear, low voice.

Stephen rose and moved with the man far enough away so that she couldn't hear them. Flustered at being ignored, Linnea glowered at Stephen's backward glance. Then noise at a small stand-up bar swarming with men absorbed her attention.

"It's not glory," snarled a commanding voice. "We have glory. Lots of it, more than we need, and more than those fucks will ever have. We're not cowboys. There's nothing we have to prove. And yet our hands are tied by a bunch of lying, shitty, cowardly wimps who've advanced by staying in."

The man with the commanding voice stood with his legs slightly apart a few feet back from a wet-sloshed bar lined with v-shaped backs in sports shirts. His head of unruly reddish brown hair had coarse gray strands that stuck out from his temples like incipient horns. He threw his arms over the men at the counter with their heads down.

When the "commander" resumed speaking, each word carried full weight. "Sent out on an assignment no one can appreciate or be responsible for. Gather information that's not enough. No, something else needs to be done ... *or picked up*." The "commander" threw out words like a knife thrower: "Lackeys ... delivery boys ... undercut ... misrouted. Humiliation ... shame ... a game. A lousy, fucking game," the "commander" declared.

Getting directions from a passing waiter to the lady's room that was at the side of the bar, Linnea came up to the "commander's" back. "Excuse me." The man whipped about. In a rush she asked, "You're Special Forces, aren't you?"

Several men at the rail glanced behind and swiveled back around. A red dragon flashed on a bicep.

"I'm sorry. Someone I know, a Special Forces man with opium poisoning, says his work boiled down to being a game ... a great game to be lost. You did say game, didn't you?"

The "commander's" face flushed. He shouted into her ear a message for his men: "Shall we?"

The men on barstools unabashedly started chanting:
I had a dog and his name was Blue.
Bet you five dollars,
He's a good dog, too.
Hey, Blue,
You're a good dog, you.

In refrains, the name Blue was replaced by surnames, descriptive nicknames, and finally first names, sadly concluding:
Hey, friends,
You were good guys, you.

Linnea couldn't move.

"Yes, the game concerns Vietnam," the "commander" spat. "Good people who did their best in spite of...."

"In spite of you screw-ups," men at the counter finished for him.

"Home is where a little dear like you ought to be." The "commander" threw his arms across the slumped shoulders of his friends.

Linnea stood rooted several strange seconds before taking the steps to the lady's restroom. She burst inside. It was empty, and it stank. She sat on the stained and tattered boudoir chair in front of a cracked partially clouded mirror and stared for as long as she dared. Somehow she'd have to find and talk with that "commander" about his delivery boy statement.

Linnea returned to their table where Stephen hissed, "What were you doing over there?"

"Those Americans have been in-country a long time. I just thought...." Her hand extended back toward the bar area that had now emptied. "I was headed to the bathroom. I heard them say 'game' the way you do sometimes, in one of your saner moments. I thought it might have to do with ... with Ap Bac."

Stephen glared. Linnea couldn't tell whether he was thinking he didn't believe her reply or about his conversation with the man he'd been talking with.

Back on the street, Stephen gripped her arm so hard it hurt. "You've got to be careful."

"I thought you wanted me to prepare for a future for myself," she said, pointedly peering at his hand squeezing her upper arm.

"I want a future for a *live* you."

They walked on without talking. A pair of young women in *ao dai* coming towards them had conical hats tilted jauntily back over their shoulders. Their oval faces glowed like alabaster. They seemed to be pristinely gliding along until Linnea noticed high-heeled gold and silver slippers exposing bright pink toenails. Their svelte, light movements now seemed cunningly clever, even feral.

"Maybe Madame Nhu has a point about keeping out our culturally bad elements," Linnea said about the women and the blast of loud American music the women were heading toward.

When they were a distance beyond warring sounds, Stephen said, "Linnea, listen to me: the opium smoker you think you're helping, your interviews with helicopter pilots, and your associations with kindly appearing Saigonese—who are suspect by our government and theirs—that's not what you should be doing." He took a deep breath. "Frankly, I wonder if I wasn't out of my mind to bring you here."

Unable to still her irritation about his secretiveness, she asserted, "I'm glad I've come. I love the Vietnamese people. What I've been learning will help them and, if I can help it, will be put to good use by us." Keeping in step, "Our gentler side, you know, focusing on people, is where we're strong."

CHAPTER XIX

Dear Clarissa,

....

Please excuse the length of this. Your father's questions need a lot to try to answer.

In short, President Diem has the power but his brother Nhu uses it. The Nhu activities that I feel are leading to a possible catastrophe are:

1) Opium— he is an addict; he manipulates opium production and people (I'll go into it in detail later). Availability of drugs to American servicemen can lead to problems as great as injuries in the field, as your father suspects.

2) Jails, torture chambers, re-education camps—with his Mat Vu secret police, Nhu is putting poets, teachers and scholars (the very ones offering constructive criticism) into camps—e.g., Poulo Condore, a prison on Con Son island for political dissidents that's said to be horrible.

3) Nhu plays for power with North Vietnam. "Extra-political activities" by Nhu that undercut his brother's regime are whispered about all over the place here. (Soon, suspicions will be substantiated.)

In short, Nhu's activities accentuate weaknesses that are attributed to Diem, creating the difficulties the U.S. is having in dealing with South Vietnam.

Senator Mansfield's trip here earlier in December is significant, I feel. He and Kennedy evidently were the only congressmen to visit Vietnam in the fifties, and sources I trust say Mansfield was almost alone in defending Diem then (in opposition to Pentagon and State Department officials who were against Diem). Mansfield's statements about the high costs of our being in South Vietnam are consonant with my feelings that easy availability of drugs could make costs even higher.

Please try to get on a congressional junket. More and more Americans are heading here (even lots of tourists!) so why not you.

With much love and a hug,

Linnea

*   *   *

Just after the beginning of 1963—the year of the hare— Linnea noted planeloads of Americans arrived as economists, sociologists, political scientists, anthropologists, agronomists, biologists, chemists, and even public opinion pollsters. They swarmed over Saigon, near-by fields and into the hills, probing and giving advice, causing Linnea to give Hmong visits a breather and to return to research, particularly in the USIS library.

In February, Linnea read in *Time* that American troops no longer had to wait until shot at before raising their firearms; shortly later, they wouldn't have to wait at all and could shoot first, including with machine guns from Army H-21 helicopters.

In March, the American South dominated the news. "Freedom Riders," Linnea learned, meant Negroes taking bus trips from Washington, D.C., to New Orleans, were making an issue of being unable to use "whites only" restrooms even in an emergency.

In early April, Linnea insisted Stephen see a news photograph of Birmingham, Alabama, police chief "Bull" Connor turning teeth-baring German Shepherds on Negroes in a march that involved young children and a minister named Martin Luther King, Junior, who was arrested.

A century after the Civil War, she said with amazement, Army troops had to escort a student named James Meredith into a classroom at the University of Mississippi.

In May, in the USAID office, Linnea brought to Stephen's attention newspaper photos and articles about the arrest of five hundred Negroes who had been obediently marching in spite of fire hoses spewing blasts and whites throwing bricks at them.

"Negroes are in our military here probably to avoid getting killed in our South," Linnea said. She wanted to share with him what she perceived as the similarity between Southern governors' mistreatment of Negroes and the Diem regime's abuse of Buddhists, but suspected Stephen would say she was going too far. At some point she might mention that the Hanoi *Nhan Dan* newspaper listed statistics proving prejudice in the U.S. military, preventing Negro servicemen from advancing, or the other *Nhan Dan* article castigating the U.S. for chemical warfare, poisoning Vietnam's water. The Hanoi paper wrote that the Americans for Democratic Action demanded that the U.S. withdraw from Vietnam, not seen in an American newspaper or magazine.

Intending to show Stephen that the year of the hare meant things were heating up, leaping right along, she said, "I've read in a Hanoi newspaper that President Diem wants America to withdraw our troops from his country. Have you heard, or do you know anything about that?"

Stephen swiveled around to face her, hands on his knees. "President Kennedy has plans to withdraw one thousand men."

"He does? That's great!" Linnea felt happily relieved that her hill project might be concluded by a political/military schedule rather than by being a fiasco.

"Maybe just a rotation," he replied in a distant tone. "The plan dates from almost exactly a year ago, April 6, 1962, to be accomplished in 1963." Sarcasm was in his voice when he appended, "However, General Harkins is about to begin an 'explosive' operation."

"And what does that mean?" Linnea asked.

"Just that he'll need more soldiers," Stephen replied with resignation.

She hadn't heard him speak quite this way before, so she let a few moments pass. She began to think that what had just happened in Hue might lead to areas she wanted to discuss. "Have you heard that yesterday in Hue Buddhists—twenty thousand of them—were fired upon?"

"And do you know why?" Stephen asked in a tired professorial tone.

"Just because they were flying their Buddhist flag on their pagoda. It was a traditional birthday celebration of Gautama Siddhartha, the Buddha. It seems Diem rejuvenated an old French edict against it. Seven children and one woman were killed, and twenty people were wounded. Stephen...."

"I'm impressed. You're proving once again that you're on top of things!" he said, rising for a tired stretch.

"Stephen, every other organization evidently flies its flag." Amidst other reports of strange actions by the Diem regime, a thought flashed. "The Hue deputy province chief Major Dang Xi is a Catholic!"

"And Diem's elder brother is the Hue Catholic diocese head priest," Stephen confirmed.

"I didn't know that," she said. "What do you think will happen?"

"Nothing," Stephen said. "Remember how passive Buddhists are."

"I'm not so sure about that, as I've tried to tell you. There's a Buddhist leader Tri Quang who may be gearing up against Diem," she said. "Won't Diem come to an understanding with the Buddhists?"

"Maybe. But with Nhu so powerful, I rather doubt it."

"Maybe soon Nhu won't be as powerful!" Linnea said. The man she's met at the Diamond Restaurant said he was the CIA contact "your friend in D.C. arranged for you to turn over some information you have." The man was cold and condescending but seemed all right, even with the speed in which he departed with the documentation in the bamboo tube.

*   *   *

"A turning point may be the flying soup tureen event, without it resulting in Witch Madame Nhu being sent abroad," Hugh said to Linnea and Stephen and a few others in late May when they all were at the Caravelle hotel for the inauguration of its plush new dining room. "No one in Hue believed the Viet Cong had fired on the Buddhists. And so, after a lot of pressure, Diem agreed to meet with several Buddhist priests to appease them."

Accepting another free drink, Hugh reported that the Palace servants told him that when Madame Nhu learned Diem had met with Buddhists to conciliate, she flew into a rage. "'You're a coward and a jellyfish,' she yelled, and threw the tureen of chicken soup at the president."

Linnea laughed along with the rest but Stephen didn't. His eyes were on waiters who were listening and slow in removing finished plates of the hotel's touted *lapin sauté chasseur*.

"Look at all these American soldiers," said plump photographer Christoph in a scratchy German-accented voice. "I never asked them to come here. They don't even have passports."

"That's rich," muttered stringer Paul. "Diem can't stand up to Nhu or his wife but he can exert power over our damned visas."

Recalling the analysis in a South Vietnamese newspaper article that Diem believes President Kennedy is distracted by what's happening in the American South, Linnea threw out the question, "Do you think the problems in our South distract JFK and affect our work here?"

"Work? What work?"

"Oh, you mean the war. But there's no real war! No Siree!" said seasoned journalist Malin coming up with some friends.

Stephen put his hand on the back of her chair. "We're leaving."

*   *   *

Heavy, gray, unmoving monsoon clouds hung over Saigon the rest of May causing humidity to condense on the skin and dampen spirits. A more or less permanent curfew stimulated earlier bedtimes that frequently resulted in troubled sleep.

Before the rooster-on-New-York-time had another chance to ruin the tail end of dreams, Linnea let herself come fully awake. It was close to 5 a.m. She heard the tinkling of cymbals, the soft, sure calls of Buddhist drums rolling like a muffled tattoo through moist streets, and decided it was again time to see what Buddhists had on their minds.

Downstairs she nudged the *bep*'s boy curled up by the front door to let her out, and followed melodies reverberating from pagodas deep in damp alleys. Nearing a familiar old Buddhist temple, she witnessed a silent line of orange robes drifting along like whiffs of fog.

In the warm darkness of the capital of a nation in conflict on many avenues, Linnea felt herself gravitating toward Buddhist paths leading to freedom from pain. Buddhism offers hope against danger, and offers guidance toward a happier after-life, but does their gentleness make it impossible for them to assert or defend themselves? she asked herself.

"Excuse me, may we talk for a minute?" she asked the tall, thin monk trying to disguise his youth by emulating the hunched elders he was trailing. With a curious glance, he slowed.

"I'm sorry about what happened in Hue," Linnea said, striding alongside. "I understand that the monk Tri Quang has come down here to the Xa Loi pagoda. I've heard he's more politically minded than many of you," she said, slowing her gait with the hope he'd walk apace.

He observed his colleagues rounding a corner a block ahead. "Tri Quang isn't political. He doesn't like power—I mean, the big powers, the U.S.S.R. and the U.S. He doesn't want Vietnam in the middle, between the two powers, or for the South or the North to be allied with either of them. Tri Quang knows things we don't."

"What things? You mean talks Tri Quang is having with the President's brother Nhu and the North?"

The young monk straightened as though stunned.   .

"Is Tri Quang going to organize the Buddhists to confront Diem?"

Looking her squarely in the eyes, "He wants to bring the South and the North together. He's been talking that way for five years."

"Five years?" she repeated. "Does Tri Quang want to lead the country?"

The young monk wrapped his robe about him. "I will catch up."

Later that day, with her head down in thought as well as to be on guard against the unevenness in pathways, Linnea headed for an old-fashioned poetry reading at a location on another nameless side street in Saigon's confusing mid-section. After walking back and forth on the presumably correct curving alley she realized that a brick and sand mortared house at the apex must be the place. Linnea pulled the bell and heard a faint ringing in the back.

A young servant girl opened the door and motioned for Linnea to step over a ledge and into a well-lighted rectangular anteroom where she could exchange her shoes for slippers. The servant led her into the softly illuminated interior with the air smelling of cinnamon.

She'd been self-conscious in earlier days, but many knew her now and even seemed pleased to see her. Quite a few young men and women were present, sitting on the floor in front of substantial appearing white haired older men in chairs at the back.

Waiting, Linnea's eyes drifted up to paintings high on the walls of the two-story home. Hung tightly together in plain wood frames, the paintings heralded typical Vietnamese scenes: sun washed purple mountains, crystal blue ponds and green and yellow rice paddies at the hem of azure skies. Most were on rice paper, a couple of them in oils, and a few reminded her of Matisse.

Tam emerged at her side. "I am glad you're here. This day is special. Our best poets will recite. I'll stay with you. Some words are from the depths of ancestry." Recognizing the first poet, Tam exclaimed, "Ah! It begins with our favorite, Nguyen Sa!"

A disheveled and wiry man of indeterminate age, Nguyen Sa had the same intelligent laissez-faire glint as the free spirited artists she remembered in Greenwich Village. When Nguyen Sa offered to recite "Stating My Intentions," he was greeted by warm applause.

"Yes, I will cry and the tears will dissolve into little bits of blood.

Let me speak at once.

If not, I will have to go seek myself like a maddened horse galloping down

the road at twilight, chasing the sun as it disappears beyond the mountains.

Let me speak at once.

When tomorrow comes the breath will still be moist and have the stench of sin

I will look at life through the eyes of a cadaver.

And, oh dear, all of me, all of life, the path ahead and the long fragrant hair—all shall become an illusion."

A weighty moment of silence gave way to extended clapping.

The next person to step onto the small corner platform was a slight, baby-faced woman named Nguyen Thi Hoang who said her poem "Confession" was incomplete.

"Let me now bid farewell to the convent
Dishonor and sin upon this body ...
My soul is drifting away from the faith ...
When was it that faith shattered?
My soul is a lonely island....
Oh, Christ, I am afraid—of being alone tomorrow."

It impressed Linnea that a woman so young could express so well the dilemma she faced with her faith. Keeping her eyes on the woman as she returned to her seat, she became startled by the tone in the poem delivered by Pham Hong Thai:

"Live and die as you live and die—
Hate the enemy, love your country
Live—your life explodes like a bomb
Die—your death waltzes in a blue river."

When the recitations concluded, and people began to exit, Linnea struggled to her feet, wishing to talk with Tam about the last poem. But Tam was off conferring with some friends.

"How did you like today?" asked Vinh, coming up from the back.

Wishing to ask the same of him, Linnea simply replied, "Very thought-provoking."

"Poetry is called the honey of men and peoples—that they should stick together," Vinh was quick to say, with an effort at a chuckle.

Linnea glanced past him at the emptying room. "Vinh, who is that man back there where you were sitting? He looks familiar but I don't think I've seen him at one of these before."

"I don't know," Vinh answered without looking to where she was pointing.

With eyes on the pavement and a grimace on her face, Linnea started back toward the center of town, disturbed about undercurrents in the poetry session, and feeling thwarted from finding a place or a person to help with what she wanted to pursue, wherever it led. Struggling with guilt over not working hard enough with her USAID contract, she wasn't conscious of subtle activities taking place around her when people were getting off work. Buses with blacked-out windows were circling and discharging Buddhist priests and nuns at major intersections. They carried placards and used bullhorns to state grievances and desires for equal religious rights. Then, just as quickly as they had materialized, the

Buddhists disappeared, like phantoms, the way it was said VC popped up and vanished for the purpose of disturbing.

Linnea overheard Saigonese on the streets expressing surprise that monks and nuns were engaging in Western-style political activities, not knowing if they liked it.

As days passed, however, Linnea noticed more and more ordinary Saigonese going along with the processions, helping in whatever way they could, such as with water jugs, in essence advertising that beliefs in Buddhism included earthly actions determining admittance to paradise. It was a subtle change that registered only vaguely on Linnea—not enough to mention to Stephen or in a letter to Clarissa.

By 9 a.m. one early June morning, Saigon's combined assault of heat and humidity had already made its way into the USAID office where Linnea steamed with the realization that it was now time for a major confrontation with Stephen … and then to depart Vietnam. Perhaps to spur him into making the first move, she stacked on her desk copies of the translated copies of the contents of the bamboo tube; her typed notes on the Bay Vien encounter in the Rung Sat swamp; what she'd been able to find out about Nhu's silent partnership in opium with the Corsican gangster "Rocky" Francisci; and information pieced together of Nhu's questionable dialogue with the North Vietnamese under the guise of cultural exchanges. A shorter stack contained notes of her recent talk with the red-haired commander from the seedy nightclub, and details about the First Transport Group routes, under the direction of Colonel Nguyen Cao Ky, flying to and from Laos in U.S. planes, possibly arranged by her boss, Stephen. She placed a heavy green and white porcelain elephant on the taller pile.

Philco, puffing hard after coming up the stairs in bounds, mopped his head with an already sopping handkerchief. "Over off Phan Dinh Phung Street," he said. "Something's about to happen. Monks and nuns—many of them—are chanting and lighting lots of incense."

USAID staffers showed scant interest in what was presumably just another respectful Buddhist demonstration against Diem, and continued whatever they were doing.

"Something's different," Philco said directly to Linnea. "I'm going back. You'd better come." His loaded torso descended the steps in heavy bounds before his shoes could be heard squishing on the pavement below.

Linnea went to the window. She watched Philco heading toward the intersection of Phan Dinh Phung and Le Van Duyet Streets, one of the busiest in all of Saigon. She wondered if Philco urged her to come, not because he sensed something was up, but because he sensed her confrontational attitude toward Stephen and felt she needed some space.

"You go," Stephen said to her distracted gaze at him in his corner window location. "Progress needs to be made with these." He tapped a finger on USAID staff status papers.

In dazzling sunlight on the street below, the colors on storefronts and signs gleamed as though scrubbed clean by recent rain. Two policemen in pristine white uniforms bicycled past, casually chatting, heading in her same direction. An elderly woman slipped up to walk beside her, looking Linnea over, her black, piercing eyes landing with what seemed like an accusation.

Linnea imagined that ahead would be a Buddhist walk-through demonstration preceded by the usual police on 'cycles going ahead and clearing the streets. This gathering might merely be larger.

Glad to be out and able to plan what she soon would be saying to Stephen, something in a call he'd made to her in New York floated into mind, "Vietnam will be a grand adventure." Now the adventure seemed an escapade into secrecy by both of them, just as their government appeared to be hiding behind noble motives and glowing statistics.

Taking the turn from a quiet, tree-lined street into the commercial Le Van Duyet, she joined men and women heading toward the main north-south boulevard, Phan Dinh Phung. In the distance she heard chanting. She paused to make it out.

Nam Mô A Di Đà Phật. It was the ancient Buddhist prayer, each word equally accented on the same monotonal note. It was familiar and hypnotic. She sauntered on.

A press of Vietnamese office workers in white blouses and dark skirts and trousers moved silently but determinedly alongside. She slowed to readjust the barrette in her moist scalp and fell behind, wishing she had grabbed a hat to block the sun beaming down.

When she reached the Le Van Duyet intersection, by habit Linnea checked the massive Cambodian consulate building on the corner with its large stone lion by the front gate.

Next she glanced at the bland, recently constructed three story apartment buildings on two other corners, and saw women and children leaning out of windows, looking below. She glimpsed the Esso station in the intersection's fourth corner, busily providing services.

Straight down Phan Dinh Phung Street, directly in front of her, proceeding slowly, came a large group of monks with a smattering of civilians four abreast, carrying white cloth banners in Vietnamese and in English:

"Charity for all religions." "Compassion for Buddhist people."

Bravo! Get it out in the open, Linnea said to herself. The Buddhists certainly deserve the same rights as Catholics. Diem should see and hear this.

As though being drawn in, people flowed into the intersection from every direction, setting the boundaries of a 30-foot wide circle.

Nam Mô A Di Đà Phật. Nam Mô A Di Đà Phật

A four door gray-green Austin A-40 sedan, its steel grill shining, crept alongside the marchers. It edged into the intersection, chrome speed strips ludicrously contradicting its hesitant entry as the closing link in a circle of humanity. Clouds of incense puffed into the air.

Nam Mô A Di Đà Phật. Nam Mô A Di Đà Phật. Nam Mô A Di Đà Phật.

A couple of tall, lean, shaved-headed monks got out of the car, their saffron robes golden in the sunlight. They moved deliberately, one monk to the front of the car. From the inside of the hood, a translucent plastic gasoline Jeri can was removed, suggesting a desire to top-off its sloshing pink fuel at the Esso station, for the container appeared three-quarters full.

A barely noticeable brown robed monk—an old man with bony features—got out and walked from the car to the center of the cement. With measured gracefulness, he folded onto a small brown cushion and crossed his legs into the lotus position.

Nam Mô A Di Đà Phật. Nam Mô A Di Đà Phật. Nam Mô A Di Đà Phật. Nam Mô A Di Đà Phật.

Monks in shades of orange and shaved-headed nuns in pale pink pressed through bystanders to be at the front of the circle enclosing the car and the seated prelate. With palms pressed together in the customary posture of passive contemplation, the monks and nuns remained still. Some softly hummed or chanted.

Nam Mô A Di Đà Phật. Nam Mô A Di Đà Phật. Nam Mô A Di Đà Phật. Nam Mô A Di Đà Phật. Nam Mô A Di Đà Phật. Nam Mô A Di Đà Phật.

More and more Saigonese pressed in from behind. Linnea looked longingly at the thin crowd in the shade in front of the Cambodian consulate. Young boys sat in the shade on the walls. An older youngster with long legs in dark blue serge climbed up onto the stone lion's back and, leaning forward with a smile, threw his arms around its neck. Off to the side on the street, approaching monks carried a banner. Shading her eyes with her hand, Linnea read, "A Buddhist Priest Burns for Buddhist Demands."

A horrifying wail snapped her head back to the circle of monks and nuns throwing themselves down, prostrating themselves in the direction of … of flames!

"My God!" she screamed, palms to her cheeks. "No! Oh, no! My God, no!"

A sheet of fire leapt up from the robe of the seated old monk and enveloped him. He didn't move. His hands were folded one on top of the other on his lap, his head unbowed, his eyes closed as though in prayer.

Pushed forward and hemmed in on all sides, Linnea stared open-mouthed in horror.

Dumbly she noted the white plastic gasoline container off to the side behind the monk, the cement dark where fuel had sloshed out. The reek of gasoline smoke and the sickly sweet smell of burning flesh poured over the intersection like a pall. Little muffled gasps of anguish and sorrowful weeping permeated the crowd.

The old monk sat upright, his features neither pinched nor twisted, his hands like Durer's.

Linnea imagined rallying people, rolling the monk over to extinguish the flames. But she couldn't move and couldn't utter a word. Someone will go to him—has got to go to him! Maybe an American!

It must be the fiercest physical torture a human could possibly suffer. Amazed and appalled Linnea realized that under frying skin the monk's living mind kept rigorous self-control, holding his agonized body erect while fire ate at his flesh with crackles mixing with sounds of lamentation.

New arrivals uttered agonizing gasps; some prostrated themselves on the cement. A white uniformed Saigon policeman with tears streaming down his face tried to break through a cordon of monks. He was held back. Another policeman pushed forward to fall flat on the ground inside the circle, apparently unconscious.

Flames danced on the monk's head. His skull blackened. He looked more like mummified remains than a man still alive.

His lashes and eyelids ignited in brief spurts and vanished as flames swarmed into eye sockets and over his charred pate. The crackling of his flesh echoed throughout the intersection.

The air from frying body parts seeped into Linnea's nostrils. She writhed.

A monk's voice on a megaphone chanted: *"A Buddhist priest burns himself to death! A Buddhist priest becomes a martyr! A priest makes the Buddhist statement!"* He repeated it, over and over, in English and Vietnamese.

The AP's Malcolm Browne moved out from between clustered monks and nuns into the center, close to the burning figure. With his silver and black camera, the journalist calmly snapped frame after frame.

Why hasn't he been pulled back, his camera knocked out of his hands? Won't Mal be blamed for photographing instead of doing something?

Fire had its own life. Whatever little fat there was in the scrawny old body, the flames liked it. They licked up from the monk's lap around his chest to his skull like long fingers encasing a religious figure.

Greasy, acrid smoke wafted into Linnea's face. She felt sick, knowing she was inhaling another person's remains! Overcome with abhorrence, she fell against the white shirt of a man's back. He whipped around with snapping eyes. Her hands lifted off as though from hot coals, her countenance a confused mixture of apologies and anguish.

Mortified, she assayed the monks on the other side of the street, calmly seated with their saffron and yellow robes draped around them. Several monks wore small round lens 'thirties-style' dark glasses and sported thick Timex steel watches. Men and women standing behind the seated monks had their arms folded, as though impatient to get on with their lives. Some of them looked casually to the right and to the left, as if for a tardy reprieve—by Diem's fire engines?

Flames hungrily lapped the old man, seemingly frustrated at having to finish the rest of an entire body's intestines and bones.

Linnea's throat pinched and her stomach pitched. She bent over to release acid from her mouth … and to grope for new air.

From almost ground level between spectators' legs, she saw the body, still rigorously controlled by a faintly living mind, finally keel over. The monk's limbs twitched convulsively in the sputtering flames of finality.

Linnea raised her arms in surrender and angry determination, and pushed and stumbled back toward the route that had brought her there. Oily smoke and incense pursued and billowed over her. Breath came hard and it pained.

She heard the bell of the Xa Loi pagoda beginning to toll.

Saigon: so beautiful, so poetic, and now so very strange. She glanced back at a crowd, some of whom seemed indifferent to what had just happened in the heart of their city.

Linnea struggled to walk and had to balance herself more than once with a hand on a dirty, moldy wall. Tree roots pushing up cement squares at dangerous angles caused her to stumble. A deep loop of a utility line hanging low on its way to an overpopulated house almost lassoed her. From an alley the heavy smell of rancid cooking oil smacked her nostrils. From another came the pungent, cloying sweetness of a tempting substance. Then, out of a crammed side street erupted a small albino boy with a macabre smile on a huge silvery bicycle, careening and coming close to running her over.

Damned, dangerous place! An immolation on the next street, and on this one....

A shawl-draped, prune-faced woman calmly sat on the ground behind a green cloth on which lay eggs mottled like marble. A street barber plied his trade: a mirror smaller than a sheet of typewriter paper dangled from a knobby tree limb; his customer in a straight-back chair swathed in a white and blue striped cloth had eyes closed as if blocking out everything but ministrations to his body. A toothless, wizened woman in a torn red shirt sat on a curb grinning, spitting betel nut juice from the black cavity of her mouth at a precise spot on the street as though playing tiddlywinks.

If they lose their freedom, they may never know or care. And I thought I knew them, she reflected with sad bitterness.

A rise in the sidewalk tripped her. She got up from the rutted cement with a scraped right hand and knee. Tiny dots of blood oozed out from around imbedded grime. She ignored the pain and continued plodding with eyes down. She felt hot, slimy and sick. Almost past a large pair of dirty footwear, she twisted back around to see the body above.

On a stoop, his wet handkerchief to his mouth, sat Philco, hardly recognizable because of the severe downward slump of his body. A small puddle of yellow vomit bubbled on the cement to his right. Linnea stepped to his other side and sat down. Philco squirmed with irritation, then, recognizing her, straightened with embarrassment. Tears had left streaks down his gasoline smoke-stained cheeks.

Despite desperately wanting succor and solace, the sight of bulky Philco—a caricature of the indomitable American—in a similar state of despair caused her to try to console while seeking help in understanding what she had witnessed.

"The single worst thing I've ever experienced," Linnea whimpered. "It didn't have to happen, did it, Philco?"

Philco cleared his throat several times. "Buddhists against Catholics ... for Diem's Catholics having discounted the people's Buddhists. It was very well thought out, a well planned ... ah, burning."

Squirming in his upright position, Philco said, "Buddhists marched the streets beforehand with banners in English, French and Vietnamese. They'd alerted Browne to document it from beginning to end." Philco's voice dropped along with his head. "This was the *coup de grace* for Diem. The pictures are going to go all over the world and there're going to be a lot of changes here—U.S. support for the Diem government, the type of aid we give, everything."

"Will we pull out?"

"Very possibly."

"What about the people?" Linnea sadly asked.

"They are Diem's responsibility. He's been supposed to help them, but now support for Diem may be nil and he won't have the time or ability."

"And us? Is there anything we can do?"

Philco looked her over. "Better ask Stephen."

Putting that aside, "Why did it have to be a burning?" she asked, flicking her limp hair like trying to rid it of smoke. "I remember there were immolations during French times here but I think I must have confused them—made them implemented by the French instead of being caused by French colonization."

"Yes, immolations have long been a tool of the Vietnamese," Philco responded. "Suicide for Buddhists is not an act of personal despair. It's a collective and honorable means of proving virtue and demonstrating the guilt of a more powerful opponent—in this case Diem's government. Buddhist priests are passive until there's a flashpoint."

Flashpoint? That was the clarion call in her first talk with Buddhist monks. "Why that monk ... was he chosen because he was old or sick?"

"I'm sure he volunteered and was chosen from several willing," Philco replied."*Thien*," Linnea uttered a word she thought she'd never use.

"Yes. That's it." Philco examined her face. "*Thien*—their incredible strength to master the inner self and make the will implacable."

Little by little, Linnea became aware that Vietnamese passing were giving them a wide berth. She wondered if they would be assaulted, anger transferring pain onto them to blame.

"That old monk reached for *satori* and I guess he made it," Linnea sighed, "*Chính Nghĩa* ... a just cause."

"Yeah," Philco exhaled.

They sat together for a while without talking.

Eventually Philco came up onto wobbly legs and flat feet to say he was going back to the villa to change. "Will you come along with me?"

"No, I'll go bck to the USAID office to be with Stephen," she said, thinking it sounded odd, for he might not be there, but at the dentist's or some other damned place, with someone else, for some other damned reason.

Linnea paused at the top of the office stairs in the doorway. Stephen's back was to her, his shirt glued to his skin, outlining the deep curvature of strong muscles lining his spine. He leaned over the new slate colored 5-foot tall AP wire printer, his hands pressing down on either side, with the AP bell, dull and insistent, ringing that a bulletin was coming through.

My goodness, she thought. Browne has already reported and the story has gone to New York and is transmitted back! She came up to read over his shoulder:

"AP June 11. Thich Quang Duc, a 77-year-old Buddhist prelate, immolated himself today in downtown Saigon. It is reported he wanted to express to the world the plight of Buddhists under the government of South Vietnam President Ngo Dinh Diem. The Buddhist act of protest follows the firing upon and killing of Buddhist civilians in Hue in May by troops loyal to the Diem government."

Stephen headed heavily in the direction of his desk.

He had barely inspected her streaked face, she realized. She followed him, though, and sat close, inhaling the familiar smell his sweat made as it mixed with the good threads of his pale coral colored cotton oxford. As close as she could be without touching him, she stared at the strong muscles in his tanned forearm, tapping away.

But he had locked himself into his emotional core, his jawbone standing out white against the tan of his cheek as he typed, stopped, looked out the window, and, as though reading something there, typed hard and fast some more.

What is so important for you to be writing right now? Linnea wanted to scream.

When his right forefinger made a final stab at the keys, Linnea said, "Stephen, I have a feeling something even more terrible is going to happen very soon."

"That's what I'm afraid of," he said, turning to her. Blood vessels pulsed at his temples. He took her hands. "There are things I haven't been able to tell you. I've been working hard;

lots of us have been, for stability—stability to enable growth. I've been trying to...." He shook his head, loosening a dark brown lock over his forehead. "Anyway, I sincerely regret your anger at me. But, frustration is no reason to go off on a complete tangent, on your own, making suppositions that can be wrong." His eyes pointed over her head to the folder on her desk.

Linnea flushed but she was ready. "I think we share basic beliefs, like that it's right we're here to help," she said. "But we disagree on means versus ends—how means, the Hmong opium, can have very bad effects long-term. That's what my research is about. I'm not trying to undermine you or to point the finger at anyone other than Nhu. I'm just trying to understand the situation here so that both America and South Vietnam can have good, proud futures."

She got up and headed for her desk. Behind her she heard him say, "The atmosphere here is so damned stultifying it makes it difficult to make much sense of anything at all."

Leaving the office soon after, they heard the bell of the Xa Loi Pagoda tolling mournfully from its concrete tower. Throughout Saigon small crowds on street corners gazed at the cloud-filled sky. Finally, with curiosity getting the better of her, Linnea asked what people were looking up at. Several women with tears streaking their cheeks answered:

"The face of Buddha is up there in the clouds weeping."

CHAPTER XX

As though trying to cleanse itself of the immolation, Saigon dripped with sweat from June heat, humidity and tensions. Periodic torrents from Stephen made Linnea, unwilling to fly away, head for cover.

Although it was strange to yearn for the countryside where insurgency steamed in pockets of the landscape, Linnea needed the nourishment in the ageless countryside—barefoot farmers hanging onto plows in deep mud behind pairs of shiny black water buffalo with horns slanting backwards like motion sidings on a roadster; or long parallel lines of neatly furrowed land against a backdrop of purple mountains with white clouds streaking high in an endlessly blue sky.

The people were the reason she had come to Vietnam, and she had stayed because of them and Clarissa's father, who said he needed her reflections a bit longer. Another reason was Stephen.

With a feeling of responsibility to Stephen and USAID, but with the Hmong produce project in abeyance due to security issues, Linnea focused on farmers, first stopping by the Saigon Operations Missions office on Ngo Thoi Nhiem Street for information before heading out. Money and effort had gone into making the headquarters impressive. When she asked about the matter of a small bridge, clearly the Missions' responsibility, the staff wanted to discuss "industrialization" and "material requisitions and disbursements," terms totally inappropriate for present-day South Vietnam, she wanted them to know.

Once out of Saigon, Linnea and Vinh headed for where Office of Rural Affairs men were living in the thatched roofed communities they were advising. The villages were in the centers of wide, well-farmed yellow and green landscapes. The Vietnamese-fluent ORA men were tall and seemed like Pied Pipers, with children following them wherever they went. In the shade inside a lean-to, one ruddy Rural Affairs guy provided details about well and windmill construction, the pumps and generators in working order, and the success in composting sites. He praised the International Volunteer Service and the Community Development Advisors who were providing carpentry tools, school and health kits, and pedal sewing machines. Importantly, he described "incipient democracy."

"The villagers have been so happy they've been cooking up a storm in our honor—stews with a few things I wouldn't want my grandmother ever to know about," he guffawed.

Linnea chuckled with a few eating challenge memories of her own.

Traveling on into Phu Yen Province, she found progress in pigs—the Pig Corn Program, that is. Pigs that had been provided by aid agencies got sick because Vietnamese by habit cooked the corn for pigs to eat. American pigs didn't like cooked corn, wouldn't eat it, and became ill. A few died before farmers accepted that corn be left in its natural state. When the pigs ate, fattened up, and began to procreate, the farmers rejoiced. With a taste of business, including loans, the farmers of Phu Yen learned to help themselves, the IVS advisor reported, making enough to prepare for the next year.

Adding a few statistics to her notebook in the jeep heading home, Linnea said to Vinh, "I'm really impressed by all the good things that are happening."

"May not last long," Vinh seemed to grumble.

Back in her room in the villa, when Stephen came in to get some pamphlets from his desk, Linnea paused from organizing her notes to say she had had "clarifying experiences in the hinterland" that she wished to share with him. He kept up what he was doing, but it seemed to her he might be listening.

"I never imagined knowing animal husbandry," she said with a lilt, describing the IVS and ORA programs dealing with the four-footed and the miraculous Pig Corn Program. "And about Strategic Hamlets," she said slowly and distinctly, "a few of them are working out and even electing officers, you'll be glad to know."

Thumbing quickly through her notebook, "The Kien Hoa Hamlet. This Vinh Ngoc Chau identifies competent Vietnamese for various positions, like for the local security forces. The villagers know that they can and should defend themselves against the Viet Cong when ARVN troops aren't around, and they're even being successful at it, I was told."

"Incidentally," Stephen began as though to join her upbeat report, "a VC officer's diary that came into our hands stated he felt the chances of the VC 'liberating the South' are only five percent when the people are healthy, prosperous and willing to fight back. He evidently was referring to hamlets in Quang Ngai, and that's given me hope."

Not wishing to dampen the mood, Linnea agreed there was progress but went ahead with mentioning that the heads of most hamlets are Diem appointees—the same elite who oppressed the villagers in earlier days.

"Diem knows that, Linnea! He's trying! Diem's National School of Administration will soon graduate of a whole new corps of civil servants."

"I hope not too late. The villagers need help. They resent the ARVN because they fail to show up in time, or not at all." She got up to come over to Stephen. They'd been talking "normally," that is, superficially, like treading water. After his review of her "evidence," nothing truly significant had been said, leading her to feel inconsequential. She feared she was losing him—losing his respect. "It's good when we can talk," she said. "I'm with you, you know."

*   *   *

On July 4th, as they walked to the American Ambassador's residence, Linnea wondered if she might be mellowing.

Reams of red, white and blue bunting and balloons festively topped the entry gate's spires, a rather ostentatious, even tacky display, in Linnea's opinion, but, to her surprise, a nostalgic lump developed in her throat. After all, America, as the primary thwart to the communist threat of worldwide domination, maybe deserved to toot its own horn—particularly in Vietnam, where, as Stephen often repeated, America had to be credible.

As though stating America's faith in openness, the gates of the ambassadorial enclave were spread wide welcoming diplomats of many nationalities in colorful native garb. The wives of Indian diplomats exuded regal stateliness, floating through the entrance in shimmering saris, burnishing the walkway and the event with luster.

"Do all these diplomatic families actually live here?" Linnea asked. "I've never seen so many, not even in the fanciest shops."

"Neighboring countries' envoys and families fly in for the occasion."

Smoothing out her dress, a mint-colored sleeveless sheath she had had copied from a photo of Jacqueline Kennedy, Linnea noticed the white-suited, broad-shouldered Vietnamese military men getting out of big Buicks with wide smiles and eager handshakes. Their medal-loaded chests accentuated their shortened frames. Some of their women wore heavy jewelry-decorated *ao dais*, while others wore Dior-style tulip-skirted silk dresses.

Stephen gave her his arm as they reached a crisply attired, square-jawed Marine at attention. Only recently had she learned that Marine Embassy Guards were not the sons of the politically well connected in safe assignments, but members of the most difficult-to-get-into and survive elite unit. To be mischievous, Linnea bent down to try to see eyes totally shaded by an extremely low-slung black patent leather visor.

Crossing into a large garden of palms and locust trees filled with little American flags, Linnea asked, "Are our embassy Fourth of the July parties everywhere like this?" She viewed waves of Vietnamese waiters in white with white cotton gloves offering guests slender chilled mugs of beer and, on silver trays, cocktail hot dogs on toothpicks with tiny glass cups of mustard and ketchup for dunking.

"This one here today could be special to express the importance of Vietnam." With glasses down the bridge of his nose, Stephen scanned earlier arrivals and headed her to the receiving line. "We need to pay our respects."

A cluster of older backcombed, beehived, and hair lacquered American women in full skirts contrasted with the elegance of others, especially the trim Vietnamese. Then a tall man with a healthy head of blond-gray hair and a matching clipped brush mustache caught and held Linnea's attention.

"Well, what do you know?" Stephen said about the man on whom her eyes were glued. "Edward Lansdale."

"What? Lansdale—quiet and ugly American? Why, he's neither! He's distinguished." Beneath his high forehead, hazel eyes radiated warmth to those solicitously surrounding him. His assured demeanor seemed totally appropriate for what Linnea knew of his philosophy and achievements.

"Funny Bunny, before you fall head over heels, remember that he's controversial—an advertising man, then military and finally a spook with antics so damned unique as to be ludicrous. He's reported to have given military officers cooking up a coup against Diem such a well-lubricated trip to Manila that they were incapable of returning."

"I rather like that!" she laughed.

"I thought you would. To his credit, Lansdale orchestrated how Magsaysay could lick the communist Huks and become the Philippine president. But you knew that."

Watching the legend, Linnea began to realize how much his thinking had contributed to her own views. She wanted to hear him now and to talk with him, if possible. But she and Stephen were two couples away from being received, and Linnea's focus had to shift to Deputy Ambassador William Trueheart about to offer his hand. His tanned face, boyishly thick hair, and flash of prominent white teeth reminded her of President Kennedy.

"We're with USAID, Mr. Ambassador," Stephen said, giving their names.

"Good for you," Trueheart said, pumping away with the right hand and clasping Stephen's upper arm with his left and moving them along. "Good you're with us," he said with a smile ready for the next in line. "Glad you could come" and "Good you're here" echoed.

Out of earshot, Linnea asked, "What's Trueheart like? Is he any good?"

"He thinks he is. It was Trueheart who pressured Diem finally into creating a committee to investigate the Buddhist deaths in Hue," Stephen said. "But the way Trueheart spoke to Diem is said to have been arrogance personified."

"Why isn't Ambassador Nolting greeting us?"

"He's sailing a sloop in the Mediterranean, supposedly on vacation. Nolting failed to put the ambassadorship—the State Department—above Intelligence and the military here, as it's supposed to be, so he's in the doghouse." Nolting was made Ambassador, Stephen continued, because he had no ties, knowledge or interest in Vietnam—better than his predecessor Durbrow who didn't get along with Diem and just let Lansdale run things.

"Then now enters arrogant Trueheart?" she asked, wishing Stephen would move faster toward the group around Lansdale.

"Nope. Kennedy's political thinking makes Henry Cabot Lodge the next ambassador."

"A Republican? Well, aren't you glad about a fellow Brahmin? When does he arrive?"

"The first of August. Remember: the Cabots speak only to the Lodges and the Lodges speak only to God. Since Lodge is none too smart, he'll need God's help dealing with Diem and, especially, with the dangerous maneuvers of Saigon's CIA factions."

"CIA factions?" She gulped. Until now, she'd felt relieved to discharge the evidence of Nhu's nefarious dealings.

Conscious of Linnea's forward press toward Lansdale, and whispered that Kennedy wanted to make Lansdale ambassador to Vietnam, but the Pentagon's McNamara opposed Lansdale because of his Agency connection and the Agency's fiasco in the Bay of Pigs. "Anyway," Stephen said, "mavericks like you and Lansdale sometimes have worthwhile ideas."

Helping her edge into the Lansdale-centered group, in a low voice Stephen said, "I don't have to tell you that many of the guys around us are Intelligence."

Without moving her head, Linnea's eyes searched for the face of the CIA man she'd met with. But attention rested on the short, stocky, leathery-faced man speaking to Lansdale in French-accented English. A strong v-wedge hairline descending into bushy eyebrows arching over eyes the color of ball bearings, making him memorable.

"You heard, *je presume*," Lucien Conein said to Lansdale, "that Madame Nhu called the burning monks 'barbecues' and said next time she'd supply the matches. Really nice people, your friends the Nhus." He twirled the contents of his glass in the hand missing two fingers, as though their absence attested to heroism.

Lansdale responded to Conein with collegial familiarity, "Luigi, you've been closer with the brothers than anyone. You must know they need to be separated." He paused. "That shouldn't mean the abandonment of Diem, however. If we treat Diem decently, accord him dignity, our influence can be regained in a healthy way and progress will be made."

"Okay," said a tall man almost Lansdale's 6'2" height standing close, "but, when we try to pressure Diem into getting rid of Brother Nhu and Madame Nhu, we get a long a monologue followed by vindictiveness. Diem may be morally good, but he adheres to the devils Nhu."

"Diem and Nhu are inextricably yoked, just like JFK with Brother Bobby," concurred a man in deep shadows at the periphery.

Lansdale admonished, "Luigi, the alternatives to Diem, the Vietnamese generals you're dealing with...."

"Oh, you observed my little session over there with our friends," Lucien Conein said with a crooked smile, acknowledging with a nod General Vinh Van Don and a group of Vietnamese military in a clutch in a far corner of the lawn.

Lansdale cautioned, "Vinh Van Don and the other generals cooking up a coup with you will only make matters worse. Do they know how to run a government? Not one bit. Are they doing a good job fighting the VC? Not at all! South Vietnam is on the defensive when it should be on the offensive." His eyes went from one face to another, stifling responses.

Lansdale resumed. "South Vietnam needs to win the people first; that's the only way a country can defeat a communist people's war. And South Vietnam needs to employ civil activity just like the communists, but do a better job at it. Believe me, friendship is more effective than firepower, and killing Viet Cong is less of an answer than building up a nation."

Linnea squeezed Stephen's arm her concurrence.

Lucien Conein answered, "If the Vietnamese people here and in the countryside don't support Diem, how can anything develop?" Conein paused to emphasize that Diem had gone too far. "Diem told his generals—the ones loyal to him—to hold back, not to fight. He doesn't want them getting messed up when he may need them to fight later, against another coup. And he's rewarded them with promotions! No. Diem's got to go."

"General Lansdale, Sir," said a straight-backed man with shaved sideburns and an oval crown of hair. "You've been away from Vietnam. There are ghost battles that magically become victories, with enemy body counts multiplying tenfold as they move up the command chain."

"Just remember one simple thing!" Lansdale intoned. "The North Vietnamese and the VC are the enemy, not Diem.

The only way to succeed is to know the enemy, its thoughts, strategies, tactics, and goals." Standing tall, Lansdale's blue gray eyes penetrated. "If the Diem regime is shattered, the dogs of war will be unleashed."

Stephen pulled Linnea's arm. "Come on! Let's see the fireworks over there."

"No, I want to hear more!" She tried to dig in her heels.

"But your hero Halberstam is speaking."

"Lansdale is my hero!" She gave him as angry a frown as she ever had.

"You can swoon over Lansdale later." Stephen pulled her along saying she needed to hear what the great *New York Times* man has to say, face to face with General Harkins.

"Halberstam isn't smart to be at loggerheads with the military. See that woman facing him? She's Brigadier General Richard Stilwell's wife and she's confronting the epitome of the enemy in her and her husband's eyes."

"You're not married are you?" Alice Stilwell tossed the question up at David Halberstam with her rosebud pink print dress shaking in rage.

Looking down with bemusement at the short, angry lady, Halberstam shook his head.

"You don't have children, do you?" she asked with a swagger. Her gloved hand went up against a possible reply. "If you did, you'd look at this war differently."

The bespectacled Halberstam took a long, slow moment to look around at the assemblage under the trees. "Mrs. Stilwell, your man President Diem does not have children. If he did, do you think we would have the benefit of an improvement in his views and actions?"

Alice Stilwell frowned, dithered, and stalked back to a gaggle of military wives.

"A reaction you'd care to share?" Stephen asked escorting Linnea off to the side with the message an obligatory toast was about to take place to the representative of the host country. Acting out frustration, Linnea snatched from a passing tray a bubbling hollow-stemmed flute of champagne and turned to find where Lansdale had moved.

Deputy Ambassador Trueheart raised his glass and started a flowery toast to the Diem representative when a loud, deep voice came from the center of an assemblage on the lawn.

"We'll never drink to that son of a bitch!" The fury in voices in unison came from a collection of correspondents around Halberstam with glasses clutched to their chests.

A hush became followed by quick swishes of chatter like fast sweeping brooms.

Linnea finished her champagne and was confused. Was ire directed solely at Diem's representative? Or were correspondents' assaults also on the Ambassador's deputy Trueheart for arrogance toward Diem?

"Oh, my," Stephen whispered. "Salt on wounds! The Fourth Estate will come under even heavier fire for that one, and deservedly, cannot you agree?"

"The journalists shouldn't have said that," Linnea concurred as he headed her away.

"But, 'Nea, dear. Correspondents are authority figures, especially when they're from New York! And please don't forget that on June 16, Halberstam's *New York Times* had the G-D audacity in its editorial to declare Diem unfit for his responsibilities."

"I didn't know that," came her sullen reply with a mental note to check it out. But she had something more urgent to do. Glancing back, she scanned the Intelligence men around Lansdale for the CIA man she'd passed the information that could kill her.

*　　*　　*

After a frantic morning trying to track down Hugh to learn what he knew about CIA enclaves, Linnea started plodding back to the USAID villa. En route, she witnessed what at first she thought was a mere scuffle.

"You were right," she said out of breath when she arrived at the villa and found Stephen at his desk in her room. "Correspondents are in big trouble. Halberstam, Sheehan,

Browne, Arnett and several others were severely hassled by the Vietnamese police today."

"Yes," Stephen replied in a tired voice, turning. "Things got out of hand."

Presuming Philco had told him, she rushed on, too excited for a simple Stephen dismissal. With as much calm as she could manage, Linnea described how the tall Halberstam with long arms probably saved the others from what could have been very bad, with men killed. The Vietnamese police must have been given the green light to go after reporters, she said, going to her rattan chair and plopping down. "Mal Browne and Peter Arnett are threatened with arrest! The U.S. and Diem must be in collusion about going after journalists … and some of us. And while the Diem regime self-destructs, we…."

"We're here to see that that doesn't happen," he said without much steam.

After a few moments catching her breath, "Did you know nightclubs are to be closed, and that the bars permitted to stay open will have waitresses wearing dentist assistant type tunics?"

"And I suppose you learned that little tidbit in the library."

"No," she snapped. "Everyone's talking about it. It's Madame Nhu's 'traditional values' program again, banning abortions, contraceptives, boxing matches, and beauty contests. You want to know why she's against divorce? To prevent her sister Le Chi, with a French lover, from divorcing her wealthy Vietnamese husband whose enormous riches will be denied Madame Nhu and her husband."

"Now, you didn't get all that in the library either, did you?" he asked with an edge.

"As you've kept saying, this place is a jungle of rumors and intrigue and just my cup of tea!" She examined her twisting hands, seeking barely developed patience. "You need to know it's not a rumor that the Saigonese feel they've lost control of their destinies … due to us."

The silence that followed seemed to shout for her to say more. "I fear," she began and stopped. It would mean nothing to Stephen that she feared she'd given the Nhu material to the wrong CIA man. He'd been angry about her notes and translations, and particularly about where she'd spent her time and energies. But the Nhu information hadn't seemed to surprise him, it now dawned. Why not? Did he know more than it appeared about what was going on?

"I fear," she finally began again, "there's substance in the latest coup talk. Know what it is? The Diem regime's fortune teller has been bribed by General Tran Van Don to prophesy that Diem will be prominent in a new government—with, of course, Tran Van Don as President."

Stephen rubbed his temples. "Either your sources are damned good or your ears are the size of an elephant's."

*   *   *

The next morning, at breakfast, Philco reported that the *Stars and Stripes* and the Armed Forces Radio announced a military victory in the Camau Peninsula where 90 Viet Cong were killed in a skirmish with only three government soldiers dead.

Throughout the day, the Camau Peninsula exercise became a hot topic, including in the poetry session that Linnea attended that afternoon. The recitations were simple and lovely. In a discussion afterwards she heard it said that the Viet Cong permitted the ARVN Camau Peninsula victory to give Diem and the Americans a false sense of security and optimism.

Linnea was at the door of the poetry gathering, starting to leave, when she heard behind her the voice of a professor she knew: "Americans have come to teach us how to fight a war they say they wouldn't have to be involved in except for our weaknesses. *Alors*, they've started this war, bringing new gadgets coupled with old French thinking."

"It's wrong to blame America for everything," she turned back to say to him, *"Thật là một điều khôi hài và hoàn toàn không thể hiểu được.* "That kind of thinking is ludicrous."

In need of a good conversation with an IVS person or other American in the USIS library, she headed for it. Deep in thought, walking slowly, she began to feel she was being followed. She turned and glimpsed a pair of Vietnamese men in shiny black pants and dark glasses dart behind a fruit cart, pretending to be selecting papaya.

Linnea hurried on, hoping she'd remember an alley shortcut. The streets and sidewalks were their usual mishmash of charcoal fires with milling adults and children of all ages, making it difficult to proceed quickly in any direction. The men were closing in, the black slits of their eyes locked onto her. Lurching towards her, they hit a cart piled high with reed baskets and wooden kitchen items, causing everything to roll off, making the pursuers hop about as though jumping through tires in a military training exercise.

Linnea ran full out into one of central Saigon's winding dirt alleys with dozens of kids kneeling in circles playing with marbles. As fast as she could, she weaved through them, careful not to disturb the games or the adults leaning against walls smoking and chatting. Almost at the end, she heard loud shouts erupt behind her. The men bursting through the alley scattered the kids' marbles, causing parents to spring into action with brooms and sticks.

Linnea had entered the back entrance of the huge Ben Thanh market with hundreds of stalls on several long, wide aisles, selling everything from meats and vegetables to garments, guns and gems. Keeping her head down and gradually relaxing without hearing any disturbance behind her, she zigzagged toward the opening at the far side. Out of the corner of her eye she caught sight of a deep green, purple and black silk patch with a gray elephant beneath a sign "Burma," the Orwellian land of intended travels. As her fingers traced the padded appliqué, a camera flash blinded her. A *Mat Vu* man with broken teeth laughed hysterically before ambling away.

Shaking, awash in sweat, her vision of the Burmese handicraft blurred with tears.

*　　　*　　　*

Safely back in the USAID villa, Linnea greeted Stephen in the downstairs hallway with as nonchalant a tone as she could manage, "I just heard the Diem's government has proclaimed the Buddhist pagodas bordellos with obscene pictures where virgins are despoiled."

"Yes," he said in a tired tone. "And there've been more immolations."

"What? When?" she asked.

Yesterday, August 5th, Stephen said, when a seventeen-year-old monk did it in Huong Tra province. "And then today, when a twenty-year-old monk did it in Saigon. Anti-suicide police squads and soldiers will be roaming the city with fire extinguishers from now on."

"Is that a joke?" Linnea pressed.

"Does it sound like one?"

"This place is going downhill fast, Stephen. Surely you know that!" Linnea headed upstairs, thinking now is the time to go. She had accomplished nothing—nothing for USAID in the hills. What had she been accomplishing in letters to Clarissa? Nothing, unless it was a record of a situation quickly deteriorating. She didn't even have the energy to pursue suspicions about U.S. involvement in the opium business.

A while later, sitting in her chair behind the screen with Stephen working at his desk, she decided to tell him about a talk she'd had with an American scholar in the USIS library. Clearing her throat, she said, "The man I'm talking about is fluent in Vietnamese, and with long relationships with students, professors and writers here. He says his friends have been abducted in the middle of the night, with no further word. A couple of our own visiting professors have been detained by Nhu's people just as they were about to leave for the States."

"I'm sorry to hear that," Stephen said with much steam.

"Things have changed, Stephen. The situation here isn't good at all," she said, close to telling him she was on the verge of leaving. "And Diem must be worried, too. Concertina wire has gone up in the bougainvillea around the presidential palace."

Stephen snapped up with loud scrape from his chair to come to stand over her. "And you saw or heard about it? You weren't down there, were you?"

"No. No, Philco told me," she said, slumping down in her chair.

Stephen looked like he suspected her of lying. "Nhu's thirteen secret police outfits are out and about looking for something to do. They don't even know each other, so they may not be the bumbling *Mat Vu* that you describe pursuing you."

Her mind clicked: If the men after her were Nhu's *Mat Vu*, does that mean Nhu knows what she passed to the CIA man? Or could pursuers be gangsters with Bay Vien? Or Corsicans in Nhu's opium trade? Or a maverick CIA group?

Ignoring sounds coming from outside, she asked, "Could the outfits on the streets be part of an American Intelligence organization, like Binoculars in the villa next to us?"

Any answer was overwhelmed by Susan's loud yell, "Horny bastards!" It came from where she was taking the sun in the front patio, and probably accompanied with a fist at the black object protruding from the upper window of the next-door villa. "You never nod or even speak when face-to-face on the street. Instead you pompously sit up there with your binoculars spying on us. Haven't you shit heads figured out we're on the same side?"

Leaving Linnea at the window looking down, Stephen muttered, "Susan should be careful about antagonizing without knowing whom she's up against. Security outfits may be in the drivers' seats right now."

A week later, Susan and Linnea planned to find out whether Binoculars was a cardboard prop or a human wearing black against a dark background to appear ghostly. Giggling and stumbling, they tried to carry a pitcher of lemonade laced with gin, a camera, a tiny table and tape recorder, and a folding chair that didn't want to unfold, into their tree-studded courtyard. Susan was swathed in layers of diaphanous silks of every color of the rainbow.

"Only mad dogs and Englishmen, eh," Susan yelled up at Binoculars' window. "Well, we're Americans, same as you, except better, you noodle."

Susan's advanced announcement had USAID staff members at the villa dining room windows, including a couple of delighted tourist friends.

Susan clicked on Stephen's new book-sized cassette player, borrowed by Linnea, for a tape to spew its sibilant sounds of enticement. Susan began a slow motion weave, her pelvis hitching up for muscles in her well-fed abdomen to undulate.

Susan's fingers, hands and arms waved in surprising elasticity, with her pink painted toenails also in the mood. As she twisted and whirled, dropping a silk sheathe now and then, it seemed like a ransom of spangles jingled from wrists with a sparkling jewel rising and falling like a blinking light in her ample belly button.

Linnea glanced up at Binoculars, snapped a few frames, and sat back sipping, waiting for Binoculars to go splat onto the ground.

Yells from the dining room indicated appreciation by a particularly ecstatic visitor who gurgled like he was deep in his cups. Behind him Linnea glimpsed Stephen edging away, probably for a telephone. Loud voices flowed from the villa window with male bodies leaning out toward Susan who, at music's end, proudly stood straight and still with barely a single stitch.

Following strenuous handclaps after repeated performances, Susan arched her back and spread her arms, first up at Binoculars with a middle finger salute, then around to the street where a few startled Vietnamese stood dumbstruck.

"Well?" Susan later asked. "Did you get a picture? A he or a she?"

"Pictures, yes," Linnea replied, "but I couldn't tell. Definitely human, though."

*   *   *

Ten days later, following a painful exchange with Hugh about the CIA and the possibility she had given information to an opposing internal intelligence element, as though to conciliate, Hugh headed Linnea to Diem's Alternative Palace for an interview with the president.

Scurrying along a street in a luxurious neighborhood, Hugh remarked, "President Diem wants some good words written about him. The best I could do was to arrange for us to sit in on the interview by a favorable journalist, the *Herald Tribune's* Marguerite Higgins."

"I looked up your newspaper articles in the USIS library over the past decade. You've written flattering pieces on President Diem about what he did for the farmers—land distribution, tax exemption, irrigation, seeds and credits. Your articles were positive and expressed hope."

"Poor man," Hugh replied, describing Diem as thinking of himself as a messiah, but without a message. After the last coup attempt, Hugh said, Diem turned inward and handed over almost total power to Nhu. Diem is aware some American Intelligence people are talking with his foes, so he's not only angry but the poor man's probably paranoid—and dangerous as hell.

"Won't you be asking questions?"

"It's Marguerite's turn. I'll greet him warmly and I'll behave respectfully, as always. But I think he misinterpreted some of my constructive comments and may consider me part of the angry mob." Out of breath, Hugh rumbled to a stop. Taking out his handkerchief to mop his dripping face, he complained, "Stop walking so fast! We're likely to be in there for hours."

When they resumed, Hugh continued, "Diem's bright and will have a lot to say—in fact, it'll be a monologue in French, the language in which he thinks, speaks and writes with basically only a working knowledge of Vietnamese. His Cambodian servants and bodyguards may be standing around and...."

"Cambodian?" Linnea asked.

"Trust, I suppose," Hugh replied, again trying to catch his breath. "Incidentally, if you have an allergy to cigarette smoke, you'd better sit by a window—Diem chain-smokes. If there's a crisis brewing or his senior ministers are urgently waiting, wanting to interrupt, he won't be rushed and will go right on smoking and talking. Maybe it won't be as bad today. He has something he evidently wants to convey."

Marguerite Higgins was already at the entrance to the Alternative Palace. In her forties, wearing a light cotton jacket over a tan linen skirt, she looked confidently professional.

The three were ushered into a room with a high ceiling decorated completely in white and gold. Chairs with brocade-covered seats were French. Air flowed from vents in window casements, difficult to determine if actually cool or only imagined. In a corner, a large stand-up fan whirled and slowly turned from side to side. And from a door behind it on the side to the right came President Ngo Dinh Diem.

The President was far shorter and nicer looking than Linnea expected. His black hair with its straight part stood out against the white, alabaster-look of his skin. The shoulders of his gleaming cream-colored double-breasted sharkskin suit sported an abundance of padding, giving him an almost round appearance.

After warmly greeting Marguerite with both hands, he shook hands with Hugh, saying a word or two in French to which Hugh smiled appreciatively. His handshake with Linnea was soft and perfunctory. Diem nodded and the three sat in chairs arranged in a semi-circle facing him. When the

President took his seat, his shiny black shoes barely touched the floor.

Linnea saw Marguerite write "Diem: August 7, 1963" in her notebook. President Diem's dark brown eyes lit up with earnestness as he began responding to her gentle, careful questions.

"I know that some Americans try to tarnish me by calling me a Mandarin ... I am proud of being a Mandarin ... It may not be similar to anything you Americans have experienced—our Mandarin-Confucian system: stability, central control, respect for authority and order. It has merits and an inner democracy ... We want to tap the roots of our Confucian tradition...."

In spite of herself, after a while, Linnea occasionally found herself nodding.

"What am I to think of the American government...? Am I merely a puppet on Washington's string? ... If you order Vietnam around like a puppet on a string, how will you be different ... from the French? I hope ... that your government will take a realistic look at these young generals plotting to take my place. I am afraid there are no George Washingtons among our military ... The West must give us a little time ... The spiritual basis of democracy is to be found everywhere in Vietnam, and especially in our villages, and we are building democracy there ... Gradually, when the conflict ends, we can move to greater democracy on a national level ... But it is impossible, a delusion, to think that a solution for Asia consists in blindly copying the West."

*   *   *

Several hours later, back on the street, Linnea said, "I'm very grateful to you and Marguerite. Diem is certainly long-winded, as you said, but he isn't weak or sinister the way I'd thought. President Diem seems to care deeply about South Vietnam. I liked how he expressed how much he wants to save the people and the culture. I think he may be right to resist Western ... well, American dictates. Diem should have the chance for a different kind of government." With a sigh she added, "Nations shouldn't have to be—and, frankly, cannot be—carbon copies of the U.S."

"I like the way you see things in this sad and tragic time," Hugh said, "and also that you've stuck around."

"The primary antagonism to Diem is really because of his damned brother Nhu." A response wasn't needed, but when nothing came forth Linnea added, "Something interesting about Madame Nhu is that she and her daughter were prisoners of the Viet Cong for four months and barely survived. Do you think that could explain her?"

Hugh laughed. "Do you think Diem's family experience of his brothers' horrible deaths by the Viet Cong contributes to the way he is? That memory may have made him unlikely to change or to come to any kind of agreement, particularly about Brother Nhu."

CHAPTER XXI

Looking up from Hugh's table in Brodard's two weeks later, Linnea could see Neil Sheehan coming up looking extremely tired. Remembering his UPI office at 19 Ngo Duc Ke had a glass storefront that could easily be bombed, she asked him, "Where do you do your work now? In your upstairs cubbyhole?"

Shaking his head, Sheehan exploded, "This place is insane! That G-D would-be politician Pham Huy Co and his grenade-throwing campaign—he should be strung up. His grenades with thousands of little pro-Co and anti-Diem leaflets inside—they're low-powered bombs! 'Not dangerous with merely a loud noise!' Ha! Mal Browne's AP messenger just now nearly had his pants blown off. We're not even getting hazardous duty pay, damn it."

Journalist friends at near-by tables concurred with clinking beer mugs. Several practically in unison said: "Bars are bugged, phones are tapped, stories are delayed or destroyed—the place is going to hell."

Sheehan focused on Stephen as though with something on his mind. "And then there's the hit list. My name, Halberstam's and others are on the South Vietnam government hit list."

"You have it?" Stephen asked. "Where did you get it?"

"Australian correspondent Denis Warner," he replied, handing over the purloined copy.

Blood drained from Linnea's face. She could be on it, and Stephen, too—because of her.

Handing it back, Stephen shook his head that neither of their names was included.

As Sheehan folded the page into his back pocket, he muttered, "President Diem says he wants us all out of here. And there's a rumor he's going to declare martial law tomorrow, August 20ᵗʰ." He gave a quick glance at his watch and hurried off.

*   *   *

August 20 began hot, moist, and electric with rumors. To prevent Linnea from venturing out on her own, Stephen escorted her, Susan and Kevin in the jeep to the USAID office, passing ARVN soldiers with fixed bayonets on every street corner. In silent amazement, they witnessed government policemen wielding Billy clubs and rifle butts at a small gathering of young boys in an alley.

Behind the closed office doors, they all talked at once.

"Are the soldiers to protect Saigon against the Viet Cong," Kevin asked, "or to protect President Diem and his family from angry Saigonese—like the Buddhists?"

"The soldiers are posted on the streets to guard against some of our Special Forces and Intelligence guys, I think," Susan said, "easily as frustrated with the Diem government as the Vietnamese."

"The situation's ripe," agreed Philco, already in the office when they arrived. "Brother Nhu has pronounced 'the Buddhists are reds in yellow robes plotting a coup d'etat.' That should have indicated there'd be trouble. Reports are rampant about arrests without reason."

Linnea tried to read Stephen's face looking at her. She wondered if he was hearing what she'd been telling him for some time. Wishing not to jump on the bandwagon, she nevertheless said, "The Vietnamese say their private chats are being taped by Nhu's secret police. They also say there are assassinations all over Saigon."

Stephen went to his desk. As Philco, Susan, Kevin and Linnea resumed sharing what they imagined was going on,

Stephen was seen to lean deeply onto his elbows, his head in his hands.

By nightfall, exhausted by tension, most of the USAID team was back at the villa deep in sleep, comfortable that hired guards were at the front and in the garden in back. But, so quietly did motorized military vehicles enter the outskirts of the city that no one was the wiser.

Shortly after midnight, hundreds of Vietnamese armed soldiers and Combat Police moved in on Saigon's main Buddhist pagoda, Xa Loi, and many other temples. Tanks and armored cars took positions at the major intersections. But trigger-happy troops roiled in confusion, not understanding why their CIA-trained roles of being defensive against VC sappers and terrorists had been changed into being offensive against they-didn't-know-who or what.

The well-coordinated action had been arranged to look like a military response to a Buddhist coup d'etat, it was reported later in a summary of the night. The Combat Police commanded by Nhu's Colonel Le Quang Tung smashed the pagodas, killed an untold number of monks, nuns and students, and dragged off and arrested more than 1,400 Buddhists. The Buddhist priest Tri Quang managed to escape over the Xa Loi pagoda walls and through a window into the USAID office. At daybreak, a "shoot to kill curfew" was announced, to be from 9 a.m. to 5 p.m.

Coming down to the breakfast gathering, Philco made the announcement that Vietnamese soldiers were on every main avenue and intersection, standing ready at the trigger of their oversized American rifles. "Jeeps mounted with .30 caliber machine guns are cruising up and down Rue Catinat," he said, "moving on to Ngo Duc Ke and Rue Pasteur. Tanks and war machines are all over the place."

Everyone sat silently looking at each other.

Philco went back upstairs and returned, angrier than anyone had seen him. The phones aren't working; the equipment is completely down, he complained. Just before that happened, he said, he'd learned the American Embassy lines were being cut, and Tan Son Nhut Airport was declared closed to all commercial traffic.

Susan was the first to recover from shock with a question: "Then, Saigon is cut off from the outside world! Steve, it's a good thing you got the guards. Can they shoot?"

A loud plop came from something landing on the gravel entryway outside. Everyone dropped to the floor, under the table, covering heads with their arms. They waited. Finally it was Stephen who, bending low, crept up to the front door and opened it. The guard had picked up the folded *Times of Vietnam* and was leaning against the wall looking over the front page. It headlined that the CIA planned a coup and was responsible for the necessity of ARVN soldiers and war instruments in Saigon's streets.

*   *   *

Several mornings later, again at breakfast, Philco reported that Ambassador Nolting's replacement, Henry Cabot Lodge, had arrived, and that street activities essentially had ceased. Without comment, he read a news report: "six foot three, with blue eyes and gray hair clipped back over the ears, with a look of confidence from under a jaunty straw hat, he carries himself like a seasoned statesman." In a somber tone Philco said the question remains whether Lodge has it in him to pressure President Diem into persuading his brother Nhu and sister-in-law to leave the country. "Lodge actually cabled Kennedy, embassy employees have told me, that Nhu was responsible for the deadly raids on the Buddhists," Philco said.

"Why, that's great!" Linnea said. "Someone's figuring things out!"

"Yes," Stephen groused, saying that in spite of the exigencies of diplomacy, Lodge didn't present his credentials, and then, when he did, he told Diem that if there were no reforms, the U.S. might support dissident generals. "And you're not going to like this, Linnea, but one American at that palace meeting analyzed the session as 'Our old mandarin whipping Saigon's old mandarin.'"

"God, Stephen. We're now to make Diem kowtow!"

As August inched its way to its end, Stephen commanded Linnea to stay put. "No matter what! No visits for any reason to anyone, anywhere, you hear me!"

Linnea remained in the villa while Stephen and Philco scurried back and forth to the office for news and, particularly, to handle an in-house matter: the monk Tri Quang, who had climbed over a wall and into the USAID office, had to be transferred in disguise to the American embassy where he became a refugee instead of the Vietnamese military's prisoner. Stephen reported the procedure as though the news would please her.

It did, and Linnea stayed put, glad to catch up through Susan's magazines on what was happening in the United States: Negro sit-ins, Freedom Riders, the National Guard escorting colored students to classes, and a horrible Ku Klux Klan killing in Mississippi. Every publication carried photographs of the Washington Mall Tidal Pool packed with two hundred thousand Negroes and Caucasians, along with the printed address of the Reverend Martin Luther King, Jr. A close-up showed the pained and purposeful face of a man who wanted to "stir the social conscience of the nation," as he eloquently affirmed.

Linnea wished she could know President Kennedy's reaction to the huge assemblage within sight of the White House. She imagined he recognized the Gandhian-like non-violence and the eloquence of the Reverend King. But it began to seep into her mind that the president might conjoin the Diem/Buddhist situation with Southern governors and Blacks—as Negroes henceforth should be called, she gleaned from a magazine.

"California?" Philco said at her bedroom door days later, carrying another pile of books he wouldn't be taking home. "What did you think of *Another Country?*"

"The author's photo on the dust jacket put me off," she admitted, taking books from the top of his armload. "James

Baldwin looks so very angry. If I hadn't lived in New York and Baldwin hadn't been a New Yorker, I might not have picked his book. He's extremely good."

Philco settled into one of her rattan chairs. "You know, the better thinkers and writers are said to be in the Boston-New York-D.C. corridor. But Bret Harte, Jack London, Bill Saroyan, and John Steinbeck are Westerner writers, and so are the new guys Kenneth Patchen, Ken Kesey and the California transplant Jack Kerouac. They're good and will probably last."

"Oh, yes, Kerouac," Linnea theatrically swooned. "He was at Kepler's—our local bookstore—and the most dazzlingly handsome man I'd seen! He recited from *On the Road* that we were all reading. An incredible experience," she said, remembering the evening on the warped, bare wood floor in Kepler's hot, book-packed back room.

"'Speeders across the sky,'" Philco said. "Kerouac, the jazz musician with words."

Linnea nodded. "Sunshine through fog," she quoted a San Francisco review.

"You see how fortunate you've been, California. Are you sure you didn't migrate to the wrong coast? There's more beat in you than you know."

"I knew Stewart Brand of The Merry Pranksters," she brightly said.

"I didn't," Philco replied, without knowing where that came from.

"At graduation I asked Stewart if the reason I wasn't in the campus 'in' group was because I didn't volunteer in LSD research, like Ken Kesey, or use the weed. You know what he said? 'It's never too late!'"

Philco laughed along with her. "Getting back to Kerouac, I hope his work doesn't suggest that drugs are essential for creativity." Philco took a minute or two as though to let his message sink in. "Incidentally, you must read *Howl* by Allen Ginsberg."

"The Saigonese poets I've gotten to know are Ginsberg fans," she responded. "I understand he's coming here. I'd never heard of Ginsberg before they mentioned him."

"Ginsberg expresses rage with tenderness and hope—a bit like you. He's writing some of the most meaningful ideas of our time, I think."

"I'll miss you very much, Philco."

"I'm not leaving quite yet!"

*   *   *

Dear Clarissa,

... Rumors swirl that President Diem receives greetings from Ho Chi Minh. It is speculated their correspondence has increased after we denied Diem's government the ability to supervise South Vietnam's own war funds. Our threats to withdraw due to Diem's failures militarily and democratically may be a bit unfair since it's Diem's brother Nhu who is at fault (meeting with Ho's representative through the French Ambassador, with the assistance of Polish ICC member Maneli). Nhu's activities can cause problems for us a long time hence.

Diem is within his sovereign rights to explore and perhaps negotiate with another government (even one the U.S. doesn't like), in my opinion. But I believe in talk, dialogue, diplomacy, and I wonder if it might be for the good of the people of Vietnam (and us) for reunification to be explored. (Stephen says my thinking is treasonous!) The Vietnamese really don't want us here.

You asked if I'm glad I came to Saigon. Yes. What I've been asked to look into has helped me grow and to learn about myself.

You and your Dad are family to me, and I'm very grateful.

With much love and a warm hug,
8/30/63   Linnea

Linnea finished penning the letter in her bedroom. Pensive with a sense of foreboding, she was about to jot a postscript about Stephen when he rushed in. While catching his breath with a handkerchief swab of his face, Linnea slid her letter under a book and pulled out a photograph of people in the American South having to march between arms-toting angry officers.

"American Blacks and Vietnamese Buddhists have guts, don't they?" she said.

"Guts may not be the right word, My Love. Guts means a single moment, a mindless, reflex response. Courage, on the other hand, requires reasoning and awareness of possible negative consequences."

"Thank you," Linnea replied with a smirk and a shake of the head.

Stephen pulled her up. "You do trust me, don't you?"

"Well," she said breathlessly, wondering what his complaint might be now.

"All right. Don't answer that. Linnea, we need to get ready."

She sat up with a cheery, "To leave?"

"President Kennedy sent word on a special communications channel of a possible bloodbath in Saigon—coups and counter coups—during which the Viet Cong could sneak into the city. With the situation confused, it could be a disaster for the whole kit and caboodle."

Linnea blinked. Very recent days had been peaceful. But once again she felt yanked around, up and down like on a seesaw.

"Five thousand noncombatants are to be extracted at any moment—that includes us. The Marines in Okinawa are on immediate alert, as are helicopter assault ships, attack transports and destroyers. It's serious, I'm afraid."

Linnea's eyes went to the armoire.

"Just essentials—toothbrush, nightie, and whatever," he said with raised eyebrows in the expression that in the past could make her smile. "Everyone who's here is doing the same."

Once they'd packed their shoulder-strapped satchels they waited, with Stephen and Philco going back and forth downtown, sharing information and answering questions.

After a very quiet dinner with the relatively few villa-mates in residence, followed by a tense night and early morning, Philco, who had been out gathering news on foot, reported that they were to remain on call and keep their bags packed. "The emergency has abated because a coup no longer seems imminent."

An uneasy calm prevailed. Linnea spent time reading, including newsmagazines she sometimes read aloud to Stephen at his desk. One day she read to him an article stating that Paul Kattenburg, who had just been in South Vietnam, believes the U.S. should get out of Vietnam honorably. "Does that mean after success or regardless?"

"Good question," Stephen replied with resignation and not a word further.

"Another report quotes McNamara as saying, 'The United States is winning.' But Vice President Johnson says, 'We need to prosecute the war vigorously.' A little confusing, no? What war? I wonder what happened to Mansfield's less than optimistic report."

Stephen shook his head. "I don't know. JFK said at one point he wonders if anyone can beat the communists. Sometimes I see your point that an all-out military victory may not be the issue or a good aim."

Linnea again uttered that President Kennedy should bring back General Lansdale, regardless of what others wanted. Lansdale understands the Vietnamese people, she said. "Kindness can be more effective than firepower is what we heard Lansdale say," and with a change of voice, "That is, if there aren't constant threats of a coup emanating from our very own embassy."

"My dear, 'Nea. Remember: that's treasonous!" He sounded tired.

"Cannot the talk of a coup by the agents of a sovereign country against an allied sovereign nation also be considered treason?" she whispered

Philco's electronic expertise became essential to the frequently house bound villa inmates. After bringing the transmission lines back into working order, he could capture on the radio transmitter/receiver the sounds of live television broadcasts in the United States. He announced that on September 3rd (September 2nd in the United States), the CBS Evening News' fatherly anchorman, Walter Cronkite, would grant young President John F. Kennedy the opportunity to demonstrate global authority by discussing the Vietnam situation. The interview would take place at his vacation home in Hyannisport, Massachusetts.

"You all need to keep in mind what Kennedy said when he was still a junior senator," Philco said, reveling in his role as a master of ceremonies to USAID colleagues settling into his equipment packed room. "'No amount of American military assistance in Indochina can conquer an enemy that is everywhere and at the same time nowhere—an enemy of the people that has the sympathy and covert support of the people.'"

"Kennedy said that?" someone grumbled. "Then why are we here?"

Before anyone else could speak, Philco adjusted the sound and intoned, "Fatherly Cronkite is granting young upstart Kennedy an opportunity to demonstrate global authority. I'm sure JFK will be asked if Vietnam is merely a proving ground for Western forces against the communists," Philco finished just as Cronkite's lead-in began.

"Mister President," Cronkite said. *"France's Charles de Gaulle has proposed a neutral, reunited Vietnam. What is your response to this?"*

"The United States rejects any such proposal that will lead to withdrawal until the communist menace is eliminated," President Kennedy answered. *"We are committed to Vietnam, but Saigon's repressive actions against Buddhists are very unwise. Unless a greater effort is made by the Diem government to win popular support, the war cannot be prosecuted effectively. With changes in policy, and perhaps with personnel, I think it can. If it doesn't make those changes, I would think that the chances of winning will not be very good."*

The interview proceeded into domestic matters before returning to Vietnam.

"Is there sufficient time for the government of South Vietnam to make changes, to be more responsive?" Cronkite asked.

There is time, or has been, Kennedy seemed to say. *"In the final analysis, it is their war. They are the ones who have to win it or lose it. We can help them, we can give them equipment, we can send our men out there as advisors, but they have to win it, the people of Vietnam, against the communists ... All we can do is help, and we are making it very clear ... but I don't agree with those who say we should withdraw. That would be a mistake."*

And then President Kennedy seemed to contradict himself. *"The Vietnam situation is being reevaluated and it will depend on whether South Vietnam's President can reform politically and banish his family from the government."*

When the interview concluded, Martin, the non-political fish expert, sitting on the floor front and center, asked, "Do changes apply to Diem, or just his family? I'm confused."

"Whoopee! Action at last," political expert Kevin chimed in.

"Reevaluation is what Kennedy said," quiet Jamie concluded. "What do you think JFK meant? The Diem regime or America's entire presence and commitment to South Vietnam?"

Kennedy meant he's committed to Diem and South Vietnam without Nhu in the regime, Linnea felt pretty sure. The purpose of the U.S. being in South Vietnam is to help the people. So, will the work of USAID and other outfits continue if the U.S. military pulls out? Would aid workers have security? Confronting communist insurrection, though, means the military.

A newly arrived young USAID staffer said, "I think Kennedy wants to support the false statistics and pie-in-the-sky attitudes of Generals Taylor and Harkins."

"Withdrawal is what I think Kennedy's getting at," Martin said.

"Doesn't anyone remember what the then Senator Kennedy stated in 1954?" Philco loudly interceded. "He said that it'd be futile and self-destructive to pour money, material and men into the jungles of Indochina without at least a remote possibility of success."

"The Special Forces the President supports and the outfits that focus on Edward Lansdale's hearts and minds are being successful," Linnea said, then, focusing on her fiddling fingers, "The interview puzzles me. It seems contradictory." She hooked eyes with Stephen.

As though prompted Stephen said, "A career naval officer told me that in Kennedy's address last year at the Academy he alleged that the days of big battles are over, that a new strategy is needed to address subversives and insurgents, instead of conventional combat tactics."

"I wonder if the military heard that?" Kevin remarked

"Kennedy's not contradictory," Susan said. "He's just in a bind. He can't hint he'll pull out when he's made all those statements about being the vanguard of freedom against communism."

"Kennedy is primarily a political animal," Jamie responded. "He has doves and hawks to worry about, so what he's probably doing is thinking about re-election next year and throwing out a morsel to both."

"Yeah," Kevin snapped. "And that'll solve everything."

"Maybe he wants to have his cake and eat it, too," Martin said. "Kennedy's a bit on the shallow side, you know."

"President Kennedy is not shallow at all," Linnea was quick to counter. "He started the Peace Corps and has supported USAID and NGOs. Good, creative efforts are helping the Vietnamese to help themselves. I hope the president knows the successes here." She glanced at Stephen.

"I feel for JFK," Philco said. "He's going to have to show real leadership." Turning to Stephen, "I've heard brother Nhu is talking with Hanoi again—via French Ambassador Lalouette—supposedly about economic and cultural exchanges. Hanoi evidently told the Diem regime that if South Vietnam has a clash with America or our forces, Nhu can rely on Hanoi's help. What's your take on that?"

Before Stephen could respond, Martin, never known to possess current information, said, "One of the latest of rumors is that the U.S. is going to attack Hanoi."

"Not a bad idea," Susan chimed in, "but we should simultaneously bomb Diem's palace."

Linnea and others chuckled.

"Incidentally," Philco resumed with Stephen, "*Le coup du jour?* Diem's *Times of Vietnam* stated the U.S. had planned a coup for August 28th."

"Postponed, canceled or still cooking?" Jamie pressed.

"Yeah," Susan urgently interjected, looking intently at Linnea. "I've heard there's the likelihood of multiple riots in the city and a big VC push to take over all of Saigon. And that we'll all to be evacuated!"

Linnea smiled, but others shook their heads and got up to leave. Stephen chided, "Susan, it was ten days ago. You were in Saigon. You should have heard about it. Where were you?" He got up, taking Linnea with him. "Oh, never mind."

*   *   *

Reports mushroomed of the jailings and murders of Buddhists, but it was news of a suicide that dominated the Vietnamese community, especially poetry meeting aficionados. Nguyen Tuong Tam, the important thinker, activist and poet, poisoned himself in protest over the Diem administration treatment of Buddhists. Tuong Tam's action stunned Linnea's poetess friend Tam who saw to it that Linnea was invited to the memorial service at a temple.

"Your death will always be a bright torch to light the dark path we must tread ... a brilliant mirror in which we who take up pens after you must look at ourselves and reflect," the esteemed poet Nhat Tien eulogized. One by one, mourners in hushed voices bestowed upon Tuong Tam the highest commendation for his sacrificial act. The voice by the scholar-priest Thanh Lang, head of Vietnam PEN, resonated: "Poetry and poets give new significance to life, to death, to the face of a loved one or a rose."

Statements of poets' intentions to play political roles gratified Linnea who wondered if she was witnessing the inaugural moment of a new chapter in South Vietnam's history.

Exiting with the crowd in a slightly elevated spirit, Linnea felt a heavy hand clamp down on the back of her neck, a strong, thick forefinger and thumb preventing her head from turning. "Walk straight ahead!" The voice was American with a New York borough accent. "Keep with the people." When the hand released its grip, something hard pushed into the small of her back, with the statement, "You're a gutsy broad to connect with Bay Vien and to get confirmation of Nhu's activities, but you're stupid because you handed over the evidence *to the wrong person!*"

"What? Why was it wrong?" she cried out. "I was told…."

"A *tay phap* (letter writer) in the central area will have a large stack of purple writing sheets on his table. You look for him. He'll hand a purple page with particulars of a meeting you will attend if you and your friend know best. Now keep going."

With a stiff stride she walked ahead until she realized nothing was against her back any longer. She turned but no American was anywhere in sight. The voice! The airport the first day!

"Where in the hell were you?" Stephen shouted from the front door when she got back to the villa. "Martin and Philco are out there looking for you right now," he said, waving his hand toward the street where the compound gates had been freshly covered with barbed-wired.

"I'm sorry," Linnea responded, heading for the stairs. "I left a message. It was a last minute decision. I wanted to see…." It wasn't the time to explain to him that a famous poet had committed suicide to highlight ire at the Diem regime's treatment of Buddhists.

"*I wanted to see,*" he mimicked, coming up behind her. He caught up when she reached the door of her room. "Well! What did you need to see?" he demanded.

Heading for her area behind the screen, "I was out trying to find out how close the Viet Cong are to particular hill people of mine," she lied. And, in fact, earlier she had been making a map of locations of tribes, not necessarily correlating them with the VC but with areas she suspected of much higher opium production.

"But, why now? What was so important about doing it today?"

"I'm sorry, Stephen. Really I am. The situation here is ... is.... I haven't been able to get out of the city, or out of this place either, and as far as my USAID job goes...."

She was cut off by the loud sounds of sirens and heavy sedans racing past. She surmised by the racket it was made by huge Cadillacs with little American flags flapping on front fenders, probably bringing Marine Corps' General Victor Krulak and the State Department's Joseph Mendenhall on a fact-finding mission. The military will talk with the military that will say that everything's fine, and State will talk to embassy bureaucrats, politicians and intelligence and may report everything's not exactly as hoped for, she mused. And then Kennedy will ask if they've been to the same country, and be more confused, just as she was.

When Stephen returned from the front window, Linnea said, "You know, Kennedy may need your input about successful enterprises with the farmers and what you hope for with the hill people. And you can quote me that the educated of Saigon intend to play greater political roles."

Stephen took the chair opposite hers. "I've told you before that many of the Saigon elite are questionable. Maybe leftist," he added in a care-less voice. Edging his chair closer, he took her hands. "Linnea, your USAID contract is more or less over. Mine, too. If we're lucky, we can have Christmas '63 in the snow."

"That'll be nice!" She replied, but hearing something in his voice she wondered what was up. In the present confusion she hadn't really thought a lot about their future together. Also, she couldn't imagine not being absolutely free to pursue whatever she wanted. "You mean, Stephen, I won't just be your Saigon smoothie?"

"Smoothie? Ha! Hardly!" He leaned back. "Can't you understand? You've got to be careful with everything you say or do, like associating with people of unknown political views, and researching the drug stuff—your opium trail, as you call it. Helping the soldier Jim is one thing but your photographs, documents and interviews, including with my tape recorder—you don't know where it may be leading."

She waited.

"You've got to be careful, even with whatever you write to your friend."

Linnea ceased breathing.

"I love you for being exceptional and for having a truly unique kind of energy," he said, leaning forward to cup her head in his hands. "And I respect your insights and even your reckless courage...."

"But?"

"You're a challenge, and a smooth one, with the silkiest skin imaginable," he said, running his hands down her neck onto her shoulders and bare upper arms as though appreciating them for the first time. He brought her forward, putting his lips to hers. The action was pristine and, at the same time, highly stimulating. In a voice close to a whisper, he said, "I think now's the time to...."

"Yes, yes," she said, acting giddy in the hope that false excitement would forestall something she didn't want to face quite yet, the unfinished business—that Stephen used her with the Hmong—told to promise transportation, when Stephen knew it would be for opium.

"I think since we've argued about everything else now's the time we should argue about coasts. The Pacific, which may be climactically comfortable—without seasons, contrast or substance—or the Atlantic where it's sometimes too hot or too cold but always friendly and definitely culturally and intellectually enlightening."

She hugged him, her head to the side. "Are you sure that's what we want?" The New York AP and Washington, D.C., had been objectives hard to let go.

"I can't let a laughing lover loose into the world," Stephen said, pulling her up.

CHAPTER XXII

The next morning, heading downstairs, Linnea and Stephen met up with Philco, obviously happy with how he'd been able to rectify and expand the electronics network.

"I guess you know McNamara and General Taylor were just here. 'Great progress in the war' they reported," he said with patent sarcasm.

"Did Ambassador Lodge stop napping long enough to talk with them?" Stephen asked.

"You know," Philco said to each of them, "I'm really glad I'm leaving. I don't like what's going on here. Some of our people imagine a Maginot Line against which to throw American troops, and I've again heard talk about using nuclear weapons." He paused to continue in a softer voice, "CIA Station Chief John Richardson has been close to Nhu and Diem and is headed home. Do you think his departure is a signal?"

Linnea saw a shadow move below the staircase, presumably only Duong or one of her girls.

"You're as bad as the rest, Philco, listening to rumors and thinking you've divined what's about to happen," Stephen answered, his tone consonant with Philco's.

Dining room conversation meandered with frustration. At one point, Susan said, "Steve, I understand Madame Nhu will soon depart for our U.S. of A. Will she be received as a head of state? After all, she's been running this place."

Giving Madame Nhu an invitation is a good idea, Linnea reflected, and she'd mention it to Clarissa. If the White House would receive Madame Nhu, her husband would go along with her. In that next letter, Linnea would mention something good about the Dragon Lady, such as that during the 1960 coup attempt, with Diem and Nhu hunkered down in a Palace bunker, Madame Nhu was the one who called two military leaders to the rescue.

"The rotten things Madame Nhu's said about Diem, indecisive weakling though he is, should have had her strung up," Kevin inserted.

"Well, Steve?" Susan asked, using the abbreviation that rankled Linnea more than ever.

Stephen answered in deadpan that Madame Nhu is not a head of state, so she wouldn't receive a White House reception. Additionally, she'd receive no help from her father Vinh Van Chuong who had just resigned as Ambassador to the U.S. over the tactics of his daughter and her husband.

"Still," Linnea submitted, "a suggestion of a White House invitation to Madame Nhu and husband could achieve the separation of Nhu from his brother Diem that's wanted."

Back upstairs, Stephen worked for a few minutes straightening up and locking his filing cabinet. "I think I need to pay another visit to the dentist's. I'm going to take you with me—not inside, of course. You can look at junk/antique shops and then we may cruise around for a piano. I don't want you away from me or off doing your own thing at this time. Okay?"

"Okay," she said. "Some dentist—no need and no after-effects, unless what you all are cooking up produces more pain in this mess."

In an area of small merchant shops at the edge of downtown, Linnea watched Stephen ascend rickety stairs above a pale sign in English: Dentistry. Finding the neighborhood new to her, Linnea kept an eye out for male salesmen indicating a Chinese shop with collectables or possibly fronting a den. A woman running a store would mean it was Vietnamese, merchandizing a degrading activity, worthy of second-class females.

The faces of passing Vietnamese seemed to express something that hadn't occurred before, that she was American, and "America supports Diem." She tried to reassure herself that the Vietnamese men with button-down collars were going about their businesses as usual, without any particular notice of her Western face.

Linnea caught a glimpse of a large collection of school children in uniforms of white shirts and dark-blue slacks or skirts coming around a corner, and stopped to watch them. Her girls' school required uniforms, eliminating clothes competition and stimulating dreams she could achieve in a man's world, she mused. And look where that's gotten me, she laughed at herself as she moseyed along.

Chanting called attention to a crowd of high school students coming into the street carrying hand-painted placards in Vietnamese and English: "Ngo Dinh Diem lost the trust of the people"; "Free Speech without Fear"; "If we cannot read the past, we will repeat it." Rhythmic chanting increased, drawing Linnea to follow them as they headed down the avenue.

Several students became aware she was going along with them, and slowed. One tall young man with alert eyes said, "Our fathers are military officers who have been loyal to Diem for years. But, men who were just corporals, lackeys to the French, are now Diem's generals. Our fathers have not been rewarded for being loyal."

"And for not being liars," a student near-by asserted, while the boy at his side yelled, "Or cowards! We will let the government know. We are protesting for our fathers' sakes."

"One of your placards paraphrases Santayana," Linnea said to the tall student. "'Those not knowing the past are destined to repeat it.' What history you are not permitted to study?"

"The war with France!" voices answered almost in unison.

"What? Why would that be forbidden?"

"Probably because the Diem government is French in many ways and is sorry or ashamed France failed and was thrown out."

The students began to move faster to catch up with the ones in the lead, Linnea going along with them. "What else are you protesting?"

Any answer was drowned out by the sound of heavy boots pounding the pavement. Vietnamese soldiers in green-brown exploded from side streets, chasing the students. Personnel carriers rolled forward, their machinery clanking harsh echoes.

Everything went into slow motion. The weaponless teenagers swarmed together, conferring with darting eyes, clutching each other. Uniformed police with drawn guns rushed at the older students standing stubbornly in place with arms crossed. A few of the younger and smaller kids started to bolt but were grabbed and held by their peers.

Linnea stood aghast with the children looking at her with questioning, pleading eyes.

Being pushed by the butt of a gun, the taller student yelled at her, "Today it's high school students. Next it'll be junior high students. Then it'll be our younger brothers and sisters in elementary school."

Running to catch up to the student being led away, she shouted, "What can I do?"

But, if the student heard, it was too late. A hand clamped down on the back of her neck. An electric ping hit her heart.

"I told you to stay near-by," Stephen bellowed.

Linnea struggled to catch her breath, twisting around to face him.

"Do you know where you are?" he yelled. "You must be six to eight blocks from where I told you to be. If it hadn't been for this protest, which I finally figured you'd get mixed up in, I'd never have found you. Haven't I pounded it into you enough times that Saigon is dangerous right now?"

"Stephen," she sputtered, pointing behind her. "Those are young high school students. They're ARVN officers' children who were only marching and now they're being taken away.

Look!" she shrieked at the youngsters being yanked and harshly pushed into trucks like rag dolls.

"Come on," Stephen angrily said with a vice-like grip to her upper arm. "We need to get out of here."

Stephen quickstepped Linnea away, and whenever she tried to turn around to see about the students being packed into vans, he pushed her forward.

"I thought I was being protective, taking you with me, warning you, watching out for you."

"Stephen...."

"Listen to me. I love you, dammit. Has it ever occurred to you that you cause me real pain? I came downstairs and expected I'd find you somewhere near—and if not on the street, at least in shops. I went in every one of them looking for you."

"Stephen," she pleaded, jumping ahead, walking backwards with hands on his chest to slow him down.

With a slight change in his voice, "Earlier I feared you've been meeting someone." His eyes were sad in a way never seen before. "I even had you followed a while back," his voice cracked in a bitter half laugh, "one tracker tracking behind a line of other trackers." He shook his head. "Can't you understand?" His voice dropped, "And about your opium trail, opium has been here for hundreds of years. The only thing new is the Americans who may use it."

"Yes, exactly: to forget being here. I don't think you see what's happening. Our new bureaucrats confront those of us who know the language and culture and are making progress. They resent us! It's like someone is maneuvering things, like opium production, creating a conflict that could be worse than what we're in now."

"Listen to me! Understand! We can't do anything about what is a Vietnamese problem, needed to be handled by Vietnamese."

She stopped. Her head fell back. She stared up at the sky until the sounds of scurrying feet returned her to the streets where frantic-faced parents were running toward where the students were still being loaded. Her heart went out to them, imagining the horrible night they were going to have trying to get their children out of jail.

"I forgot to ask," Linnea ground out the words with each step she was forced to take. "How were things at the dentist?"

"What?" Stephen asked, his eyes sharp in every direction.

"Your session at the dentist's. No problems, unless whatever you and your friends are drilling for creates more pain—in fact, agony!"

Stephen tightened his grip to her arm.

Eventually they came from a dark side street into the gaudy area close to Rue Catinat where the smells of rancid cooking oil and the harsh calls of hawkers now seemed welcome. And so was American slang issuing from a larger number of newly brazen soldiers tracking Vietnamese women in skin-tight *ao dais*.

They passed a *tay phap* letter writer sitting behind a square board on which brightly colored papers curled at the corners. In the center was a large stack of purple sheets under a rock. Linnea's eyes met the *tay phap* man before scanning for whatever could identify the place later.

Inside Brodard's, Stephen took Linnea to the large, round corner table where Hugh was performing like a managing editor with a new bunch of green stringers. Pulling out a chair to put Linnea next to Hugh, Stephen immediately left to head to someone at the bar.

As soon as Hugh was free she exploded: "There must have been 800 students! I learned from one of them that they're children of Diem loyalists. If that's true, and I'm sure it is, why were they arrested? That's not good thinking."

Hugh laughed. "As you know, Linnea, the Diem regime continues to assassinate itself. In the words of Graham Greene, Diem is a patriot ruined by the West. He idolizes the past, doesn't comprehend the present, and is unaware how to care for the future."

A stringer ran up, talked rapidly, listened intently to Hugh, and took off.

Maybe it's not as over as it appears, Linnea had been thinking. The West can make a change by giving Diem new advisors. If the U.S. thinks of itself as a patron, and from what Tam showed in Frost's inaugural poem it does, then America has a responsibility—politically, culturally, historically.

Linnea's musings produced a wee smile that became enhanced by *Time Magazine's* Charley Mohr belting out a bitter refrain with the names of Madame Nhu, her husband Nhu, President Diem, General Harkins, and any other that rhymed to give spice to his song.

"Mohr over there," Hugh said, "is singing his heart out, probably for the last time. His piece about Saigon's goons and spies and white mice policemen became another article his *Time* editors refused to print. He evidently roiled them with, 'Vietnam is a graveyard of lost hopes, destroyed vanities, glib promises and good intentions.' Personally, I think that's good prose. Anyway, *Time* is now shelling its troops. Mohr may be about to receive the cable that he's fired, but it'll be too late; he's already quit."

When Stephen returned, Hugh said, "I have something to tell you."

"And I've got something to tell you," Stephen replied in a low voice. "A Foreign Service officer just told me our Chancery is about to be burned with an attempt made on the Ambassador's life."

Linnea and Hugh searched Stephen's face; he was serious.

"Well, things are definitely looking up," Hugh said almost happily. "What I wanted to tell you—and I reserve judgment on whether this isn't just as important—is that the AP's Mal Browne and his New Zealand photographer Peter Arnett are about to be arrested."

Linnea and Stephen scanned the room.

"They're not here," Hugh said. "They don't want to be too easy for the *Mat Vu* to find. Diem's police might as well arrest us all. The latest is that for the next two weeks we won't be able to get any stories out. Martial law is due to begin again, either tonight or tomorrow."

"'Nea, I have work yet to do this evening. Shall we?"

As she began to rise, a powerful explosion threw her down. "God!" she shrieked, folding under the table.

"That felt close—definitely closer than the Chancery," Hugh said.

"What do you think?" Stephen shouted into Hugh's face. "Should we wait for a *plastique* to be thrown in here and try to catch it, or should we ascertain the severity of the Viet Cong's latest calling card?" Flames bounced off Brodard's windows and mirrors.

"Stephen," Hugh answered with practiced calm. "The Viet Cong will never hit a foreign press hangout. They think we're on their side, as told by our very own authorities." Rising, fully energized, he proclaimed, "It's time to show we're on the job."

Linnea stayed close behind Stephen and Hugh edging toward the fire. A dozen Americans in khaki lay on both sides, propped against walls, stunned and blankly staring. Wounded and crying Vietnamese males and females, from deep inside the bombsite, their clothes bloody and in shreds, struggled to drag themselves away from the wreckage. Behind them flames crackled from the cabaret that looked like it had been opened with a serrated sword. Bodies strewn over the sidewalk were buoyant, as though they might get up and walk away. But blood seeped darkly into the cement beneath them.

Stephen and Hugh moved about, speaking to the wounded, helping with a dangling arm, putting pressure on a gaping wound. Sirens screamed. Military Police vans honked their way onto the street, discharging MPs who, for a second, stared at the devastation on a street known for laid-back joy.

Edging forward, following wherever Stephen and Hugh moved, she expected they'd tell her how to assist. She had to watch her step. The explosion had blown out the windows, doors and metal awnings of shops, depositing radio parts, broken perfume bottles, and bolts of filmy silk to eerily flutter in the debris. Small fires replaced the lights of downed electricity.

In the flickering light, Linnea stepped hesitantly around broken glass. She bent to see something glittering. A gold chain with ruby-red stones sparkled on an ankle above red sequined platform high-heeled shoes. Upright, it looked like a plastic manikin. Looking closer, the amber-colored calf had a few red nicks. The knee was ripped and in flaps, with white bones and tendons and black blood like parts of a spent firecracker. The lithe young go-go dancer, trying to make a living for her family!

The Viet Cong didn't have to do this, Linnea's mind screamed. It's like the village we came upon after the Frenchman's—school children hysterical, pointing to the severed heads of their teachers with eyes open and mouths frozen with a final instruction. So cruel! And so is Madame Nhu who didn't want music or cabarets or even laughter. This is as much her doing as the Viet Cong's.

Wildly screaming and crying out, she eventually was clutched to Stephen's chest. He brushed at wet clumps of hair clotted on her hysterical face and gently rocked her back and forth.

Leaving Hugh to continue as best he could, Stephen carried Linnea past Brodard's and the Majestic to the dock and the inky black Saigon River. He held her at the edge where she retched and heaved until it seemed she tasted her own blood. After a while, Stephen lifted her into a taxi for a jolting ride back to their villa sanctuary.

In September, when Linnea saw and heard Nhu's Cong Hoa Youth Group march through Saigon like Hitler's *KristalNacht*, shouting threats against anti-government activity, fear overwhelmed her. When she learned that journalists were changing the places they slept each night, communicating by courier, she wondered how far in the rear she should be in the USAID villa.

When the Cong Hoa were heard as far away as the USAID compound, those who could leave the city to do so on quickly remembered or suddenly designed assignments.

"Whether or not you're angry with me," Stephen soon said, "isn't it time for us to experience accommodations at the Continental Hotel?" They checked in, but after only one night moved to the Majestic from which they took day trips up the Saigon River, out of Saigon.

$$*\qquad*\qquad*$$

Dear Clarissa,

Thanks so much for remembering my birthday. It reached me today, on The day, and at a time when Saigon is succeeding in becoming a mess.

....

Diem is good and moral, and he could be a strong leader in an insurgency, if he had good advisors such as Lansdale. But he needs to be separated from Nhu. The need is urgent, even if it may initially be difficult for Diem to function without his brother—a relationship close like JFK and RFK.

With regard to our support of the South Vietnamese regime, I cannot understand why our government continues to give Nhu funds for his secret police and private military forces when it's known that by Nhu's command Colonel Le Quang Tung stormed the Buddhist pagodas and killed and jailed monks, nuns, students and even bystanders.

A Gandhi saying resonates: "What you do is inconsequential, but not to do anything is consequential." *Saigon's intellectuals, the poets I've told you about, are motivated to participate in politics. They are important to the future here, if they are not jailed or killed or don't become exiles.*

Hurriedly, with love and a hug,
10/6/63   Linnea

CHAPTER XXIII

In the afternoon in late October, curled up in her chair, totally absorbed in reading *To Kill a Mockingbird*, Linnea became startled by the way Stephen rushed in.

"Listen, Linnea. I've got to go downtown this afternoon. I want you with me. I don't trust the safety of the villa anymore."

"You don't think the guards and the fence make it safe?"

"The barbed wire advertises that Americans live here. Any one of those bicycles or cycles on the street could have someone with a tube packed with *plastique* to hurl in here. It'll be better if you're with me. And," Stephen added, "you're going to stay where I tell you."

"Saigon is increasingly spooky," Linnea said after they were left off in an uneasy crowd around the Majestic and started walking up Rue Catinat. "Imagine that the Buddhist monk Tri Quang still has to be a refugee in our embassy! It's not a good situation, is it?" She waited a few seconds and then slowed to fall behind to squeeze Stephen's narrow waist and push her head between his arm and his side. "Boo!" she said. "Are you there?"

"'Nea, what's the matter? Why give me trouble? You think I don't know what's going on, that I'm not aware of undercurrents!"

"It's just that when something's on your mind, you close down. Completely." She got back beside him and mimicked his long strides. "You're so damned distant sometimes."

Stephen draped his arm across her shoulder. "My Dear 'Nea, I've been pretending to be a nonchalant French *colon* who considers it bad form to be nervous about bombs and grenades blasting Saigon apart." He was referring to the gunfire at the Hoa Lu stadium on Dinh Tien Hoang Street, the bomb dropped on the Presidential Brigade Headquarters, and the Radio Saigon takeover by rebels and the bloody recovery by Diem forces.

"Okay. I'm sorry, Stephen. I'm also sorry to be saying I'm sorry all the time. It's just that I've been watching Saigonese and our people pack up to leave, and it's sad." She didn't have to say again that it was time to leave. "The Special Forces, the IVS and our USAID programs have been effective, and can be more so if they could continue with people with language skills and cultural knowledge. I care about the Vietnamese."

"I know you do. And so do I." Stephen didn't say anything until a block or more later. "You need to know that before you arrived, communists began with the educated, the scholars, the artists and intellectuals. Communists get inside organizations, like poets' groups, to suffocate thinkers and silence society."

"Stephen, the Vietnamese poets are not squelched, and they can make a difference."

Stephen slowed and turned to her. "My Dear Linnea. Please understand what I'm trying to tell you. There's a lot going on. Vietnam may be the tip of an iceberg."

"Oh, Stephen! Vietnam is not *strategically* important."

"As I've said before: Vietnam *isn't* strategically important, and that's its importance." He reminded her to think of a line running from the 38th parallel in Korea, through the Taiwan Straits across the 17th parallel here and down the center of Berlin. Vietnam is the focal point of an ideological struggle, he said, between two sides but involving every nation on earth.

As strongly as she could, Linnea countered that Vietnam's land and people, particularly the hill people, shouldn't be used as a means to an end.

Stephen's eyes panned to the right and left as they neared the bombed out cabaret where the smell of smoke remained heavy. Establishments near the cordoned off area were closed. But, in spite of curfews and martial law, a few nightclubs exploded with neon lights and electric sounds, as though flaunting both Madame Nhu and the Viet Cong.

"Where are we headed?" she asked in a desultory tone.

"The rooftop bar at the Caravelle will be a good place."

"Stephen! Linnea! You have to be off the street." It was Martin, rushing at them. "It's just come across the radio. A 7 p.m. curfew."

"Thanks, Martin," Stephen replied, appearing somewhat relieved and even glad to see him. "We're headed for the Caravelle. Come along."

"Oh, I don't know," Martin said, looking up and down the street. "I guess right now I should hop a cab." A moment later, "It's strange how they all disappear in times like this. Cabs must have radios hooked directly into intelligence systems."

"There'll be cabs at the hotel," Stephen suggested. "And I don't know that our villa is all that safe. Tonight I'd rather be up high out of the way of *plastiques*. Neutralist diplomats live and work in the Caravelle whom neither Diem's government nor the VC will want to get killed."

"Ah. Good point," Martin said. "I've been thinking along those lines, too, of course."

"Good. Then to the Caravelle we go," Stephen said.

They progressed three abreast past the sharp eyes of the gigantic Sikh doorman in his rich red costume, a dagger at his waist and layers of white turban above an upward curled, waxed mustache. The swank lobby glittered with new gold- and silver-colored appointments.

The rooftop lounge was filling up by the time they reached it, requiring them to wait before a table could be set up near the outer perimeter. The skyline had changed from the last time they'd been there. New, tall gray American apartment buildings stuck out in distasteful contrast to the quaint red tile roofs of old two-storied French buildings. The American Chancery and Dinh Doc Lap palace even took an effort to find.

"What time is it?" Stephen asked Martin as they waited.

"You're really something, Stephen. Of all people, you should have a watch. One of these days someone's not going to give you the time of day."

"Okay. Okay. You're right. I do have a watch. A gift from a friend," he said with a stiff wink at Linnea. "I simply forgot to put it on."

Linnea stared at him. Stephen hadn't used the watch in months, presumably because he didn't like jewelry of any kind. Why lie?

"So what's the time," Stephen demanded.

"Almost 7," Martin replied, hiding the face of his watch from the sun.

The menu offered hamburgers, lasagna, omelets, minestrone, quiche and crepes and, in small print at the bottom, Vietnamese *pho,* noodles hot or cold, *bún cha* or *bún thang.*

"Decided?" Stephen asked.

"This place is so non-Vietnamese I might as well have a hamburger," Linnea replied.

"I think I will, too," Martin said.

Stephen signaled the waiter, gave their orders along with his own, lasagna, and ordered a carafe of French wine. Do you want anything for starters?"

"I think I'll have a Johnny Walker Black over ice," Martin replied.

"Me, too," Linnea responded, testing Stephen's reaction to her unusual request.

After giving the order to the waiter, Stephen asked, "Martin, when you heard the radio, what was said?"

"The curfew time, as I told you. Also that a planned coup has been discovered and scrapped, and that Diem's loyalist troops—the best ones he keeps close—have moved tanks into a defensive position on the palace forecourt. Earlier machine-gun fire, the announcer said, was simply a testing of weapons."

"Anything else? Any music or significant background noise?"

"Now that you ask, I remember just before the broadcast cut off there was a barely audible voice in the background saying *cha cha cha*. Very strange: *cha cha cha*."

"Yes." Stephen held Linnea with his eyes as though counting seconds. "I need to do something. I have to go downstairs and make a phone call and I might have to go out, close by. I'll probably return just as my lasagna arrives." Stephen pushed back his chair.

"Sure! You wanted me with you! Then you leave!"

"Listen, I'm not the one who gets out of bed in the middle of the night to walk city streets; asks fool questions of everyone from military officers and pilots to dope dealers and frauds; and pow-wows with killer pirates!"

Air left her lungs with a squeak.

"Okay, 'Nea." Stephen squeezed her shoulder and planted a kiss on the top of her head. "I'll be back soon. Martin, make sure she doesn't leave here. The dinner and drinks are on me."

Linnea's eyes cast down at her lap. When she looked up, she found Martin staring at her.

Eventually they decided to special order a generous supply of Vietnamese appetizers: *tôm khô* dried shrimp, minced beef kebabs and tiny fried spring rolls with lettuce, mint and *nước mắm*. Then, with drinks drained but appetizers unfinished, they ordered a second round.

Linnea broached sailing, their primary mutual interest. "I very much enjoyed our sail—I started to say our blue water sail—but the ocean's now graying over with American navy steel. Why do you take your sloop upriver?"

"Because by boat I can get to places in the interior and see things ... like prehistoric people and old stone monuments. And the sight of a sailboat, canvas up or not, startles the natives into thinking I and my craft are supernatural," he chortled.

"You know," Martin said a couple of hours later, "I've never heard of a woman sailor—who really likes racing. You actually sailed for Stanford?"

"The only female then on the West Coast. Sometime we had to launch boats through the surf. It wasn't easy." She thought of Philco's gift to Martin and her own recollection of yellow streams arching aft over transoms and smiled over recalled events. "Did you sail in the east?"

"No. I heard of a frost bite series, but in freezing storms doing the macho iron men in wooden boats stuff...." He shook his head. "Not for me. And I'm sure there were no females."

Linnea looked behind at the noisy influx of humanity by the elevator. "What are you going to do with your sloop when you leave here?"

"Oh, probably sail out into the South China Sea. More likely over to Malaya—Malaysia, I guess its new name is."

"Alone?"

"I might pick up a crew. People around here migrate or, as they're beginning to do, emigrate. I can pick up someone one place and drop him at another without a problem."

"Men can do things like that," she said peevishly.

"Things are changing," Martin responded. "Hang in there."

His awareness of gender equality issues surprised and delighted her.

"Are you ready for me to bring the food now?" The waiter appeared, mopping his brow, and remained standing, looking over the edge. "What about the other gentleman?"

Martin and Linnea looked at each other. "What gentleman?" Martin raised a nearly empty glass. "Two more of these, please."

The waiter nodded and with reluctance returned to the surge of people without a place to perch.

The sky had turned darkest blue with air weighty with a suggestion of rain.

Linnea and Martin had exhausted anything either one could think of to say or ask.

"What time is it, Martin?"

"You, too? Nine fifteen."

"Man, look at the crowd trying to get in here. It's a good thing we arrived when we did."

Linnea glared at the Western businessmen and a few women searching for a place to sit.

She turned back to the skyline. Tears started to well, even though suspecting Stephen had said what he did out of nervousness about something to do with his work. She rose and, steadying herself, reached for the ledge. She remained until tears subsided. Returning to her seat she asked, "What time is it?"

They both laughed.

"It's now nine-fifty. Believe me, I'm going to do something about this. At the PX there's a great lady's Mickey Mouse watch I'm going to get you—Minnie, I guess it is."

"I'm sorry, Martin, but where can he be?"

All of a sudden the terrace filled with a high pitched, whistling screech, followed by a deep whoosh and a crisp rat-a-tat-tat.

"God! What was that?" Linnea asked Martin at the rail, searching the streets below.

Linnea struggled around the table and chairs, peering over, hunting the source.

"There it is," Martin shouted hard on the heels of the second round of automatic fire, and pointed at flashes of red and white. "My gosh. Look at the people running, and it looks like they're all heading here."

Plopping back down, with her head hanging, Linnea morosely said, "Stephen can't run like the people down there. He sort of lopes—not a run, and not even a terribly fast walk."

"What?"

"Polio. Stephen walks all right, but his left leg is atrophied."

"Well, he's probably just downstairs either waiting for a phone or still talking on one. I suppose you want me to go down and check."

"Yes, please. Would you, Martin?"

321

While Martin was gone, several American men asked if they either could have the two empty chairs or sit with her. The way they examined her made her furious. Before another approached, Linnea fumbled fruitlessly in her mesh bag for the gold bamboo-motif band brought from New York, and put her purse at Stephen's place and tipped Martin's chair into the table.

With her back to rooftop arrivals, Linnea sipped her refill and worked to compose herself. Occasionally someone ran to the balcony edge on either side of the table, searched the source of sporadic gunfire, and, turning, took a good look at her, producing her sour face.

The waiter presented himself, mopping his forehand with a napkin, taking a glance down at the street and stretching his back at the crowd pressing onto the terrace. "Signal when you want your orders, but it may be too late," his voice trailed as he returned slowly to duty.

Linnea scrutinize the dense throng in front of the elevator and made another survey of the streets around the Caravelle.

Excited chatter exploded behind her. Military types who had earlier leered now raucously laughed. She closed her mind to them and even to the racket in the streets below.

Writers were right, she decided. Saigon is hypnotic and magical. But the greatest peace and purity surely are in its past.

"Linnea, look who I've found!"

Linnea remained in a slouch, intending to show Stephen she'd hadn't had thoughts of him. "Oh, Hugh," she smiled, sitting up. "I'm glad to see you. What are you doing here?"

"The same as you," Hugh said, removing her satchel and plunking down into the chair, "trying not to get mowed down by a tank or a machine gun or bombed by a revolutionary on a bicycle, or by all the loose screws rushing pell-mell into here!" He finished out of breath, with an angry glance back at the mob trying to push its way forward.

"When did you ... how long have you been here?" Linnea asked.

"About an hour. Downstairs is a madhouse, and the elevator has so many people trying to squeeze into it you'd think drinks are up here are free."

"When I found Hugh," Martin said, "we covered the lobby as much as we could. You know, it's very possible Stephen is in the hotel in one of the embassies or consulates here and that he's just become absorbed in people or their radios."

Casting about, Hugh tried to signal a frazzled waiter. He then rose to announce, "It'll be easier at the source. I need something stronger than the urine-colored fluid in that carafe," he said of Stephen's recently plunked down order of wine. "Martin? Linnea?"

"Yeah," Martin responded. "A Johnny Walker on the rocks."

"The same," she said with a thick tongue.

"Thatta girl," Hugh said, moving off to the bar, mumbling about the need for a bottle.

"Martin, what do you think has really happened to Stephen? I don't think he's in the hotel. Could he be at the dentist's?" she asked pointedly. "Please tell me."

"Linnea, I would if I had any idea. Stephen's sharp and always knows a little better than the rest of us what's going on. He may have been delayed or prevented from leaving wherever he had to go. A lot of people must be marooned all over Saigon," and, glancing in the direction of the palace, "every rooftop has people. Perhaps Stephen's on one of them trying to signal us."

Linnea examined the shadows made by fires and lanterns, and stood up so that Stephen at least could recognize her scooped neck white blouse, if not the denim skirt onto which she'd sewn squares of Hmong embroidery. She became elated at arms waving until she realized they belonged to a woman. She slumped back down into her chair.

Hugh returned with drinks and small talk with Martin, his eyes on a sullen Linnea.

"Hugh likes lasagna, Linnea, so let's get the dinner into our stomachs. I'm sure Stephen would have wanted it that way," Martin said, rising to find the waiter.

Would have wanted? Past tense, like he's dead? Linnea's wide-open eyes began to fill.

"Sorry. Our waiter had to give our dinners away but will try to get us a new order soon.

Biting her lips, she hid her face in the fresh drink. "Is this a double or a quadruple?"

"Just a double. The bar is jammed," Hugh said. "If liquor runs out that could mean real trouble. I'll try again for a bottle. We may be stuck here a while."

Linnea left her eyes on people milling about on a rooftop, dancing around bonfires as though Indians around campfires. Words and laughter flowed in the heavy atmosphere.

"What's needed up here right now is a band, don't you think?" Hugh said to Linnea.

"No sooner said!" Martin interjected.

A rooftop radio blasted loud American band music followed by Vietnamese. When the music ceased, a voice came on, alternating from Vietnamese to French to English.

"Remain calm. South Vietnam is about to be liberated from misrule."

Rooftop dwellers looked at each other. Then, twist and cha-cha music blared into the night air and coalesced with a cacophony of rooftop radios.

"Madame Nhu banned those pieces," Linnea said. "What's happening? She's out of the country, but the government station still wouldn't play that music." She saw Hugh and Martin's eyes meet. "Well? Why that music?"

Unperturbed, Hugh took a few moments before replying, "I don't know whether it was a rebel station controlled by General Minh or General Don ... or...."

"Or a Viet Cong station," Martin completed the presumed thought.

Oh, God. Where is Stephen? Linnea asked into space.

A good half-hour later Martin said, "In a moment I'll try to go down to the lobby again."

She mulled it over. "Maybe you should wait until I get back from the bathroom. Two of us shouldn't be gone at once or we'll lose our chairs and probably the table."

"Good thinking," Martin said, obviously relieved.

Linnea was in need of the bathroom anyway. Filling the tiny lavatory two heavy-set older American women chatted about what Linnea considered total domestic rot, the sparkle of huge wedding rings blinking "future assured." Linnea waited and, with the arrival of the whirlies, closed her eyes and leaned back.

"Are you not feeling well, dear?" said the woman in a too-tight orange silk Shantung.

Linnea pulled herself off the wall and pointed, "Sweetie, you're next" and the woman mindlessly trundled into the stall.

As the only person in the down elevator, when the door opened she barely squeezed out through a swarm of bodies pushing in. An unruly mob at the registration desk demanded rooms. Souls at the entrance struggled, making it difficult to tell whether the Caravelle's huge Sikh doorman was helping or hindering.

The lobby had so many people that they swayed rather than moved. It seemed that if some were short and some tall and thin, progress might be possible. Also by crawling.

"Eek," screamed a woman's high voice. But males cried, "Dammit," and "What the hell!" sometimes with a stomp or kick.

On all fours, Linnea winced, sucked in her breath, and slithered toward the front door. Through a sea of pant legs, she smelled air from outside, both fresh and acrid. A sudden surge of bodies coming in pushed her backwards. Scrambling, she lowered her head ram-like and plowed ahead. Then, with knees scraped and painful, she had to stop.

Polished brown calfskin shoes connected with sharply creased khaki were in her way.

She moved to the left.

The shoes and pants moved the same way. She sprang to the right to quickly press forward, and the same shoes and pants legs blocked her again. As fast as she could move with legs pressing on all sides, she sprang frog-like to the left. Like a magnet, the khaki-legged nemesis was there, to the right or to the left, back and forth.

Finally, resting back onto haunches, she pounded the toes.

"Can I help you?" Khaki Man's laughing American voice spilled over her.

"Yes. Move along," she said, with a wave of the back of her hand. "I have to find Stephen ... my, my…. He's outside." A surge pushed her back. "I need to get out of here."

"Have you considered the service entrance?" he asked.

"What? No," she said, rising to try to see to the side of the check-in counter.

"I'll help you," Khaki Man said, pulling her up. "Pregnant lady! Pregnant lady about to puke," he shouted, getting her as far as the phones. "Rather than immediately exiting, perhaps first a phone call?"

Linnea wobbled.

Khaki Man propped her against the wall next to the phones.

"Miss. Miss, you can go next," said a short, plump, bald-headed man gaping at her well-equipped attendant and getting out of the way.

"Oh, no. You've been waiting," Linnea said extra sweetly.

"Yes, I have," he said, then glancing at Khaki Man. "Please," and backed off.

Linnea approached the French designers' prissy excuse for a communication instrument and carefully lifted the unnecessarily curving receiver. She gawked at the faces eyeing her and carefully dialed numbers she rarely used.

"*Toi Day.*" ("Here I am,") Linnea said.

"Linneeea. You all right? Sound strange," Duong said.

Lifting her chin to her audience, in Vietnamese she said, *"Từ tiếng Anh sang tiếng Việt. Cám ơn. Tôi khỏe mạnh. Còn Anh thì sao? Stephen có ở đó không?"* "Thank you, Duong. I'm fine. And you? Is Stephen there?" She glanced at Khaki Man looking up to the ceiling.

"No. Susan, Philco and others, all in Philco's room, listening to radio. No Stephen."

Linnea appeared stymied. Finally, "How's everyone?"

"The same. I'm feeding the guards and the *bep's* kids. Many mouths."

"That's nice."

"Not for long!" Duong replied.

"Has there been a phone call from Stephen?"

"No. Yours first. If Stephen calls, what's to say?"

Exactly. "Say? Oh, nothing, I guess." She bit her lip. "Thank you. Well, I guess it's good-bye, Duong," and she put the handle gently into its cradle as though resting an anvil on a basket of eggs. Her eyes smarted.

"Young lady," Khaki Man said. "Where do you need to go?"

"Dammit," Linnea snapped at eyes the khaki color of his pants.

Waiting to join in the next push to the elevators, he asked, "Drinking all day? Or just since curfew?"

"My husb Stephen," she explained, had complained about her, hadn't come back, and there had been gunfire.

"If he's anything like you, no problem." He gave some sort of signal to the people around them and bodies parted for him to pull Linnea onto the elevator.

"Over there," Linnea said. "Our beachhead at the edge."

Guiding her, they wound their way through many more chairs, tables and bodies than it seemed possible the terrace could hold.

Hugh and Martin, startled and speechless, slowly rose.

"Hugh and Martin, this is....", she came close to calling him Khaki Man.

Hugh collected himself and pushed out Linnea's chair in time for Linnea to drop into it. As though programmed, her ankles crossed and her hands folded ladylike onto her lap.

"I take it you're friends and not the young lady's missing husband," he asked, correcting Linnea's bobbing head and sloping body.

"In fact," Martin interjected, "they're not even mar...."

"Now, Martin. They've been busy."

"You and everyone else, always in awe, giving him the damned benefit of the doubt," Martin complained.

"Well then, what is she doing here?" Khaki man asked, again checking her sliding tilt.

"USAID, and that's Stephen's outfit, too," Hugh answered.

"It's Stephen's outfit," Martin testily stated, "and she's his obedient little lackey."

Hugh shook his head. "I don't think so. She has a good mind, she's been researching important things, and she has a future. She's achieved far more in the hills and lowlands than anticipated, and, from what I can tell, understands better than most what's going on here."

"Interesting," he said, correcting her forward pitch. "She's been in the hills?"

"She has a masters in the ethnic groups," Hugh said, appreciating his attention to her.

After aimless talk, Khaki Man gave Martin and Hugh a semi-salute and departed.

"When did Stephen say he'd return?" Hugh asked.

"After blasting her, he said he had a telephone call to make and a short visit somewhere close and would be right back. That was many hours ago," Martin said, glancing at his watch.

"I'm glad I could obtain the bottle," Hugh sighed as he reseated himself. "This is going to be a very long night. Do you have anything you need to do, Martin?"

"Well, I guess not. There's nothing much I can do except stay here," he answered, facing the drooping Linnea as a loud rat-a-tat-tat began below.

Hugh responded, "You're safe here with a bunch of drunken diplomats and, of course, with Linnea and me," seeing her head drift in the direction of her navel. "I think I'll give her my jacket and, with your help, park her under the table. Let's hope this fine drizzle will cool off tempers and whatever else's going on down there." Hugh waved his arm at the edge and the steady collection peering over it.

"And it's very possible nothing's going on," Hugh continued. "Simply a Diem trick—an appeal for sympathy, understanding, and more time. The coup leaders may have cold feet and are undecided whether to launch all-out attacks on the Palace or, more likely, to let things go for another day. Coups are quite taxing, you know."

"More diplomats, correspondents, businessmen and high ranking military and special forces operators are on this balcony right now than I've ever seen assembled at any one place before," Martin said, looking around. "Impressive. And they're talking to each other!"

"Then this is a very good public relations effort that Diem is engineering," Hugh joked.

"Hugh! Listen," Martin said, turning around to the sounds of a radio getting louder. Music abruptly stopped and a man began speaking in Vietnamese. Hugh quickly identified it for surrounding tablemates as General Minh's voice.

"The armed forces have rescued the Vietnamese people from eight years of misrule."

The same announcement was replayed three times before twist and cha-cha music resumed.

Martin asked Hugh, "Well. What do you think of that?"

"A bit premature. Nothing's really happened as far as I can see," Hugh answered.

A massive explosion came from the direction of the palace. Another boom and then a vroom reverberated across the Caravelle terrace. From below, the rumbling of tanks moving on asphalt felt its way into rooftop chairs. Then, filling the sultriness came a voice over a loudspeaker. Sober souls shouted for the increasingly boisterous groups dotting the terrace to stop yammering.

"My loyal troops are racing to defend us. Bless you." Squeakily high in stilted Vietnamese, then in flowing French, came a distant but unmistakable voice. *"You will be rewarded. Bless you."* The utterance sounded desperately light and false in the heavy night air.

Many heads turned to Hugh who quietly confirmed, "President Ngo Dinh Diem."

"What's happening? Will there be fighting? Are we in the line of fire?"

To all questions from surrounding tables, Hugh answered that he didn't know. "But whatever the case, we'll have front row seats," he added with a grin.

Hugh and Martin alternated using the bathroom and watching over the lightly snoring Linnea, her head on Hugh's expansive, expensive white linen jacket under the table.

It was well after the bewitching hour when the terrace assumed a peculiar mixture of tension, fatigue, and happy alcoholic euphoria. Some Caravelle refugees slowly danced, perhaps inspired by the American Chancery roof where exuberant young staffers cavorted around enormous bonfires probably made from reams of paper that someone deemed in need of burning.

At 3:30 in the morning, when many had given up on the development of any real excitement, a single deep thud became followed by silence, suggesting the evening's conclusion.

Then the night sprang alive with a million muzzle flashes in every direction. The deep boom of a 75-millimeter tank gun came from the direction of the palace. From the Caravelle rooftop, the avenues leading to the palace streaked with tracer shots.

A few terrace dwellers raced to balcony edges while others sneaked up to peek over and duck back. The braver souls reported column after column of ARVN airborne troops marching alongside two-dozen armored cars. A rattle of 50-millimeter machine guns stuttered pervasively, impossible to locate, they said. The barrage went on and on, a truly bizarre display for most of those on rooftops who, until now, had never seen military action of any kind before.

"Hugh," Martin shouted at the person calmest of anyone, for it was his third war as a journalist. "Do you think there's a possibility that all those fireworks aren't by the Saigon military? Do you think the Viet Cong might have infiltrated?"

"A possibility, and they'd be very clever and bright if they did so right now. But despite the VC's Fifth Column and extremely good intelligence, I don't think they're quite that well organized ... yet, that is. They might even bring the craziness of this stalemate to an end. If a coup effort to topple Diem is successful whoever Diem's replacement might be, he'll be as much a disaster but in an entirely different way."

In another brief lull, Hugh continued for those close enough to hear his remarks. The Vietnamese nationalists capable of leading Vietnam, he said, were killed either by the French or the communists. Diem survived in American monasteries and cleverly made friends with Cardinal Spellman and then junior Senator Jack Kennedy. So, to suggest to Catholic Kennedy that Catholic Diem be replaced is tantamount to treason. "Therefore, in summation, this bit of confusion could be a false coup."

As he finished, the huge boom of 75-millimeter tank guns shattered Caravelle rooftop dwellers' nerves, and amidst the racket, Linnea began to emerge.

"Martin!" Hugh shouted. "Protect yourself!" Hugh raised hands surrender-like in the air.

Linnea stood up, yawned, and rubbed her eyes. She saw a bottle of Vichy water, poured, and greedily drank. "Anything happen I should know about?"

"You may answer her, Martin." Hugh had taken out his notebook and, with a stubby pencil, was hurriedly writing in small, neat block letters. He looked at his watch and wrote that a loud and constant barrage, started at 3:30 a.m., continued for a half hour.

"A lot of activity is going on over there. Isn't that the palace?" Linnea asked.

"Yes," Hugh answered. "It looks like it's surrounded by attackers with machine guns."

"What's that?" Linnea asked, pointing up at the sky.

"It looks like a T-28," Hugh squinted at the plane in a cross beam of spotlights, "heading for the palace." He stood up. "Wow! This is getting good! Look over there at the Saigon River—planes diving with cannons streaming shells down into Diem's two-boat navy. And they're firing back! First rate!" Hugh sat back down, rapidly scribbling.

To Linnea, still standing, it seemed like a newsreel. With nothing aimed at the Caravelle, she and the rest were just observers. When the thought arrived that something could be misfired, she ducked down, crying, damn you, Stephen!

On and on, and after every boom with an explosion of white and red, a cheer went up from terrace dwellers.

"Did you see that? It looks like the Saigon River exploded!" Linnea exclaimed. "What about your sloop, Martin? Isn't it moored there?"

"I moved it down into the Mekong last week," Martin answered, his eyes glued to the fire on the river. "Interesting how the subconscious sometimes helps."

"Boy! Look over there!" Linnea pointed again at the palace where rockets were lobbing down onto it. "My lord!" she responded to tank gun echoes.

The palace's glass cupola lit with dancing crimson flames, mimicking wind-up animated wedding cake figures.

"If the palace is on fire, what does that mean?" Linnea asked, as Martin ran to the radio.

"Diem and his brother may fight to the end, or scurry away in one of the tunnels I've heard they've constructed under the palace. At least they'll be dry! Linnea, may I have my jacket back? This drizzle is getting to me."

"Oh, yes, of course, thank you," she said, pulling out the soiled mass of wrinkles and shaking it. "I'm sorry."

Martin returned, saying, "General Minh's tape recorded voice proclaiming the armed forces have rescued the people is still being played over and over with lots more twist and cha-cha music in the background."

"What about the Armed Forces Radio station?"

"Just that the situation is being watched very carefully," Martin responded.

"If Diem is deposed, could this Minh become President?" Linnea asked.

"Perhaps," Martin replied. "Stephen likes Minh, without holding great hope for him."

"Well, is Minh any good?" Linnea pressed, blocking thoughts of Stephen.

"What's he like?" came from a near-by table.

"He's a well-respected military leader," Hugh said to those leaning close, reporting that he's called Big Minh because he's 6 feet tall—unusual for a Vietnamese. He's affable and has been called *beo*, meaning fat boy, which he doesn't seem to mind, Hugh said, commenting that he grins a lot, showing off the single tooth in the front of his mouth left by a Japanese torturer during World War II, probably to remind people of his travails and bravery. I almost forgot, Hugh concluded: he's good with ladies and plays tennis with a strong backhand at the Cirque Sportif. "That's important to a ridiculous few."

Linnea offered, "Ambassador Lodge plays tennis," and, abashed, bowed her head.

The situation couldn't be a Viet Cong attack, or the fighting would be all over the city and not concentrated on the palace, Linnea decided. That meant Stephen might be safe somewhere. After standing to scan rooftops, she glumly sat down.

Machine gun fire and the occasional pop of a bazooka produced smoke and the reek of cordite.

When a very pale ray of light rose in the east, it inspired some of the tipsy on the terrace to bow with outstretched arms and shout "Bonzai!"

"Look over there!" Martin shouted. "A white flag is flying in a palace window."

Hugh looked at his watch and wrote down the time. He made a few more hurried additions, and put the notebook into his jacket pocket. In a low voice, "We need to be down in the lobby before everyone else to get a cab or cyclo. Ready?"

The three slow-walked to the elevator. When they reached the lobby they found they were not the only ones to recognize that daylight meant an end of curfew.

At the entrance, Linnea asked: "I noticed you recorded times with your notes. For a bird's eye view in sequence?"

"I was really doing it for Neil Sheehan. The UPI powers said he had to go on an R&R to Tokyo, even when he begged them that he was certain a coup would happen any day. I'm sure he's going to have a fit when he knows this happened while he was gone. My notes are from a perspective others might not have. Incidentally, Linnea, you and Stephen should be at Brodard's tomorrow night—or, rather, at the end of this day, tonight—for the full scoop on everything. Especially if it's a real coup."

"I'll tell him," she grumbled.

"Just let Martin get you home," Hugh said as Martin ran up with his hand on a rickety cyclo with its very thin-faced, frightened and weary looking old Vietnamese man, yelling, "I've got one! I've got one!"

"I'm within walking distance," Hugh said, giving his trademark regal wave of three straight middle fingers and setting off.

"You take it, Martin," she said when Hugh was far enough away not to hear. And then, hoping Martin would go on without her, thinking she had an idea where Stephen would be, she lied, "I know where Stephen is. Thanks for everything," and headed out fast in the direction of the Palace. Air thick

with cordite and streets chewed up by tanks made walking
difficult.

CHAPTER XXIV

The rising sun cast light enough for Linnea to see adults venturing outside to look around with blank expressions. Children, however, scampered about, picking up and playing with spent cartridges littering the streets. Older youths draped flowers over rebel machine guns and the turrets of tanks aimed in the direction of Diem's palace.

With the morning growing brighter, avenues began filling with dancing and clapping. Streams of student-age boys and girls ran down roads coming from one of Saigon's biggest jails, singing and leading adults, some in saffron robes, many limping or holding a damaged arm.

The sight of portraits of Diem being ripped and dragged behind anything that moved made Linnea sad. She wondered when she found Stephen, presumably with Diem, whether under present circumstances Diem would remember her from the interview.

At an intersection, several husky men worked feverishly at dismantling the statue of Vietnam's legendary heroines, the Trung Sisters, commissioned by Madame Nhu with one of the sisters the image of herself.

Linnea reached the white fence of the palace and hesitated. Everyone always says Stephen knows how to take care of himself, she was thinking, hoping the same for herself.

Red-scarfed gun-carrying soldiers ran in every direction into and out of the palace grounds, making it hard to determine which soldiers might be defenders and which ones rebels.

Linnea watched and waited. A single shot zipped from the far side of the palace without a volume in reply. Hugging the side of the two-story house, Linnea tried to figure out the directions of the men in red scarves. An equal number appeared to be going in as coming out.

She stayed in the shadows and peered inside the palace grounds. When it looked like the coast was clear, she edged along the palace fence and searched for an opening.

A sharp crack came from above, causing Linnea to fall flat into the debris of stones and empty casings, burying her head deep below rapid rat-a-tat-tatting and hysterical shrieking.

When gunfire ceased, Linnea opened her eyes. At ground level she could see nothing. She edged up, one leg after the other, dusted herself off and inched toward a hole in the palace enclosure.

Another sharp crack made her fall. Like a duck in a shooting gallery, she whammed down into the dirt of a flowerbed. After a lengthy spell with an absence of gunfire, she rose again and picked off leaves, stems and petals to make for the palace entrance.

The once gleaming marble of the steps drew her into it. She edged along a formerly grand hallway, littered with broken glass from smashed chandeliers. "Oh, my!" Linnea said aloud at the beautiful brocade chairs and huge potted palms covered with shell fragments and plaster. Bullet holes in the walls and a stream of bright red blood indicated there'd been a violent fight only shortly before.

"That's Nhu's room," she heard a man yell about a room off the entry corridor. A wild-eyed figure sprang from it dragging tiger skins lifted from the floors. The looter saw her startled face and adjusted his red rebel scarf at his neck to indicate rebel status. His cohorts followed, loaded down with bric-a-brac and bottles of whiskey. They left behind them a once richly appointed large office where red-scarfed soldiers continued chipping at gold filigree fittings for their pockets. In the back of Nhu's desk hung what had been a life-sized, sensuous portrait of Madame Nhu. A bayonet jutted out from her lower abdomen.

Staring at the desecration, she made her way through broken glass to the foot of a wide stairway. Swiped by soldiers rushing past, her eyes stayed with the silk negligees thrown over shoulders like bodies being hauled away.

The next suite was obviously Madame Nhu's room because an extremely sweet aroma drifted out past a pair of stuffed tigers with glassy eyes still undamaged and on guard. Once sumptuous surroundings inside were strewn with filmy gowns, ripped apart and stomped on by muddy boots as though under the mounds of silk might be the malevolent owner's well-formed little body. Drawn by the perfume to the bathroom and closets, Linnea marveled at the black Venetian marble washbasin, the huge pink sunken tub, and the multiple racks with long lines of stiletto shoes. On an untouched make-up table stood huge bottles of perfume labeled *Vent Vert.*

Back at the foot of the stairs, she heard from above, "No sense in trying rooms up here." The calm, definite words issued from a dignified looking older Vietnamese man in a suit and tie, coming down a step or two to head off the men in red scarves. He stepped back up to disappear along a dark side hallway.

That man is too distinguished to be here and not protecting something. Linnea bounded up the stairs. The first thing she came upon was a door with a plaque, "Vo Van Hai, Private Secretary," and across from it a room with a door slightly ajar. With her fingertips, she pushed it open, half expecting to find a body. Inside, in contrast to Nhu's large and luxurious lair directly below, the President's room was small and ascetic—a monk-like bedroom. A double-breasted ivory colored sharkskin jacket lay across a chair as though its owner had just stepped out and might shortly reappear. The suit looked the same as the one President Diem wore in the interview with Hugh and Marguerite Higgins.

Heavy footsteps coming up the stairs made a rocking chair move. A Kennedy gift? She made a hasty exit down the dark side hallway, hoping that there she'd find Stephen and probably the brothers.

Two hours later, when Linnea landed back at the USAID villa, kitchen smells drew her in to Duong chopping on the long wooden table worn down at its edges. Light coming in from the eastern window gave an aura to her lustrous black hair. Duong looked up. They examined each other—Duong fresh and Linnea a mess.

"Have you heard from Stephen?" Linnea asked.

Duong shook her head and turned to close the faucet dripping noisily into the large rectangular metal sink behind her. "One by one they came in through the night, *Bep* told me."

Linnea turned in case Stephen had slipped by unseen. But, feeling a need to express something, she turned back. "I'm sorry about the ... the coup attempt. Do you think President Diem is in another palace ... or abroad?"

"Ngo Dinh Diem is good person. He did good in bad times." Duong shook her head, her fingers slicing and chopping, eyes on her work. "Perhaps he loses ability to hear."

Hear? Linnea paused. Hear, Duong had said, rather than listen, which would mean listen to Americans, the often-heard criticism of Diem. Does she mean Diem lost the Mandate of Heaven because he couldn't hear the oracle, or couldn't hear the warnings about his brother's corruption and malfeasance?

"Will it be all right if Diem departed, or even resigned and is succeeded?" Linnea asked, trying to remember the full name of Diem's vice president Tho who, presumably, could succeed to the presidency.

"In time," Duong said.

"Yes." Anxious to be on her way, "You're sure there's no word by a messenger?"

"No. Mr. Stephen is busy person."

To Linnea's recollection, that was the only time Duong said anything remotely good about Stephen.

*　　　*　　　*

More than seven hours later, sweaty with worry and undefined guilt, a message came from Linnea's feet to bring her fully awake. Her toes touched what seemed like a bony leg. She rolled over. Eyelashes presented a beautiful black feathery line against tanned and lightly freckled skin on the white pillowcase. His rich dark brown hair splayed out wildly, smelling of gunpowder.

Linnea sat up, her legs tucked beneath her.

Stephen's eyes popped open, an impish grin spreading over his face.

After looking at each other without speaking, Linnea demanded, "Where were you?"

"A short distance away," Stephen replied. "I could see you. You stood up and waved," he said, tugging at the sheet covering her.

"You saw me?" She crossed her arms over her breasts. "Oh, don't play games. I have been worried sick. Why didn't you wave back?"

Stephen yanked at the sheet and, unsuccessful, lay back with hands behind his head. "I was doing good work. I was helping take care of a couple of transportation matters, and got stuck at the ambassador's."

"Couldn't you have gotten a message to me?"

"A curfew—shoot on sight—remember? A lot was going on. I was trying to get to you this morning. Everybody had guns—and a rather extraordinary assortment at that. Our Marines had to move into defensive positions." His freed left hand crept under the sheet.

Linnea slapped it. "Didn't you.... Couldn't you have...?"

"You were with Martin. You were safe. There was plenty to eat and drink where you were. Come to think of it, I've had nothing for a long time and I've wanted your nourishment. Can't you comfort a tired old soul?"

If she couldn't get him to explain himself this time, she felt she'd have to give up.

"You always want to know what's going to happen," he said. "Well, you're going to be the first to know that vacation arrangements did the trick. Ambassador Lodge last night says there'll now be a successful, shorter war."

She frowned. "War?"

"Now, come on, Linnea. Come down here. I need you."

At an early dinner, the few who had had a normal night's sleep heard from others who struggled home some time in the morning. Descriptions of the dancing and clapping on the jammed streets suggested that the Vietnamese people were relieved and happy. Others reported that many in Saigon remained anxious and cautious, like always.

"The Diem-loving *Times of Vietnam* offices were burned — totally wiped out," Kevin reported with glee. "They won't be publishing any more."

"This coup certainly had more to it than other attempts," Martin said.

"I wonder what changes there'll be?" Linnea asked. "I wonder if Hanoi will choose this time to do something."

Stephen turned to her, about to say something, but, before he could, Duong entered.

"A delicate balance of the primary flavors for you," she said, "the sweet, the sour, the bitter, the salty and the peppery. Medicinal herbs assure physical and spiritual health. Here is special *cơm rang* rice, and this dish," she pointed, "is mussels and their water with banana flowers and peanut sauce. And here is your favorite, *gỏi đu đủ*, green papaya salad with chopped peanuts and shallots.

"And this plate, my friends," Duong continued, huffing from the exertion of showing heavy platters all around, "is seared vegetables like the heavens: the red tomato slices, the sun; the very thin starfruit, the stars; the figs cut in quarters, the phases of the moon. On the bottom are green banana slices, bumpy with seeds — that's our imperfect earth."

"You are a true artist, Duong," Linnea proclaimed.

Others concurred, with Martin saying, "You help our karma, Duong."

Ignoring him, Duong continued, "I've added shredded purple basil, morning glory leaves, and red pepper, and a second salad, chicken with lime and red onions. You smart people know I teach you our food is crispy and smooth, cooked and raw, sweet and sour, and hot and cool."

With hands on her hips, Duong stretched her back to proudly watch over the plates still coming and being placed down the center of the long table until it became covered with symmetric patterns and colors. The array was so beautiful that no one wanted to be the first to disturb it.

"This is your most magnificent creation yet, Duong—fit for an emperor!" Linnea said, and, realizing it might seem she was referring to President Diem, quickly added, "We are most honored."

"Thank you. I hope you will keep respect for the past, and have hope for what can be. Yet," she tacked on with a wink at Linnea.

As soon as Duong and her helpers turned back to the kitchen, Martin quipped, "At least one Vietnamese appreciates our presence enough to show it," Martin said.

When stuffing abated and talking resumed, everyone compared notes about the previous night. Stephen directed a question to Susan, asking where she'd been.

"Oh, Steve, I was stuck in a house across from the palace." Susan's eyes met Linnea's.

"Then you must have been on the ground floor and seen everything," Stephen said.

"Not exactly. You see I was on the second floor. The rebels were on the ground floor with machine guns going non-stop."

"Trapped?" Linnea said. "By yourself?"

Susan cocked her head, suppressing a smile.

"But it wasn't awful," Stephen said. "You weren't alone. American or Vietnamese?"

Susan stuffed something into her mouth. "American," she eventually blurted.

Linnea tried to read Stephen's face.

"Seeking comfort in a man's arms, what were you scared of most, Susan: yourself?" Stephen paused. "The American?"

After another pause, "Or the rebels who had other interests than what you two were noisily doing upstairs?"

Amid guffaws, Linnea fixed on Susan, wondering if Susan had seen her on the street going into the palace—something she hadn't yet revealed to Stephen.

Nervously laughing and rolling her eyes, Susan said, "I had a good view of...." Whatever she was going to say became drowned by words of anatomy.

When it quieted down, Stephen looked at Linnea a sustained second before leaning forward to Susan, "Weren't you at all concerned about being blown apart by the Claymore mines Nhu lined the streets with around the palace, which could be detonated at any moment?"

Linnea's sharp intake of air was audible.

"Oh, Steve," Susan swiftly said. "I'd like to think you make these things up but you always know too damned much to be kidding."

"It's true about Nhu's Claymores," Martin said, reading Linnea's face with curiosity.

"Well, anyway, our Chancery wasn't burned," Jamie remarked, tired of whatever was going on. "And Ambassador Lodge hasn't been assassinated."

"Right you are," Kevin said. "I pray Lodge doesn't act like a gambler with a straight face and let things ride. Kennedy might ponder and weigh the cards, but Lodge is the kind who will let things commence—whether good or bad—just so he can get on with a nap."

*   *   *

More hard-news correspondents were collected in Brodard's that night than Linnea had seen before. Hugh's huge round table, now surrounded by two chairs deep, had everyone talking over a tabletop sopping with beer foam.

"Oh, my dear Linnea," Hugh said, rising as she and Stephen neared. "You come over here and sit by me." He dragged from another table a chair and jammed it in next to his. "Stephen the deserter can just find his own place."

"Hugh, *mea culpa*," Stephen responded.

After Stephen ordered and settled himself, he replied to senior correspondent Lyman, "Yes, General Tan That Dinh controls nearly all the forces in and around Saigon. As a 'rice Catholic' for a good political future, Dinh's been absolutely loyal to Diem."

"I've learned," Lyman began in a low, even-paced voice, "General Dinh's coup committee decided that because of his close relationship with Diem, General Dinh should be the one to call Diem and brother Nhu to encourage them to give themselves up."

"Yes," Stephen replied, focusing on paying for drinks. "That might be how it was."

The correspondents around the table became quiet and still.

Lyman resumed. "General Dinh, however, didn't realize that Diem and his brother were not in the palace when he called them. Diem and Nhu had had the phone lines switched, and scurried out around 8 p.m. through a tunnel to either a Red Cross Land Rover or Diem's aide Cao Xuan Uy's small Citroen 2CV—I haven't confirmed which—that took them into Cholon."

"You've worked pretty fast." Stephen looked with interest at the senior correspondent.

Lyman continued, "General Dinh didn't realize that Diem and Nhu had been driven to the Cholon home of their friend, wealthy Chinese merchant Ma Tuyen."

"You mean, at eight o'clock last night," correspondent Paul asked, "they weren't even in the palace and all that fighting kept going on with Diem's defenders dying?"

Ignoring him, Lyman resumed. "When General Dinh finally told Diem and Nhu that he was in with the coup leaders and that it was all over, Diem probably didn't believe him."

Linnea ceased breathing. Everyone seemed to be eyeing Stephen.

Stephen focused on Lyman. "Diem was given the option to be flown to his favorite seaside resort or out to another country, both options set up. He chose to go abroad."

Without emotion, Lyman said, "Yes, Diem and his brother did agree to be collected at Saint Francis Xavier Church in Cholon, after taking communion. An M-113 armored personnel carrier came to the church to take them to the airport." He paused. "But, from what's been learned, the military man in charge of the M-113, Major Duong-Huu-Nghia, had a grudge against Nhu and maybe both brothers." Lyman's dark eyes pierced Stephen's. "Somewhere between Cholon and Saigon, the major had captain Nguyen van Nhung take care of Diem and Nhu."

"You mean kill them," Paul said, launching a barrage.

"It's rumored they committed suicide."

"Suicide? A Roman Catholic commits suicide? Sure," said Paul, shaking his head.

Nodding, Lyman continued, "Head-in-the-sand Ambassador Lodge has been spreading the insane suicide notion of a pistol inadvertently left beside them, but he has had to backtrack when told their hands were tied behind their backs!"

"CIA man Lucien Conein says he and the U.S. had nothing to do with it," Malin inserted, "and that's a lot of garbage."

Diem is dead? Killed like a sorry dictator in South America? Linnea felt sick.

Lyman kept his eyes on Stephen. In a deep voice, he said, "The order had to have come from high up, probably Big Minh here ... *and* our administration in D.C."

Eyes roamed as though culpability sought an owner.

Stephen reached for a pack of Camels loose on the table. He fumbled with a small box of moist wooden matches to finally get a cigarette lighted. She had never seen him smoke before.

Hugh whooped at the correspondent coming through the door. "Sheehan! You're back." The UPI's correspondent, Neil Sheehan, just returning from Tokyo, looked depressed and angry. "I have notes for you from a bird's eye view."

Everyone had something to say to or ask the man who had witnessed the actions of Nhu's agents against the Buddhist priests and nuns, and who had predicted the coup, but been forced to miss the action.

After awhile Paul asked, "What do you think will happen now?"

"Probably one coup after another," Hugh replied, "heading nowhere but down."

Linnea kept her eyes on Stephen. Going through her mind were her words in a letter to Clarissa, suggesting that President Diem didn't inspire trust. Had she conveyed rumors that President Diem wanted to abandon the U.S. in favor of Ho Chi Minh? Her stomach turned over as though with food poisoning.

Stephen looked ill, his eyes deep in their sockets, his cheeks red as though slapped.

Linnea went around the table to him. She leaned over his back to surround his head and neck with her arms, her cheek to his. "You've tried very hard, Stephen. You attempted something for the good of the Vietnamese people and for America, but because of...." She took in the surrounding faces one by one, as though expressing embassy and military accusations that correspondents create an atmosphere for a calamity. But are journalists any more responsible than the U.S. government ... or herself?

"You were trying to accomplish an orderly transfer of power," she said, her voice cracking. Struggling to speak clearly and distinctly, "You're an extremely decent man, Stephen. There's been a terrible mistake ... that's not your fault."

CHAPTER XXV

Following the Diem and Nhu assassinations, Stephen wrapped himself into so severe a cocoon of silence that Linnea had to bite her tongue not to let feelings fly. She was mad, and dying to state that assassinations shouldn't be part of American foreign policy, that deposing an elected head of state is not a good precedent.

"I don't believe anyone authorized Diem's death," he uttered one afternoon from his desk in her room. "Our embassy has been weak and stupidly arrogant with Diem, maybe causing Nhu into dealing with the North. Perhaps I contributed."

Linnea went across to him. "You aren't any more responsible than anyone else," she said, wrapping her arms around him as if to share culpability. To absolve herself, she intended to learn what was happening with Nhu's opium network—to find out whether the United States had taken it over, as suspected.

"I appreciate that you know this meeting is important to me," she said in the taxi heading for Cholon, edgy because the meeting was set up in the purple pages of a letter writer's, and also because she was unsure where the finger would point. "The CIA man is about to head back to the states, and, it's suggested he's willing to share a few things, possibly why my USAID efforts have been undermined." She glanced at Stephen for a reaction. There was none.

Several minutes later, after getting past a street clogged with rattan vendors loudly shouting, she said, "You've noticed, I trust, that fewer *Mat Vu* are around now."

"Didn't I say your observation skills are indispensable?" Stephen said without much steam.

She could later share that the head of the Social and Political Study Organization, Dr. Vinh Kim Tuyen, the ruler of the Can Lao street vendors, cyclo drivers, and taxi dancers, has supplanted Nhu's *Mat Vu* secret police. She suspected that Tuyen, who had been close to Nhu, might now be running opium from growers to labs, through Bonaventure Francisci, and that that might be confirmed in the meeting.

"The Corsican overlord of the opium business, the place could be his," she said, hoping that tonight's information would cause Stephen to realize that she had been on to something.

"By the way," Stephen asked, "your Saigonese intelligentsia friends are happier, aren't they, with the new South Vietnamese government?"

Linnea began a slow, almost casual response. "Yes, certainly. Many are less fearful now. You know, I'm sorry I haven't made you join me at poetry gatherings so you could see that the Vietnamese are intelligent, educated, and caring, just like you." All they want are a few rights—free speech, freedom of assembly, and the chance to help Vietnam, she mentally appended. Then she remembered the wife of Professor Nguyen Van Tran entering a poetry session in tears, describing how her husband had been taken away the night before.

"Well, haven't things improved?" he came close to snapping.

"Stephen, professors, lawyers and civil servants are being taken away in the night." Seeing Stephen's jaw muscles twitch, she rushed to say, "The Saigon thinkers and the Montagnard chiefs and provincial leaders all count on us ... and Big Minh is cruel to them!"

It took several seconds before he said, "A war's starting."

She was startled. He had never said anything like that before. If it's war, it doesn't have to include us, she came close to exploding.

Entering the Cholon area, Linnea attempted to return to the benign areas of their work. "Has anything come through about my request for more fertilizers, pesticides and livestock for the Montagnards."

"No. Nothing."

"I fear people in Washington don't know or care about the Vietnamese any more than our new bureaucrats here do, setting up their fiefdoms." She recalled an American official's suggestion of dropping the Sears catalogue over North Vietnam and VC hangouts to impel surrender for a richer life. "Remember the plan for the Hmong to be given cowboy hats to get them in the John Wayne mood? God!"

The tiny chuckle that escaped Stephen's lips encouraged her to say, "My crop substitution idea is no joke, you know. Kanesh is the fast-growing China grass that's like hemp or silk, and can be great for making parachutes."

"You've had many good ideas, Linnea." Stephen said, squeezing her hand. "Incidentally, I just read about a helicopter kit for downed pilots that can be assembled in ten minutes. Imagine a pilot landing hard, pulling out instructions 'no tools necessary,' and putting up his hand to VC rushing at him, 'Hold on, now, I haven't finished.' Your ideas definitely are more likely to fly."

They had a good laugh, the first in what seemed like a long while.

The Citroen edged into the red glowing, paper lantern lit streets, and had to weave until it could stop in front of a restaurant cabaret that at first looked barely different from surrounding worn, brown, wooden structures. But Linnea observed thick exterior planks and a heavy roof and sturdy front door that suggested fortification.

Looking around while Stephen paid the driver, Linnea realized that this street was built on especially tall and probably stout piers sunk deep into mud of a Mekong tributary. She imagined the underbelly, from where men in slim, dark barques with opium and its derivatives would swiftly, silently glide to ships in the South China Sea.

"A lot goes on beneath the streets here," she commented as Stephen took her elbow for them to step onto a bridge-like entry platform. "Boa constrictors, lots of dank tunnels, and huge rats ... I've heard," she added when he looked at her like a parent hearing a child with a fib.

Once inside, Linnea was entranced. The interior was as dim as in a set from old black and white movies of Shanghai in the 'thirties. Under a ceiling with slowly rotating fans, lamps with silk shades and dripping tassels spread muted light over small round lacquered tabletops, accentuating shadows beneath patrons' hollowed eyes. Thick clouds of cigarette smoke hung over clumps of huddled Chinamen. Crushed yellow-brown and red and white American cigarette wrappers dotted warped planks on a sloping floor. Being led to a table in back, she saw small white paper envelopes changing hands, perhaps as samples of shipments.

When they were seated, the slim, olive skinned European at the entrance became identifiable probably as The Corsican. Under thick dark hair and a gleaming forehead, a thin, straight mustache lined his upper lip. His look of studied disdain recalled reports of a Corsican proprietor totally business-like the night a stiletto was stuck into a customer's gut while he sat talking with his killer. The Corsican, according to the story, handled the murder without any feeling other than concern for the interruption of business and the blood on the floor.

A short, energetic Westerner coming jauntily through the door was so colorless and with a face so bland that, if he weren't an American in Chinatown, he might not be noticed at all.

Linnea tapped Stephen's arm.

As the Westerner approached, he seemed aware of his own presence—as though he bore a scent to be noticed only by the purposefully observant for him duly to note. About her same height, five foot six, his compact physique hinted of solid muscle.

The Westerner nodded at Stephen, acknowledged Linnea rooted in her chair, and took the place offering an eye on the entry.

The Old Spy's eyelids were diaphanous; when lowered, his eyes appeared to be looking through them; when lifted, large blue-gray irises pierced in startling directness. A wet comb had been put through thinning ash-blonde hair. His crisply pressed yellow plaid shirt had the scent of having been recently ironed, perhaps by a well-run brothel.

After taking a quick, thorough look around, the Old Spy demanded of Linnea, "What stimulated you to come to Vietnam?"

Startled, Linnea glanced at Stephen, considered saying global importance or career advancement and, instead, responded: "We had a lot of Asians in Southern California where I grew up who gave us intriguing things. Europe was the focus of families and in school, so I became drawn in the other direction, to an Orient few knew or studied."

"That can't be the reason?"

Her eyes were drawn to the hairs of his bushy, yellow blond eyebrows that seemed the texture of steel wool. "I also had an extraordinary Far Eastern history professor who had been in the Foreign Service in China, Japan and the Philippines and wrote our textbooks." She glimpsed Stephen examining the man and imagined he didn't mind if she kept talking.

"Our professor always came to class carrying biographies he'd pass out with the imperative that we know people, histories and cultures and how they shape events." Thinking that was enough, Linnea concluded, "Asia is interesting and different."

"Well, you're different, all right." He paused. "You both may just have found yourself as a part of history, although some of what's going on here right now probably never will be admitted or recorded."

A waiter appeared as though summoned. The Old Spy named his bourbon, and requested it neat and doubled. He indicated that the tables near them were to be left empty and, when the waiter departed, said, "I'm going to provide a grounding to put your roles into context." With that, he extended a name: "Jack, as in of all trades."

Before he could begin, Linnea asked: "What's really going on here, Jack?"

"Oh, what's going on here is just 'sporty,'" he said, using the term for spying. "I agreed to meet because information," he flashed a piercing glance at her, "may have gone to a wrong party."

Linnea's eyelids flickered as though from a blast of sand.

"Before that, though," Jack said, "some perspective. France made opium a major industry here to bring money into its coffers for draining swamps, building bridges, and constructing prisons—lots of them, though not many schools. The sizeable Chinese population had a built-in market of addicts, and workmen needed pains made effervescent. And nothing's better than a nice dark, quiet den for coddling bits of balled opium over a tiny flame, now is there, Linnea?"

Linnea reddened.

Stephen's long legs remained spread under the table as though waiting, unconcerned.

"Okay, speeding right along," Jack continued, "the Corsicans here were instrumental in getting the Montagnard morphine base to Saigon for shipment to France for processing into heroin. From Marseille docks—the docks we stupidly helped stabilize against the Commie rats—fleets speed across the Atlantic with small, white muslin bags to stressed out New Yorkers, abetted by our dear French friends' Secret Service." Jack paused to pan the room.

"Nhu-the-Addict invested in the Corsican opium enterprise—in fact, as a full-fledged partner—flying the morphine here. But, our forces haven't liked unknown little planes flying into Saigon air space, so, the planes have gone below the radar to drop opium bales into the shallow waters of the Delta for pick up and processing."

Jack stopped talking to examine four men in skullcaps and long black silk Chinese robes moving onto a low platform. As the ensemble began playing their zither, drums and a shrill violin, two young Chinese couples moved onto a small cleared square of floor and started dancing, undulating like being moved by a river magnet on currents below.

Resuming, Jack said, "The opium continues to be grown by the hill tribes now serving as our American spotters and trackers. To reward them, we buy what they have to sell. Right?"

Stephen drew his legs back under his chair. "Yes, we've in essence paid some Hmong for their services by buying what they've had to sell until other, new crops...."

"Right on," Jack interrupted. "Self-sufficiency and economic viability. The Hmong need buyers—a good, steady, reliable one. And who is the best big spender in this whole wide Goddamned world? Our old Glory, of course! *Papaver somniferum*," Jack continued, jangling the gold bracelet on his wrist. "It's the most versatile of one hundred kinds of poppies, and can be smoked, cooked and eaten."

Linnea couldn't help it, but she swallowed.

"I'm here to talk because I'm wondering where things may be heading. Before Nhu was *permanently* put out of business," Jack said, "his opium enterprise was being wrestled away from him."

"Okay," Stephen snapped. "We've bought from the Montagnards for the sake of trying to control a situation." Get on with it, his voice indicated. He glanced at Linnea looking at him.

Jack's attention went to noise at the entrance where the Corsican was indicating that Vietnamese men entering were to be escorted out. He watched the action getting rougher. "A Corsican in Chinatown repaying the Vietnamese for their historically bad treatment of Chinese. Nice!"

"Are you the red-hot who designed a scheme to control opium, and for you own profit?" Stephen asked, nodding at Jack's bracelet that sparkled without scratches.

Jack raised his hand. "You and I are not of the 'goodness prevails' school. We know damned well goodness can't win by its sweet dear little self. Vietnam, as *the* current combat arena of a Cold War, requires that we utilize every indigenous resource we can, in a business-like way, of course."

The waiter bearing down on them had a tray with three drinking glasses, plump individual vials of liquor, and a tin-lined lacquer ware bucket with ice.

As soon as he departed, Stephen leaned over his elbow at Jack. "An increase in opium has temporarily occurred, and may have been purchased to keep it off the market."

"If the opium is taken out to sea and dumped," Jack said, puffing at a long, narrow cigar. "But it isn't taken out to sea and cast to the wind or dumped in a hole for destruction." Jack used the long fingernail of his little finger as a swizzle stick and sucked it. "Let's get back to the hills where tremendous communications have been necessary for picking up for delivery."

Stephen flicked away an ash landing near him.

"More and more round brown morphine balls from South Vietnam's hills are now transported to the far northwest of Laos … to Long Tieng … for refining into heroin."

"Long Tieng?" In a voice like a low growl, Stephen said, "Our men are fighting the Pathet Lao and other communist outfits, not transporting opium to a Laos CIA station!"

"Lao tribesmen," Jack said with patience, "have been establishing sites in their Northwest with the delivery of building materials, and chemists are coming there from around the world."

Stephen's hand clenched. "A couple of mavericks like you may be setting something up. Building materials flown in? Not on your life, and your implication that...." He was cut short.

As if by prearranged signal, the Corsican proprietor materialized, towering over them. He faced Jack who said, "I've been telling a bit of the history of this Pearl-of-the-Orient and how powerful you are and how well you take care of people. They're a little late in appreciating how things have always been done here. But because of something stumbled upon and corroborated," Jack pointed the top of his head toward Linnea, "there's a bit of vulnerability."

Her head down, with closed eyes, Linnea fumed, this Corsican was to be the focus, the culprit, for the U.S. to know to confront.

"Help may be needed some day," Jack continued with the Corsican. "I'll feel better leaving this hellhole knowing your special care can be provided ... if and when, of course."

The Corsican nodded. A card flipped from between his fingers to land near Linnea's hand. He walked away, leaving the impression he already had all the information needed.

At the edge of her chair ready to rise, Linnea said, "We don't need...."

"I'm owed a favor. I'm leaving and can't collect. So, I'm transferring my *on*—obligation—onto you. And, my dear little lady," Jack started to laugh, exposing tiny yellow teeth with serrated edges, "the favor has to do with an airline." His glee accelerated until he had to flick away tears at the corners of his eyes. "Like Air America, Air Opium!"

"Oh my God!" Linnea whimpered.

A screech from Stephen's chair moving back from the table said he'd had enough.

Jack talked fast. The Corsican here, he said, is the cousin of Rocky Francisci, the owner of the airline that had Nhu as a partner. Chiang K'ai Shek's Koumintang units came down into Indochina when Mao took over China and they acted as a tripwire against the PRC—the enemy of our enemy is an ally. The KMT troops settled in the Mekong where Burma, Thailand and Laos meet—now, due to opium, called a golden triangle. Jack paused only briefly to look at the back of hands sprouting thick blond hairs.

He resumed, explaining that the United States, under both Truman and Eisenhower, needed Chiang's Koumintang to be a possible fighting force against Mao ... and permitted them to support themselves any way they could. The old Chinese triad gangs, the Trieu Chau, helped the KMT soldiers into the heroin business. The crux is that the Chinese have emigrated to every nation and corner of the world and the Chinese triads have a representative in every one. "The Corsicans are still in business, but are about to be eclipsed by Chinese," he looked at both of them, "after our own hopefully brief involvement."

Linnea saw Stephen' jaw muscles ripple over grinding teeth. She put her hand on his arm. Glancing down, seeing the Corsican's card, Linnea murmured, "You don't owe us."

"I've read your stuff," Jack said to Stephen. "Your questions and complaints ruffled feathers higher up. With fine, original thinking, and good writing, you looked ahead on how USAID and its Rural Office can help—instead of through a myopic frontal assault on communism. You're good, and your efforts toward a successful end game reminded me of the old self."

Linnea looked from Jack to Stephen, for once glad with what she'd just heard.

"You're quite a team." Jack said with lids half-mast at Linnea. "I saw you in the hills once. Actually I saw, heard, and smelled you. You were splendid, telling the Hmong you wanted them to keep their traditional ways ... their identities, when you looked scared to death."

Sweating profusely, she took a fresh look at him.

"I was in a dark corner. That chieftain is a very wise man—with the good qualities of *tri* and *dung*. He'd never seen the sea and you came from across the seas—conceived right, bred right, schooled right. You and he were a world apart." Jack gave as sincere a smile as his small shark-like little teeth would permit.

"That head man could see what has now happened to his young men," Jack said. "Even eight-, ten-, twelve-, and fourteen-year-olds are not returning. It may be a culture curtailed." Jack cleared his throat. "Special Forces and Operations folks have been in the hills, hiking alone in the dark ... spooks in spooky places ... doing good. The work has been dangerous but manageable; then we started being hamstrung by military heads who can't make decent decisions and who treat us like dirt." After a good sip, "The Montagnards are critically important ... more so than our powerful weapons."

Montagnards as proxies! Enough! She wanted no more of Jack's career end swan song.

"I know you agree it's not evil to retain the loyalty of the 30,000 tribal groups for whom opium is their only currency," Jack said to Stephen. "The Viet Cong currency—know what it is? *Papaver somniferum*—the only paper currency in the world based on a vegetable."

Jack focused on Stephen and then Linnea. "Sure, crop substitutions may eventually work, but the powers-that-be cannot hold Montagnard hands while opium is eradicated and sensitive little coffee and kidney beans begin to grow. Our objective is beating Commies, isn't that right, Stephen? While your teammate here has been poking around, including down here in Cholon, you may have looked the other way, or pretended to do so, is that not right?"

"Let's get back to your laboratories in Laos. That's way and the hell ridiculous!" Stephen jabbed his finger at Jack.

Jack put his hands up. "But doesn't USAID supply building equipment and materials?"

Stephen shook his head. "Not for that!"

Jack intoned: "A collateral matter—transportation. We fly forces up to northwestern Laos and, rather than come back empty, planes return with a finished product. Then there's distribution—via ships lying right out there ready to take it all over the place, including warships going back home." Jack snorted. "Our government hadn't wanted US military presence in Vietnam known, remember? So warships couldn't dock any longer where people could see them in front of the Majestic Hotel, right? Well, if a ship can't be seen coming in, how can countless little parcels be seen going out? Get me? And that's why I'm talking with you."

Stephen, seething, pulled back from the table. "We won't let that happen."

"Where there's demand, it'll be met." Jack said that the U.S. in furthering freedom sometimes had to do despicable things. Anyway, opium in the short term may not be so bad, he continued. England today isn't a nation of addicts even though for centuries its infants were born or grew to be addicted because of what Shakespeare called the 'drowsy syrup' the parents used themselves or with crying babies.

"The godless out to defeat the godless," Stephen groaned onto the tabletop.

"If gospel truth is needed, try Matthew: 'Behold I send you out as sheep in the midst of wolves; so be wise as serpents and innocent as doves.' Doesn't that describe you both?"

The ensuing silence was deafening.

Slowly and clearly, Jack said, "Be assured: you and I and others may have prevented a nuclear war by being here and facing off both Russia and China, preventing a major worldwide conflagration." Jack scanned the room as though tallying good guys and bad. "Sometimes assassinations happen … they just happen, and that is too bad because they can lead to disastrous consequences."

"Stephen, we'd better…." she began, grasping Stephen's arm.

"I've talked with you," Jack said to her, "because your actions, inquiries and documents have led somewhere that has made you enemies." He let it sink in. "Materials for the laboratories in Laos have enabled an improved opium from the old morphine ball used in dens. Heroin Number 3 has a dangerous potential because it can be heated on a spoon or on the lid of a tin can by a cigarette lighter underneath and its fumes inhaled through a straw or rolled paper. 'Chasing the dragon' can be done anywhere, even by soldiers hunkered down in a rice paddy."

Jack took a last swallow and intoned that unconventional but effective forces are going to be replaced by the strictly conventional and ineffective. The gung-ho military will see that our troops make a big splash with lots of firepower, weapons of every conceivable kind, doing things the way they've always done them, for a sorry little conflict without a clear conclusion. "And then there's the dragon for more and more Americans arriving on these shores," Jack said. "The dragon's deeply rooted — and this is his territory. His hold is subtle and he's going to try to wring our people dry."

"There." Jack stood. "I've warned, and I've introduced you to a principal player. Be careful. Play the game well.

Exit soon." He disappeared through a large party of entering Chinese.

It was several long minutes before Stephen readjusted himself, his face drained. He was agitated—including for a waiter's attention. Standing, waving arms railroad crossing style he succeeded in getting their waiter to come running. After indicating a repeat order, Stephen took off his glasses, pulled a handkerchief from his rear pocket, and meticulously wiped.

Chinese at near-by tables looked them over. Linnea felt conspicuous and vulnerable.

Glasses back in place, Stephen began, "I feel like I've been wallowing in mud with a horde—the loose and lost embassy personnel, the green journalists out for a scoop, the sleazy businessmen arriving along with volunteers in well-intentioned organizations or religious groups—cuckoo or crooked, or both. This place is attracting and creating the worst."

"Yes," Linnea mumbled. "I've been telling you: good, knowledgeable, courageous people are leaving, including Vietnamese intellectuals—professionals who could be leaders."

"So many agencies, so many personnel, and who's the final arbiter?" Stephen continued like a lecturer who didn't hear a student's question. "Perhaps it's that damned military honcho Maxwell Taylor who snowed Kennedy by also being an author, going full speed ahead, with General Harkins here as water boy. And McNamara...." He shook his head.

She gripped his forearm with both hands, hoping to keep his voice down.

"The situation here has run amok. My making sense of it all, putting it into something intelligible to be read by the right people, well, I feel it's too late."

"Oh, Stephen, it's not." He reminded her of a pooch rolling on its side, exposing its jugular yet with eyes open, waiting, perhaps to defend itself one last time.

"I've sent a wire that I feel I've been used and that I don't want the damned editorship even if it's offered." He sat back with eyes focusing far off.

"Oh, no, Stephen! You've wanted that Council position! These have just been confusing days." She bowed her head. "I'm deeply sorry. I wanted you to know my inquiries and research have been honest, and that opium is one reason for the U.S. to get out of here. Jack was more than I bargained for … perhaps a plant."

"To reveal that honest, hard work has been for nothing?" Stephen cocked his head and squinted at her a few sustained seconds. "A plant to reveal what?"

Recoiling, she said, "I've been worried that, what you call my 'opium trail,' might be leading back to … to…."

"Ha! You think I was the mastermind?" he huffed. "You think I wasn't aware and wasn't trying to do something about it?" With a full exhale, "If what Jack suggested is true, someone higher up wants me out of the way." Shaking his head, "Well, who's going to believe what you and I know, or that Jack described? It'll be lost in all the false information issued by our ever-optimistic government about our being ahead, winning, and the Viet Cong about to be defeated." He swallowed almost all of his straight brown liquor.

Linnea's perspiration-soaked back recoiled from her rattan chair like from the nails of an instrument of torture.

"I don't believe morality and integrity must be thrown to the wind," he said. "Decent goals don't need black arts and dirty tricks, the ends justifying the means—your constant criticism of me. Responsibility and accountability matter—on that at least I think we agree."

"Yes, we do, Stephen. Please, let's…"

"The North Vietnamese and their communist allies are *not* going to defeat us. They won't have to. They'll simply outlast us, as the old Frenchman said, and we'll defeat ourselves."

"Come on, Stephen." She fumbled for her purse and rising, grasped his arm.

"Even our intelligence agencies are going after other agencies, like snakes in a pit."

"Like Binoculars next door? Agreed!" She pulled his arm.

"My file on the swelling number of people here who may be up to no good—and most of them, damn it, don't even know it—and your research and your missives...." He gave a wicked sideways grin to the blush on her face.

With her arm around his waist, heading for the entrance, she mumbled, "I've feared opium can maim us badly, that's all."

Outside, a flood of tears singed her cheeks. She had pushed out of her mind what Tam had sputtered on the phone just after the Diem/Nhu assassinations. Jim, who had impelled Linnea's exploration into the effects of opium, had died in a "meaningless" jungle incident, sent to the wrong place with the wrong equipment at the wrong time. A spear entered from below through the length of his body, stopped at the neck, leaving him alive long enough to suffer.

"Oh, Stephen," she choked.

The driver of the carriage they acquired was as worn as his nag. As they set out in balmy air, Linnea sensed this might be a last night to travel through Cholon and Saigon before their departure, and became absorbed in the vortex of life on the sidewalks. In a twenty-four hour period, the Vietnamese would be cooking, eating, gambling, playing games, fornicating, sleeping, birthing, dying—everyone and everything connected and predictable like succeeding beats of Buddhist drums. Tonight, sitting beside the bobbing, drowsy Stephen, Linnea felt acutely alien, even lonely.

When they reached the familiar section of large old villas with tall, full-leafed tamarind and plane trees and the scent of jasmine, they returned to the atmosphere of security and peace in the place they called home, the USAID villa.

The noticeably quieter environment caused Stephen to stir.

They helped each other up the stairs. After changing into light cotton nightclothes, and sitting in the neutral zone of her room, in the little area of rattan chairs and books behind a screen, Stephen seemed to sober up. The sweet frangipani breeze dancing in from the rear window seemed to encourage them to share.

"Thank you for believing in me," Stephen said, "if you still do."

"You know I do. All I've wanted is openness." She looked down at her fingers beginning to twist, wondering how Stephen would use this moment. With a fresh voice, she said, "I've wanted to get out of here, as you know, but I've felt tied to the Vietnamese, wishing to stay to help them. But, to show how confused I am, I've sensed something is brewing in the U.S. I've had an almost overwhelming urge to return," and she remembered to tack on, "to either coast."

CHAPTER XXVI

Linnea arrived well ahead of Stephen for brunch on November 23rd to save a place for him because the villa was overflowing with visitors, an increasing occurrence as though Saigon had become a hot tourist destination. Plates of one of Duong's special quiches of mushrooms, onions, diced chicken and Chinese greens were being passed around with a bountiful selection of fresh papaya, mango and starfruit.

When Stephen arrived, he came to the chair next to hers and gently squeezed her shoulder. She smiled up at him to express how much she appreciated, three weeks after the assassinations, that he was beginning to talk wth her as he had in the past, in New York.

Speaking with her mouth full, Susan said to Linnea, "I hear really good junk shops are on Rue Vinh Hung Dao, just this side of Cholon. Care to scrounge for some of the old things you and others are collecting?"

"Sure. Just name the day and time," Linnea replied, wondering if Susan's stated quest was to establish an alibi for an assignation of some kind.

Philco dropped from the stairs onto the shiny floor at the dining room entrance, landing like a heavy infant bird pushed out of a nest, and that, on the ground, wasn't sure what to do, although desperate to fly away.

Hugging his huge black battery-operated radio, Philco surveyed the assemblage with sad eyes and waited. No one paid much attention at first. The Armed Forces Radio

Network, the butt of jokes rather than a totally reliable source of information or entertainment, blared its identification several times.

Philco turned up the sound. An awkward voice struggled to make a professional delivery. *"The President of the United States, John Fitzgerald Kennedy, has been shot in Dallas, Texas, while in a motorcade, and now has been declared dead at Parkland Memorial Hospital. Repeat. This is a bulletin: The President of the United States, John Fitzgerald Kennedy, was shot in Dallas, Texas, and has been pronounced dead."*

Eating ceased. Everyone stared at Philco, willing a "War of the Worlds" technological trick. But Philco's blanched face indicated something horrible had happened. Listening to the radio from earliest hours, he had garnered the courage and responsibility to be the purveyor of the worst of all possible news.

"John Fitzgerald Kennedy, the 35th President of the United States, and the youngest ever to hold the office, died today after massive wounds to the head...." The words went on and on, over and over, as though trying to drum truth into listeners' ears.

Asides faded. A fork bounced. Eyes darted in search of an indication of collusion—that there suddenly might be a cry, "Fooled you!"

Linnea felt as though blood drained from her head. Her neck seemed as cold as ice. She turned to Stephen with a pale face: It couldn't be! He covered her hand with his own and held tight. His eyes along with all the rest returned to the large black box spewing forth the most incomprehensible horror.

The radio continued to cackle the same message, like a hypnotic mantra, a force-fed loop of information, with changes of word order as though alterations would imbed and confirm. New details with changes in announcers' voices kept everyone listening as though there might be a chance something could change the horrible news. But nothing altered the basic message or assuaged the unbelievable, unbearable shock.

Hope and anticipation had been Kennedy since 1959 when Linnea saw and heard him on a warm spring day in Stanford's Memorial Auditorium. She'd been mesmerized. Kennedy expressed the desires of her fellow students to be distanced from society's belief that glory and togetherness had been in the past, during World War II. She and friends expressed misgivings about parents' concentrations on money, like buying a place in society, and yearned to get away from the Mylar glossiness of post-war years. Vibrant, articulate Kennedy recalled inchoate American values, the buried integrity that if not taken for granted had been overlooked or abandoned in the fifties. Kennedy espoused the power of the possible. Whatever the challenge, it could be met with success—and Linnea embraced that belief.

Her mind screamed: we're in Saigon because of President Kennedy! We're out here doing for our country what it says it needs and wants. He tapped our souls, gave us purpose, and he empowered. Kennedy cannot be gone! It was with Kennedy's inspiration and the encouragement of Clarissa and her father that she had come to Vietnam to help America and the Vietnamese people.

Linnea felt rudderless, like she was being drawn down into a familiar dreaded well of loneliness. Struggling with family shame and pain, she'd been cut off and adrift from everybody and everything until this USAID venture. Now with Kennedy's death it felt like it was the end of feeling connected and motivated with a purpose in life.

The Vietnamese staff, who had scurried back and forth from the kitchen to the dining room, shuffled to a stop to stare in amazement at Americans with faces down, many with heads in their hands. They could not imagine what had happened. The cocky, sometimes arrogant, always self-assured Americans suddenly appeared destitute.

"What happened?" one Vietnamese whispered to another. "They lose family ... all at same time?"

"Well, that's that." Politically saucy Kevin became the first to speak. "JFK had been playing with fire. He counted on the CIA about Cuba when he should have relied on the military, and he's waffled with the military and the CIA here, even making the ridiculous selections of Lodge and Taylor on their handsome looks instead of intelligence and integrity."

"What goes around, comes around," Jamie concurred.

"Fuck you!" erupted from several strained throats.

Philco curled over the radio like a wounded armadillo.

Two men rose and walked to windows before an outside that seemed the yellow whiteness of an atomic flash.

The radio blared on and on. Gradually, repetition produced a salve that life would go on. The voices of familiar national airwave correspondents throbbed with reassurance while the reality behind their delivery pierced the heart. Listeners sank into a struggle against an undertow, to grope for a tiny toehold in unfamiliar fathoms to come up to be changed from that time forward.

Others may have once, briefly, experienced sadness over the death of a warm and understanding grandparent or the loss of a beloved pet, Linnea bitterly thought. But no one has groveled as much as she, afraid of rejection and loss, number one with no one. I wanted to achieve something, she mentally moaned, to be needed and not to grow old empty and alone.

Stephen rose and pulled Linnea up to him. They held each other, lightly patting each other on the back, tapping out a permanent imprint of a time and place.

Susan came around the table. She and Linnea and then Susan and Stephen grasped each other. Throughout the room everyone gave and sustained silent hugs, startling the staring Vietnamese.

Not able to stand it any longer, Linnea ripped away and with tears streaming headed for the staircase, squeezing Philco's shoulder as she hurried past.

"We're all going to the chancery," Stephen said later that morning, catching her in the center of her room and holding her.

"What?" she asked weakly. "Why?"

"Protocol. Good sense, too. Shared grief. We need to show unity in this tragic time. The flag," Stephen's voice cracked, "is at half staff. Marine guards are wearing black armbands, and there are books of condolences to sign. There's already a long line, and Vietnamese of every...." He shook his head and turned away.

Downstairs to wait with everyone else, in the only black she had, a Jackie Kennedy look-alike sleeveless linen dress, Linnea noted through puffy eyes that the USAID contingent had never all before been this well-dressed at the same time.

Stephen's arrangements for drivers and vehicles made her grateful he was in charge when she felt so bereft in a most perplexing situation in a country so far away edging toward war.

It was several days later, after sadly examining AP photos of Jack and Jackie sitting regally in the final motorcade—reminiscent of the assassination in Sarajevo triggering World War I—that Linnea felt in need of being with Duong in the kitchen flowing with aromas, this time it was *thịt kho nước dừa*, pork in coconut milk.

Duong hummed as she delicately stuffed minced pork, vermicelli, and onion, shrimp and mushroom into bite-sized very thin rice flour wrappers. She already had prepared a large platter of mint, basil, parsley, thin carrots, cucumber slices, bean sprouts, lettuce leaves and wedges of lime for *chả giò*, the delicious spring rolls that were a USAID staff favorite.

Linnea wanted to be set to work, but Duong didn't need help. Linnea lifted a paper-thin slice of carrot from the platter and nibbled. "How is your family?" she asked.

"Ancestors and family are happy back together in village, not in hamlet. Land is everything to us. Is it not that way in states?"

"Land is important to us, too." Linnea took another carrot slice and watched the dexterity with which Duong's fingers rapidly filled the rice flour wrappers and sealed them. "I'm sorry for what has happened," she said, meaning what the hamlet program had done to Duong's family and also the deaths of both their presidents.

Duong looked up and asked, "When are you and Mr. Stephen to begin your family? The brightest and healthiest are made when mother is young. With the father it doesn't matter," Duong said, back to her usual Stephen dismissal.

"Yes. Well, we may do it differently. We may...." It had been a long time since she had thought of it or even considered discussing it with Stephen. "I, we will probably adopt. Do you know what adopt means?"

"Yes, of course. We do that all the time. When someone can't afford a child, it goes to relatives. Lots of us brought up not by father and mother. But why?" Duong's rich brown eyes held Linnea's.

Linnea felt a pinch in the corner of her eye. What is this? Why after all these years?

Duong left her fingers in the minced mixture to focus on Linnea.

"I cannot have children." Linnea swiped her hand over her lower abdomen. "Tumors. Growths," she said, her hands going into the shape of a small watermelon.

Duong's food covered fingers lifted to point at Linnea's lower body. "There?"

"Yes. But the tumors are gone now," Linnea said in case she was misunderstood.

Linnea couldn't understand Duong's Vietnamese that followed, but she was sure she comprehended the tone: Bad. Bad. Bad for you! Your karma not good ... maybe deserved.

"*Qui*," Linnea said, hiding how she felt by using the Vietnamese word for ghosts. Yes, *qui*, in hot pursuit of one like her. Hungry ghosts out in the dark of night, going after those without children, the cast-off, with no one to moan over ashes or to take care of the bones.

"Mr. Stephen? Because you visit dens?"

With tears flowing, Linnea ran upstairs.

*   *   *

Linnea couldn't shake feeling bereft and empty. When she awakened before dawn the next morning, she got up and stumbled out through the heavy front door, not caring whether she would be followed or even attacked. Her feet carried her through the gradually awakening central Saigon area where she found a vehicle to take her into the dank atmosphere of southern Cholon. Once there, she wandered aimlessly, trying to deflect a cavalcade of worries.

President Diem—she'd contributed to his assassination with the information on Nhu's political activities with Hanoi.

Opium—she'd connected Nhu with Corsican gangsters and the Khun Sa and Matuyen Green gangs undermining Saigon and the government, but achieved nothing and roiled others.

Like a child, she wanted to impress Stephen. But in her USAID assignment, she'd felt set up, and suspected he was responsible for orchestrating opium to Saigon. Had she ruined his career plans? Had she destroyed their potential deeper relationship?

Strange stray thoughts pursued as she meandered twisting alleys. Keeping her eye out for a den to lie down in for memories to dissipate and vanish, she trudged on. Absently pausing at a large box on a sidewalk with tawny-colored almost hairless puppies yipping and falling all over each other, she sighed "Taffy," the name of her beloved childhood cocker spaniel. When Taffy gave birth, her own mother had been unusually tender to Taffy and the puppies … and Linnea stole their pabulum, rushed upstairs, locked her bedroom door to sit on the floor eating the puppies' food sprinkled with her tears.

With the memory came her mother's voice: You're a bitch! You think your Daddy loves you because you don't wear thick glasses like your brother. You can't see that you hurt people.

With vision clouded and her head hanging, Linnea moved on. Once, she barely pulled up before being run over by a man in a brown bowler hat sitting tall, looking straight ahead, pedaling fast on a bicycle with pots and pans piled high and a bird swinging wildly in a tilting cage on top. The rear of his load had a piece of cloth waving aft like the birgie on a sloop sailing away, leaving her in its wake. Morose, she plodded on, passing Chinese men dragging yelping animals for slaughter, preparing to surrender on a mat and let the world go on without her.

Hours later she found herself at the lip of the Mekong River. She stayed at its edge, hugging her knees, watching sampans and barques, and wishing she could be as simple as the people in them. The nine dragon fingers of the Mekong, its waters flowing from the Tibetan plateau, hypnotized her with thoughts of the myriad cultures the river passed through. After awhile, as though emerging from a beautiful opium trance, she acquired a place on a sampan traversing the Mekong, heading farther away, until eventually reaching the Hau River, the Great Serpent's lower branch. It may have been the despondency in her face, or that she mumbled in their language that enabled her to be given a place on a sampan and ignored.

By late afternoon, with a change of sampans near the town of Can Tho, Linnea reached the Cai Rang floating market, a destination long imagined as a place of peace and purity. Narrow wooden skiffs, tightly joined and gently knocking, had women sitting cross-legged under conical hats exchanging gossip along with durian and soursop. Rambutan and mangoes, pineapples and papaya, and flowers in yellows, reds, greens, oranges, browns and purples spread over the skiffs like the world's richest patchwork quilt.

On the far shore, Linnea sat for a long while, hugging her knees, looking back at the women. Her mind cried out for them to protect themselves and their children from the military action likely to begin now that Kennedy was gone. Her sad eyes remained on the floating market until colors shredded by the skiffs sculling away. It felt to her like she had been seeing the happy face of a friend known to be about to die.

Slowly, heavily she headed onto a narrow green spit between brown ribbons of the Mekong, and sauntered toward a clump of trees out of which peeked a small Buddhist temple. The simple wooden structure built on a slight rise to the surrounding land might catch a breeze. Its clean swept interior appeared expectant. A golden Buddha on a table against a wall bathed in the light of several tiny votive candles. The Buddha's head, hands, feet and blank black eyes gradually assumed a lifelike glow. Comfortably seated on a small orange and yellow-dyed fiber rug facing the Buddha, Linnea surrendered into feeling she was embarking on a journey.

She stayed under the gaze of the Buddha, gradually identifying with the Siddhartha, also from a privileged background, who sought clarity in challenges by sitting under a Bodhi tree until achieving lucidity that led to nirvana.

Voices approaching the pagoda broke the spell and hurried her outside. It had become dark. Muted candlelight identified a few dwellings scattered in trees on narrow islands between gurgling rivulets. Linnea groped along a path onto a broad plain without knowing where to head until she saw a shed with a roof of banana leaves. She called out; no one answered. She edged forward and stepped inside. The hut was stable but barren as though used as a shelter from a beating sun or the thrashing of monsoon winds and rain. Using a dried palm frond, she swept a place in the dirt and sat with her back against the side, the top of her head just above a crude window-like opening.

Animal shrieks and bellows applauded the spread of darkness. The wood whined in sampans pulled ashore as their seams clamped tight in defense against growing coolness in the night air. From behind scattered high clouds a few quiet stars peaked in a sky with a distant, pale purplish moon.

Would the Binh Xugen bandits, swathed in black with berets sporting a badge of snarling tigers, find her? Did their leader Bay Vien know she was there? Or could an end come with the murderous Viet Cong, killing simply as a part of a night's work?

As time passed, the pain in the back of her neck subsided. Like a Buddhist tired from trying to shun evil, Linnea surrendered bundled muscles and let the mind go. Why had she investigated an opium trail? Was it to impress Stephen? Or, in some strange way, was it to pre-empt rejection?

From the direction of the temple, a soft communal monotone swirled through the trees and drifted in to her ears. The blackness around became so total and intense that it was their voices that maintained a tenuous connection to the world. Over and over, like a good night prayer, she repeated lines from *The Tale of Kieu*,

"Night fell on the path she had traveled.
The sky seemed endless, with no horizon,
Even seeing the moon made her ashamed,
The moon, her witness to broken vows."

Steps lightly determined in the spongy earth made her stiffen. In darkness, lying on her side, she forced her eyes to remain shut while her body would take it. Would it be by the stab of a knife in the back, a rope swiftly looped around the neck, or death by a sharp blow to the head? She waited. And waited. At long last with an intake of air, she rolled over.

In the deep early gray a small, barefoot boy with his back to the faintly dawning light stared at her backpack and said nothing. Linnea reached for her bag and searched its contents. The boy stepped forward, accepted the Dentine gum, and silently disappeared.

Linnea got up, stretched, and went outside to sit on a rock and gaze at fields growing pineapple and papaya, and pears and loganberries until it seemed she was seeing with new eyes. A light rain during the night made grasses glisten. The air smelled good and sweet. The rising sun gleamed its nourishment, without humidity, at least for a while.

Passing the tiny temple, she glanced in to see a soft morning light washing the Buddha's face, suggesting a smile. She walked with a lighter step.

Arriving at the villa in the late afternoon days later, Stephen lunged up at her from where he had been slumped over his desk. "Oh, 'Nea. My God! I've looked everywhere for you. I've been out of my mind!" Dark shadows hung under his eyes as he rushed up to her. "Why do you do things like that? I, Vinh, Kevin, Martin, Susan—everyone has been out searching for you … in all kinds of strange places. Are you all right? Where have you been?" Then, "You weren't with someone, were you?"

Shaking her head in response, "The Cai Rang floating market down in the Delta," Linnea said, dropping her backpack. "I had some thinking to do. I know I should have told you. I didn't know what … where…." She buried her head in his chest.

After freshening herself up in the bathroom, Linnea came out to find he had made drinks and was waiting for her in her sitting area. "You've been down deeper and longer than anyone," he said. "What is it? Is there something I can do to help?"

Relieved to see him looking better than a few minutes before, Linnea still didn't know what to say.

Stephen sat at the rim of the rattan chair, looking into eyes beginning to fill. He offered a handkerchief that Linnea declined … and then snatched to wipe wet cheeks and a dripping chin and to blow her nose. After taking a few moments of trying to acquire the calm clarity of her Buddhist meditation, she finally began.

"The twin assassinations did something to me. I'm sorry, but I've felt there's a connection between the two." Shaking her head against a presumed forthcoming negative response, "I know there's not." Nevertheless, she had put together Nhu's connection with the Corsicans and their connection with the Mafia; and the reputed Mafia involvement with JFK's father's activities and conceivably in the Bay of Pigs fiasco; a mad Mafia man could have been in Dallas. But those synapses were the kind of thing that enraged Stephen, so, instead, she said:

"The French-accented CIA man with the missing fingers who was against Diem is probably Corsican and hence Mafia. I turned over to one of our CIA agents, not him, the material I collected on Nhu that recorded his approaches with North

Vietnam. I fear that that information became ammunition," she paused, fighting against saying by her own government, "for the killing of Nhu and his brother President Diem."

With a hand waving him off, her voice cracked. "President Kennedy was family to me. I felt close to him. I thought he could be a great leader. Also, he was a close friend of the father of my friend Clarissa, the Interior Secretary. He was the one who encouraged me to come here."

"And all this time I've believed USAID and I are the reason," Stephen said.

"Oh but you are!" Yes, he is. She would fight it no more. If he knew what it was like when he left New York for Vietnam…. "I missed you … very much when you left for here."

Linnea took a good swallow of her drink. Clearing her throat, in a soft voice, "You are interesting and intelligent and kind. I've felt comfortable with you, and even energized by you … like a confident, ambitious child." Shaking her head, "Clarissa knew about you and how I felt. She had given me the will to go on when I lost my family at the same time as my surgeries."

"And you've been writing Clarissa," Stephen gently said.

"Yes. I tried hard to understand the situation here, and explaining how I viewed things in letters was, well, not only good exercise, but enlightening" She paused to anxiously glance up. "And one thing seemed to lead to another. Clarissa's job is to draft reports for her boss on the Foreign Relations Committee, so we dialogued about Committee concerns."

"And she and or her father would ask you to look into something," Stephen said.

"Yes, sometimes. I wanted to prove that I could comprehend and write … because, as you are always reminding me, I must think of my future. Well, I have been … and, and, and, I've wanted to be worthy of you … your selection of me for USAID."

"Good God, Linnea! You give me heart problems. You know how I feel about you!" After a moment or two he took her hands. "I just want to know if you wrote Clarissa and her father that Diem should be ousted."

"No, I did not! I said what everyone was saying, that the brothers should be separated. Particularly after hearing President Diem, I wrote that if Diem could be separated from Nhu, we could help Diem with informed advisors—with people like you, Lansdale, and knowledgeable, non-threatening ambassadors. And I suggested that there could be a transition from Diem to elected officials with the help of Buddhist leaders, such as the one you helped save, Tri Quang."

Stephen gazed over the upper rim of his glasses. "What else? What did you write about the American presence here?"

Turning from side to side, speaking quickly, "I described that, when I arrived, the men in SOG, Special Operations, the IVS and USAID spoke the language and got along with the people. I reported there'd been a sea change, that recently arrived Americans didn't have direction or seem to want to know about the land they are in. And, you might as well know, Stephen, I mentioned that the South Vietnamese military's style of raping wives, daughters and even grandmothers, has made it seem like our military is needed to train ARVN soldiers. I may have mentioned that those saying 'The U.S. has never lost a war and cannot will not lose one now' are not the American presence that's needed here."

Linnea couldn't determine whether Stephen was smiling or frowning. "You see," she said, squirming, "I've learned from our relationship, our disagreements. Well, the situation here seems like a conflict between lovers," and rushing on, "that a friend shouldn't get involved in."

Linnea anticipated a reaction. When there wasn't one, she bowed her heard for one last statement. "I complained to Clarissa that Nhu's *Mat Vu* secret police and army continued to be financed by us, with laudatory films about Nhu, right up until he was assassinated. And, I shared with Clarissa that the Vietnamese don't want us here, and if we remain on their soil, it will possibly unite South and North Vietnam sooner than we know."

"You wrote Clarissa that the U.S. should withdraw from Vietnam?"

"Yes! No! Well, not exactly. I said I believe that the proposals—De Gaulle's and others'—for reunification of South and North should be considered."

"No power has ever controlled both the Red River and the Mekong at the same time, you know that," Stephen said.

"No *foreign* power," she said, facing the floor. "I haven't done any good here. I've let you down ... and, and...." Sighing for all she was worth, "I haven't wanted to be a bitter, brain dead, briefly useful female somewhere, and so I followed you here. And in the process, I've learned I love you."

He pulled her up, wrapping her in his arms. "My Intriguing One! Don't you realize? We're on the same track! Assassinations and all the other things haven't derailed us. There's a future ahead for us, and it'll be a good one."

Shrouded behind cascading mosquito net, Linnea explored Stephen's body as though on a treasure hunt for breath-quickening areas once passed over and intending to find. With her fingers massaging, she licked the soft area below his ribcage, and working south, hoped he'd wait and be patient and give her time.

Stephen drew her up to his chest, his fingers massaging the soft, moist place known to excite. With slow carefulness he stroked and pressed and teased until her head fell back and her chest arched. With her hips greedily rising in a thrusting tempo to enhance his own, they reached a shuddering new height in a glorious burst of joy, clasping each other awash in sweat.

Lying back exhausted, Linnea giggled, "Oh, Stephen!"

Later, staring up at the canopy, Linnea said, "You know it doesn't seem possible that a single sharpshooter, could change history like that."

After several moments passed, Stephen said, "What bothers me is that the guys JFK collected onto his staff and cabinet gave him a wide range of views. Johnson is West Texas, not Boston Harvard. He's been a wheeler-dealer in Congress, and I suspect there's dislike and distrust between the Kennedy team and those who toady to Johnson. LBJ may do his 'good old boy' thing domestically, with civil rights, so that the JFK men in place can be left to make foreign policy decisions, with the military prevailing on top of the State Department and the CIA."

"Who is on top makes a difference," she said, rolling over to creep up onto his chest.

CHAPTER XXVII

Their departure date delayed again, Linnea had the chance for a final assessment of the Saigon scene. The streets had the same incessant traffic with clouds of dust and the smells of everything from fish sauce to fresh dung. Muddied oxen still clumped along, saliva dripping from dirty rope muzzles, drawing carts piled high with all manner of goods—fresh and alive but not long lasting in the tropical heat. The *pouse-pouse*, pedicabs and cyclos still abounded but were being pushed aside by American jeeps, Buicks, and huge, ungainly buses, producing a canopy of fume-laden humidity encircling from overhead. And the clamor! The sounds of Saigon rose in a cacophony of motor scooter horns, bicycle bells, blaring radios, motorcycle backfires, squealing brakes, and high pitched shouts about every kind of item to eat or for sale.

Saigon no longer could be described in Somerset Maugham's words as a "blithe and smiling place," she decided. Many Vietnamese were abandoning their graceful style of life in an all-out embrace of American culture for profit. At the dock in front of the Majestic, ships disgorged consumer goods—televisions, tuner-amplifiers, sewing machines, toasters, fans, air conditioners, crates and crates of liquor, the packaged items Post Toasties and Texas rice, and surfboards—before curious and increasingly covetous Vietnamese.

The central district rejoiced in an orgy of neon lights swirling in and around practically everything. Dance halls had reopened. Hostesses resumed wearing the form-fitting outfits that Madame Nhu had banned. Bars named the Florida Club and Uncle Sam's, featuring fast strutting go-go dancers, spilled out onto roadways with the rhythms of Chubby Checker and the vocals of Paul Anka and Frankie Avalon. It seemed strident Americana had smashed the quaint and slightly moldy colonial world, and left it barely tottering amidst glitz.

Over sixteen thousand American servicemen were now in South Vietnam, and in Saigon they frequently seemed to outnumber Vietnamese. When Linnea passed the Continental Hotel, she sadly realized that the era of casual sidewalk cafes of barely two years ago was over. Observation *à la* Graham Greene of the passing scene was now permanently blocked by thick mesh against plastique bombs hurled by Viet Cong sympathizers on fast-moving Vespas. Behind the canopy on the veranda, American servicemen sat with tense muscles and alert eyes; and in the hotel upstairs, four military men were to a room. Contractors with free rein erected gray concrete apartment buildings, completely destroying what was left of the city's charming profile.

Military buses, with metal bars over windows covered by chicken wire, made its soldier passengers look like prisoners going to jail, confusion and frustration on their faces. The bombing of a movie theater, with soldiers and dependants killed, necessitated heightened security that disinclined an appreciation of the land and people. To Linnea, Saigon pulsed like a marketplace fish—opened up, partially filleted, and prolonged with a barely beating heart.

On a final trip to Cholon's market and Vinh Hung Dao road junk shops, Linnea hoped to find an old scroll of a hare, Stephen's lunar sign. After crawling through a tangle of floor urns and layers of dust into a low ceiling back room where the shop owner said he had put aside treasures, and finding nothing of interest, Linnea started backing outside.

"Do you like groveling at my feet? Or are you still groping for someone?"

"Oh, my God. You!" It was Khaki Man.

"Well, I am impressed," he said at her recognition. "Tell me, did you ever find your husb?"

"Yes, I certainly did," she replied, brushing her skirt. "What are you doing here?" She had never seen an American in this part of Cholon, much less inside a shop.

"Probably the same as you. Trying to find something priceless amidst the junk." He ushered her outside. "I found a lovely Khmer bust recently, unfortunately probably cut from an architectural masterpiece and bootlegged. Before that I bargained for hours for a seated Maitreya from Tibet that I'll treasure. And you?"

"I found a Tibetan Thanka!" she nodded. "I'm trying to find a Chinese scroll of a hare … or perhaps a tiger." She stepped away as though to depart.

"Well, then, we have something to talk about. Come on. There's a tea shop with overhead fans somewhere near-by … if I can find it."

A black and white diamond-patterned tile floor gleamed from a recent wash. Between it and the revolving fans, a layer of flies and mosquitoes circled complacently. Chinese customers looked from under black felt hats at the tall American and momentarily suspended talk.

"Here you have your choice of tea leaves of a hundred varieties from all over Asia," he said, seating her. "Some of these guys may be brokers, sampling until kidneys give out. Incidentally, the bathroom's back out there."

A waiter came with wrinkled orange paper menus. Linnea didn't examine hers. Sitting back, fanning herself, she watched Cholon residents of every station and occupation hurrying about their business in the hot, swarming street outside. Fathers carried children on their shoulders, holding them upright by hands gripping their feet, and pairs of men in dark shoulder board suits with wide-brimmed hats animatedly talked with their hands, like in Manhattan's jewelry district.

After a few questions in Cantonese with the waiter, Khaki Man ordered.

His language fluency propelled her into saying, "I presume you're Special Operations."

"That's right. Going home to be switched under Army control."

"Is that good? From what I've seen, your group has been helpful and successful."

"Yes, we've done well. But after Kennedy's death and Diem's replacements—the mystery military heads we never see or hear—the situation has completely changed. The Vietnamese military officers don't know how to lead, the ARVN grunt knows it, and so they're looking to depend on us."

"That's too bad. And it's sad," she concurred. "Some of our best USAID efforts are being phased out, or are becoming run by bureaucrats—seven times as many of them stay in their air-conditioned villas now as go out into the field."

"Probably just scared. The unconventional tactics in counterinsurgency no longer may work, I'm afraid. We're up against not just the locally grown VC but the North Vietnamese army, and to our government that'll mean our standard military."

A pair of fast-moving Westerners on the street outside caught her attention. Two conversing men followed. And then, slower, an American came along. He seemed to pause to look into the teashop directly at them..

"Oh no!" she gasped.

"What's the matter?"

"Oh, I guess I forgot about ... about his dental appointment." She fumbled in her purse for a handkerchief.

"I take it your husb just passed."

Stephen said he had seen her on the roof the night of the Diem coup. Had he seen her with Khaki Man? Her scalp crawled with sweat.

"Your Caravelle rooftop friends told me about your USAID work with the Montagnards. You and I were probably in the same hills."

Light headed, her fingers twisting the handkerchief, Linnea started describing frightening or confusing times with Montagnards, the victuals she'd felt obligated to eat, like fried lizards and bats' wings, and as she went on she started laughing, grateful to release mundane experiences that often seemed too simple or inconsequential to share with Stephen.

"You and your friend are lucky you found each other," Khaki Man said after awhile. "You two have been in the thick of things during extraordinary times. Is he aware of your fear of having your wings clipped?"

How had he figured that out? "I don't know."

To her distracted gaze, he ruminated about not having the education she and Stephen shared, and not starting out well. Alone a lot, he knocked around, he said, was a real scrapper, on the verge of trouble. "A teacher one day took me aside and marched me over to the register in the local college where another teacher headed me into the ROTC. Low and behold, for the first time in my life I clicked. I've loved leading men, facing challenges, and adjusting to situations."

Khaki Man described a life in America so remote from her own that it was fascinating. All she could say was that in spite of similar backgrounds she and Stephen had seen things differently.

"Everyone who's been in Vietnam up to now has been here for a worthwhile purpose and sees things differently. Special Forces, SOG, and CIDG are good but are going to be phased out by our military that some think has been thoroughly thinned of skill since World War II. Well, we'll see. I hope that whatever our military does here, it does so quickly and gets out."

Another pot of Dragonwell, "the Imperial tea of the West Lake," produced a pressing need. Wearily she asked, "Could you go back there with me in case I can't locate the bathroom?"

"You've needed me before," he said, rising to lead the way.

Finding only one thin wood-plank door with wide cracks, she yelled. "God! Nothing but a big hole! And over water!"

"Forget the scenery, and ignore the echoes. We need to antique scrounge!"

After they found an 18th century Mandala from Mongolia for him to bargain for and acquire, they gave each other a parting hug.

*　　　*　　　*

"You are not to go down to Cholon or even somewhere closer," Stephen said so vehemently that it scared her. Danger wasn't heightened, even if Americans in Saigon were a temptation for the Viet Cong.

Feeling cooped up, Linnea made it a point to be downstairs near the front door when Susan began going through family mail. "Do you think the VC will strike this place?" she asked her. "For some reason, Stephen is extremely tense."

Susan responded with a description of Stephen yelling at her "for nothing at all!" She handed Linnea a stack of cartoon clippings that Linnea looked over and decided to confess she didn't always understand "Peanuts" or find them funny. Susan replied, "Don't worry. My mother has to explain the ones closest to home."

Upstairs, Linnea examined the books Philco had left, including records, many of which had lost appeal, like Peter, Paul and Mary's "Puff the Magic Dragon." Once loved Broadway show tunes seemed saccharine, superficial and out of sync. Even Josephine Baker recordings and Sinatra's "Come Dance With Me" didn't do anything for her. But Joan Baez's voice resonated with provocative words that fit. She remembered Baez as a Stanford professor's young daughter, who, at the conclusion of student seminars in the faculty residence, came into the living room with her big guitar to play and sweetly sing.

Philco had pointed out to her *Pham Duy* music on Rue Catinat featuring the gamelan, the same instrument in a haunting recording, *"Pacifica Rondo,"* composed by a San Franciscan named Lou Harrison. Linnea listened closely to Philco's records. The new music truly evoked "the sounds of stars appearing in a night sky," as the dust jacket stated, amplifying her yearning to embrace changes going on in her absence in the United States.

*   *   *

While packing up records and books, Linnea said to Stephen at his desk, "I feel like I've been here for far more than two years, and have aged!"

"You're as feisty and energetic as ever, Dear Linnea, and you have what it takes to write something comprehensible about this time and place. You should, too, because new arrivals need a bit of perspective." He sustained a look at her.

"Why, Stephen! Thank you! But you're the one whose reflections will matter."

Stephen turned back to his people cards and the papers on his desk.

"Is there a chance of hearing some live music some place one last time?" she asked.

"What do you have in mind?"

"Well, La Cigalle has a Miss Yen Hung who sings like Edith Piaf."

*   *   *

After the cabaret, Linnea and Stephen walked down Rue Catinat to the Majestic rooftop lounge where a puffing Hugh found them and pulled up a chair.

"Glad I found you two … together. I've decided to call up the troops for a little concluding chat."

"Which troops?" Linnea asked.

"The thinking contingent!" Hugh replied, feigning disappointment. "Vietnam is now a major news story, and the press is heading here from all over. The wet-behind-the-ears guys should have some perspective. I'll be in charge, of course, instructing those strange people with wires, microphones, cables and cameras—the NBC television news guys," Hugh wrinkled his nose. "And, because thinking isn't always necessarily exclusively the domain of journalists, I've invited a mid-level embassy man, and assorted others of varying inclinations."

"When and where?" Stephen asked. "Or hasn't your brilliance gotten you that far?"

"My dear man, of course I've decided. Next Tuesday night at 7:30 at the Caravelle rooftop bar. And the reason for that spot ... other than splendid memories?" He winked at Linnea. "Less likely of being taped by the Vietnamese of various political allegiances or by one of our own ubiquitous secret services."

They were the first to arrive, at Linnea's insistence, bringing cocktail napkins in case of spills, soy kernels, cashews, and *tôm khô* dried shrimp. Hugh already had several tables dragged together, and more than a dozen chairs placed around them, with more available. Bottles of Jack Daniels, Beefeaters, Smirnoff, Canadian Club and small green glass Coca-Cola, Canada Dry ginger ale and quinine held center stage on a Lazy Susan.

Correspondents were familiar. Two women, one blonde and the other brunette, arrived separately but sat together. A couple of unfamiliar men with halo-like haircuts and expansive chests stuck close, and a short, pale-faced man entered, knowing only Hugh who secured a seat for the man near him.

The whirl of the Lazy Susan indicated that with Hugh's news outfit paying, the liquor might as well be liberally consumed.

Stephen, seated on Hugh's left, saw to it that Linnea on Hugh's right had a well-fixed gin and tonic.

Linnea estimated that Hugh had arrived in the delicate zone between barely fueled and adequately tanked. At around 9 o'clock, with chairs filled, Hugh struck something metal against glass. He began lightly, saying that for the price of their drinks, and as an Asiaphile and senior correspondent about to go on extended leave, he had a few important observations to share. Because Hugh was well respected and genuinely liked, patter ceased.

"One of these days the U.S. is going to pack up and go home," he began, and the press is going to be blamed for the confusion that has existed here all along. It's going to be said that we've misrepresented the situation, confused the American people and encouraged them to turn their backs on a noble cause."

The senior representatives of major news organizations remained silent and the rest followed their lead.

"That's not the real issue, though, is it?" Hugh asked, enhancing his Missouri accent, as though advertising heartland purities. "What is the main worry for a free world?"

"Misinformation."

"Nuclear proliferation."

"Owners and editors."

"Bureaucracies," Linnea muttered.

"Whoever said arrogance wins the price," Hugh said with an encouraging glance at her.

"The arrogance of power.   Elitism. Exceptionalism. Information control. The right of the government to lie! That's the issue. It's critically important." He took a deep breath to attain a stride.

"It may seem shockingly early to be appraising Kennedy, but I think we must," Hugh said, with a wave of his hand, as though to forestall disagreement. "There's been a sea change. Some say it began when Ike had to admit he'd lied about our U-2s as Khrushchev handed him the wreckage. But it really achieved artistry with Jack Kennedy." Hugh persisted, "We loved him and there's no question but that we'd give anything to have him back. He was President during a terrible time and had to call the most difficult shots."

The mention of President Kennedy slowed hands to the Lazy Susan.

"Let me paint a picture. We've been living in fear since the 'forties when we developed the bomb and the Ruskies stole it. They built a wall, and we had to send our U-2s over to see what was happening on the other side. One fell down just before the '61 Vienna summit and Khrushchev yelled at Kennedy that he'd bury us and that our grandchildren would grow up communist. Then the Soviet Yuri Gargarin circled the earth in 'The Eagle,' thumbing a Bolshevik talon at our own national birdie. Finally, Russia had the temerity to send missiles to Cuba to try to zap us from closer range. Major fear. Agreed?"

Concurrence wafted the tabletop.

"Okay, enter paranoia that we're weak and the world is about to be gobbled up by communism through wars of liberation. The world's in a real mess, yes? And, with the loss of China and now Laos, Vietnam is where JFK said we must put our finger in the dike, where America's credibility and determination are on the line. Kennedy entered the White House with a mandate that information could and should be controlled by the Executive Branch, the Papa Knows Best philosophy."

"Masterminded by Pierre Salinger," senior correspondent Lyman agreed.

Hugh rushed on, "When Salinger says the government is telling the truth, you know it's lying. Salinger said that a wide-open democracy can't defend itself against an enemy operating in secret, and that it has to prevaricate." Hugh fingered his glass. "Every time I saw or heard a Kennedy news conference, especially when Kennedy got everyone laughing, I knew the press was in his hands—flattery to the face while pockets are being picked, that sort of thing. His great charm and easy charisma set things in motion which are going to be hard to stop no matter who is president."

Kennedy being analyzed this way made Linnea anxious for Hugh's point.

"Hugh's right," Malin said, leaning forward. "Go into the Oval Office, or just into the White House, and you want to be a believer and on the inner team."

"But if you criticize," colleague Lyman took it further, "you're ostracized. Remember what happened to *Time's* Hugh Sidey. His critical analysis of Maxwell Taylor ruined him."

Sitting up, Linnea asked, "When did JFK say information should be controlled by the Executive Branch?"

Lyman answered her: "In campaign speeches, and absolutely demonstrated it during the Bay of Pigs fiasco. Everything was blacked out, zipped tight. Kennedy was exposed when facts finally came out about the Bay of Pigs, like the Cuban exiles trained in Guatemala with the CIA practically swimming behind and pushing boats to Cuba's shore. Our colleagues were leaned on hard by the White House and didn't report it."

"Kennedy faced a helluva lot of challenges," Hugh intoned above the chatter, glancing again at Linnea. "But that doesn't mean the President, the White House, or our government or military has a God-given right to control information. Do we want to be manipulated tools or a responsible press?"

Had she acted responsibly? Linnea asked herself.

Hugh's fingers tapped his glass without lifting it. "How are you guys covering the war? How do you get your information? To save time, the press here is told what the military wants it to know and some of it, as we well know, has been false information." His eyes scanned the faces. "Do you get to go out and see the war? No. You're kept away except for the tightly controlled and stage-managed."

"We're responsible for your lives!" One of the taut-muscled, crewcut men said.

"Nonsense. We could report on Ap Bac," Sheehan's UPI stringer said, because it was close and we could get there on our own."

"I also was at Ap Bac," Linnea said into the din as loudly as she could, "and it was different from the way some in our military said it was."

"Or as our allied ARVN commanders experienced it," Stephen said, leaning forward to benignly scowl at her. "Truth isn't always one-sided."

Hugh put hands on either side of him like arms separating quarrelling children. "For you newcomers and others who don't know, Homer Bigart is a two-time Pulitzer Prize winning correspondent—World War Two Pacific and Korea. He's possibly the nation's most respected journalist, working for *The New York Times* well before Halberstam arrived. Bigart for a long while constantly requested a helicopter ride to get a look at how things were progressing.

"Enter JFK friend and Washington insider Joseph Alsop who no sooner arrived at Tan Son Nhut than he was whisked off in a helicopter by the army. And what did Alsop report? 'The war is going very, very well. Intelligent, unified, energetic leadership, making solid progress.' If that isn't information control, I don't know what is!" Hugh paused to wet his throat while others threw comments at each other, with Linnea sensing more had been going on than she realized.

"Alsop wrote that the press in Vietnam transformed a courageous Diem into a quivering affliction with a galloping persecution complex," Hugh continued. "Homer Bigart saw things differently—as America's 'doomed policy led by unimaginative and deceitful men, attempting to save a regime more concerned with its own preservation than with the welfare of the people.'"

When talk died down, Stephen, in his most distinctive voice, said: "There are definite times when information has to be controlled. Clear and present danger negates the public's need to know." He paused. "In World War II, the press didn't get to go to the front. They were taken into confidence by the military, respected ... and the U.S. persevered and won."

"That's just it," a newly arrived journalist said. "There's no front in Vietnam because the VC are all over the place, and there's no respect, because the 'big picture' information briefings at Tan Son Nhut aren't what I need. My editors want to know who, why, where, when, what...."

"And how!" Paul remarked for a quick laugh.

Hugh plodded on. "Of course there are times when bona fide national security must prevail over the right to know, but curtailing freedom of the press shouldn't be a habit or an objective ... nor a mandated policy."

The short, pudgy man with neatly combed hair, short-sleeved shirt and bow tie indicating mid-level embassy employee, made several stabs at being heard in his high-pitched voice. "Cable number 1006 dated February 20, 1962, written by Carl Rowan, Deputy Assistant Secretary of State for Public Affairs, sent jointly by State, Defense and USIAD, described Guidelines."

"Well?" impatiently snapped several people practically in unison.

"Item number 4 stated that details about numbers of Americans here and about material—planes or ships, whatever—should not be reported to newsmen. Correspondents should not be taken on missions whose nature is such that undesirable dispatches are highly likely to follow. No casualty information is to be released."

"Thank you," Hugh said in a tone suggesting the man now had permission to leave.

Linnea leaned past Hugh to read Stephen's face.

Following an extraordinary period of quiet, journalists exploded.

"It's absurd—trying to do my job, being in danger all the time, only to learn...."

"It's disgusting—a theatre of the bizarre."

"What does our government think it's doing?"

"We've been considered our government's mouthpiece like South Vietnam's reporters who actually are. Then we're blamed for undermining the South Vietnamese government...."

"And accused of being communists...."

"...and our government gets on our backs."

"A puking, vicious circle."

After Hugh fixed a careful drink, "The plan may not have been full speed ahead. Remember that Kennedy in September said he would reappraise the situation. But LBJ has said, 'I'm not going to lose Vietnam or see it go the way of China. Once elected, the military can have its way.' Well, that's not what our Founding Fathers had in mind. Personal politics are not to determine wars."

"Kennedy wasn't going to pull out," one of the military men calmly said. "There's too much at stake, especially with China becoming nuclear last year."

"We can get into that," Hugh said in a rush, "but let me finish: Some of us—you, really," and he indicated Lyman and Malin, "may have to play extraordinary roles for our nation in looking at what our government is doing in the name of national security."

"But we're in a shadow play — we see, we know, but if we write, it's rewritten," Malin said, mentioning *Time* changing 'Madame Nhu's destructive influence' to 'she's a fragile, exciting beauty and the bravest woman in South Vietnam.'"

Hugh rapidly suggested, "What about a government disclaimer printed alongside a report from the field? I'm talking about Halberstam's *New York Times* story that the *Times* editors couldn't quite believe. That's despicable."

"Halberstam shouldn't be treated that way," Linnea said, glancing at Stephen sprawled in his chair, glasses down his nose, taking in everything. "But I want to point out that Halberstam's story of June 17 misrepresented facts about Catholics and Buddhists." She proceeded, reporting her research that the Diem government officials are not all Roman Catholic. In the National Assembly, she said, five are Catholics, five are Confucianists, and eight say they are Buddhists. Of thirty-eight governors of provinces, twelve are Catholic and twenty-six are either Buddhists or Confucianists. And in the ARVN, three generals are Catholic, but sixteen are Confucians or Buddhists. "Halberstam wrote in July that the majority of South Vietnam's people are Buddhists when they actually are Confucianists, Taoists and animists. And a *Times'* editorial page even parroted Halbertstam's inaccuracies," Linnea said, leaning forward to see Stephen smiling.

"Thank you, Linnea. You have the ability of the best. If the Fourth Estate is to be anything, it must be as accurate as humanly possible." Hugh sipped his drink and turned to Lyman. "When you started reporting about missing U.S. government money and property, sloppy accounting procedures and the insufficient direction by our military leaders, what happened? You were accused of writing distorted information and false reports. You weren't, but did you challenge?"

Lyman nodded. "We went along with the presumed wisdom of a higher authority — editors and/or our government."

Hugh's voice lost steam. "Governments come and go. Truth doesn't; it transcends. What is victory but Pyrrhic if we staunch the enemy and lose our souls." Hugh took a deep breath. "And truth is most vulnerable when the search for it is arrogantly controlled."

Or mishandled, Linnea was thinking, noticing newsmen in private thoughts, either preparing an argument, or mentally drafting a story.

"If what you know to be true is being controlled," Hugh said, "you have an obligation and a duty to report it, no matter what it takes or where it takes you ... into the many fingers of our government here—state, the military, the spooks, or Washington, or even our own employers. So, be diligent!"

Nervous laughter bubbled as respectful, appreciative glances went to Hugh for his final statement: "And if you aren't diligent about truth, there's likely to be a quagmire into which we'll all sink ... and it'll be a long, long time before we can crawl out." Hugh proceeded to fix himself another bourbon of his usual strength.

CHAPTER XXVIII

"Hugh conducted quite a session," Linnea said when she and Stephen were having a nightcap, hemmed in by boxes ready for shipment. "What is your take on it?"

"Hugh seems tired. He collected an interesting group, especially the embassy bloke reporting Item 4." He cocked his head. "You were terrific to speak up the way you did. I just hope newsmen and everyone else will remember that our government exists for the good—and is here for the sake of doing good."

Linnea took a few extra moments. "If we can behave like a friend, with empathy and humility." Her mind clicked to the resignation of Clarissa's father from the Cabinet. "What I mean is that since nuclear war no longer commands the situation, America can promote our stronger, gentler powers, don't you think?"

*   *   *

In the morning, the sounds outside suggested another coup might be beginning. But recognizable noises were tanks coughing and rumbling or plane swooshing and helicopter whack-whacking in and out of Tan Son Nhut as though in a constant air show. These sounds were more like machine-gun fire. Linnea rolled onto her back listening.

"It's definitely not machine-gun fire," she said about the regularity of beat and the continuity of the grinding, pressing in on their very room from both ends of the street.

"Chain saws," Stephen said.

"What are they doing?"

With a sigh he answered, "Because we are in the direction of the airport, and tanks may have to use this street, the trees along the sides are being cut down to widen the road."

"Those beautiful big, old trees?" Linnea was up, out of bed, heading for the front windows. "But that's awful! Whose tanks? In which direction?"

"My Darling 'Nea, that is the question all right," Stephen said, coming up behind, wrapping his arms around her. "We don't know that the Viet Cong have them, but with what the ARVN leaves and loses, it may not be long before the VC are driving tanks down this road right here." Resting his chin on the top of her head, twisting toward the second floor window of the compound next door, "Not our problem any more."

Binoculars was leaning out the green shutter-encased window, training on the USAID front gate. No one yet knew which American Intelligence outfit Binoculars was part of and it continued to be an issue with everyone except Stephen, until this moment. A Vietnamese man was at the gate carrying something, probably for Stephen.

"Why are they so interested in us?" Linnea asked Stephen rapidly getting dressed.

Later, Linnea placed in a suitcase her final acquisition, a boxed Chinese scroll of a hare, and looked over to see what Stephen was doing. "I think you feel the answers to a great puzzle are inside those cards of yours," she said. "They contain notes for a book, don't they?"

"Maybe. Some day people may wish to know who was here the critical first years of the 'sixties and be interested in thoughts and activities, good and bad."

"Do your notes include what Old Spy Jack confirmed?" she asked.

"Yes, 'Nea, they do. Merit and morality may be ignored, but costs can't be. Millions of dollars a day for our military could finish the United States financially."

Including the costs caused by stimulants, Linnea speculated.

Many people needed to see Stephen. Linnea was astonished at the cross-section ringing the gate each day. Besides Vietnamese, there were Caucasians, many not American, some of them probably with peculiar connections and reasons for being in Saigon.

Visitors went in and out during the daytime. In the evening, her room remained disturbed by flecks of dirt on the floor and the harsh smell of cigarette butts in the newly acquired yellow kryptonite ashtray on the little Japanese refrigerator, even though restocked liquor would not be consumed before departure.

Linnea did her reading downstairs by the front window in the cool, cross breeze in the tall ceiling dining room where she could observe comings and goings, including a good view of Binoculars' window. When Binoculars shifted toward the compound gate, it signaled the bell was about to be rung. If it was an individual of special interest, Binoculars stretched out over the windowsill as though with a camera, renewing her hope of a headfirst fall. Visitors had either been forewarned or sensed Binoculars and made a point of scurrying from the street to the villa as though running a gauntlet with hands, newspapers or briefcases at the Binoculars side of their heads.

Linnea kept on perusing newsmagazines and newspapers, alternately impressed by accuracies about Vietnam and outraged at mistakes. It gnawed that she could easily do as good a job as several newly arrived reporters, some of whom now appeared to write their stories in hotels and on balconies. If departure was delayed again, she felt certain an article with photographs about the Montagnards would be of interest to *Life* or *National Geographic*.

On a following morning, when Linnea looked up by habit at the window of the villa next door, Binoculars wasn't there. It crossed her mind that something might have happened downtown. But, there hadn't been as many bombing incidents lately, and Saigon streets momentarily appeared safer.

"How could anything elsewhere be of greater interest to Binoculars than our villa?" Linnea said in a light voice to Stephen as they stepped out the front door.

Stephen hugged Linnea in the shafts of sunlight coming through the courtyard's old *cay dura* and *cay cha la* palm trees. Linnea was about to share that when she'd passed the hall table, she had glimpsed envelopes with return addresses from publications she'd sent story proposals.

But the moment passed as she watched Stephen's tall, lean body walk the ancient seldom-used motorbike toward the gate, intending to take it downtown to sell. In his pastel button-down Oxford cotton shirt, his tortoise-framed glasses accentuating his smoothly sculptured Brahmin jaw, he was what he looked like: a confident, purposeful, honest intellectual. A proud smile curled her lips.

Stephen began weaving, trying to keep in balance, laughing at himself. His backpack appeared bulky, and he wobbled. Linnea dashed up to say she could take his backpack when she went in the jeep in a few minutes to the office. But he declined and headed off. He waved, but came close to falling over, like a circus clown.

An inveterate preppie, Linnea said to herself, as she watched him join the collection of Vietnamese on every conceivable kind of moving object heading downtown. A vague impression registered that Stephen's slender body resembled the slim, wiry Vietnamese.

Moments later Linnea and three other staffers were in the jeep at the gate, waiting to go out to their increasingly clerical jobs at the office. It was hot and Linnea looked forward to movement.

The two young boys of the *bep* were ready at either side of the chicken-wired gate to open and close it in one quick, smooth motion. Linnea looked up to give a toothy grin at

Binoculars and saw Venetian blinds clacking, as though the room had been left in a hurry.

Duong came out of the villa, speaking sharply between gulps of air. What was it now? Jeep-mates whispered, complaining that after Vinh arrived in the morning, Duong had become surly. She had slammed down whatever was in her hand, and when coriander was requested to go with an omelet, it was never delivered.

"The croissants disintegrated—heated too long," one new staff member mentioned his irritant. "Now is she trying to make amends? She's setting a record for waddling."

Duong banged the side of the jeep and dragged herself puffing to the driver's side. She spoke rapidly, rubbing at perspiration streaming from her scalp. "What's she saying?" someone asked Linnea about the dialect Duong spoke with the driver.

Finally, the motor revved and the jeep bounced across the concrete slab to the street. After a moment's hesitation the driver made a hard swerve to the right—away from the usual direct route to the downtown Trung Tam district. The driver sped up and didn't answer anyone's questions about the reason for the change in route.

The driver's behavior disturbed Linnea. She should and would tell Stephen.

The road became increasingly rough, recently chewed up by tank treads. The houses they started passing were gray, pockmarked, crumbling structures mixed in between with recently erected fiberglass and corrugated sheetmetal shacks.

The jeep took another right, and eventually seemed to be headed back in the direction of "Civilized Central Saigon," as the increasingly perilous Saigon sarcastically was called.

Linnea heard and even felt a sharp blast.

"Close," the new USAID passenger remarked.

Probably less than a mile away, the other added.

"That explosion was enormous," Linnea agreed. And it was excessive, sucking air out of lungs, far more than the Viet Cong's usual "we're here" scare tactics.

A black cloud billowed into the pale blue sky like a sports arena overhead balloon, marking the place on the street near the USAID villa.

"My God! You have to go back," Linnea screamed at the driver.

The driver hesitated as long as he dared and then demonstrating better driving skills than ever before, turned and retraced their route. Linnea rode high in the front seat, standing some of the time, trying to see ahead.

Vietnamese sirens were ostentatious. They even sounded sophisticated and out of context for the tropics.

Would those sirens be so loud if the injured didn't have the strong possibility of including an American?

CHAPTER XXIX

Mechanically, Linnea attended to final details at the villa and in the USAID office, and stood at Brodard's glass and teak front door to look in at where Hugh had held court.

She thought she could see Hugh's attentive waiter at his table with a swelling crowd of stringers. She imagined him welcoming her; she'd sit down beside him and be included as a working journalist. Then Stephen would slide in next to her and squeeze her hand. Hugh would lean forward to ask her a question, and, with Stephen listening to her, she'd give her answer—and be as proud and happy as she could possibly ever be.

Through tears, she couldn't tell whether Hugh was there or not, or whether she'd enter if he were.

Linnea closed and locked her USAID villa bedroom door and seated herself primly on a rattan chair, as though waiting for Stephen to come from his desk to join her.

The sun blasted in one window, hovered midway, and began to creep across the floor and out the back. The roof creaked with scurrying birds and rodents and changes of temperature from morning to noon to night. On the second afternoon, the sun created a violent salvo of deep burnt-orange and splattered itself across the floor for a harshly red-brown finale.

Linnea mentally tallied things: Stephen's well-worn phonograph records, the tired turntable, the new tape deck and versatile speakers had already been sent. Linnea might rendezvous with them later—at least with Mabel Mercer singing "By Myself," which she imagined she could hear at that moment.

Stephen's cameras and typewriter she'd given to Susan for distribution; it was a comfort to know they might continue in use. Nothing remained to decide about in his file cabinets: they had been emptied, she didn't know when or by whom.

There had been booze left to finish, and she was into Stephen's favorite Mount Gay rum. Its sweetness returned the memory of the cold saltiness sailing his sloop down the East River heading for South Carolina in the spring of '61 shortly after they'd met and before Saigon.

Linnea thought of poetry. The words of that delicate young woman, Nguyen Thi Hoang: "My soul is a lonely island ... Oh Christ, I am afraid of being alone tomorrow."

She hummed, "Too late now to forget my love-how could I ever close the door, be the things I was before."

A challenging thing it was to follow Stephen to Saigon, and to struggle for clarity in trying to make a difference. She imagined witnessing a scene change in a *ceo* water puppet show, going from a placid tale with soft rhythms of everyday life to hearing the eerie whistling of silver bombs falling out of a clear blue sky.

Had she done anything worthwhile at all? Getting Tam a poetry writing scholarship at Stanford was the only thing she could think of.

In the cold emotional well into which liquor had taken her, she experienced the excruciating pain of guilt, that she had caused Stephen's death. Like sadistically screaming demons, with arms flailing for a good kill, horrible images descended.

"Who are you?" Stephen had asked her in New York. "A survivor, you say. What does that mean? We're all survivors."

"Yes," she'd replied. "But a survivor is a person who consciously has had to make a difficult decision and by doing so develops strengths overcoming a fear of failure."

"You made me strong and you made me happy!" she screamed out loud as she let herself pass out, with loud oxygen-searching snores and a mind grasping for a thread of a future.

Susan heard muttering, tried the lock, and took it upon herself to be a rescuer. Along with two new villa residents, she tore down the door and inserted herself into the realm that may only briefly once have been hers.

Linnea didn't show anger when finally awakened. She mumbled about pretty purple poppies producing brown beeswax and taken to a clean, white laboratory in Laos—"like the parasite"—she said with bitter laughter.

Susan and the others, already on edge and in a mood for dramatics, discussed what should be done.

Linnea watched Susan as though from a great distance. When she finally realized what was happening, Linnea struggled to say: "I'm not on drugs. There's a camouflage over everyone and everything here. I'm the least, last person for removal. I know Vietnam, and I'm going to stay where Stephen ... remains."

*　　*　　*

Vinh came to say goodbye and seemed embarrassed by the sustained embrace Linnea gave him. He had prepared something to say:

"You remember our Vietnamese proverb: 'Force binds for a time; education enchains forever.' Stephen was an intelligent, finely motivated and well-educated American. He sought to learn. Now he's no longer chained, and his spirit lives here unrestrained."

Linnea couldn't speak. Through watering eyes, she glanced at Duong under the frangipani tree by the villa steps and bit her lip.

Vinh continued, "You have free reins and there are things you need to do. Remember the poem I once quoted, "If the wings of your heart have not yet spread, then go knock on the door of life. When life has come, the heart will flap its wings, and poetry will soar."

Departing through the villa gates the last time might have been more excruciating if attention hadn't been drawn to Binocular's villa, still smoldering—firebombed by Corsicans, Linnea heard it whispered, a bitter smile crossing her face.

* *
* * * * * * * * * * * * * *

During the early years of the Vietnam War, author Jane Miller Chai was Editor for Asia at the Japanese Reader's Digest in Tokyo. At the Associated Press headquarters in New York, she was a division head, with focus on Asia. In recent years, she has taught at the Naval Postgraduate School in Monterey and on the San Francisco peninsula on the subjects: Southeast Asia, Central Asia, and the Silk Road (from China to Rome). She is the co-author of *Pacific Security* with Dr. Claude A. Buss, her Far Eastern History professor at Stanford University. She adopted two Asian boys.